THE ROMEO
A Levi Hart Thriller
Richard Craig Anderson

Excerpt from *Siddhartha* by Hermann Hesse, translated by Hilda Rosner, copyright ©1951 by New Directions Publishing Corp. Reprinted by permission of New Directions Publishing Corp.

Published by Hellgate Press
(An imprint of L&R Publishing, LLC)
2305 Ashland St., #104-176
Ashland, OR 97520
email: sales@hellgatepress.com

Editor: Harley B. Patrick
Book design: Michael Campbell
Cover design: L. Redding

ISBN: 978-1-954163-91-1

Printed and bound in the United States of America
First edition 10 9 8 7 6 5 4 3 2 1

THE
ROMEO

A LEVI HART THRILLER

. . .

RICHARD CRAIG
ANDERSON

PRAISE FOR
The Romeo

I read a lot of books. Often I hear that a certain book is "a real page turner." This one, The Romeo, *actually is!*

Author Richard Craig Anderson, in a continuation of his Levi Hart Series, has crafted a storyline that incorporates two elements that make this an extremely satisfying read and unusually well-crafted piece of fiction. First, the author's real world experiences reveal the hard- edged realities of actual undercover work and the sacrifices that work requires. Second, he shows that any relationship based on true love and respect is of great value to those engaged in it.

A thrill-packed story underscored with a touching relationship of both love and respect between the two key characters, one gay and one straight, makes this an incredibly literary experience for everyone.

GARY CLARK, GLOBAL TRAVELER
AND LITERARY CRITIC

The Romeo *is a stirring thriller. Its emotional impact is deep, the authenticity stunning, its message vibrant.*

K.B., EUROPEAN COUNTER TERRORISM CENTRE

Richard Craig Anderson has crafted a suspenseful novel about a young patriot who must leave everything behind in his top-secret role as an undercover agent. It all starts when a very likely form of 21st century terrorism shuts down worldwide electrical power grids, opens dams, and stops the world's essential operations.

The struggles of one brave operator sacrificing his marriage, health, education and genuinely risking his life are intertwined throughout the story. Every hero pays an unseen price, and this one is no exception. The book is a page turner detailing an alarming and all too likely scenario.

JEFF BOOTY, RETIRED FEDERAL AGENT

Rick Anderson's latest novel, The Romeo, *weaves a tale of domestic terrorism across the country. His protagonist, code-named "The Romeo," battles with a band of urban guerrillas, chasing them from coast to coast. Relying on his military skills and mental munitions, Romeo risks his life, friends, and others until the crisis ends. Anderson's book is a fast-paced thriller from the first page to the last. His familiarity with the thriller genre guarantees a raucous journey of master storytelling.*

MICHAEL PALLAMARY, BEST-SELLING AUTHOR OF "DAYS OF EIGHT"

This story is dedicated to the memory of

Robert Stephen Anderson, 1950–2023.

•   •   •

This story is inspired by true events,

especially Kid's story.

PART I

. . .

Cyberwar targets the computer control systems that operate chemical, electricity and water plants, and those that guide transportation throughout this country. The collective results of these kinds of attacks could be a cyber Pearl Harbor...

An aggressor nation or extremist group could use these kinds of cyber tools to gain control of critical switches. They could derail passenger trains, or even trains loaded with lethal chemicals. They could contaminate the water supply in major cities or shut down the power grid across large parts of the country...

DEFENSE SECRETARY LEON PANETTA
SPEAKING TO REPORTERS IN 2012

Every intelligence agency across the globe employs men and women groomed to engage in sexual activities. The men are Romeos. The females? Sparrows. This has been a dark reality of espionage long before and ever since Mata Hari.

SEXPIONAGE: THE WASHINGTON POST, 1987

Chapter One

· · · · · · · · · · · · · · · · · · · ·

Present Day • April 26 • Beaver Dam • Eureka, Arkansas

IT WASN'T SUPPOSED TO HAPPEN. Not like this and especially not here. No, way; no freakin' way.

Yet the dam's floodgates were all that stood between the seventy-mile-long lake, and the many campgrounds and homes downstream of it—and in precisely 13.89 seconds, a hacker would left-click his mouse and open those gates.

As for the lake itself, gray birch trees with tapered, sharp leaves and black triangular patches on their bark surrounded it. Native Americans once created slurries of the bark to dab onto infected cuts. Other trees of the birch family smelled of hops, and the abundant red spruce trees were previously used as sounding boards on musical instruments.

Sloping mud flats now marred a few spots along the shore, and the fish population had been dying off over the past five decades, leaving everything smelling of hops, sour mud, and pine scent from the whispering pines whose shadows looked like stalking black cats.

That evening long after the regular work crews punched out for the day, a high cirrus cloud reached out and was grappling with the moon for possession of the night when the gates began to screech and groan while slowly opening of their own accord.

Steve Hill was the sole grave shift engineer, and the aging man gasped and went bug-eyed while wondering why the gates were moving. One fact he did know: millions of gallons of water were already shouldering their way through the breach, like so many elementary school kids streaming outdoors for recess through a too-narrow door.

"My God," he whispered, his face gone white. All at once he clutched his chest and tugged at his collar. His immediate thought: *I can't die. Martha needs me —*

Steve's wife Martha absolutely did need him, ever since she'd slipped into a deeper phase of dementia and he began changing her diapers, never marring with a misstep that portion of his vows that commanded, "… in sickness and in health."

The tumbling waters collapsed the Perry Campground's infrastructure first. As luck would have it, the facility was closed for renovation. Nobody died.

The Bluffs Campground vanished next under the flash flood's torrent, all of it gone with neither a bang nor a whimper. Perhaps by design, it too was down for repairs.

Meanwhile, the roaring waters tripped smartphone alarms that sent staff members racing from their homes toward predetermined back roads. From there they could reach the floodgates' large auxiliary valves. Then they might — *might* — be able to manually close the dam's yawning gates.

Steve Hill meanwhile pushed past his chest pain and was madly checking the dam's computerized systems when the gates inexplicably swung shut. Once he got control of his trembling hands, he alerted the Federal Emergency Management Agency.

FEMA oversees the 91,000 dams across the United States, and its experts scrambled to discover the reason behind Beaver Dam's impertinence. A low-level techie finally spotted the problem—a system vulnerability had exposed the soft underbelly of the dam's computer to a hacker. FEMA tried but could not uncover so much as a whiff of a suspect—although FEMA did find a way to take credit for this singular consolation: that nobody died as a result of what became known within inner circles as, *The Beaver Dam Episode.*

Two agencies disagreed. DHS's Cybersecurity and Infrastructure Security Agency exists to track and share information about the latest cybersecurity risks, vulnerabilities, and attacks. And its director declared that there had been a death: a local resident who went into cardiac arrest as floodwaters rushed past her home with the sound and fury of a runaway freight train.

The chief of the Joint Cyber Defense Collaborative went further when she announced, "The Beaver Dam Episode pummeled the souls of the scores of analysts, engineers and policymakers who predicted such an episode years ago." She added that her people considered the episode a precursor to exponentially greater floods to come. While still on camera she stifled a sob before adding in a strangled voice, "We're in trouble."

Chapter Two

· ·

The Next Evening · Olympia, Washington · West Coast Time

FBI SPECIAL AGENT Dustin Smythe whimpered and said in a strangled voice, "I'm in trouble."

Not knowing if his earlier plea for help had been heard, he thumbed his iPhone's SOS feature and activated it, then ran another hundred yards before stopping to catch his breath, only to realize that he should have gotten his bearings before fleeing the dark cottage. Now he was lost amid the abundant green trees and shrubs that rendered the dark skies even darker.

Unfortunately, he had no weapon—a consequence of working deep cover—so he asked himself in a hoarse murmur, "Jesus, what do I do now?"

The twenty-five-year-old agent had no answer. Born into wealth and educated at Princeton, he had relied on his PhD in English Lit and Daddy's influence with a certain U.S. Senator to be admitted to the FBI Academy. He barely squeaked by, finishing at the bottom of his class. Even so, he still got his Special Agent credentials.

Dustin's sole purpose in becoming an agent was to impress the ladies. Three years with the Bureau, he told himself. "Then I'll fill an associate professor slot at Daddy's alma mater."

But neither his PhD nor Daddy's deep pockets had prepared him for this or any other deep cover assignment. And now he was in deep shit.

Snap.

Dustin whirled. *Where'd that come from? What do I do?*

So he ran blindly, crashing through mossy deep woods where unseen ferns slapped his face as if conspiring to slow his escape.

He ran until he could run no more, his heart jackhammering against his sternum, his breathing coming in loud stabs.

Snap.

He spun around, eyes huge. A sob escaped his lips. He cried out, "Mommy!"

Then...

...BANG!

He never heard the shot, the hypersonic bullet striking the back of his head before the sound reached his ears, his body remaining upright for five full seconds before crashing against a forest floor now littered with pink gobs of his brains.

Dustin Smythe's killer stood over him seconds later and smiled, his teeth gleaming even in the dark while a wisp of blue smoke and the stench of spent cordite from his .40 caliber pistol hung in the air. He grunted and asked, "Did I not tell you never to refuse me?"

After adjusting the military-grade night vision goggles he'd donned when the chase began, he turned and strolled away. But he was hungry in the wake of the kill, and he said aloud. "Perhaps I shall scramble some eggs, just as I scrambled his brains."

•   •   •

At that same instant • Cambridge, Massachusetts

Kid Bailey rested a palm on his smooth chest and shifted his hips while regarding the sleeping young woman at his side. Her beauty and zesty odor of newly sliced lemons loomed large in the tall, lean and very good-looking young man's sniffer.

Speaking of odors, he sniffed one of his pits. Ugh. He needed a shower. But it could wait until he slipped away from this girl's side at dawn to see another girl — Tisha, the tall Kenyan he did his twice a week five-mile runs with.

Following the run, a trail of their shoes, socks, shirts and shorts would lead from her front door to her bedroom, where they would share some laughs before he hopped into her en suite shower. And should she poke her head inside and ask to join him, his smile would pierce the billowing steam clouds like a lighthouse beam, for he was quite fond of her.

Afterward, he would don fresh clothes and race off to a study session at a Harvard frat house. On the heels of that, he would go upstairs for a one-on-one session with Conor, whom he'd met while sitting in on an LGBTQ+ club gathering.

Then it would be off to the library before charging over to Britney's for another of their intimate study sessions that always left him smelling funky, and in need of another shower.

All that was yet to come. Right now he brushed his fingers through his heavy brown hair and sighed, for although it was just past midnight he was hungry. So after a brief internal debate, he left the woman's side and went in search of his briefs.

Because he tended to cast his clothes in all directions — a bad habit since childhood — he squatted on the floor Asian style to look for them, his long slender back shimmering beneath a slim beam of moonlight that made it past the curtain.

"Ah," he whispered after spotting the fire-engine-red Calvin Klein hip briefs. They were beneath the bed, and normally the happy-go-lucky yet oftentimes too glib-for-his-own-good Kid wouldn't bother reaching for them—or putting anything on at all for that matter. But two girls were sleeping in the next room with the door partly open. So he reached for the Calvins, and after pulling them on, he padded downstairs to the kitchen to see what might be in the fridge. For some reason, he felt like scrambled eggs.

Chapter Three

· ·

A few hours later · Washington, D.C. · Federal Bureau of Investigation Headquarters

THE SILVER-HAIRED BRIEFER approached the podium and regarded her audience of five men and one woman. They were inside a special room used to discuss classified matters, and the listeners were seated around a brown oval table with a scattering of freshly filled coffee cups and two platters of donuts.

The briefer cleared her throat. "Good morning. What I'm about to reveal does not go beyond the seven of us. Not without Presidential authorization. Is that understood?" She peered over wire-rimmed readers at each person in turn before announcing, "Very well. We're going Top Secret/SCI as in, Sensitive Compartmented Information. And yes, I'm required to state what SCI means." She rolled her eyes. "As if."

She continued. "For the record, everyone here holds the proper clearances combined with the required need-to-know. The project code name is, *Stranger*. Questions?" She looked around the room.

"Very well. Yesterday, April 26—which perhaps not coincidentally happens to be Audubon Day—the Beaver Dam's floodgates opened unexpectedly. Public knowledge, and all that. What's not known is that the Bureau previously identified an affiliation of Green Anarchists who've been developing plans to take down our nation's infrastructure.

"They'll open dams throughout the country, sending trillions of gallons of water crashing down upon Small Town, America. We're also talking power grids; water supply systems; oil pipelines; shipping and air traffic control, not to mention myriad other assets." The briefer arched an eyebrow. "Everything, everywhere, all at once."

She glanced at her notes. "The anarchists are based in Olympia, Washington. Last August, the Bureau sent an agent to infiltrate them. He managed to blow his cover within two days. A second agent lasted long enough to discover that our persons of interest have found a hacker, and we've reason to believe he's behind Beaver Dam.

"Even worse, the hacker has the wherewithal to utilize AI in shutting down not only the country but the entire planet. Sadly, the agent could only provide frustratingly generic details. For example, the player is a twenty-six-year-old male. He weighs more than six hundred pounds, and he lives in his mother's basement."

Nobody scoffed at the hacker's size, although someone asked, "Is there a name?"

"Ag, short for *Agamemnon*. In Greek mythology, Agamemnon is the King of Mycenae. By some accounts, he was killed in his own home."

The briefer sniffed. "Agamemnon could simply be a code name. So far there's no trace of anyone even remotely matching his description." She lowered her voice. "At least not in official records such as birth certificates, health reports, and the sort."

She squinted at the FBI's faultlessly attired Assistant Director. "We also face a dilemma. Even if we identify and arrest Agamemnon, the anarchists are said to have a failsafe system. It's why a deep cover operative must first identify Ag before ferreting out any safeguards. We cannot take down the others until this is accomplished.

"There's more," she said in a subdued tone. "We sent in a third agent. Several hours ago he sent an iPhone SOS. Police tracked its pings and found his body. He'd been shot in the back of the head at close range. We suspect one of the anarchists. If it's who the earlier agent thinks it is, the suspect is likely to have known he murdered an agent. Assuming this is accurate, it could mean that they're so close to achieving their objective that he doesn't fear arrest."

She scanned everyone's faces and spoke with the formality of a physician telling parents that their child was dying: "Accordingly, the President of the United States has ordered the Bureau to stand down while Vanguard infiltrates the group and cancels their Apocalyptic plans."

In the discussion that followed, the Bureau's Assistant Director fumed over the decision to assign the investigation to a private company—even shaking a finger at the company's three reps. They simply regarded him with unreadable faces.

· · ·

Two Hours Later · Washington, DC · Vanguard International Headquarters

Levi Hart, president and CEO of *Vanguard International* stood just under six feet. He had fair skin and thick umber hair that he brushed straight back. Now in his forties, the former FBI Assistant Special Agent in Charge and life-long ladies' man still maintained a swimmer's build. He also retained a high sense of humor that helped him mask the lifetime of evils he'd seen.

His face at the moment revealed nothing of the new evil he'd just learned of during the highly classified briefing. But its urgency showed itself in the simple fact that he had yet to change out of the dark suit he'd worn to the White House before heading over to FBI Headquarters. Now he and two others were gathered in his office of rosewood paneling, black leather club chairs, and leather sofa.

The office included a wet bar tucked away in an alcove, and its steaming coffee service provided hot stuff—Navy stuff—and its rich aromas filled the room. His domain also boasted the usual scattering of framed photos.

One photo paid homage to Mark Cohen, who had ascended to the presidency after terrorists assassinated his predecessor. After serving out the remaining three and a half years of the murdered president's term, Cohen got elected to his own term and was now in the middle of a second term. This made America's first Jewish president the longest-serving chief executive after FDR.

A man of great humanity, he all but adopted Levi a few years ago after Levi infiltrated a gang of skinheads that were bent on killing Cohen. Although Levi prevailed in the mission, it came with great personal, emotional, and physical costs.

It's why Cohen fastened around Levi's neck the Star of David that his only son was wearing the day he fell victim to a campus shooter. The President said while presenting it to Levi, "I know you are of a different faith. Even so, I want you to have it."

Another photograph honored Vanguard's founder, Heath Baker, who did four tours in 'Nam as a Green Beret and finished his last gig as a bird colonel. He retired, got a Harvard law degree, and established a prestigious practice in the wealthy D.C. suburb of Chevy Chase, Maryland.

When 9/11 erupted, Baker formed Vanguard International. Its purpose: to supply supremely trained and experienced operatives capable of performing complex criminal investigations, and able to conduct deep cover assignments. To accomplish these tasks, the operatives carried the rare credentials of Special U.S. Deputy Marshals.

They were also veterans of the notorious Tactical Pistol Course—the TPC. It's straight out of the movies, with split-second timing combined with deadly accuracy. In real life, those who successfully shoot the course rank among the top *one* percent of the world's shooters.

After Heath died of natural causes, Levi took over as CEO. Right now he was leaning back in his Aeron chair while thumbing the switch on a Sony flat-screen remote. A video of Defense Secretary Leon Panetta's 2012 remarks instantly appeared.

> *"An aggressor nation or extremist group could use these kinds of cyber tools to gain control of critical switches …"*

Levi hit PAUSE and turned to Cati, who appeared understated yet elegant in a simple white knit blouse and matching skirt. The one-time FBI Special Agent in Charge and current Vanguard operative was also Levi's second wife—the woman he fell in love with following the brutal murders of his first wife and their young son.

Next, he glanced at Marty Fischbach before hitting the remote's PLAY button. "Marty? Cati? Take note of Panetta's phrase, *or extremist group*. It's why I think Beaver Dam was a test meant to gauge this group's capabilities before they hit even harder." Levi rubbed his chin. "Whether by design or chance, their target selection presented the least threat to life. But then they go and murder a Bureau agent."

Putting down the remote, he turned to his Rhodes Scholar wife with a PhD in global studies and explored her face for clues.

Cati's only tell came when she squinted at the scar on the side of his neck, a scar that spoke of a knife-wielding terrorist who sliced through Levi's external jugular. The resulting massive blood loss sent him into cardiac arrest. Clinical death followed. The merest quirk of fate intervened when his team got to him in time to perform CPR. But by then his dead wife and son were already reaching out from a blazing white light; reaching out to guide him home; his son running toward him with outstretched arms while crying out, "Daddydaddydaddy!" The event has haunted him ever since.

Cati looked past the scar and said, "There was also that bit about a cyber Pearl Harbor." She made a sound. "We must stop them at all costs."

He nodded. "That's my thinking." He stood and stretched. "Marty? What's your take?"

In his life, Marty Fischbach achieved a number of remarkable goals. Those who knew him weren't surprised when the tall airline captain married a Miss America contestant. His friends also took it in stride when he only bid on flights that got him home each night to be with his two young sons.

After retiring, Marty traded his airline captain's blues for silk suits and came aboard Vanguard in the dual roles of chief operating officer and operative. It's why he held the credentials and clearances that got him into that Top Secret/ SCI briefing.

In response to Levi's question, Marty hunched forward in his club chair and rested his elbows on his thighs. But he could only speak in general terms since Levi's office wasn't a designated Sensitive Compartmented Information Facility—a SCIF.

"A dam opens on its own. We have a dead agent. We're unsure of a connection." Marty looked from Levi to Cati. "Sadly, time is not our ally."

Levi regarded his COO and said, "We have two additional obstacles. First, the Bureau kept sending in deep cover types. But come on. Fake identities and backgrounds? They're what trip up most operatives. We need a civilian, one who can hide in plain sight."

Marty spoke up. "Originality, rather than predictability."

Levi pointed a finger at him like a pistol. "Precisely." He sat in his chair. "Second prob. We're dealing with millennials and Gen Zers. It's why we also need someone both young enough and capable enough to infiltrate this group."

Cati spoke up. "Unfortunately, we've nobody younger than thirty." When Levi let out a long breath and regarded her with his expressive blue eyes, she stepped closer and touched his arm. "We have no choice. We'll have to use him." She arched her eyebrows. "Do you concur?"

Levi's mouth became a straight line, and his fingers formed a steeple under his long jaw. Once the logical side of his brain concluded that the bitter totals jived with the rough realities, he blew air from his cheeks and let the steeple collapse. "Yeah, I agree. Hell, isn't it why we've been grooming him?" He sighed and said, "Marty?"

Looking as if bad news might break at any moment, Marty said in a funeral voice, "Yeah, you're both on target. Yes, we're all past our prime. And yes, we have Kid... Kid, who doesn't just light up a room when he enters; he turns off the darkness. But he might have to literally sleep with the enemy. And that'll kill his soul."

Levi frowned. "No kidding, Marty. This is a job for a Romeo. It's why…"

"It's why—" Marty hung his head and said to the floor, "It's why we trained Kid for this eventuality." Then he jammed a hand against his eyes as if to shield them from an intrusive light. "Oh, Kid. I hope you'll find it in your heart to forgive us for that which we are about to do."

Chapter Four

· ·

The next day · April 28 · Cambridge, Massachusetts

KID HAD BEEN christened 'Levi Hart Bailey' in honor of Levi Hart, who not coincidentally had been his mother's lover before she fell for and married a certain Michael Bailey. Michael and Nadia Bailey in turn nicknamed their son 'Kid' to avoid confusion.

At the moment, the product of all that love and honor remained engulfed in a battle of sorts inside Harvard University's Countway Library, where he sat at one end of a long table occupied by five other students.

Kid's conflict involved the angry comments he'd just composed—a rebellious screed that cried out against the wrongs brought down on society by bankers and politicians; by right-wing whack-jobs and—oh, yes—by organized religion. Next, he added a message renouncing yet again his trust-fund status—despite drawing generously from it to support his education and expenses, along with the luxury townhouse his parents let him use gratis. For good measure, he pledged to support groups demanding action to reduce global warming.

After proofing the message he hit SEND and nodded, pleased that his opinions, beliefs, and thoughts were flooding a wide variety of social media sites—although he often wondered how many of his friends actually bought into what he said, or labeled it drivel.

Those who did believe him shook their heads at the anti-government anger they saw brewing in him for the past three years. Nor could anyone deny the irony of such ugly rage emanating from this beautiful boy, for Kid was an Adonis; long, lean, and lanky with thick brown hair that flowed like the gentlest of ocean waves, coupled with a triangular face, striking blue eyes, and a pleasing skin scent of sunlight and fresh water.

Blessed as he was with the body, the looks, and the hair, he once enjoyed a brief career as a much sought-after model. Every high-end magazine wanted Kid, since he could look fabulous in nothing but a burlap sack—as he did for a Paris photo shoot—or in nothing at all for that infamous Milan shoot.

Whether from a love of travel or of people in general, he became fluent in four Romance languages: Italian, French, Spanish, and Portuguese. He was also conversant in German and—Kid being Kid—Finnish. But his honest language became his most universal—the one with which he radiated pure joy and a loving personality wherever he went; an obliging young man who made friends easily, dressed well, and danced with sensual, sometimes naughty and often hypnotic moves.

As if these traits were not enough, in high school he captained the varsity lacrosse and water polo teams—and it bears pointing out that in the latter sport, he sent hearts fluttering every time he appeared poolside in his sky-blue Speedo.

And yet he'd never been arrogant or conceited. Indeed, he dated all women—full-figured ones along with women of color and those with translucent skin; blondes, redheads, and those with bald heads. But he never slept with a gal simply because he could. Rather, he first sought a woman's friendship. Whatever followed, followed. And make no mistake: Kid had enjoyed a multitude of friendships, along with those things that followed.

Or as one lover put it, "It's the friendliness of his penis that makes him so very irresistible."

All at once the noise in the library had become too much for a quiet Saturday. Perhaps the late April morning's unseasonably warm temps were to blame. It's why he was wearing an indifferently buttoned blue aloha shirt festooned with red orchids, baggy black cotton shorts, and black Flojo flip-flops. Harvard, despite its varied political stances, frowned on the latter. But Kid always pushed back against the absurd rule forbidding such footwear.

Now here he was inside the Countway Library with its sweeping avantgarde renovations, its expensive decorative accessories that never called attention to their costliness, and the second floor's organic wooden bookshelves populated by volumes of books with their old-paper odor.

The sum of it all now grated on him. But finals were nine days away, he was third-year pre-med, and he needed to make a stellar showing in a pre-med program that exists only in theory. That's because undergrads pursuing a medical degree must complete any number of math, science, biology, and—ugh—organic chemistry prerequisites, so they're lumped together and referred to as 'Harvard pre-med.'

After heaving a sigh, he gathered his books while thinking he could grab a sandwich before an upcoming study session. But by the time he had a finger on the laptop's power-down key, a decidedly obese and acne-scarred student native to Nassau appeared at his elbow—an act that jerked Kid back a decade in time.

He was twelve when a high school footballer taunted a new boy who hailed from Haiti. The boy was Kid's age—but Kid knew how to fight. So he lit into the high schooler and knocked him to the ground. "Leave the new guy alone," he warned before stomping off.

At the current moment, Kid chatted briefly with the large man until he turned to go. But when Kid pulled him close and kissed his cheek, his big friend said *sotto voce,* "You are so *very* pretty. If only you were available. I might then have at least a fighting chance of luring you to the dark side." Kid laughed along with him, and after they confirmed their next study session the guy walked away.

Kid was reaching for the laptop again when a long-limbed girl with blonde hair, an oval face, and fine-looking hazel eyes entered his field of vision. A green HARVARD T-shirt clung revealingly to her breasts, and her jeans spoke proudly of hips that ached for release. The male students turned as one to ogle her. One of them even sighed aloud when she gave her head a casual toss that sent her long hair flying with a regal flair.

Seconds later she grazed a long manicured fingernail along the back of Kid's neck and spoke in a hushed voice in keeping with their surroundings. "Hi, lover boy."

His eyes lit up. "Britney, babe."

She stepped behind him and grabbed a hank of his hair, then tugged until his chin tilted toward the ceiling. "Love the lazily undone shirt. Very raffish." Letting go of his hair, she slid a knowing hand inside the shirt and moved her cool palm across his smooth chest.

Kid moaned. "Mmm. I always love it when you touch me that way."

"I know you do. I also know what else you like touched."
She swept her palm down his belly to his waistband and
began worming her fingers deep inside.

"Behave," he said while clamping his hand against hers.
But after she pulled her fingers free, the corners of his mouth
lifted. "Wanna fuck?"

"Are barns lavender? I—" She frowned and jutted her
jaw at his laptop. "Oh, Kid. Not another posting. Why so
much anger?"

"It's not anger," he said self-righteously. "It's indignation."

She looked heavenward. "Your parents must be so proud.
Listen, this stuff can bar you from HMS."

"Harvard Medical School cannot stop me from exercising
my free speech rights." He flicked his eyes at the screen. "I'm
supporting the activists who did that sit-in on L.A.'s I-5 to
put an end to global warming."

"That's noble of you. Only, why take the chance? Wait till
you've been accepted before firing off these… these *epistles*.
I mean, damn… you get so irritated lately."

"I'll take it under advisement," he blazed.

"The prosecution rests." The girl sighed but then she put
her mouth close to his ear. "Let's go to my place. We'll get
naked, do some lines and fuck. Well?"

"I'd love to. But come on, Brit. Finals begin next week."

Not to be dissuaded, she pressed her breasts against his
neck and combed her fingers through his thick hair. "Let's
renegotiate. Why don't we have our fun and *then* hit the
books."

"Well, when you put it that way—"

"I usually do." She smooched his cheek when he began to
gather his things, and she laughed joyously when he stood
and offered a lazy seductive glance just before locking an

arm around her waist. Seconds later the jaunty *slap, slap* of his flip-flops against the floor marked a stark contrast to the subdued library.

Several guys watched with mixtures of envy and undisguised lust. One student nudged a buddy's arm and said just above a whisper, "Pretty Boy's been hittin' that since last fall."

The buddy reared back. "How can you be so sure?"

"Christ, she told me. Said he nails her three, four times a week. At least. Then there's that Kenyan babe. The one in second-year chem/bio?"

The buddy's jaw dropped. "Tisha? That utterly stunning marathoner?"

"That's the one. Word is, he's knocked her *up*. Can you believe it?" The student chuckled. "But wait, there's more. He's also been going *down* on Dakota." When the friend's eyebrows knotted together, the fellow student added, "The swim team captain. Tall lean guy? Know who I'm talking about?"

A nearby student named Mateo scoffed. "Jealous, are we?"

"No. But—" The guy exhaled in a rush. "But I see him leave Dak's room all the time."

The first buddy slowly shook his head. "Fucker gets around, doesn't he?"

•   •   •

Barely twenty minutes later Kid's and Britney's clothes were strewn across her studio apartment's floor, their torsos glistening from thin veils of perspiration and the rhythmic *creak, creak, creak* of her bed echoing against the walls until Kid gasped and Britney made a sound.

They smiled foolishly at each other, their bodies gone limp. But when Kid eased away, Britney reached out with beseeching arms and wailed, "Why?"

"Just taking a break," he mumbled. A split-sec later and with his briefs in place, he glanced at the hand mirror atop the nightstand with its remnants of cocaine lines. He could almost feel a sharp and bitter taste in the back of his throat, and following a swipe at his nose he padded to the room's only window.

He stuck his head out in search of a soothing breeze on the one hot day that her a/c had gone tits up. Finding no wind, he frowned and was pulling his head inside when Britney came up from behind in her white lace Victoria's Secrets — secrets denied to everyone but Kid — and yanked his Calvin Kleins down. As they clumped around his ankles, she stood behind him and whisked her fingertips up and down his flanks.

"Oh, you are such a naughty girl." He craned his neck and his smile dazzled — which made her cry out from pure joy.

"Guilty," she said, and stood next to him. Kid draped a casual arm around her shoulders. She planted a palm against his bare bottom. Then they stood quietly and gazed at the goings-on outside. After a moment she kissed his ear and whispered, "Coming back to bed, lover boy?"

Kid responded with a basso-profundo voice. "Ladies and gentlemen, the movie you are about to see has not yet been rated."

Her hand lingered on his bottom as she sang, "Rated X, I hope." She caressed his butt and climbed atop the exhausted bed with its sweat-damp sheets. But when he bent down to hoist his briefs into place, her voice trilled like a song when she asked, "Why bother?"

Kid shrugged and stepped out of them with an indifference that eluded so many others, and after nudging the now-flaccid, fire-engine-red Calvins to one side with his foot, he turned around with a natural grace and regarded her thoughtfully.

"My, aren't we being so very European?" In her glee, she giggled like the tinkling of glass and began undoing her bra. That is until he gave her a wave-off.

"I'm not comfortable with you doing that, babe."

She grimaced. "Oh, all right." She let go and asked, "There. Happy?"

"Thanks."

A cricket sounded from a far corner while he examined the studio apartment's yellowing walls, the threadbare rugs, and an ebony incense holder atop the nightstand—its burning joss stick sending sickly sweet smoke curling toward the ceiling to mask the enduring odor of hashish. There was also that hand mirror with cocaine residue—though they hadn't smoked hash or done any lines. Not today, that is—they were here to study for finals.

Nor had there been any sex; not now or ever before. Their sweat-streaked bodies simply bore testament to the day's sweltering heat, while the bed's creaking had come from Kid moving his body in time with Cyndi Lauper's *Girls Just Wanna Have Fun* on Brit's CD. As for their goofy grins, they signified nothing less than two of God's children at play to a music's beat.

That left their state of undress. Long ago they got into the habit of doing their study sessions while sitting cross-legged atop her bed. They only shed their shoes at first. But in time the devilish athlete and the brilliant beauty began a game of daring to see who would show the most skin. It didn't take long before they routinely pared down to the barest essentials—i.e., his briefs which he had to adjust often to maintain modesty—and her lingerie. And though they had always been celibate, they did kiss and touch. That's because she worshipped him, and he truly cared for her.

So the question of why two healthy and vibrant college students didn't indulge in steamy sex came down to this: Kid was happily married to Jennifer—whose side he'd left earlier so he could scramble some eggs. He was also the father of the twin girls in the other bedroom, the soon-to-be father of a son, and the proud wearer of a simple gold wedding band.

To his inestimable credit, Kid always told his wife everything about his study sessions. Jen in turn so trusted him that she thought nothing of their quasi-naked activities and didn't feel threatened by their casual kissing and caressing.

Not that Kid wouldn't mind making passionate love to the eye-catching and evocatively constructed Britney; deep down he did and if single he would. But not even the romantic guitar version of *Ojos De La Tierra* now playing in the background could lead him astray.

All at once Kid stretched in a way that caused his long and utterly nude body to appear dagger-like, his fingers reaching for the ceiling while his toes splayed like a cat's to maintain balance.

"Mmm," Britney said. "No wonder you wowed 'em as a model. The camera must've *loved* you. Tall. Slender. *Perfect* symmetry, along with your erotically bare chest. There's also that graceful line of your back and long neck. Damn, even your hands and feet are exquisite. Oh, did I forget to mention your cute ass?"

He blew her a kiss and stalked her with the sure grace of a panther, his manhood jiggling and jouncing with each step like an elephant's tail swishing at flies. After joining her in bed, he smiled a smile that warmed her heart.

"Babe? Were he alive today, Botticelli would surely sell his soul for the privilege of having you sit for him. And have I ever mentioned that you drive me into deep raptures with your kittenish sex quality?"

"Speaking of sex…" She bit down softly on her lower lip and asked, "Did you sleep with those two models? You know the ones; those hotties from that nude photo spread? The Milan one, I mean."

"Hey, come on." He frowned, only to reconsider. "Look, I'd just turned eighteen. Jen and I weren't married yet… in fact we were taking a break from each other. So yeah, we partied."

"I'll bet you did." She fought a growing smile. "So, darling. How does one say *ménage à trois* in Italian?"

"*Terzetto*," he blurted just as her music went from Spanish guitar to *Adagio for Strings, Opus 11*.

"Ah, yes. *Trio*. Bravo! As for you? *Che bello*."

Beautiful as he might be, those who bothered to look beyond his surface attraction also found his confidence intriguing. Britney herself once told a gal pal, "His appeal was instantly obvious. Devastating charm. Effortless, subdued; lethal."

Others who had known him before he married remarked that his lovemaking was playful and passionate, naughty and nice; sassy in between and at all times nuanced—a synthesis of heart, mind, and spirit.

Not that he didn't also love the simple fun of fucking. He did, and he could be both a little devil and St. Christopher combined, safely bearing the adventuresome to the far shores of Pleasantville with occasional side trips to Ecstasy, while always, always guiding the journey to its ultimate destination deep within the Land of Pillow Talk.

But while Kid enjoyed a childlike innocence of it all—a lusty young lad moving through life while gazing, smelling, tasting, and touching—he couldn't help but be aware of the dual-edged reputation he acquired along the way.

At least he'd tempered that cutting edge—first by marrying Jennifer, and then by pursuing his passions: those of husband, father, future surgeon and lifelong student.

THIRTY minutes later Britney and the unclothed Kid were still immersed in their books. As the back and forth continued and rivulets of sweat coursed down their bodies, Kid turned the page of a philosophy study guide. "Next question. Does God exist?" He glanced at her. "You're required to defend your thesis."

Britney peered at the discolored ceiling. "Logically speaking, no. The short answer is that there's nothing more complex than an Almighty Creator. However, physicists will argue that the beginning of the universe had been heralded by irreducible minimums. Now then, theories with foundations built upon simple premises are awarded greater credibility than those with complex, statistically improbable..."

"Okay. Quit showing off—and enough with the Occam's razor crap." He flashed a smile. "Next question..."

"Yes. I want to suck your cock. Definitely."

Kid grimaced. "*Next* question..."

"Speaking of questions," she began, "I've been meaning to ask for the longest time. Why aren't you circumcised?"

Kid blinked in confusion. "The longest time? Wait, how'd you know I'm uncut before today? I—" He rolled his eyes. "Ah. The photo spread."

"Of course, my prince. I do have that magazine, you know. The one with those glorious images taken in Milan? Those famous full-frontal pinups that line every girl's mirror the world over? The images that were taken by a photographer whom I'll happily shower with kisses for capturing your, um, essence? Or should I say…"

"The photographer wanted to adjust my junk for each shot." To her look of concern, he shrugged. "It's part of the biz. Straight shooters pursue the pussy; gay shutterbugs are out to fondle, and then some. So I made my boundaries clear. Issue resolved."

"Interesting." She looked away, then at him. "Regardless, your cock? Quite lovely."

Kid lifted a hand. "Why is being uncut even a topic for discussion?"

She shrugged. "It sets you apart from other guys? I mean, come on."

He grunted. "Yeah, well it's a huge turn-off for a lot of girls. American ones, at least."

"Hmm, never thought of that. I personally think it looks cute and I'd like to knit it a sweater. Anyway, you're definitely not Jewish. Not unless there's a Bris amiss."

"Shalom," he said to the ceiling.

But she wasn't ready to drop it. "You, with those two equally unclad beauties."

"Brit? It's like this. I posed, I got paid, I pushed the job aside and forgot about it." He frowned. "That whole nudity thing… the photos, and all that… hell, I'd walk the streets buck-assed if our society would back the fuck off."

"I know, Kid. Governments are evil and you wear flip-flops at Countway to demonstrate your rebellious nature." She swiped an arm across her sweaty brow. Then as Etta James'

At Last swept through the room, she narrowed her eyes and pointed at his crotch. "So. The amiss Bris. Why do you still have your foreskin?"

Kid raised an eyebrow and adopted a John Wayne accent. "Well I'll tell ya, little lady. My folks back on the ranch thought it an offense against Mother Nature. I'm intact, as God intended… wah hah." It was a canned response; one he'd supplied a thousand times.

And yet he held back on something: he *was* a Jew, by virtue of having been born to a Jewish mother, which under Judaic custom made him a de facto member of the tribe. Enter the spoiler: Kid and his younger brother had been baptized Catholics—their surname *was* Bailey, after all—and in his youth he served as an altar boy. Then again, Kid owned a gold and black yarmulke, and he wore it with pride on major Jewish holidays.

Kid was about to pose the next academic challenge when Britney abruptly said, "I need to pee," and scampered from the bed into the bathroom while leaving the door open. "Hey," she began, her voice muffled by the small room and some late Beatles now playing. "I um, heard a rumor just this morning that you've knocked up three girls this semester."

The toilet flushed, followed by the sound of tap water and two pumps of a soap dispenser. She emerged seconds later, but after studying his face her shoulders slumped. "It's true. Isn't it?"

He mumbled while reading from a textbook, "I've knocked up five, actually. Or seven." He looked up from the page he'd been scanning and squinted at the wall. "Wait. It's eight now. I think." He shrugged. "Hell, who knows? I've lost count."

She flinched as if slapped. "Five maybe *eight*? Then… then why won't you make love to *me*? And don't use marriage as

an excuse. Not when you're screwing every co-ed in sight."
All at once a sob escaped her. "What is so *wrong* with me
that you won't…"

His eyes softened and he leaped out of bed and put fingers
to her lips. Rumors of him impregnating girls had plagued
him since high school—the Lothario; the seducer bedding
all the babes when he wasn't going to other guy's beds.

He'd never been able to stop the urban legends, and
unknown to all he now had a legitimate need to perpetu-
ate them. But he was forbidden from revealing the reason
why; not to Britney or anyone else. A crazy-making part of
it was that Kid couldn't deny that the reputation stroked
his male ego.

Finally, he spoke from his soul. "Don't believe everything
you hear. I'm not bedding co-eds and fathering children as
I'm alleged to be doing. Sure, I worship women. Just not
that way."

"Well, I have this friend? Mateo? We passed him in the
library. He claims you bottom for the swim team captain.
Dakota."

He urged her toward the bed, and after laying on his back
he pulled her into his arms. Then while Yo-Yo Ma and Yitzhak
Perlman began playing Dvorak, he idly ran the pad of his
big toe up and down her silken calf. "Dak and I are friends.
Nothing more, nothing less; I'm neither gay nor bi-. Hell, I
didn't even experiment during my angst-filled adolescence.
That doesn't mean I'm not gay-friendly; I am."

Following this, he arched his far leg and planted his foot
flat on the mattress, then nuzzled the top of her head with
his lips. When she began caressing his hairy inner thigh
a minute later, he sighed. "Mmm. I like it when you do
that." But when she unexpectedly traced a tapering fingertip

down the long length of his exposed penis and toyed with its fringed terminus, he gripped her wrist. "No. Only my wife touches me there."

"Oh!" She pulled her hand away as if burned, and her face flushed red. "Sorry. I didn't mean to violate your boundaries."

He shrugged. "Don't sweat it." Then a little smile crept across his lips. "Besides, I liked it. Hey, I'm a guy." He shifted his long legs and winked at her.

•　•　•

Agamemnon finished scanning the personals for his latest ad: *"Looking for a warm and fuzzy soul mate to share my life with…"* Yet the women he dared reach out to wanted nothing to do with him. Even prostitutes gave him the brush-off.

And Ag sensed the life go out of him each time—unwanted, unloved; untouched.

It's why he felt so grateful when a woman called six months ago and asked him to use his magic; entreating him to right the world's wrongs while striking back at the scorning, the mocking, the… revulsion. *Yep, I'm gonna show 'em. Gonna show 'em all.*

•　•　•

Britney snuggled against him and planted her cheek against his sweaty chest. Following a silent moment during which he raked his long fingers through her hair, she whispered, "I can't get enough of listening to your heart."

Kid touched the back of her neck, and after reveling in the fine hairs he found there, he whispered, "I am passionate about the sound of your voice."

The stifling air seemed to lighten until she moved a bit to kiss his navel. Then she was looking up with pleading eyes and asking in a small voice, "Make sweet love to me? Please?"

"I—" He traced a fingertip along her eyebrows and down her cheek. "Babe? I feel a deep love for you. The thing is, I'm *in* love with my wife and she's the only woman for me."

Britney choked back a sob. "Your wife doesn't have to know."

"I would know," he gently told her. "So would you."

She looked at the wall and nodded. "You're right. I um, accepted long ago that you would never cheat on her. And I'm happy that you and she have this gift in your lives. But I love you. So is it asking too much to let me adore you as I do?" Now on the verge of tears, she wrapped an arm around his naked waist and held on for dear life. "Please let me love you."

"Oh, Brit." Kid held her close and made soothing noises while she trembled and sobbed against him, her great salty tears streaking down her cheeks and splattering against his chest.

In time she hitched and snuffled and whispered, "I'm so thankful for having you in my life."

As her music mix switched to Jesse Cook's *Mario Takes a Walk*, Kid brushed his lips across her cheek. "Thank you for being my friend."

He caressed her, kissed her, and offered words meant for her ears alone. In time they got back to studying, finishing just as the last of her tunes shifted to Elliott Smith's *Miss Misery*, when Britney looked into his eyes and said in a ghostly way, "We've only one more study session before exams. Then I won't see you again until the fall semester. Will I?"

"Hey, know what? I'm taking some summer flex courses. Why not take some with me?"

The corners of her eyes crinkled. "Tell me which ones. I'll make it happen."

He smiled and eased away from her, and while still naked he gathered his study materials and put them in his backpack. After getting dressed he went to the door. But while gripping the knob he looked over his shoulder at her and mouthed, *I love you.* An instant later he was out the door and closing it behind him.

KID stood there on the other side. He knew Britney sensed his presence, and part of him wanted to step back inside; to clutch her while burying his nose in her hair and inhaling; to hold her in his arms awhile longer.

But the other and far stronger part of him wanted to go home to the pregnant wife he loved above all else, and the two children he adored. Kid decided in an instant, and a great calm descended upon him as he walked away.

On reaching the first-floor vestibule he pushed open a scarred brown wooden door and stepped outside just as a car with a broken muffler whizzed past. Then when a brace of pigeons took sudden flight with furious beatings of wings, he looked up to watch them circling beneath a bright sky.

But while moving onto the sidewalk his eyes were drawn to a nondescript charcoal gray sedan parked at the end of the street, its motor chugging, and the hairs on the back of his neck instantly stood on end.

He touched his neck while wondering, *what's this all about?* He shook it off and unlocked his BMW with a chirp-chirp, only to look around when those hairs stood up again. *What the hell?*

He looked for the gray car. But it was no longer there.

Chapter Five

. . . .

12:00 noon West Coast Time • Olympia, Washington

AT ALMOST THE same time that Kid was sliding behind the wheel of his car, Lizbeth was grabbing the blue Morton Salt refill and slamming the pantry door shut. With it safely clutched in her nicotine-stained fingers, she shuffled toward her termite-infested home's tiny kitchen table, her frazzled slippers offending the floor until she reached the sagging table. After plopping onto a chair she released a long sigh.

Her morbidly obese son meanwhile never bothered to look up as he dabbed some gravy on his plate with a piece of low-grade store-bought cornbread.

While he crammed it into his mouth, Lizbeth lit her fifth Benson & Hedges Menthol Luxury since getting out of bed an hour ago. After dragging deeply at it, she closed her eyes and exhaled, the blue-grey smoke jetting from both nostrils to drift downward before rising to join the dust mites and mold that were constant components of this house.

On the heels of another drag and a gulp of cheap whiskey, she shook a defeated finger at her son. "Ain't you had enough to eat by now?"

"No." He struggled to his feet and asked, "Is there any food I can take with me?"

Lizbeth stared at him for a few beats before slurring, "Ag, you fat fuck. Don't you go asking for no more to eat. I got enough bills to pay without feeding your six hundred pounds of lard-ass. Or is it seven hundred now? Christ on a jumped-up crutch, it sure looks that way. Now go on. Get your butt downstairs so's you can play with your fuckin' computers. Or whatever else it is you play with... *loser.*"

She pulled at her cigarette and held the smoke for a few seconds before exhaling with a rush. "At least them computer gadgets keep you outta my sight. Now go on. Git. An' take a shower. Clean your face while yer at it. Might maybe you'll clean up some a them zits you always got."

Agamemnon's eyes burned with hate. "I did not ask you to get pregnant with me. But you did and now we're stuck with one another."

Lizbeth's face turned scarlet as she stood and drew her skinny, tobacco-ravaged frame up to its full five-foot-four-inch height. "Git outta here, you sad sumbitch!"

He said through barely suppressed anger, "I'll get, all right. I'll also get you. Along with the people who wouldn't help me get away from you." He turned his back on her and started for the basement door.

She screamed, "Where in hell you think you're going? Get back here when I'm talkin' to ya."

A sudden calm swept over Ag. "Where am I going? What're you, simple?" A hesitation. Then, "I am going to call Cleo. Why? Because she likes me."

Lizbeth scoffed. "Who's this Cleo? Another hippopotamus? The female version of *you*?"

A vein in Ag's forehead throbbed and he spat on the floor. "Bah!" Following this, he held himself upright like the U.S. Marines he'd once seen do in town and began walking, his cane thumping against the bare linoleum as he descended into his basement sanctuary.

Chapter Six

. . . .

At that exact moment • 3:12 PM East Coast Time • Cambridge, Massachusetts

JENNIFER BAILEY'S DELICATE oval face was framed not by night but by ebony hair; hair graced with a luster that spoke of starlight. Tall and lithe when not pregnant, she had on a black tank top and yellow sweatpants. A former model herself and holder of a master's in modern art, she embraced life, worshipped her husband, and lavished loving care on their twin daughters.

At the moment she was reading a thriller while the twins were immersed in their coloring books. But when the front door opened with a slight squeak, her eyes lit up and she did a little dance before charging down a photo-lined hallway to greet her husband.

She was about to rush into Kid's outstretched arms when she saw his eyes and came to an abrupt halt. She asked in a low voice, "What's wrong?"

"It's the strangest thing," he began. "While leaving Brit's I got this, I don't know—this feeling. Jen? I felt a coldness pass in front of my soul."

"Oh, my. That's not good." She entered his arms and bussed his cheek. "Hey? Have I told you lately that I love you?"

Levi Hart Bailey, aka Kid, snapped out of his *whatever* and planted a palm against her growing belly. "You have. And

I love you *and* I love this baby." Kid was about to kiss her mouth when he spied his daughters running toward him. "And I *adore* these two *munch*kins!"

As the twins closed the distance, he captured them in his arms and began tickling them until he reduced both girls to wriggling heaps of laughter.

Jen meanwhile leaned forward and sniffed at Kid. "You smell like a dead carp."

"Carp?"

She shrugged. "Why be generic? To just say *fish* would be oh-so-boring. But the idea of a bottom-feeder is *so* you. Anyway, didn't you shower at Tisha's?"

"I did."

"Did you get her to wash your balls? Was her wife there? Oh, and how was the run?"

"Tisha did not join me this time. She never does my balls, just my back—although there was this one time. Clarice was not there, and we had a good run; did the five in under thirty-six. In other news, the air's out at Brit's. It's why I'm malodorous. I'd have showered at her place, but I wanted to get home to you and the girls."

"Hmm, I kinda like the ripeness. Why not hold off on the shower?" She caught his eye and monkey-grinned him, which made them both laugh.

When the younger twin walked toward her, she caught Kid's eye. "What about Conor? Did you see him?"

Kid replied with beer-commercial joviality. "I did."

She asked while cleaning a smudge from the twin's cheek, "Do his frat brothers know you're tutoring him?"

"Christ, no. They... well, some of 'em would rag him for being dyslexic. The homophobic ones? They'd give him extra grief." He shrugged and got back to his daughters.

A short time later Kid and Jen were in the kitchen feeding the children while chatting about their day. The well-appointed kitchen smelled of warm food and spices, and vases filled with roses and white frangipani added nature's odors to their little corner of the world.

Kid shifted Lana—the younger twin by nine minutes—from one arm to the other before picking up a plate of finger food and holding it in front of the toddler's face. She glared and abruptly shouted, "*Mine,*" and grabbed a beef strip with one tiny hand while digging her other into a pile of mashed potatoes. Then while Lana shoveled both foods down her pipe, she regarded her father as if daring him to intervene.

Her father only smiled and wiped her chin. "Remember what I told you about sharing. And? I love you, Lana."

Jennifer adjusted a white linen napkin over her black T before offering a spoonful of applesauce to Lara, their more sedate older daughter. But as Kid wiped Lana's chin, he said in a low voice, "Britney's fallen in love with me."

Jen shrugged. "Why wouldn't she? I mean, get real. You're gorgeous. And did I forget to mention how much fun you are to be with?"

Having honestly forgotten about Britney yanking his briefs down and touching him so intimately, he said in a subdued voice, "She also asked me to make love to her."

Jen fed some diced broccoli to Lara. "That's what, the fifth time? So what'd you tell her, you randy little stud?"

The randy stud snorted. "What do you think? I told her the friggin' truth. That she has to wait her turn because there are fourteen babes ahead of her."

Jen asked while fighting a smile, "Where am I in that line? Oh, and your answer better be good, Young Mister. Or you're fucked."

"Oops. Make that fifteen before she gets her turn."

Jen ran the edge of the spoon along Lara's chin to scrape some spilled food away before saying matter-of-factly, "If any other guy babbled away as you so often do? I'd laugh 'em out of the room. Or have them committed. With you? Different matter altogether."

He enjoyed his wife's unfazed attitude, the result of never keeping secrets from each other ever since they met in preschool. They were casual lovers by fifteen yet never a couple, per se. Instead, they generously championed each other's successes in dating and even sleeping with a variety of fun and interesting others before they fell head-over for each other. It's what helped them appreciate how essential integrity is to a happy marriage; it's why Jen didn't mind him constantly getting hit on, or routinely showering with a lesbian.

He offered Lana a carrot. She made a face and pushed it away. He smiled. She giggled. He made silly faces at her and was wiping her mouth when he looked at Jen. "Babe? I realized long ago that I can always tell you my deepest darkest thoughts, and know you'll still be there for me; that you're my true north and that I..." Kid's voice caught. "And that I adore you."

She happily mouthed, *As I do you.* After a heartbeat, she looked at him and asked, "Have you given further thought to a name? Or has your feeble brain forgotten?"

"I. Am. Not. That. Vacuous." He looked mindlessly at her to prove it.

Jen chuckled as expected. "I suppose you're not."

"Nope." He took her hand in the close confines of their ultra-science, flower-graced kitchen. "A name—" His voice trailed away as he groped for the right words. "Jen, you're twenty-five weeks. And sometimes… sometimes I jerk awake at night thinking about a name for this one. Because I'm already so in tune with our baby and I…" A tear rolled down his cheek until he blurted, "Michael."

Jen reached out and touched her husband's arm. "After your papa. Awww. So sweet. I like it, although I should have thought you would want *Levi Hart Bailey, Jr.*"

"No. I want him to have Papa's name."

"Okay. Only?" She hunched her shoulders and raised her eyebrows as if tip-toeing behind someone. "Umm, what about… *Huckleberry?*"

Kid gasped and stared at her as if seeing E.T. standing in a corner. "Huckleberry? Cripes, I freaking love it!"

A bit of pain flashed across her face. "I was afraid you might. Seriously. How about, *Michael Levi Bailey?* That way he'll have both his paternal grandfathers' names along with a portion of yours."

He tried it on for size: "Michael Levi Bailey? Yeahhh, there we go." He shifted in his chair and wagged his eyebrows at her. "Huckleberry would be kinda cool, though. Then again, why not name this one after *your* dad?"

Jen turned pensive. "That's generous of you. Tell you what. Let's keep that option for our next boy."

"Hmm. I'm ready to try for that next boy right now." He regarded her with star-bright eyes and a glittering smile before quietly saying, "So we're good with *Michael Levi Bailey?*"

"We're good," she said while wiping Lara's mouth.

"Thank you," he said from the heart, and while looking down at his daughter he asked, "Did you hear that, Lana? You're about to have a baby brother. His name will be Michael. Can you say, *Michael?*" He watched her face go through the gradations of confusion to annoyance to a look that said *More food!*

. . .

"Damn," Agamemnon said into his Bluetooth. "That's a helluva an idea. I confess that I am at a loss for not thinking of it myself. I most certainly doff my cap to thee, fair knight."

Ag was seated beneath a splintered wooden ceiling beam flecked with cobwebs, his chair within easy reach of a plate of coffee cake. As his caller rambled on, Ag shoved a piece down his hatch.

In response to a question, Ag brushed crumbs from his lips and glared at a monitor. "Oh my God! What's this magic *window* I've been staring at? Damn! I never knew I could do that with these computer things!"

He took a deep breath and said in an equally condescending tone, "Of course I can mask the I.P. address, you dolt. What do you think I've been doing all this time?" He munched more cake. "For example, I make the I.P. appear to have originated in Zagreb. Only, it's always too late by the time they figure it out. By then it's coming at 'em from Nairobi."

Ag listened a bit, then screwed his eyes tight and nodded. "Now then. Once we proceed the worldwide stocks will crash within minutes. Wall Street; Nikkei; the London Exchange. They'll go ballistic and self-destruct."

While the caller laughed, Ag tilted his head to one side like a dog listening to its master. The caller finally spoke. Ag listened and replied, "Yeah, of course it'll take time. Six weeks, maybe eight." He canted his head again and listened, only to roll his eyes. "Yes, tonight's exercise is still on. Why wouldn't it be?"

When a dial tone filled Ag's ear, he reached for another piece of cake.

· · ·

Kid spent the next hours studying in the cedar-beamed family room in between breaks to play with the children. At six o'clock he dropped everything to prepare a filet of sole — for not only could Kid pose, wear clothes, dance, and think deep thoughts — he could cook.

He'd learned from the best — his mother, a gourmet cook and owner of the five-star restaurant that transformed her and his papa into multi-millionaires. His folks even sent him to Paris soon after he turned sixteen to learn the art from the world's finest.

Following tonight's dinner and with the twins in bed, Jen sniffed at Kid and winked. "You've always been a stud in the kitchen and a chef in bed. Plus you smell so *raw*. Mmm, I want you." And so around nine that evening Kid took the darling of his young life to their bed, where they made eager love to each other within the limits of her pregnancy.

· · ·

10:52 PM · Cleveland Air Route Traffic Control Center · Oberlin, Ohio

The air traffic controller perked up and listened when a flight called in: "*And Cleveland Center, United twenty-three oh one.*"

The controller glanced at the information strip near his elbow. It had the essential data: UNITED 2301. AIRBUS 320. PHILADELPHIA TO CHICAGO. To confirm the aircraft's position and altitude, he keyed his mic and spoke crisply.

"United twenty-three oh one, Cleveland Center. Say your altitude and ident."

"Ah, Cleveland. United 2301's at angels thirty…"

That's all the controller heard as the crowded ATC center went dark. Only the automated battery-powered emergency lights prevented people from stumbling into consoles or chairs. Even worse, the emergency generator failed to kick in, leaving the pilots and controllers unable to communicate.

The power returned precisely three minutes and twenty seconds later, leaving everyone from controllers to White House Situation Room staff scratching their heads at an intriguing fact: the three-minute, twenty-second outage matched United 2301's aircraft type: Airbus-320.

. . .

The persistent chirp of Kid's smartphone clawed him from the trancelike sleep he'd fallen into following the evening's passions. But while reaching for it he fumbled the play and dropped the ball.

After feeling around on the carpet and locating it, he pressed the green icon and held the phone close while mumbling with brain-dead earnestness, "Dooja domma dab?"

"Listen up," Levi's detached voice said from the other end.

Kid instantly sat up and gripped the phone. "Dad."

"I'm parked down the street. Gray sedan. Cati and Marty are with me. Tell Jen you'll be gone for two hours. Your Uncle Marty will stay with her and the children. Get dressed. As in, now. Then step outside."

"Yes, sir." He pressed the END icon, unaware that by stepping outside he would become entangled in a series of unstoppable events that would threaten not only the death of his body, but that of his soul.

Chapter Seven

· ·

At that same moment • Olympia

AGAMEMNON'S NOSE CRINKLED as he cursed the environmental quality of his otherwise spotless basement room. It crinkled because he could still smell the mildew that not even the mainframes' ozone tangs could mask.

The mustiness always puzzled him, since he worked hard to maintain a bright and orderly living area. Ag had two air purifiers equipped with HEPA13 filters, and he used an exterior door that opened from the split-level home's basement to the rear yard—because opening the interior door at the top of the stairs would let dust in. Or worse, it would invite a run-in with his mother.

Ag lived on Social Security disability payments that let him equip his basement room with a microwave and fridge. He also had a toilet and a shower. And yet despite his best efforts at hygiene, he'd surrendered long ago to oily skin and acne.

He had also grown to accept how others regarded him: the morbidly obese freak with uneven eyebrows and dark, bowl-cut hair; the ogre whose sausage-sized fingers hampered his ability to navigate a keyboard.

There were other physical deficits, beginning with a respiratory system that couldn't keep up with his physical demands, so that he ended up wheezing from the slightest exertion.

Then there was his heart, which labored to supply blood to his massive body while still leaving his extremities cold and occasionally blue. Ag needed a cane to walk, he had trouble squeezing into his mother's ancient green Ford Explorer, and had to struggle even more just to escape it.

And yet long ago he vowed to live with these problems, if only he could take girls out on dates. But those who even deigned to talk to him would soon roll their eyes and end things with a curt, "It was good talkin' to ya." Translation: Get your skanky-ass bod away from me.

In short, he lived a life of thorough rejection. To his credit, he didn't deceive himself or cast blame elsewhere. He'd pigged out all his life. Now he lived with a damaged body and a self-image that barely rose above self-loathing.

Then one day he experienced a splendid turn of events when a woman befriended him. She wasn't just any woman either, but a beautiful one who had gone out of her way to speak to him. One time she even rested a hand on his thigh. Oh, Father God and Sonny Jesus—how it made him blush; how it made his heart race. It made his day, and Ag wished he were talking to her now.

Unfortunately, right now he was talking with one of *the others*—a label that made him grunt and think, *Christ, I sound like an Amish farmer referring to 'the outsiders'… 'der Engländers.'*

"Tell me again of the results," the accented voice came through Ag's Bluetooth.

"Simple," Ag began in a chin-up, shoulders back professorial voice. "We will simultaneously neutralize all electrical power in America. Everywhere."

"I am intrigued. Please to tell me more."

Ag leaned back in his reinforced chair and began holding court. "There are three main grids, all interconnected with one another. There's also a fourth. The Texas Grid, which for reasons only Texans can explain is not tied into the other three. Now then. A sudden influx of AI-induced problems will compound and escalate until the entire country sinks into complete and utter chaos. No electricity. No power for gas pumps. There's more."

He licked his lips, unable to remain still. "Say farewell to GPS. Bid adieu to refrigeration. Wave bye-bye to Wi-Fi or any other means of communication. Every city, town, village, and hamlet will be isolated and rendered vulnerable to roving gangs in search of food and medications. The..."

"Medications? Why do you make the mention of this?"

Ag scoffed. "Are you for real? Christ, even gang bangers become ill. They have diabetic children in need of insulin. They..."

"Wait," the voice said. "All of this due to loss of power?"

"Of course." Ag looked up to the Heavens with a why me, God face. "It's America's worst nightmare. The few enlightened government types who have been warning of this for years go unheard, because nobody has time for doom an' gloom stuff."

"You call this a nightmare why?"

"Jesus, what don't you understand? Everything... *everything*, comes to a screeching halt. No lights. No trucks to deliver food or medicine."

"You will do this how?"

"Oh... my... god. Did I not just tell you? I'll utilize AI. It'll replicate, duplicate, and then some. AI can both outsmart *and* work faster than humans. It'll even go into a self-survival mode by erecting roadblocks to prevent a restoration of power. Dams will open. Drawbridges will malfunction."

Ag pounded a fist against his console. "These fuckers who seek to humiliate and dominate will finally see how powerless they truly are."

"Well, that is our plan," his caller said. "A return to the nature. So. This scenario that we have outlined. You can do all this when?"

"Are you daft? Didn't we discuss this just the other day? Look, I need to hack into three more websites. They include a utility transfer grid and two comm centers."

"This will be how difficult?"

"What, to hack 'em? Listen, and listen good. Any barrier devised by a human brain can be defeated by another brain. By throwing AI into the mix? It becomes an unstoppable tsunami."

"Again," the voice demanded. "A timeline."

Ag hesitated. Lines etched his oily forehead until he spoke in a quiet academic voice. "That depends."

"On?"

"On how soon you want this to happen. It's almost May. We can move by July; August tops. But," he began, his voice changing its tone, pacing, and syntax to that of a criminal confederate. "*If* we were to wait until winter—if we wait until *Christmas*—the results will be magnified a thousandfold by polar vortex temps." Ag sniffed. "We don't have to stop with the USA, you know. We can make this global."

A long silence ensued, broken only when the voice said, "I will most assuredly get back to you on both the timeline and this global scheme. Now we move to the other matters, sí? I should like to know more about this AI. Does it have the connection with this thing called deepfake? Hmm. Perhaps we should do the dinner this Wednesday and discuss these matters. My treat. What do you say to this?"

Ag hesitated. He'd intentionally held back on mentioning both the encryptions and the encryption keys required to unleash his AI devils — a tactic he chose after gaming scenarios that had him wondering, *what if they decide they can manage things on their own, and kill me? Only, they can't manage without me. Sooo... .* "Love to," he finally told his caller.

·   ·   ·

Minutes Later — April 29 — Boston Time

Boston's streets are studded with stores, banks, and other businesses. Scattered among them are nameless office buildings housing a clutch of secure rooms hardened against spyware to permit select government personnel to meet in secrecy. Some of these offices house classified information, and procedural methods are used to keep the secrets secure. These below-the-radar sites are known throughout the spy biz as Sensitive Compartmented Information Facilities.

"Let me guess," Kid intoned as Levi entered an underground parking garage beneath a nine-story office building. "This is a SCIF."

He still hadn't received a reply by the time they stepped into an elevator. One inside, Kid gave his biological father a once over.

Levi was wearing a suit that Kid knew had been tailored around the Sig SAUER P-229 .357 magnum pistol in Levi's shoulder holster. As for Cati, Kid had to study her carefully before spotting the heat she was packing within her black and white casual wear.

The elevator doors whisked open. The instant they stepped out, Levi led the way through myriad hallways that were designed to confuse intruders. All at once they encountered a security checkpoint manned by two armed guards.

"I believe you're expecting us," Levi murmured while showing his ID. Next, he held up his smartphone and displayed a QR code. One of the guards scanned it with a reader and studied his computer screen before glancing at Levi and nodding.

Without needing to be asked, Levi handed over his phone and opened his briefcase for inspection. The other guard meanwhile gave the still-frowzy-headed Kid a once over and decided against wondering why a young man wearing an Aloha shirt, black shorts and flip-flops—and who smelled like six-day-old socks—should be allowed entry.

After Cati and Kid followed Levi's lead, the first guard asked, "Does anyone have any thumb drives or other media that can carry information from this facility?"

Levi answered for all of them. "No, sir."

"Very well." The guard passed Levi's briefcase and Cati's purse through an airport x-ray machine. "Procedure," he commented. "I know you're armed. Still—" Once the items came through he tilted his head at a glass-topped pedestal on the other side.

Levi went to it and placed his palm against the glass, then opened his fingers wide and held still until a small green light glowed. When a muted *beep* concluded the verification process, the guard used a physical key to unlock a hardened door. "You may pass through," he intoned.

From there the trio ventured down a series of sterile passageways before reaching a heavy wooden door with the innocuous placard: *Room Twelve*. Levi pushed it open to reveal a richly appointed room of dark paneling, an elliptical conference table, and deep leather chairs.

Kid rasped, "Show me the coffee."

"Over there." Levi pointed at a service tucked in the far corner. "I called ahead and had it readied."

"Anyone else?" Kid asked while lurching for it. When Levi and Cati shook their heads, he poured a cup and took a tentative sip. It was good, and he closed his eyes and groaned with pleasure.

Following a second sip, he faced Levi and Cati and said without fanfare, "You're activating me. Aren't you?"

.   .   .

In Olympia at that same moment

Alessandro Costa, aka Sandro to those he felt worthy enough to enjoy that level of familiarity—sniffed as if someone had passed gas without so much as a 'pardon me.' Not that the odor would matter inside his hemp-saturated backwoods cabin.

Tall, slender, handsome, and in his late-twenties, Sandro had black hair, grey-green eyes, and compelling dark features. But whenever the self-styled English manor lord smiled it never reached his eyes. The only exception came when he had his Siamese cat Malee in his arms, for he cherished Malee, a Thai word for *jasmine flower*.

The incongruity of a Catalan Basque Separatist seeking English-style nobility disturbed those who met him—not that they would say so in his presence, especially while he was doing drugs as he was right now by taking another hit from a bong, closing his eyes, and exhaling harsh khaki-colored smoke that rose toward the ceiling. He felt chill, only to feel his disposition go sour when his cell vibrated.

He thumbed the icon and listened while the caller spoke. The more he heard, the greater the grip he took on the phone. In time his face turned red. Then he erupted in fury. "Do not tell me what I am to think, you… you Nubian *bitch!*"

The caller shrieked. "Don't you dare call me that, you wanker! You failed *solicitor!* Or I shall gouge your bloody eyes out and shove them up your arse! Straight away, too!"

"Point your condescending finger at thine own self. For you are nothing more than the over-educated loser." The Spaniard pressed his lips so tight they turned blue. "Shut up and listen to me, *bitch.* I know where I am with the fat-assed one. So do not question my progress. However, where are *you* with him? Will he deliver? Or must you sleep with him?"

"Sleep with him? Christ, are you completely mad?"

"You would enjoy sleeping with that… that *thing,* sí? What do these Norteamericanos call it? Slumming?" He took another hit from his bong.

The female caller fired back. "Bollocks to you for telling me to shut up. Am I clear?"

Sandro drew a sharp breath and released it. "Do you not see that all I want to know is whether or not this… this *hippopotamus* will deliver on time? Yes? No?"

"He's assured me that he will. July for certain. I make it a bit under ten weeks from this day. It's either that, or we push back until Jolly Saint Nick time."

"Very well. But he *can* make good by the fourth day in the month of July, no?" He was about to say more when Malee rubbed against his leg, which made him smile.

"He can deliver by then," the woman said. "Complete shutdown, beginning at noon on the Yank's Independence Day… though I prefer doing it on Christmas Day."

"Either option will serve our purposes. Well? Do we elect to proceed?"

"Global economic collapse," she whispered. "The best thing? The most scathingly brilliant part of it all? They shall never know what hit them."

Sandro ended the call and said to the empty room, "Dustin Smythe never knew what hit him, either. Dustin, of the Bureau of the Federal Investigations. Sí, this Dustin, he said to me that his name was Leonard Whiting. Of the *Romeo and Juliet* motion picture? Bah! Also, he would not have the sex." Sandro rubbed his chin and thought, *This means the F.B. of I. will send another of the undercover types.*

.   .   .

Boston • The SCIF

"Yes," Levi told Kid once they were seated at the table. "We're activating you."

A tight-lipped Kid opened his mouth enough to say, "All right. Spill it."

Levi grunted. "Yeah, right away. Because I'm dying to violate the Espionage Act." He turned to his wife. "Darling?"

Cati pulled a manila folder from her bag and guided it across the table to Kid. "This document certifies that effective immediately you are an employee of Vanguard International. This makes you eligible to receive selected classified information."

"Understood." Kid read the document's fine print and signed in blue ink from the Mont Blanc pen Levi supplied.

After retrieving the writing instrument, Levi shifted in his chair and looked at Kid. "By direct presidential order, I am permitted to circumvent certain security requirements and lawfully disclose to you an abstract that contains Top Secret, Sensitive Compartmented Information."

"SCI," Kid mumbled. "Above Top Secret."

"Yes. And ORCON."

Kid nodded rapidly. "Originator Controlled. They decide who can be in the know. Do I have it right?" He studied Levi's face for verification.

"Excellent. Ready?"

"Wait." Kid took another swallow of coffee before sitting back and saying, "Go."

"First, tell me how you feel about environmentalists."

Kid's face dissolved into a potato sack of confusion. "Feel? Hell, how else could I feel? I'm indebted to them and their cause. They're great people. Number one on my list of heroes."

"Good answer, seeing as you are to infiltrate a radical faction of Green Anarchists."

The young man scoffed. "Green Anarchists, my ass. It's shorthand for eco-terrorist Nazis who splash buckets of paint on eighty-year-old women because they're wearing fur coats. My, such stalwart young lads—though I've noticed they never enter biker bars and douse *them* with paint for wearing leathers. Nooo. Although of course, Greeners don't wear leather because they scream about being oh-so-compassionate vegans. Or take that pair of true believers who recently threw cans of tomato soup on a Van Gogh to protest—wait for it—offshore drilling."

He rolled his eyes. "Yeah, attack a masterpiece, since god only knows how deep a tie-in poor old Van Gogh had to oil production." He looked from Cati to Levi, their faces unreadable masks. "Okay, they did it for the publicity. I get it."

Levi said, "Our gang-of-interest is located near Olympia, Washington."

"Well of course they are. And bless their little hearts. Yes sir, state capitals are always grand venues for crusaders. Why, I hear on the down low that some capitals can only be reached by yellow brick roads." Kid glanced at Cati who was sitting with a calmness that belies a coming storm. "Why me?"

She replied with an unfaltering gaze. "You have special skill sets."

"Which are?"

"Ones that will become self-evident."

"Right. Because what I lack in experience, I make up for with inexperience."

"Listen up," Levi said in a curt manner that forbade argument. "Three deep-cover FBI agents have tried to infiltrate the group. The first quickly blew his cover. The second lasted a month before an old friend recognized her in passing. Totally innocent encounter, but the agent had to assume she'd been compromised. So she started a blistering argument with the gang's leader. To nobody's surprise, the leader gave her the boot before they could make her."

"Good thinking on the agent's part," Kid said.

"I'd have done the same." Levi pointed a finger at Kid. "By chance, she remained long enough to learn they'd found a hacker. Not just any hacker, either. No sir. They acquired the mother of 'em all. He's somewhere in Olympia, he's off-grid, and he can shut down our nation's entire infrastructure with the flick of a switch. Possibly the whole planet's."

Although Kid's eyes widened, he remained quiet and alert.

"Think about it. He neutralizes electrical power throughout the United States; he prevents emergency generators from kicking in. Jacks up oil and gas line pressures to create explosions at refineries. He'll open the floodgates of nine thousand dams. Instant destruction on a scale too massive even for me to imagine.

"Complicating matters will be a total loss of communications—especially cell phones. Victims can't call for help from overwhelmed first responders…"

"Darling?" Cati rested a palm on Levi's arm. "Perhaps we should tell Kid what occurred just a few short hours ago."

Levi pushed his bottom lip forward in thought. "Ah, right." He caught Kid's eye. "Your Uncle Marty, Cati, and I flew into Boston yesterday afternoon to hold this discussion."

Kid bolted upright. "The gray car. Outside my lady friend's apartment."

Levi said, "Yes. It was us. We were about to approach you when I received a call from the White House. Hell, we came to this very room for a telecon. I was about to call you again before being interrupted by a game-changer…"

"… Some three and one-half hours ago," Cati interjected. "We got caught up in its aftermath, hence this late-night meeting."

"Here it is," Levi began. "Cleveland Air Traffic Control experienced a sudden power failure. Everything. Electricity; comms; even the generators failed to kick in. This fits the profile of what we've been discussing. Hence this new imperative."

Kid winced as if he'd bitten into a lemon. "I get it. No way to process credit cards without electricity. People can't get their money from banks since tellers have no way to pull up accounts. An end to civilization as we know it. A return to bartering. Armed gangs wandering throughout in search of food; raping and killing all who stand in their way. Humph. These jerk-offs have *such* a great vision of utopia."

Cati caught his eye. "It's why you must infiltrate them."

Kid scowled. "Hey, I'm on it... *okay*? Christ, I'll even put up a suggestion box. What I wanna know is, how great a peril can it be? I mean, this hacker's undoubtedly into dark webs and deep webs, yadda, yadda. Let's say for argument's sake he succeeds in cutting power. But what the hell? Floridians lose electricity for days and weeks at a time from hurricanes. Yet they manage until engineers restore power."

"Your argument's flawed," Cati fired back. "Consider this scenario: the entire nation's without power. In theory, we could game the situation and decide that while great harm's been done, we shall resolve the problem with good ole' Yankee ingenuity."

"Yankees? Gimme a break. I'm thinking you lost the thread, right?"

Levi glared. "Knock it off."

"Yeah, yeah." Kid gulped some coffee and drove a fist into an open hand. "All right, all right. Got it. Yankee ingenuity. I'm on it. But?"

"But our foreign enemies will have begun circling overhead." She arched a splendid eyebrow. "Sensing weakness, they'll dive like hawks for the kill. China, Russia, North Korea; even Iran could launch a nuclear attack. We'd be wide open."

Kid countered by saying, "We'll have ample global military assets to retaliate."

She looked at him. "You're the President of the United States. Do you save your nation's honor, only to plunge the world into one hundred years of nuclear winter? Do you end all life on Earth? Or will you go belly-up for humankind's sake? In another scenario, imagine if these terrorists succeed in doing this on a global scale. Our enemies, not knowing where the attack originated, strike out in all directions with missiles, bombers, and ballistic subs."

"Got it." Kid mumbled before swearing under his breath. While processing all of this he slipped his right flip-flop off and absently worried his big toe against the carpet. Finally, he exhaled in a rush. "Why do eco-freaks feel so entitled to thrust their agendas upon the world?"

"You've got 'em nailed," Levi agreed.

The son snorted. "You think? Come on! I've read their manifesto." He raised his hands to the ceiling. "The language is so structured, so... loaded with legalese that it ends up a mockery of their ideology. Sure, I'll concede that anarchists don't pose as great a threat to our way of life as Antifa or white supremacists or other whack-jobs do." He frowned. "Still, I'm on it."

Cati's dark skirt swished as she crossed one slender calf over the other. "Kid? The anarchist movement is expanding with a continent's confidence. Worse still, this particular unit embraces the Gaia Hypothesis. Do you know of this?"

He made a point of rolling his eyes. "Don't insult me, Cati. Yeah, I know Gaia. It's centered on Darwinism and bio-chem synthesis. Except in their view, it's humans that stand in the way and should therefore be destroyed. Not too unlike Stephen Hawking's fears of AI running amok." Kid shook his head. "Fuuuck. Talk about 'open the pod bay door, HAL.'"

Levi cut in. "The hypothesis has been interpreted as a neo-pagan religion." While loosening his tie he added, "This matters to us because anarchists form loose relationships known as affinity groups. Some become heavily armed even while seeking a suspension of the Second Amendment.

Armed or not, they're vicious thugs who until now have been content to carry out small-scale raids and disband to hinder efforts to track them. If they do have an Achilles heel, it's that they stay in touch with one another."

Cati cleared her throat. "We believe this faction's behind the recent Beaver Dam episode. Now they stand on the precipice of the mother of all disasters, with an eye toward doing their deed by the 4th of July some ten weeks from now. Or they might wait until Christmas Day."

"It's why we need you," Levi said. "Not someone like you, but *you*."

"Because?"

"Because you have a PhD mind and can win a bar fight. Because you grew up within the shadow world that your papa and I inhabit. You're gregarious. Others are drawn to you. It's why we had you rant online against governments."

The son looked at the man who sired him. "To establish my bona fides." Falling silent, he began imagining walking hand-in-hand through fields and gardens with Jennifer, their twins, and their future son. He and Jen had plans; they had hopes for their children. He grunted. "Why not swoop in and round 'em up?"

"I wondered when you'd ask." Levi raised an index finger. "Failsafe systems. Should we pounce too soon, a protocol might trigger a Hail Mary pass that'll unleash the Furies." He gestured at Cati.

She spoke up loud and clear. "Back to business. These anarchists hang out at an old coffee shop. Mom-and-pop place. Owners are aging hippies. Husband has a gray last-chance ponytail; wife wears long skirts and lots of rings. They're anti-gov in general and vicious toward cops in particular. But they're not the problem. It's these two." She handed Kid some grainy surveillance photos. "The Bureau has ID'd them as anarchist ringleaders. I think it's best to begin with the woman."

Kid studied the woman's full-on photo and read aloud from an attached printout. "Twenty-five. Born in Ghana. Parents moved to London soon after. Attended Jesus College at Oxford. PhD in economics—" He glanced up and said from the side of his mouth, "Which the Brits call a D.Phil. Let's see, what else."

He studied the page. "Hmm. Unable to find work. 'Overly educated,' some say. 'Far too obnoxious,' others claim. Moves to Ulster where she becomes disenfranchised with governments. Vocabulary's a patois of English and Irish slang terms. A devout Christian, she claims Egyptian descent and calls herself Cleopatra." He snorted. "How convenient. A black Cleopatra. Christ, why didn't she just get a job promoting that recent movie?"

"Probably," Levi mumbled.

The son continued. "Where was I? Ah. Her name is Cleopatra Koufie." He squinted. "Wait. Koufie. Isn't there a Ghanaian footballer by that name?" He shook his head without waiting for an answer. "So. Cleopatra. Cleo for short. And whaddya know? As a child, she had a sled named 'Rosebud.'"

"You know better than that," Cati scolded. "Also? You failed to mention her dream of becoming a fashion model—a dream her father stifled. You and she will have that in common. Make it work for you."

"Roger that," Kid said, only to pause while reading from the slip of paper. "Next on the hit parade is Alessandro Costa, aka *Sandro*. Late twenties. Basque separatist. Vicious psychopath. Rumored to be the group's enforcer. Heroin addict. Openly gay."

Following a brief silence Levi said, "Your Uncle Marty and a pair of new Vanguard people will be your handlers."

Kid nodded rapidly. "New. Meaning they weren't at the Castle."

Castle is the Secret Service code word for the White House, where Levi and Michael Bailey—the man who raised Kid as his own—made headlines when Vanguard got into a firefight with a group of heavily armed skinheads bent on killing the President. Michael took a bullet in the neck and only survived because Levi braved a hail of gunfire to reach his side, stick a finger inside the wound, and prevent a total bleed-out.

Levi now said with wide sweeps of his arms, "The newbies are a married couple, and to our great fortune they're already positioned. Doctor Jacob Berg and Gillian Robertson. The good doctor hails from Wyoming and he's doing a residency at Olympia's premier hospital."

Cati cut in. "Gillian's Canadian by birth, she's a naturalized U.S. citizen, and a titled flyweight Ultimate Fighting Champion."

Kid perked up. "Holy crap! The one who dyes her hair neon red? I've seen her on UFC. Man, she's kick-ass! MMA all the way. They call her The Savage." He narrowed his eyes and spoke as if reciting a grammar school lesson. "Ah, I see. She's a crowd-pleaser. Nobody will suspect her of leading a double life."

"Affirmative. Back to our physician friend. Jake drives a black F-150 with *Naked Jake* stenciled on the tailboard, courtesy of his college buddies after he posed nude for live art classes. This led to an invitation to pose for a fund-raiser honoring USS Arizona's last surviving sailors. Jake's portrait of a horribly burned sailor in a tattered uniform raised more than a hundred grand alone."

Kid nodded like a bird pecking at seeds. "I like him already."

Cate nodded. "They're superb operatives. And as you pointed out, their bona fides let them hide in plain sight. As for Doctor J? Why, who would be surprised if he formed a bond with a med student?"

Kid blew air from his cheeks. "Copy loud an' clear."

Cati smiled at him. "Marty's fully briefed on this mission… one of only eighteen people on this planet including you who are in on it. Jake and Gillian know only that they're supporting a deep cover mission." She glanced at Levi. "Anything else?"

"Yes." He looked into Kid's eyes. "As an operative, you'll enjoy limited immunity from prosecution for certain crimes."

"Huh? What're you talking about?" He swallowed a slug of coffee and waited.

"The group might test you, maybe say they're low on funds, ask you to burglarize the homes of wealthy capitalists. Fill in the blanks from there. Anyway, you're protected so long as you don't participate in acts of violence…"

"As in, robbing banks," Kid muttered.

"Right. Crimes against property without a threat of physical violence. That's the key. If caught, you won't be prosecuted so long as you were acting under color of your mission."

"Understood."

Levi hunched forward. "Son? There's one more item we need to discuss. The FBI sent in a third operative. Local police officers found his body the other night near Sandro's home."

Kid maintained his composure. "Got it."

"As anyone might imagine, the Bureau wants a piece of Sandro. Only, they've been ordered to stand down. So do your best to develop evidence that can lead to his arrest."

Cati quietly said, "The agent's name was Dustin Smythe."

Kid scoffed. "Why thank you, Cati. Thanks for making him a real person to motivate me. How kind of you."

Rather than feed Kid's anger, Levi stated in an official voice, "This ends the classified portion for now. While you decide whether to accept the mission, I am obligated to caution you not to reveal what we've discussed to anyone under penalty of imprisonment. Is that understood?"

"Come on, Dad. Gimme just a little break. I'm on it, okay? I don't talk. Not to Jen, not to Mom. Not nobody." And yet despite his resistance to the task, Kid felt his pulse quicken.

Levi cleared his throat. "Your papa and your mother are due in on a morning flight. She and Jen need to know that we're sending you into harm's way. But they can't know the full details. So we'll do some role-play to paint a picture in broad strokes while avoiding specifics."

"I take it Papa's been briefed?" Kid thought to himself, *After all, he is on Vanguard's board of directors.*

"Yes. If you accept the assignment he'll talk to Nick, since he'll need to be in the same loop as Jen and your mother."

Kid's half-brother Nicholas—same mother but fathered by Michael—was a sophomore at Johns Hopkins University.

"Now listen," Levi continued. "Following tomorrow's discussion you can decide whether to take this on. I suggest we meet at your home."

Kid said as if reading from a grocery receipt, "I'll prepare an early dinner. We'll talk afterward. Twelve noon?"

"Excellent. Questions?"

Kid looked down at his flip-flop-shod feet and wiggled his long toes. *Time to grow up,* he told himself. Raising his head, he looked at his father. "No questions, sir."

"Didn't think so. All right. Let's get you home to your family. First, though—" He stood and pulled Kid to his feet and looked into his eyes. "Son? I'm such a slacker. I mean, I just cannot stop loving you more with each passing day—ever since the moment you came kicking an' screaming into the world." After a heartbeat, he pulled his son into his arms and kissed his cheek. "Oh, Kid. I love you completely."

LEVI and Cati dropped Kid off half an hour later. After thanking Marty for watching his family, he and Jen got back in bed. The thing about Jen is that she grew up alongside Kid. She knew from an early age what Levi, who sired Kid—and Papa Michael, who raised him—did for a living. She also knew this day might come. So they held each other in silence while pondering how badly their world was about to be ripped asunder.

Chapter Eight

· ·

April 29 · Twelve Noon · Cambridge, Massachusetts

WHEN THE DOORBELL chimed, Kid glanced at the clock and told Jen, "Right on schedule."

The young husband was wearing an immaculately tailored two-button Ralph Lauren of impeccable Italian craftsmanship in wool sharkskin, with flat-fronted trousers and gleaming Bally lace-ups. The sky-blue button-down shirt he selected went well with a dark blue tie, whose white dots lined up with a precision born from attention to detail.

And he wore it all with breathtaking elegance, the formal attire rooted in childhood when Sunday dinner required jacket and tie for gentlemen young and old, and evening apparel for ladies.

He opened the door and found Levi and Cati on the other side. Levi had on a cobalt-blue Givenchy suit, while Cati wore a chic Paul Ka peach-colored dress with faultless grace.

Furrows erupted across Kid's forehead. "Where's Uncle Marty?"

"Caught the early bird to Reagan National. Somebody's gotta mind the store."

"Of course." Kid hugged Levi and kissed his cheek before turning to greet Cati. "My, don't you look beautiful in that peachy delight? Gosh, Cati. I'm never able to decide what has the higher octane—your brains or your beauty."

Cati revealed the merest hint of a smile before putting a palm to his cheek. "If I didn't know you so well, I'd accuse you of flirting."

"Guilty as charged," he teased and draped an affectionate arm around Levi. "Where are Mom and Papa?"

"Should be here soon."

MICHAEL Bailey and Nadia Bailey were amicably divorced but they arrived together half an hour later. Kid's mother was a tall raven-haired beauty of Russian-Jewish descent, and she presented in a black Diane Von Furstenberg with the understated poise so common to old money—a trait she shared with Cati.

Kid embraced her. "The twins are napping, and... and here's my Jen!"

Jennifer strode down the hallway in an ivory maternity dress and Manolo Blahnik shoes. Nadia, who had watched Jen grow alongside her son, went to her at once and held the younger woman's head between her hands like warming loaves of bread.

Michael Bailey stepped forward next in a gray Soho single-breasted Armani. He stood tall as always, with blond hair and big brown eyes that still melted hearts. Yet Kid could never shake the notion that his papa's unspoiled face contradicted an unutterably cruel childhood that sent him fleeing his home only to end up a street kid who was forced to sell his body for food.

Despite his stunning good looks, Michael bore only a passing resemblance to Kid, who at the moment was planting his forehead against Michael's. "I love you, Papa."

Michael whispered, "My precious, irreplaceable son."

Kid segued with statesmanlike elegance by asking after his papa's wife. "How's Monica?"

Michael grimaced. "You know how it is. Stage four. What's there to say? She's coping. Anyway, thanks for asking." He clamped a fatherly hand on Kid's shoulder.

The son asked, "And the baby?"

"Growing like a bean sprout." The corners of his eyes crinkled. "I'll brag over some new photos later."

"Great. Well? Dad and Cati are in the living room."

THE ice in Levi's scotch rocks tinkled the instant Nadia entered the room. He put down the glass and kissed the cheek of the woman he once lived with and loved completely—only to step aside for her sake after she fell head-over for Michael.

But when Nadia delivered a son just shy of seven months later, all eyes turned to Levi. If there were any doubts that he fathered the child, they faded as the newborn grew: Kid's striking blue eyes matched Levi's, while Nadia's and Michael's were brown. Kid also had Levi Hart's triangular face, plus his hands and feet. And years later when Nadia sat next to Kid to review his full-frontals, she commented with total ease, "Oh, look. You have your father's penis."

As for Michael and Levi, they'd been best friends for years and had saved each other's life at least once. It's why Michael embraced the newborn Kid to the max and raised him as his own. As for Kid? He felt blessed by having two fathers.

EARLIER in the day the beneficiary of two fathers set about preparing a *Coq au Vin* which turned out to be an impressive version of the classic red wine chicken stew. Its tantalizing aromas filled the home, and Jen's table boasted six place settings of robin egg blue-and-white speckled china. There were also two high chairs, and she had placed uncorked bottles of Châteauneuf-du-Pape at either end of the SCAN dining room table. Jen of course would drink sparkling water.

Once everyone took their seats, Kid stood and raised his glass and said with a reverent voice, "Wine is sunlight, held together by water. And to Galileo's poignant observation, I offer this brief coda: family is also sunlight, held together by intimacy."

During the ripple of applause that followed, Jen took her husband's hand. *"Nice."*

While still standing he turned and looked into her eyes. Then with glass held high, he spoke slowly, quietly; humbly. "To Jennifer, who taught me to conjugate the verb, 'to love.'"

The endearment had been so unexpected, so heartfelt, that the room fell into stunned silence. Meanwhile, a choked-up Jen put a hand to her chest and tilted her head at Kid.

FOR dessert, the young couple offered a *Poire avec Orange* version of poached pears: light, simple, and bursting with a mimicked marmalade flavor. The rich food came with a bonus: it made the twins sleepy, which let Kid and Jen put them down for a nap.

Then while Beethoven played softly from hidden speakers, Kid turned to the guests and spoke two words. "The library."

Everyone retired to the elegant room of rosewood paneling, brown leather furniture and graceful oak bookshelves populated by philosophies, histories, and novels. The young couple also had books on art, architecture, and travel—along with other books just for plain fun.

Once inside the library with its scents of old books and Murphy Oil-polished wood, Kid sat atop an African-wood settee. After Jen settled next to him, his eyes followed the others as they jockeyed chairs into a semi-circle around them.

All except Michael, who went to a small bar snuggled between matching casement windows and lined up six Baccarat crystal glasses. He'd brought an extremely rare eighteen-year-old Glenmorangie scotch whiskey, and after breaking its seal he poured a generous measure into five of the glasses, and Evian into the sixth for his pregnant daughter-in-law.

He handed them out and raised his drink. "I want to propose a toast to the son who has grown into as fine a man as any father could ever hope for; and to Jennifer, whom Nadia and I have adored since you were five years old. And, well, we kinda decided to keep on liking Kid, even after he learned to walk and run his yap."

Everyone chuckled and tossed back a healthy slug, with Kid closing his eyes to savor the warm balance of floral lushness; of honey brushing against fig with just a touch of campfire smoke.

A short silence followed until Nadia cleared her throat. "We all know why we're here." She looked at her daughter-in-law, who regarded her in turn with a calmness so in keeping with the young woman.

Cati crossed her ankles and leaned forward. "Nadia? Jen? Last night we provided Kid with details classified so far above top secret that they require a code word. Fewer than fifteen other people on this planet are in the loop."

Jen spoke for herself and the mother-in-law who had endured this often enough. "Mom and I understand, and we appreciate the gravity."

Cati nodded and faced them to begin some role-play. "Upon completing his final exams Kid shall pack some belongings and travel to Olympia, Washington. Once there, he will seek out any local anarchist groups—assuming there are any." She glanced at her notes in a false sense of spontaneity. "If successful, he must befriend them."

"Okay," Nadia and Jen said in unison.

Kid understood that this talk of a random group served as a bulwark to keep key details from Jen and his mother. This was meant to shield them from being tricked or coerced into disclosing that Kid went to Olympia with a target already in mind.

"His mission," Cati continued, "is to give life to the internet postings he's sent out in recent years. He'll do this by becoming an anarchist."

Michael began speaking. "In his zeal to do something that matters, Kid has renounced his trust fund status and left his family."

Feeling half in and half out of this hole being dug for him, Kid stole a look at Jen and began his role-play—but his was spiced by the true anger he now felt as last night's revelations hit home. "Let's see if I have this straight, 'cause I've been rethinking this. I'm to drop out of Harvard, leave my family, and move to Washington State? Is that correct? Did I hear you right?"

"You heard," Levi Hart said.

"Kid?" Nadia broke in. "You've known since childhood that your papa and Levi have always believed in their calling. In return, you believed in them. It's why we had to literally drag you away from the ICU after your papa was shot…"

"… Except I wrangled loose and…"

"… And draped yourself over him to protect him…"

"… And to love him," Kid said just above a whisper, his eyes riveted on Michael's.

Jen had just opened her mouth to speak when Nadia said simply, "You believed in your fathers. Why? Because you're a man in love with decency, as Don Quixote was."

"You're also the best hope our nation has," Michael said in a quiet way that commanded attention.

Levi turned to Nadia and Jen. "President Cohen personally ordered us to take this job. But our operatives are too old to penetrate the groups, so we need a Gen Zer—a compassionate one who also has a set of balls."

Kid thought back to the day he put down Kobi, the Rhodesian Ridgeback he'd raised from puppyhood. Kid was fifteen when one day Kobi stood on shaky legs and whimpered. His nose felt warm. They rushed him to a vet who said its kidneys were failing, and that the pain would soon be unbearable. So Nadia and Michael prepared the boy for what needed to be done for Kobi's sake.

"I'll give him a sedative first," the vet explained amid antiseptic odors, adding while flicking his eyes at the exit door, "Anyone would understand if you chose to..."

"No!" Kid said, adding from between clenched teeth, "I will never abandon him. *Never.* I'm part of his pack. Kobi would know I was cutting and running." Looking up at the vet, the fifteen-year-old boy spoke with a man's steel. "I will stay with him."

The vet nodded, and Michael and Nadia took their places on either side of their son. Just before the vet began the injection that would stop Kobi's heart, Kid picked up one of his floppy ears and whispered, "It's okay. It's all right. I'm right here. You're not alone."

He began caressing Kobi's paw when the life-ending drug flowed through a transparent I.V. catheter, all the while whispering his life-affirming mantra into his beloved dog's ear: "It's okay. It's all right. I'm right here. You're not alone..."

"He's gone," the vet had to tell him.

"It's okay," Kid kept saying into the unhearing ear. "It's all right. I'm right here. You're not alone."

Michael and Nadia massaged their son's shoulders as he got it out of his system. Almost a minute passed before he whispered into his dog's ear, "You've been a good boy. Now go to your bed. Go to your bed and... and sleep." Only then did Kid step back and sob against his papa's chest.

That was seven years ago. Now he asked in a fifteen-year-old's voice, "You said I have to go to Olympia. Does this... um, does this mean—" He swallowed hard, and the blood drained from his face as he turned to Michael. "Does this mean I have to fly?"

His papa spoke to him. "No, son. Don't worry. It's okay. You'll be safe."

But Kid was tugging at his shirt collar and breathing heavily. "Listen. I'll deal with flying if it's for a good reason. I did it for Paris. And Milan. I..."

"You are to drive," Cati said. "Although this does use up valuable time, a cross-country trip fits the profile we've begun developing for you."

"Yes, profiles," Michael began in a low tone. "Do you recall me telling you that the best authors of spy fiction were those who did the job in real life? Fleming? Forsyth? Le Carre? All three have been there, done that, and seen firsthand that state secrets derive from three sources." He started counting off on his fingers. "Patriotism. Bribery. The bed. It's why their stories speak the truth. It's how Mata Hari became a legend."

Kid winced and held up a hand. Although this hadn't surfaced at the SCIF, he sensed what was coming next. He also understood why they were discussing this in front of Jen. "Wait, wait, wait. Are you suggesting I sleep *around*?" Feeling as if he was taking sniper fire, he turned his hands into fists and said as if betrayed, "Hold on one fucking second! You need me to be a goddamn Romeo. Don't you?"

Levi said, "Yes. And, no."

Kid scowled. "What the hell kind of answer is *that*?"

Michael said, "Son? We're preparing you and Jen for possibilities and outcomes."

"I've got your outcomes! Hey, listen up. I won't cheat on Jen. I just won't!"

To his surprise, Jen touched his shoulder. "Even a blind person can see that you're being asked to intervene in a monumental event of some kind. If the cause is that great? I'll understand. Okay?" She waited until he nodded before adding, "I'll support whatever decision you make."

Levi looked Kid in the eye. "I once worked a mission with an Israeli agent. Mossad. Former IDF major. Married with children. He had to have sex with a man to get the job done. It didn't change who he was—a true warrior who cared enough about others to act against his grain."

Now Cati cleared her throat. "Come on, Kid. You know how your father and I met."

He winced. "I… yeah."

Cati had been deep cover and acting as a Sparrow—the female version of a Romeo—and she slept with a murderous psychopath to take him down.

But Cati hadn't finished. "Levi was also compelled to sleep around—albeit while single at the time. There's also Eva Marie Saint in *North by Northwest*. She…"

"Also slept with the enemy... for the greater good."

Michael went to Kid and knelt on one knee. "This is a job where a lot of rules don't apply. They can't apply, because this job often wrecks the lives of good people in their quest to avert calamity."

"Save it," Kid said, his face scarlet, his next words raw and explosive. "I don't need to rationalize, *okay*? I can compartmentalize with the best of 'em. Are we *clear*?"

Michael gripped Kid's wrist. "Son? If having a relationship brings your mission to an earlier resolution—not to mention what's at stake—isn't it worthwhile?"

"I—" Kid's mouth opened and closed several times until he grunted. "Damn. Why didn't I see that one coming?"

Nadia coughed politely. "This troubles me. We're asking Kid to surrender everything for what... some tenuous concept? My god, give me a break!"

Cati stood at once. "Nadia? A moment?" She tilted her head toward the hallway. Nadia followed. There were some muffled words. Some were harsh; others subdued. In time they returned and took their seats.

Nadia folded her hands on her lap and cleared her throat. "Kid? It seems a grave danger exists. I only want to say, do what must be done. I'll always be with you."

"Like any true hound," Michal began, "at our urging these past few years you've kept your sex life ambiguous. Are you a guy who cheats on his wife? Or do you honor your marriage vows, and by default earn the trust of others? It could also be a bit of both."

"Nobody's pure. Is that what you mean?"

"Affirmative. Sometimes a few warts make you appear more genuine."

The son waved a hand in front of his face as if shooing flies. "Yeah, yeah. It's why I've done what you wanted; I've fed the damn legend. Christ, now I'm just too sexy for my shirts."

"You've worked hard," Cati said by way of deflection. "Now comes the payoff. As a mole, you'll enjoy impeccable credentials as a Gen Zer. Or as a lover if need be."

"I—" Kid's breath came sharp; his eyes lost their focus; he clasped his hands together and stared at the floor.

"Kid?"

He looked up at his mother, so stunning in her black Diane Von Furstenberg even though she would also command attention in a T-shirt and jeans.

"I've listened to both arguments. I admittedly had my doubts. But I want you to recite the passage toward the end of JFK's inaugural address. You know the one—the speech's raison-d'être."

He stared at his mother as if peering into her soul. In time he stood and lifted his chin and spoke from memory. "Now the trumpet summons us again—not as a call to bear arms, though arms we need—not as a call to battle, though embattled we are—but a call to bear the burden of a long twilight struggle, year in and year out, rejoicing in hope, patient in tribulation—a struggle against the common enemies of man: Tyranny. Poverty. Disease. And war itself."

Nadia stood and picked it up from there. "Can we forge against these enemies a grand and global alliance, North and South, East and West, that can assure a more fruitful life for all mankind? Will you join in the historic effort?"

Michael saw his son nod, and after trading a glance with Levi he raised an eyebrow; Kid would do what they asked of him.

CATI said after a brief pause, "Assuming an anarchist group does a due diligence on you, they might buy into your online anti-gov, friend-of-the-proletariat persona."

"Even so," Levi said, "To be credible you'll need a precipitating event that pushes you over the cliff."

Cati caught Kid's eye. "Otherwise they'll question why a third-year Harvard pre-med abandons wife, children, and studies for the Pacific Northwest. It's one thing to rant and rave on the internet; quite another to have guts enough to follow through on your beliefs."

Michael shifted his long body, making his leather chair squeak. While studying the reduced contents of his glass, he said as if talking sports, "The war in Ukraine works in our favor. Think, soaring gas prices."

"I see it," Kid said with an edge of excitement. "Rising prices have forced a reopening of the gas pipeline. *And* our dear Congress is now promising to allow offshore drilling—not to mention *fracking* of all things. There's even talk of lifting EPA standards meant to reduce global warming."

Cati, ever the lady, grunted. "These assaults upon nature are what transformed you into the prototypical nut-job."

Nadia said, "While I'm not privy to your mission, I can read around the edges."

Kid made a sound. "Imagine my shock at learning that a Stanford PhD has to read between the proverbial lines. Come on, Mom. Don't bust my balls."

Nadia continued as if he hadn't interrupted. *"Really,* Kid. It's quite simple. Being a nut-job makes it easier for them to buy into your story."

"The disenfranchised trust-fund slob," Jen said.

"Quite." Nadia offered her daughter-in-law a radiant smile. "You despise being wealthy. After all, haven't you been posting that *ad nauseam*? Maybe you've slept around; perhaps not." She studied her son through narrowed eyes. "If you're lucky they'll interview a few high school classmates who'll say you never could keep your dick in your pants..."

Jen laughingly blurted, "Or couldn't keep from boinking cheerleaders in his car during lunch hour."

Nadia sipped her drink and said, "Let's hope they hear the stories. It will help gain their trust."

Cati cut in. "Only, you really might have to sleep around."

· · ·

Olympia, Washington

"We have our assets in the readiness mode," Sandro told a third member of the loose affiliation of patriots standing against eco-disaster and government domination. "Two more months. Then we send the 'Yew-knighted State of 'Murrica' back to the Stone Age."

"With the rest of the world to follow," the young woman added.

· · ·

"Papa?" Kid waited until Michael looked his way. "You and Dad have always been my heroes." He wet his lips. "What I'm trying to say is, I need to test myself. Will I bear up? Will I cut and run?" Kid searched Michael's face for clues. "I need to know if I have what it takes to stand up and *be* somebody."

Michael asked in his gentle way, "Don't you think becoming a physician isn't test enough?"

"It is." Kid paused, only to surrender and just say it. "I need to do this for my ego."

Michael smiled. "Ah, yes. Now we're making progress." He went to Kid and touched fingertips to his cheek. "I wouldn't want you or anyone else at my back if they didn't have a damn healthy ego. Okay?" He looked into the eyes of the boy he'd raised. "Are we done here?"

There were no more words. They'd said it all.

To provide time for both Kid and Jen to assimilate this life-changing event, Michael went to the bar and refreshed everyone's drinks.

Levi said after accepting a glass, "Kid? If this mission goes into overtime and into the next academic year, we can't guarantee that Harvard will take you back."

"Right. Next, you'll tell me how a well-placed phone call from the President of the United States might help." Kid swirled the liquor in his glass. "Puh-leeze. Harvard's so left of center, I doubt they'd take a call from Joe Stalin himself... much less from our just *moderately* lib prez." He frowned. "It's all right. There are greater priorities in life." He glanced at Jen, who nodded.

Cati cleared her throat. "Jen? You'll be expected to give an Oscar-caliber performance. It shall begin this way: you must call your parents the morning after Kid's departure."

Jen leaned forward. "I'm listening."

"Cry a bit. Tell them Kid left you with little more than a credit card, a bank account, and a promise to send money for you and the children. Then ask... in fact, *beg* your mother to abandon her medical practice and come to Boston. You'll say you need her to help with the twins." Cati paused. "Jen? Your parents must think this is real."

"Because?"

Michael said, "Anarchists are equipped with blazing intelligence coupled with a survival acumen honed during years of struggle. They're also well-financed. They'll hire top investigators to check Kid's story."

Michael turned to Jen and began speaking in the manner and voice that cops use when telling parents that their child's just been killed. "Sweetheart? You'll file for divorce a week after he leaves."

Jen gasped and gripped Kid's hand.

"You'll claim adultery. Claiming this comes with an advantage under Mass law, since a spouse must all but walk in on their partner to prevail. It's why we had Kid build an image that he sleeps around."

"But why a divorce?"

"The filing signals whatever group he might infiltrate that he's legit." Michael sloshed the scotch in his glass. "Jen? They'll know you filed even before Kid hears it from you. The more genuine he comes across as a regular person whose life is open for examination? The more likely they are to trust him."

Jen stared at him with graveyard dismay. "You want me to actually *divorce* my husband?"

"Yes. For this mission to succeed there can be no halfway measures. Contingencies, Jen. This is the 'just in case' portion of planning a job."

She released a burst of nervous laughter. "I'm tough. I can see this through. I ask only that you bear with me while I grow into this."

Kid brushed his lips against her cheek. "If anyone caves it'll be me." He narrowed his eyes at both fathers. "Only, I won't cave." Then while gazing at some unseen thing he said, "It's all a question of how far I'm willing to go to protect the people I love. With Jen's help, of course." He turned to face her.

"Nice answer," Jen said while snuggling against her husband.

Now Levi said, "In accordance with Massachusetts law, you'll post announcements in the Pacific Northwest's major newspapers since that's where Kid said he was going. Then you'll follow through and divorce him. In the best-case scenario, Kid completes the mission, and you cancel the proceedings."

Cati coughed. "If not? Worse-case? You and Kid remarry afterward."

Kid nodded. "Yeah, I get it. Make it all real. Don't fly if you're not prepared to get air sick, 'cause these people don't supply barf bags. They—" His voice trailed off.

"Kid?" Cati began. "This bears repeating: they will see through any attempt at deception. It's why you must be who you are—a world-famous model; the son of men and women who've been in the news and are wealthy enough to provide all this." She swept a hand at the polished library. "To nobody's surprise, since it happens so often in moneyed families, your wealth is among the reasons you've become consumed by rage."

Levi's quiet voice came across loud and clear, "We need the genuine article. Not some Bureau agent doing improv."

Kid blazed up. "I get it, Dad. I'm not stupid." His nostrils dilated as he drew a sharp breath just before muttering, "To trap a lion, you tether a goat." Then he said to the floor, "God I wish I smoked."

•   •   •

Agamemnon craned his neck and glanced at Sandro in the basement's dim light. When the Spaniard nodded, Ag held his breath and hit ENTER. Seconds later he peered at the huge screen while his sausage fingers moved across the keyboard. "It's done," he announced in a subdued voice. He pointed at the screen. "Look."

Sandro regarded the red-lettered notice meant for government agencies only:

EMERGENCY

HIGHEST ALERT

TOTAL SHUTDOWN DETECTED

IMMEDIATE ACTION REQUIRED

"Wow," Sandro whispered. "Just... wow." His grin grew as he slapped Ag's shoulder.

The big man whispered, "Rest easy and sleep well, Amtrak—for you've just been sidelined for the next twelve hours. As in, you are *completely* down."

•   •   •

Kid went to the mini bar and grabbed the nearly depleted bottle of Glenmorangie. When he held it aloft Levi and Michael nodded, so he poured a finger's worth into each glass and handed them out. After tilting his glass at Jen, he tossed back a gulp.

Then while idly tapping a finger against the fine crystal glass and making it resonate with a *ding-ding-ding*, he looked at her. When an unspoken message passed between them, he said over his shoulder to the others, "I'm in. All the way."

Nadia said just above a whisper, "Despite my reservations, I knew you would be. I..."

Levi's phone rang. He took the call, listened, and clenched his fists. Following a quick intake of breath like someone about to plunge into icy waters, he said, "Notify me of any developments." After ending the call he faced the others.

"That was Marty. Amtrak's down throughout the nation. All trains have ground to a halt. Computers are locked tight. Nobody knows who hacked them. Even the Alphabet Agencies are mystified." He held up a hand and wagged it. "Could be anything or anyone. Might be the Russians… Iran. So let's not get melodramatic and blame it on a specific nemesis. Not yet."

Kid said in a droll voice, "Quite the coincidence."

Levi glared and said in a low, menacing tone, "Don't you dare show me such disrespect. Don't even dare."

Kid winced but lifted his chin. "Sir? I have no excuse. Please accept my apology."

"You do have an excuse," Levi replied in a sudden, fatherly manner. "We've come into your home to jerk you from all you know and value."

"Yes, sir."

Levi winked at him. "Moving along, Hacksaw will oversee your activities from our Ops Center."

Even his closest friends described Quenton Jones, aka Hacksaw Jones, as an unmade bed of a man who loved the ladies and was loved back. He had been with Levi and Michael since Vanguard's inception. Prior to that, he worked as a locksmith while putting himself through William and Mary, hence the Hacksaw moniker—or Hack for short. He also capitalized on his African descent to blend into regions other team members had to avoid. Now he would do his utmost to assist Kid, whom he'd known and cherished since the boy was thirteen.

Cati smoothed some wrinkles in her peachy dress. "Turning to other matters. Kid? You might be wondering why we're not performing multiple surveillances on Olympia's various anarchist affiliations. The short answer is that they're quite clever and extraordinarily cautious. They are known to sweep their immediate areas for bugs and cameras. They're also on constant lookouts for tails. This is not mere speculation; we are certain of this. Were we to spook them in some way? Why, they'll simply burrow deeper."

"Understood. The justification for my new life as a mole." Kid also grasped that although the Feds were probably allocating satellite assets to track the gang, only human intel could ferret out possible failsafe protocols. It's why they came to him.

He tapped a fingernail against the rim of his glass and said to nobody in particular, "I'll buy next semester's textbooks and bring them along to remain in the loop." He drew a deep breath and asked, "Anything else?"

Cati said, "Yes. This. Take it on faith that any anarchists you meet will monitor you at all times. They'll employ cameras and audio eavesdropping devices."

"They would be sloppy not to," Levi interjected. "And these people are anything but."

"Kid?" Cati began. "No matter where you go—even if you should step inside a public toilet—assume it's under visual and audio surveillance. You must extend this caution even to your very clothes."

Michael coughed. "We've encountered adversaries with microphones inserted in their teeth. I once discovered a tiny transmitter sewn into some clothes after I picked them up from a dry cleaner. They'll need physical access to your iPhone to bug it, but they can still plant a mic in your home or apartment. We'll address safeguards later."

Cati said, "Continuing, should someone bump into you on a street? Or if a stranger remarks that you're skinnier than the mannequin he just saw in a men's store around the corner? Take these as cues to check your pockets for a note that's been slipped to you, or to visit that store and glance at the skinny mannequin. There could be a subliminal clue attached to it, or a note stuffed inside its inanimate hand. Go with your gut. You won't be in error."

Kid nodded and clenched his glass. "Will I be here when our son is born?"

"We can't guarantee that," Michael said bluntly.

The room fell silent until Levi said, "Kid? You'll have a codename. *Stranger*. Be alert if and when anyone mentions it."

Kid locked eyes with Jen. "Camus. *The Stanger*. And Heinlein's *Stranger in a Strange Land*. A human raised on Mars comes to Earth in early adulthood. He's to interact with and eventually transform the culture."

Levi nodded. "Excellent."

But the son glared at the bio-dad. "Why not use Romeo as a codename? I mean, Christ. Isn't that what I'll be?"

The bio-dad raised an eyebrow. "Your mission, your call. Very well, we'll use Romeo." Turning solemn, Levi faced the young adult and said, "Go, Romeo."

Kid scoffed. "Go, Romeo? How about, let's just get this the fuck over with?"

Levi let it slide. They had just turned Kid's life on its head. He had a right to vent.

.   .   .

"It's what you trained for," Jen reminded him.

They were in bed after putting the twins to sleep; after Kid spent half an hour massaging his wife's shoulders, lower back, legs, and feet to help her deal with pregnancy's discomforts.

After ministering to her, Kid propped himself up on an elbow. "Jen, don't you feel I'm cutting out on you and the girls? On our son?"

Jen spoke slowly, feeling her way. "Remember the guy who attacked us at the fast-food place?"

Kid met her eyes. "I see what you mean."

Levi and Michael had been on a desperate mission to prevent a Russian oligarch from releasing information that would trigger worldwide panic. A disgraced reporter caught wind of the search and confronted Levi. When the team derailed the reporter, he went after the then-fifteen-year-old Kid and Jen to force Levi into showing his hand.

Jen said, "You and I weathered it together. Humph. Imagine that punk, pointing that friggin' Taser at us."

Kid's face turned to stone. "He also had that hideout pistol. Remember?"

"Of course." She reached for his hand. "But what I so vividly recall is how you jumped between me and him to shield me with your body."

"Christ, did he really think I wouldn't punch his lights out?" Kid made a sound. "Yeah, we weathered it all right."

Jen said with a flip of her head, "That's the thing. Listen to me, my love. I am so proud of you for pursuing your dreams. Come on. A chest surgeon?"

"Thoracic," he said from the side of his mouth.

"*Thoracic*, muriatic, whatever. The point is, how many people go after *that*?"

"Not many," he admitted.

"Now imagine how I'll hold you in mega-high esteem for sacrificing so much more." Looking sidelong at him, she added, "For us… and for your own needs."

He chuckled. "You read me like a book."

"You're a regular Yellow Pages." Creases etched her forehead as she put a hand on his arm. "Suppose you were a police officer. You shoot and kill someone in the line of duty. I wouldn't like it. But I'd understand and accept it. Sweetheart?" She grazed her fingers along his hairy leg. "Here's the deal. I won't like it if duty compels you to sleep around. Will I grasp why? Yes. Will I be okay with it? Hard to say."

He kissed her cheek. "Of course."

She grew quiet, only to come back with a stronger voice. "Kid? Should duty require you to have intercourse? I won't think you stepped outside the marriage bed. Okay?"

"Jen, I—" Kid held his arms out to her.

She deflected him. "Hold on, Sparky. I have one condition. When the mission's over? I'll expect you to tell me if you had sex. A yes or a no. Just… no details, please." A look of searing pain tore across her lovely face. All at once she trembled against him and wailed, "I'm terrified." Then she burst into tears.

·   ·   ·

At that same moment in Olympia, Washington

Ag straightened up in his stout chair and growled, "Gotcha, sucker!"

Days ago he targeted a Hoover Dam employee who'd been bragging on social media about his sensitive position at the iconic dam. The poor sod even boasted that he exercised power over the computerized systems that operate the floodgates, adding, "Not only that, but can't nobody hack into *my* site."

With the patience of a predatory animal watching its prey, Ag spent a week gleaning keywords and phrases from the braggart's Facebook page. Next, he compiled a list and ran a search program that looked for repeated phrases. That's when Ag shouted his *gotcha*. Moving with a lion's assurance, he typed the password that got him through the computer's backdoor.

• • •

The woman lived fewer than two miles from Agamemnon and she had come far in life, from humble beginnings to a world-class education.

Feeling restless, she stepped outside and looked up into the clear night sky. The stillness was absolute. She could even hear the growl of tractor-trailers whizzing along the interstate some four miles away. At the moment, everyone within her sphere had gone to bed for the night. She nodded, for that's as it should be. In her view, orderliness must prevail at the risk of anarchy, and chaos could only be circumvented with a population that evolved from superior bloodlines. The kicker was that the orderliness she yearned for could only be born from apocalyptic chaos.

Her people—her soldiers as she called them—were orderly enough. They possessed discipline, and she'd purged the ranks of those who lacked it. Those who made the cut showed courage, a capacity to learn, and an acceptable level of obedience. But only a small band of her one dozen followers were suitable for what also had to be done. It's why she needed one or perhaps two more men or women of good stock.

A breeze ruffled her hair as she regarded a nearby confluence of two gullies where spruce and fir and other flora grew.

There were also wild animals foraging nearby, and she could smell them when the wind was right; could even pick up on their urine. Animals were fine; part of the natural order. Yet she required more; she needed someone of substance to serve as a catalyst.

She turned her face upward again. The lack of ambient light so far from the city revealed nebulae, star clusters, meteors, and an assortment of other Messier objects. Their methodical transitions and movements, as ageless as her fears, had come full circle from the year past. Now the Christmas season as measured on earthly calendars grew closer. Sure, she had laid a good foundation. But she wanted more than ever to bring in that catalyst in the form of new blood. And if a male candidate should hold promise as both a poet warrior and a lover? That person would move to the head of the group's line.

PART II

. . .

Chapter Nine

· ·

May 9 · Cambridge, Massachusetts

AS DUSK MERGED with night but before the evening birds began warbling their songs, Kid dropped two backpacks laden with clothes and textbooks into the trunk of his 750Li BMW.

He loved everything about this car, beginning with its black sapphire metallic exterior and caramel interior. His papa bought it in 2014 after raking in his first million—but only after Levi talked his deprived childhood friend into buying it.

Michael, who came from trash and knew it, asked, "Why spend that kind of money?"

Levi had clamped a hand on his shoulder. "Because you deserve to be good to yourself."

A few years later Michael gave the car to Kid as an eighteenth birthday gift. It would replace the black Trans Am he'd bought with money earned from years of mowing lawns and packing grocery bags. But Kid sold the Trans Am and prized the Beamer ever since.

Now he turned to Jen. "I serviced the Lexus a month ago. It's gassed up, so…"

"… The girls and I will be fine." Jen held their daughters by the hands.

"Oh, wait." Kid removed his wedding band and handed it to her while reaching into a pocket to retrieve an identical one. It was suitably tarnished, and their wedding date was inscribed in it. Marty bought it from an off-grid jeweler with cash so Kid could have a 'throwaway ring,' the idea being that once Jen announced the divorce, Kid could dramatically remove it from his finger in front of witnesses and toss it. He put the ring on and looked at her.

They'd said everything earlier. Now he picked up Lara and Lana in turn and hugged them. But the girls clearly sensed something momentous, and when they began to fuss he made faces and googly noises until he had them laughing.

All at once it turned into a last kiss, a wave at the children, a climbing into the car, and driving off.

Kid told Britney of his plans the other day and considered stopping by her apartment for a last farewell. But common sense told him not to. So he sped past the exit to her apartment.

A moment later with streetlights now pushing at the gloom, he rocketed toward Memorial Drive—that highway scar of the automobile age—and hightailed it to I-90 before he could change his mind.

He reached the interstate within minutes and set the cruise control for seventy. Next, he gave silent thanks for the solace offered by the lonely highway, where shadows looked like stalking gray cats amid the green prison walls of bordering trees. Soon enough he settled in for the 3,082-mile trip to Olympia.

His route would take him to Mount Rushmore, and after bidding adieu to the four presidents he would angle slightly north to skirt the northeast corner of Wyoming. Then on to Montana and Idaho before reaching Spokane. A final six-hour drive would see him in Olympia.

Thank goodness for this BMW. The 700 series was designed with long trips in mind, a precision-engineered machine that sheltered its occupants in a nearly soundproof cocoon. Thus sequestered, the young man would have time to think about what he had embarked upon.

After leaving the metro area's ambient light in his rearview, he lavished in the rich feel of the leather seats and their smells, still vivid in the ten-year-old car, the tires air-brushing over the usual imperfections in the roadway with only the occasional whirring to remind Kid that he was driving.

Later, he cranked up the stereo and settled back for a long trip, one that in time would lead to a very dark place in his soul—one so dark that it would make him yearn for those stalking gray cats and green prison walls of trees.

But Kid could not yet see that danger. He still had to round a few curves in the road before he would begin losing touch with those things that meant the most to him. Right now all he really knew was that he could not go back to how things were. Not now and not ever.

Chapter Ten

. . . .

Two Days Later • May 11 • A rest area somewhere in Wyoming

KID CONTINUED DOWN the empty interstate despite feeling the exhaustion of the past days to his core. But when the coffee fueling him since midnight kicked in with a demand for relief, he pulled into the next rest area.

The place spooked him the moment he parked next to the cold and unimaginative main building. The entire rest area came off as dark and forlorn, the only sound coming from a parked eighteen-wheeler, its chugging Diesel sending a *potatopotatopotato* noise echoing off the building. There were no other trucks and zero automobiles.

Stepping out into the chilly air did more than the coffee to revive him since all he had on were a gray hoodie, blue nylon athletic shorts, and checkerboard Vans. After deciding to dress more warmly tomorrow, he headed for the men's room.

His nose crinkled the instant he entered. The place reeked of urine, the filthy floor looked as if it hadn't seen a mop in days, and a pair of feeble overhead lights cast dark shadows. There were four industrial-grade metal sinks attached to one wall. Metal urinals lined another. Half a dozen stalls took up the far end. At least one of them smelled of unflushed feces.

He went to the first urinal and got busy, wanting to get it done and get going. He almost finished when a car with a loud muffler pulled up near the building. After flushing, he was washing up when a behemoth wearing leather and denim entered.

It wasn't until this Goliath turned the deadbolt on the door and began looking around, even stooping to peer under the toilet stalls, that Kid went on high alert. The guy had to be pushing six foot six and two-fifty. He also had ex-con written all over him, from his shaved bullet head to the amateurish tattoos covering his neck and arms.

Kid's eyes darted left and right to get a sense of this small field of battle. Then the son of Levi Hart and Michael Bailey moved his feet and legs to tactically blade himself for combat, his arms and hands at the ready. This didn't mean he was without fear; he had a healthy dose of it right now. He also knew how beneficial a bit of fright can be.

Goliath edged closer while jabbing a forefinger at Kid. "My, my. Ain't you a pretty boy. An' that must be yer Beamer out there. Wait. Did I say, yours? I meant, mine. Now gimme the keys." He pointed at Kid's fake wedding band. "The ring, too. Along with yer wallet and phone."

The taunting daredevil athlete knew how to put opponents off their guard, first by feigning submission and then by spinning off in unexpected directions. So he held his hands in front of his chest as if praying and said with a Cockney accent, "Please guvnor. Don't take from me. I promise not to sass ya none. Truly I do."

The ex-con pointed a finger at Kid and bellowed, "Gimme yer stuff! *Now.*"

Kid made his eyes appear to be wide with fear. "Oh no, guvnor. Not the lash."

The thug snarled and said, "Don't wise-guy me."

"I wouldn't do that, guv. Oi. I'm just a poor British lad what's on 'oliday. Just a bloke from 'umble beginnings, I am. Father a vicar and all that. Church of England, don't ya know?"

"You'd better get moving," he growled.

"Right, guv. I shall." Kid pulled his wallet from his back pocket and fished the cars keys from another. Then he held them aloft. "See? I'm doing as you command. Only, that superb BMW isn't mine. I nicked it from an aeroport's long-term car park. So fair warning, mate. I've not had time to change the registration plates. And wouldn't you know? The constables are on the lookout for it. Yes, quite."

"Hey! Brit boy! I don't care where you got it from. Ya got that... mother*fucker*?"

All at once Kid gave a wave-off and said in his real voice, "Wait, wait, wait. Did you just call me a motherfucker? Well that tears it." He pocketed the wallet and keys and squinted at the thug. "You had a good thing going there, my friend. But because you were rude? I've decided that giving you my stuff's gonna be a big no. " He dropped his voice an octave. "Ya got that, *ass*hole?"

The ex-con's face turned red with rage. "What'd you call me?"

"You heard me... asshole."

"Why you little—" Goliath pulled a switchblade from a back pocket and snapped it open with a *click* that echoed off the tile walls.

Long ago when Kid and his younger brother Nick were children, Levi and Michael began preparing them for close-quarter combat—including against knives. They also instilled in the two boys this ironclad principle in the event of mortal combat: Defy. Deflect. Destroy. Kid had already defied. Now he purposely dissembled as a means to deflect.

Then he would lull this thug into dropping his guard before he destroyed.

Kid began the deflection by saying, "Maybe we can make a deal, big guy."

The thug's face wrinkled in confusion. "Deal? What kinda deal you talking about?"

"The kind where you get the fuck outta here before I bust your nose. Well? We good?"

Goliath looked at Kid with a snake's cold eyes and thrust the knife blade at him. "Jist fer that I'm gonna cut your tongue out. Then try an' mouth off to me."

Kid squinted while rubbing his jaw as if deep in thought. "Hmm. I take it the first deal fell through. Well? You leave me with no other choice. I'm just gonna have to kick your ass."

A shadow clouded the man's face. Then came the snorting and huffing that signals a level of anger that overshadows skill and judgment. It's why Kid now stared straight through the big man with a street fighter's glazed-over eyes and spoke in a low monotone. "Enough with the games. You do not want to take me on. Walk away from this one. Do it now."

Most bullies would have read the message between the lines and looked for an honorable out. But Goliath either couldn't read or he didn't care because he took a step forward, only to stop with a quizzical expression when Kid didn't back up.

"Walk away from this one," Kid repeated in a low tone. "Or I will hurt you."

The big man hesitated. He put away his knife. Then he charged.

Kid feinted right and leaned back. But he miscalculated and caught a fist against his jaw. A missile went off behind his eyes and exploded. Shaken and off-balance, he realized how badly he'd undersold his opponent.

Goliath grunted. "Not so smart now, are you girly-boy?" He rushed forward and landed a fist against Kid's head that sent him staggering.

Dazed by the blow, he lurched drunkenly against a sink and clutched it just as his knees buckled. The room went dark, and he crashed to the grimy floor like a rag doll, his limbs going every which way.

Goliath grabbed Kid's arm, jerked him to his feet, and backhanded him.

Kid's teeth clacked, and blood blossomed from his nose.

Not done yet, the thug sent him flying across the room until Kid crashed onto the pissy floor. Goliath yanked him up at once and punched the side of his head. Then he bashed Kid's face against a wall before spinning him around and pressing him against it.

As blood gushed from his nose, the thug kept him pinned in place with a meaty hand against his throat. Kid fought to remain conscious, but the room kept getting darker. Seconds later he broke out in a greasy sweat when the thug opened his knife with a loud *snap*.

Then he cringed when Goliath gripped his cheeks between two fingers and pressed cruelly until Kid's mouth puckered like a parrot fish. After placing the blade against Kid's lower lip, he whispered, "Say adios to your tongue… motherfucker."

Despite being dazed and weak from the blow to the head, Kid understood that he was about to lose his powers of speech and taste. Still in the fight though, he clenched his teeth tight.

"Don't matter none," the thug muttered. "I'll take yer eyes instead. Startin' with this pretty blue one here." He placed the point against the corner of Kid's left eye.

That's when Kid drew from some deep place—and went to rockets-full.

As if exploding from a launch pad, he shoved the thug's knife hand aside, while at the same time he grabbed Goliath's balls and squeezed with a vice-like grip he never knew he had.

As the bastard cried out, Kid clamped down on Goliath's nads until the giant doubled over and howled with real pain.

Though still dizzy, Kid head-butted him and followed through with a fist against the ex-con's cheek and felt the thin zygomatic bone collapse as Goliath stumbled backward with a roar.

Then Kid got ready for real battle.

It wasn't long in coming. The enraged bull somehow pushed past the incredible pain in his nads and narrowed his eyes. Incredibly enough, he still had his switchblade. Now he charged with knife in hand and homicide in his eyes.

Kid had defied and deflected. Now to destroy.

He bid his time and dodged at the last instant.

Goliath reached for Kid—only to grasp empty air.

As he stumbled, Kid gripped the ex-con's right wrist and jerked him forward. Then he wrapped his arm around the ex-con's elbow and clamped down. Using the joint as a fulcrum, he yanked the forearm back with brutal force.

The elbow snapped with a sharp *crack.*

Goliath screamed.

The knife fell to the floor with a dull *clunk.*

Kid's right arm uncoiled.

His edged hand struck the thug's neck.

Perfect brachial stun. Total blood disruption to the brain. Goliath's eyelids fluttered. As he fell to the floor Kid slammed a knee against his nose. Cartilage crunched; blood poured from both nostrils.

"Told you I'd bust your nose," Kid said while stooping over the inert thug to check his eyes. Although they had rolled back into his head, Kid knew he had no time to waste before the son of a bitch came to.

First, he tore off two pieces of a paper towel in a dispenser and stuffed them up his nose to staunch the bleeding.

Moving quickly, he undid Goliath's belt, jerked the giant's arms behind his broad back, and used the belt to secure the wrists. He retrieved the switchblade next, and cut the thug's pant legs completely off. After slicing strips from the denim, he bound Goliath's ankles and knees just as the thug's eyelids were opening.

Kid worked his way up and tied the elbows together until they nearly touched. His attacker screamed in pain, but Kid didn't care what this would do to the ruined elbow; he meant to render him incapable of attacking again.

Now to call 911. But his phone would leave an electronic trail for law enforcement to follow, and he had to avoid encounters that could derail his mission. So he fished the punk's early-generation cell from his pocket and made the call.

With that done—and while Goliath struggled with his bonds—Kid pulled out the phone's SIM card and pocketed it to send to Hack for analysis. Next, he propped the open switchblade against a wall and stomped it, snapping the blade where it met the handle. After wiping his prints from the knife and phone, he dropped the items next to the ex-con.

Following this, he checked his face and nose in a mirror. To his surprise, the bleeding had stopped. *Must've only been a few capillaries,* the pre-med student decided. After gingerly pulling the paper from his nostrils, he flushed everything to avoid leaving any DNA.

One more clean-up chore remained: his face, arms, and legs were smeared with urine from being tossed about on the floor. So he washed up at the sink and dried off with paper towels, then used the towels to clean his bloodstain from the wall. *Sure,* he told himself. *Even a half-assed crime lab tech with a UV light will find blood remnants. But this isn't a homicide scene that would justify the expense. Besides, I doubt if there's a tech within a hundred miles.*

There were troopers though, so he moved fast. Using a fresh paper towel, he fished Goliath's wallet from his jeans, flipped it open, and memorized the license info. He couldn't photograph it with his smartphone, since that would also leave an E-trail. Finally, he caught Goliath's eye and said, "Ya shoulda left me alone when you had the chance… motherfucker."

He walked outside where security cameras had almost certainly captured images of him and his license plates. Or maybe not. He would worry about that later.

For now, he surveyed the mottled gray 2002 Chevy next to his BMW. After memorizing the license plate and sticking a twig inside the right rear tire's valve stem to flatten the tire—just in case—he got in his car and drove to the far end of the rest area's exit ramp, where he parked and left the engine running.

Moving fast, he popped his trunk, stripped completely, and traded his bloody hoodie, urine-smelling shorts, and shoes for a fresh sweatshirt, jeans, and sneakers.

Then he got behind the wheel and waited. Twenty minutes passed before a trooper assigned to this barren highway stormed into the rest area. The instant he dashed inside the men's room, Kid dropped the transmission into gear and scooted away with his lights off. He drove a quarter mile before he turned them on and floored the accelerator.

After drawing a deep breath and releasing it, he thumbed the Beamer's MAKE A CALL button. When an automated voice responded, Kid said aloud, "Call Papa."

The phone rang twice before it picked up. Kid described the encounter and added the driver's license and vehicle registration data.

Michael spoke with iron in his voice. "You performed superbly. Don't worry about the authorities. We'll handle them if they come looking for you."

"That's a relief."

"I'll have Hacksaw track this punk down and have a discussion. I guarantee he'll never attack anyone again. Ever."

They spoke a bit more before Kid ended the call and had the car's system call his brother. "Nick," he said when his frowzy-sounding brother picked up. He heard Nick's sleepy girlfriend in the background.

Brothers who are close have a secret communication. Nicholas sensed that his older brother needed to talk — and talk they did for the next ten minutes.

"Thanks," Kid said afterward and drove on, only to jump when the car's Bluetooth speaker sounded. He pressed ACCEPT.

"Hi, Kid. Cati here. I am given to understand the details of the attack. Moreover, I'm told that you royally kicked some ass. Now then. Levi's been called to the Castle on an emergency. He said he's damn proud of you, and to assure you that we've got your back."

"I… hold on a sec." Kid glanced in his rearview as a set of highlights rapidly closed the distance. Thinking it might be a trooper looking for him, he narrowed his eyes and made a plan to deal with it. But he relaxed when a beige Buick coupe flashed by in the fast lane.

He talked with Cati, grateful for the call since he needed to hear a woman's voice right now. But he wouldn't call Jen until tomorrow. She and the girls were asleep. No need to bother them.

Kid ended the call by telling Cati, "Tell Dad not to worry."

A second later his mother called. "Hey, Kiddo. Just got off the phone with your papa. He told me you're in good spirits."

The kiddo spoke matter-of-factly. "It wasn't pretty, Mom. The bastard busted my nose."

"So I hear." She cleared her throat. "I also heard what you did to him; how you paid him back. You sound good, despite what happened."

"Mom?" He took a breath and turned somber. "He almost had me."

"I know," she said, her voice flat and no-nonsense.

Kid licked his lips and said after a pause, "Know what else is eating at me?"

"What's that, my darling?"

"I got too cocky. Figured I could handle him, no sweat." Kid exhaled in a rush and let his shoulders slump. "At least I learned a lesson."

"Your resilience is admirable, kiddo."

"Thanks, Mom. You just gave me a boost. I can deal with the rest of it. Only? I don't want anyone telling Jen. She's asleep and there's no need to disturb her. I'll do a Zoom call first thing in the morning. She needs to see my face when I tell her."

"Aw, Kid. You sure do know women."

Kid's breath caught. "Mom? I—" Swiping at sudden tears and unashamed of the tremor in his voice, he said, "I love you."

After they ended the call he sped up to eighty, only to shudder once it hit home just how close he'd come to being taken down. Goliath's fist against his head had sent him reeling. If he'd passed out? The ex-con would've blinded him, which led Kid to admit once more that it was his sarcastic game-playing that got him in trouble.

All at once this first brush with such pure evil had him trembling so hard that he couldn't stay in his lane, the encounter troubling him in ways he'd rather not think about. With no switch to turn it off, he resigned himself to assimilating it.

And so he drove further into the darkness while trying to push it aside. What he could not yet see was this truth: that the harder people try to forget, the more they remember—and he most assuredly did not want to remember what had just happened to him. At least he took a degree of comfort in knowing he would never see Goliath again.

Chapter Eleven

· ·

May 13 • Olympia, Washington • Fifty-three Days before July 4ᵗʰ

KID JERKED AWAKE in a nameless motel room, his pulse racing until he realized he wasn't locked in combat with an ex-con. Even so, he lay in bed for several minutes before getting up, and after settling in with a cup of joe he made a Zoom call to Jen. To his utter relief, she had taken the news in stride.

THE next day saw him in the state capital, where he checked into a chain motel room with chain décor down to matching curtains and bedspread. Dismal though the room might be, at least he'd realized this much of his journey.

Following a cup of chain coffee, he phoned home.

He perked up when Jen answered. "You wouldn't believe how green everything is. Well, green but with gray skies. The air's also cooler than back home."

"I miss you terribly and the girls are asking where their daddy is. I told them you went to help a friend and that you'll be home soon. You will be, won't you?"

"God, I wish I had you guys in my arms right now."

They talked for two hours. Following the call, Kid considered his next move. Logic dictated that he go to that coffee shop café where this bunch of anarchists were hanging out.

So he hopped in the car and got going. But the ride through stop-and-go traffic grew tedious, and apathy was already setting in by the time he reached the café.

He parked and gave the faded dark green clapboard building a once-over. Then he grabbed his textbooks along with a laptop and walked to the main door, where he stopped to survey the place—the stranger in a strange land in a dark blue hoodie, white jeans, and cerulean blue flip-flops.

The ceiling was low, and cheap chairs were scattered pell-mell with white stuffing poking through brown vinyl seat cushions. As for the tables, well they were nothing more than a jumble of low-budget thrift store refugees of various sizes and materials.

Mundane walls had faded into a mustard color, and checkered linoleum floors went here and there without logic. A large blue neon coffee cup with a Wi-Fi emblem in its center adorned the wall behind the barista's faux granite countertop. Espresso machines and coffee makers flanked both sides of the cash register, and thin wooden shelves featuring multi-colored pastries served as a backdrop to the exhausted odors of coffee, ozone, and sweat.

There were only a few customers, and Kid saw that many of them were shirtless or shoeless or both—a regional oddity he'd been told to expect.

Here I am, Kid thought while buying a basic java from a pimply barista with way too much attitude and too few skills. After getting a bowl of hummus and some falafels, he carried the lot to an empty table littered with crumbs, used napkins, and other detritus.

Following a sip of coffee that turned out to be not half-bad—which wasn't the same as being half-good—and after a bite of humus-saturated falafel that was oily to the point of repugnance, he got out his laptop and went about getting a signal.

•   •   •

Agamemnon glanced at the Pacific marine layer blanketing the region and sighed. Just last night he'd prayed for a clear day this far into spring. *No such luck,* he told himself as he struggled into his mother's SUV. Following a drive to the city's west side, he turned down a meandering road and lowered his window to pick up on the sweet-smelling evergreens and fresh air.

Three-quarters of a mile later, he pulled to the side just short of a wooden mock-up of a massive fallen tree trunk. Its bottom faced the road and white lowercase letters on it spelled out: the evergreen state college. Ag scoffed. He had long since come to regard the college as little more than a hangout for Gen Zers in search of Walden Pond. But what really fueled his scorn were the many young men and women in Evergreen logo t-shirts who taunted him in public.

Ag finally shut down the engine, which sent the neglected motor clanking and shaking while going through its death throes. But he was more interested in the second hand on the dash-mounted analog clock, and he watched as it swept to within a hair's breadth of twelve noon. When it reached its zenith, he looked up in time to see her emerge from who-knew-where, knowing that had he blinked she would have eluded him completely.

The woman, whom his ravaged mind regarded as a goddess, went to the passenger side and got in. Just her act of glancing at him made his breath catch. "You... you're so—" His face turned crimson, and he looked away.

"Dearest Agamemnon. Relax." She placed a tender hand on his forearm to end his misery. "We're friends. No need to go grafting. Not for me."

He looked at her graciously and opened his laptop. "I penetrated two more—" His face flushed deep red again. "I… I mean, I *breached* two more." He pointed at the screen with the eagerness of a little boy saying to his mommy, *See?*

She examined his face before asking, "Firewalls?"

"Affirmative. Two more to go. Then you just wait an' see. We'll have our hands around their throats. Jesus, no wonder the Feds view the Dark Web as a security threat. It is! How else could I've gotten this far?"

She moved her hand to Ag's thigh and suppressed a smile when she felt it tremble. "That Amtrak thing? Baby, you did gooood and Momma's gonna treat you real special for that."

Ag grinned crazily at the compliment, despite knowing in a dark corner of his soul where he didn't care to look that she was using him. At least he had the cojones to admit that even a bogus human touch trumps none at all.

Now she looked at him with bedroom eyes and spoke in a lover's undertone. "You had better get going, sweetheart. I need you to work those firewalls." She reached between his legs, and said with a wicked smile, "Yeah, baby. Work it! Work it for me!"

But she abruptly pulled her hand away. "It's getting late, so I had better crack on." She leaned close and kissed his cheek.

He shuddered.

She vanished.

AG trembled as the flora magically absorbed her, and once his excitement withered he drove to the café. He had to struggle to get out of the SUV, and needed his cane and three wheezing pauses to catch his breath before he reached the café and with its aloof mom-and-pop owners who were quick to point out that this was not a café, but a collective. On the plus side, the café/collective/whatever featured a variety of coffees. The downside was its abysmal Wi-Fi.

He reached the counter but looked away to avoid facing the willowy, carrot-topped, and totally indifferent barista. Speaking to the floor, he ordered a double-shot espresso with drip coffee and chocolate.

Minutes later and with drink in hand, he chose a corner table near the main door and settled his six hundred-plus pounds onto a stout chair, followed by a gratified moan. Once he caught his breath, he took an experimental sip of the double-shot-drip-choc coffee and closed his eyes. "Mmm."

After another sip and a quick darting out of his pink tongue to lick the corners of his lips, he put the coffee aside, opened his laptop, and spent the next nine minutes working the keyboard while sipping coffee. When he reached the bottom of the cup he tilted his head back to gulp the dregs, only to sense a presence at his side.

Turning with a quick snap of his shoulders, he frowned at the young man hovering nearby. "What is it? Come on, come on. Spill it. I don't have all gud-damn day."

The young man said equitably, "I can't get my laptop to connect to the Wi-Fi. Maybe you can help me?"

Ag glared and asked in a deep rumbling voice, "Why? Because I'm the fat guy? 'Cause I must be the nerd who knows everything about computers?" He made a face and waved a hand as if shooing flies. "Get the fuck away."

"It's not that," Kid said at once. Moving closer against the background noise of café chatter, he rested a hand on one of the big man's shoulders.

But Ag stiffened and growled, "What the fuck are you doing? I'm not *homo*. Get your hand off!"

Kid yanked it away. "Sorry. I'm just one of those people."

"*What* people?"

"The touchy-feely kind?" Kid shrugged and smiled disarmingly, as if saying, *I know it's dumb but that's how I am and anyway I'm sorry to have offended you.* "Please hear me out," Kid began over. "I saw you working the keyboard. I figured you must've gotten a signal. It's why I thought you could help." Kid locked eyes with Ag and without hesitation, he planted a hand on Ag's shoulder. "Okay?"

Kid had in fact been unable to get a Wi-Fi signal, he really did see the morbidly obese guy with obvious skills, and truly thought he could connect with him—if only to use a Wi-Fi connection as a reason to approach him. Of course, given the location, Kid had wondered if this large man might be the guy who lived in his mom's basement—or that he might know the guy, if only socially. Either way, he pressed on by giving Ag's shoulder a slight shake.

"My name's Kid. What's yours?"

Ag's body slumped, and when he could trust his voice he said, "It's like this. Nobody ever touches me." He vigorously rubbed the end of his nose. "I ah, just didn't know what you were after. That's all."

"Understood," Kid said in his honest way. "Friends call me Kid."

"Okay. Friends call me Bill." Ag—whose name on his birth certificate *was* William and not Agamemnon—took a deep breath and held out his hand. "Nice to meet you."

"Likewise," Kid said as they shook. "Sooo, Bill. The Wi-Fi?" Pointing at Bill's empty cup, he asked, "And can I get you another of those?"

Ag leaned back and appraised his new friend. *Tall and lanky. Brown hair and a happy-go-lucky face to go along with his designer hoodie, jeans, and blue flip-flops.* He also noted the young man's wedding band. "I see you're married."

"Yep. Wife, twin daughters, and a son on the way."

"Good, good." Ag paused before saying, "I've also got a wife… and *four* children. The thing is? I'm not good with computers. Fortunately for you, I'm current on the peculiarities of this shithole's Wi-Fi. Tell you what. Give me your laptop and yes, I would like another." He pointed at his cup and impulsively summoned a word from some primordial place in his memory. "Please."

AG drained his third double-shot-drip-choc coffee an hour later and gave Kid another look-over. They had talked. When the young man told him why he'd come to Olympia, Ag felt his way by speaking to the wall beyond Kid. "Might be that I'll be here again tomorrow. Same time." He stopped right there, afraid to get his hopes up; afraid that having never had a true friend he could trust with any secrets—beginning with the deepest one involving his favorite hard porn sites—that he felt destined to never have a friend.

As for why he'd taken a liking to Kid, it was the lad's story of giving up everything for a cause; not that Ag didn't think it idiotic to turn away from so much money and opportunity. Even so, he respected the young man. It's why he prompted Kid once more. "Tomorrow? One o'clock?" Ag held his breath.

Kid's sparking eyes and glittering smile lit the room. "Absolutely." Holding out a hand, he added, "I'll be here."

Feeling a buoyancy he'd never known, he shook hands and even let the stranger help him stand. "Much obliged," he mumbled.

Bill—Ag—wanted to say more about their day together but didn't know how. So he looked at the floor and said in a low voice, "Thanks for not finding me repulsive."

Kid wrapped a friendly arm around the big man's shoulders. "Never in a million years," he said in his open way, only to add with a droll smile, "Fatboy."

Ag snorted and glared at him until he cracked a smile. "Pretty *boy*." Still smiling, he walked slowly to the door, paused, and said, "Great meeting you." He meant it, for he felt that this ships-in-passing encounter *had* been great. He also truly respected the simple, authentic way in which Kid met his eyes and nodded.

"Bill?" Kid said as Ag was halfway out the door. "One more thing. I'll need a place to stay. Can you recommend anything?"

Ag opened his mouth and almost said, *You can stay with me,* only to recall the name his middle school classmates saddled him with: Holden Caulfield. He also needed to exercise great caution, because two feds had tried to worm their way into the group. So what rolled off his lips was this: "Just hang around here. You'll find what you're looking for."

KID thanked him and stepped outside to watch the large guy go down the street, all the while thinking *Bill, you have no idea who or what I'm really looking for—but I don't think you're him.* Once his new buddy rounded the corner, he called his brother Nick and they chatted awhile.

Next, he called Britney, whose soothing voice over his Bluetooth had kept him company during the dismal days and dark nights of his journey. When she answered, he said what he truly felt. "I sure do miss you."

"You think? Jesus, I still can't believe you walked away from everything." Her voice turned soft. "Kid? I miss listening to the beating of your heart. Now listen and listen good: you'd better tell me when you're feeling lonely, so I can hop a flight and soothe your weary brow. No shenanigans. I promise. Just friendship."

He spoke quietly. "That's so sweet of you."

"Where are you, by the way?"

Feeling homesick and not thinking it through, he blurted the name of the café. They spoke a bit more before he shoved the phone into his pocket along with any memory of the conversation.

Following a glance at the lowering clouds, he shook from the cold and went inside for more coffee. On impulse, he grabbed four spinach pastries and got a table in a dark corner, where he sat amid a light background buzz while breaking out his books.

The hours passed, and when darkness draped the café Kid felt a growing sickness of the heart. Although he trusted the intel that identified this café as the anarchists' hangout. But even though he knew that Uncle Marty was somewhere nearby, a loneliness descended upon him like a cape he couldn't shrug off.

Part of this had its roots in the fact that Marty wasn't really his uncle. They weren't even related by blood. But they had bonded long ago, and the captain of the skies was forevermore Uncle Marty.

And so he finished the food, and minutes later he trudged outside and drove to his lonely room inside the impersonal chain motel.

Chapter Twelve

· ·

May 15 · Olympia

THE NEXT MORNING Kid put on a shirt and shorts and drove to the café while humming a nameless tune. Since today's traffic under scattered clouds was sparse, he arrived earlier than expected.

Once inside he bought caffeine and two pressed cakes of seaweed, flax and wheat, got a table, and was opening his laptop when the Ghanaian woman in the photo—Cleopatra Koufie—strolled through the door.

Seeing her sent his pulse taking off like a greyhound running the track, because having slept with his share of beautiful women, this one left him feeling energized. Hell—his breathing sped up just by watching the imperial manner in which she swept past a table of noisy students.

He took her in with a practiced glance: five-seven; one-thirty; slender. As for her skin, he thought, *Ahh, what skin.* It was the color of the caramel candies he'd loved since childhood.

She had on a black satin blouse with sleeves reaching to just above her elbows, with matching pants. The clothing's colors went perfectly with her skin tone, and this dazzling woman wore her black hair drawn back and parted in the middle and teased out into curls that fell upon trim shoulders.

Then there were her eyebrows, dark and angled above mascara-enriched eyes in a way that resurrected the Cleopatra of history. In keeping with royalty, her manicured nails were long and lacquered, and four silver rings adorned the fingers of her left hand.

Kid watched her buy an espresso and a European cream tart topped with fat blueberries. To his great luck, she started his way. He decided to touch gloves with the enemy by flashing an engaging smile, then bury his face in the laptop screen with an indifference certain to pique her curiosity.

Sure enough, she stopped at once and peered at him while her mouth formed a silent O. The tipping point arrived when she stepped closer with a ruffled brow to ask with a lilting British accent, "Where do I know you from, love?"

Kid looked up from his screen and stood as fine manners required. "I could equivocate by insisting that I'm nobody, just a stranger in a strange land…"

"Heinlein," she said at once.

"My favorite author. Me? The name's Kid." He smiled and regarded her with liquid, woman-loving eyes.

"Cleo. Short for Cleopatra." She put the espresso on his table and offered her hand.

He took her fingers in his and held them for a second before letting go. "I'm pleased to know you, Cleo. As for your question, I modeled a few years back. Guess I was in the right place, yadda, yadda. Anyway, I got lucky when some photos made their way to the majors. *Vogue; Cosmopolitan.* Couple of others."

Moving closer, she skewered him with her eyes. "Yes. *Cosmo.* 'The Lovers Embrace'. Some four years ago; that photo spread which shall live in infamy. Plus that legendary spread for *Vogue*?" She canted her head to one side while a new-age couple in rainbow tie-dies, billowy skirts, and balloon pants trooped past with cups in hand. "I believe you also modeled for another Milan shoot." Her eyes looked up and to the left. "Ah. Three years ago. Dolce & Gabbana. Am I not correct?"

"You've quite a memory. Bravo!" He clapped and showed clean white teeth.

She studied him with a slight squint of the eye, a sideways movement of the jaw. "*Memory?* Don't be daft. For God's sake, man! They were full-*frontals*—and quickly bandied about across social media's far-flung corners."

"Then the burning question is whether you required a magnifying glass as most do when checking my junk."

Her face opened up. "Mmmmm. See? I knew there was something I liked about you. Yes, you seem filled with equal parts mischief and modesty."

Kid raised an eyebrow before driving a spear into the enemy. "Modesty is the virtue of slaves."

She rolled her eyes. "Aristotle. And God is a comedian playing to an audience that's afraid to laugh."

"Voltaire," he fired back.

"Impressive. Also? I did not require the aid of magnification. Nature graced you at birth." She edged closer and undressed him with her eyes. "You're even prettier in person. Quite girlish. Feminine, even. Clearly gay. Only, please tell me that you might at least be bi-."

He said poker-faced, "I see you use sex as an icebreaker."

"Sue me. Remind me later and I shall provide the name of my solicitor. Well?"

"I have lady friends. Does that answer your repugnant personal question?"

"Perhaps." She arched an eyebrow. "Are you not going to ask if I prefer the ladies?"

He looked sidelong at her. "Please tell me why you find it necessary to come across as a whore."

As the sound of crashing dishes carried from the kitchen, she drew herself up to her full five foot seven and regarded him through eyelids turned to slits. "Is that how you see me?"

"The question," he began with a direct look, "Is whether you see yourself as one."

The clock ran out, the buzzer sounded, and she gave her head a regal toss. "Brilliant reply. Cool, crisp. Cutting edge, and all that. You're certainly not a tosser."

"I've never thought so." When he saw her peering at his left hand, he held it up to show his wedding band. "Yep. Happily married."

"Yes. Quite. Saw it right off. I assume you're married to a bloke. What's his name?"

"Does it matter?"

"No. Not really." A silence hung between them until she said with a brooding quality, "You've nice eyes. They're… direct. They don't look away. Also, you are married to a woman, yet you felt no need to clarify this."

"My wife's name is Jennifer." He swept a hand at his table. "Would you please join me?"

Reaching out, she touched cool fingers to his cheek. "Of course."

He held her chair as any gentleman operative who might have to sleep with a loathsome enemy would, then spent thirty minutes working into an otherwise mundane conversation that he'd left his family behind to come here.

She lifted both palms toward the ceiling when he finished. "You claim to protest environmental issues. Yet what triggered you to abandon your family? Because I'm finding it difficult to accept your decision."

He nodded rapidly. "The talk of reopening the pipeline got to me first. But it was the offshore drilling stuff that pushed me over the edge." He looked deep into her eyes. "Increased coal mining's next."

Cleo settled her espresso cup in its saucer and looked point-blank at him. "You've been here two days now?"

"Nearly three."

"I see. Do you require accommodations?"

"I do." He was watching her face for a reaction when he spotted Marty Fischbach at the service counter. *Damn. How'd I miss not seeing him come in?*

"What type do you seek, love?"

"Hell, I'm open. I mean…" He made small talk about his remaining financial resources after repudiating his wealth, while Marty got a coffee and a snack. But when the operative chose a distant table and sat with his back to him, Kid wondered why until he realized that Marty could see him in a window's reflection.

Several silent seconds passed before Cleo squinted. "Oi! You told me you're married. A moment ago you let on that you've twin daughters and are expecting a son. Shall I assume then that you are totally straight?"

He gave her a look. "What is it with you and sex? Earlier you tossed out a not-so-subtle inquiry about whether I'm bi-." Pausing for effect, he spelled it out. "Not that it's anyone's business, but I have slept with guys." He held off clarifying that the encounters were sleepovers he had between the ages of five and eight with other boys his age.

Cleo showed a small smile. "Good on you, then. Flexible nature, and all that. Tell me more about when you're with the guys. Are you top, bottom, or vers?"

"Looking to pimp me out, are you?" He held up his ring finger again.

She sniffed. "That's shite. Unless you plan on summoning your wife and children here."

Kid blew air from his cheeks. "They'll just get in the way."

"Oh? How so?"

He narrowed his eyes. "Did I not just finish telling you? That government is oppressive? That it should only exist to collect garbage and handle taxes? That our planet's in danger of collapsing upon itself? That I'm here to make a difference? Or to at least try, damn it."

The woman from Ghana put on a face as if she'd entered a room only to hear people shout, surprise! "Wow. You're just what the Pacific Northwest needs. Another social justice warrior."

"Shove it," he fired back. Then he did what good deep-cover operatives do by showing total indifference to her, and any group she might be affiliated with. "I left my family. Don't like it? Go piss up a rope. Now back to the question at hand. Do you know of any rooms for rent?"

Cleo bit off a piece of her blueberry tart, and after swallowing she asked, "For how long? Because as I see it, mate? A bloke who leaves wife and children behind is not intent on returning to them anytime soon."

"Kiss my ass and listen up. My marriage isn't lessened by the purity of my beliefs."

She reared back in mock surprise. "Oh my! I am totally gobsmacked. Permit me to guess. *Seven Pillars of Wisdom*."

Kid narrowed his eyes. "A fan of T.E. Lawrence, are we? Come on, gimme just a little break." He said in a softer tone, "I haven't read the book. Who knows where I dredged that up from."

Cleo settled her elbows on the table and leaned forward until her face was inches from his. "What… a… nice… mix; the classic education combined with bourgeois street slang; the whole served up with a heaping helping of honesty."

Her face threatened to glare at any moment. It's why she surprised him with a gleaming smile. "I like you, Kid. Yes, you're all right. Oh, and I wouldn't mind the opportunity to literally kiss your arse. It is quite cute, you know."

Kid summoned up a droll voice. "So I've been told. Well, segue time again. I like you as well." He didn't. Cleo was the enemy and he felt real anger at having to be here—yet this was tempered by his awe and admiration for this very strong woman.

"Ah. Cheers, mate. Brilliant, that. Yes. Absolutely brilliant. Not to mention that fortune favors you today. For it so happens that I know of some available lodgings."

"Yeah?"

"A flat. More precisely, a refurbished garage situated to the rear of an established home. The landlord should be there. Senior citizen, don't you know? Wait one while I ring a bloke who'll know if it's been let." She walked a short distance away to make the call.

.   .   .

Sandro stared at his smartphone in irritation until he saw the caller ID. "Sí," he barked while rousing himself from the drug-induced stupor he'd fallen into. "No," he replied in response to a question, adding, "I must have our friend conduct, how do you say… further probes for weak spots. Then…" He narrowed his eyes and pressed his lips tight after the caller interrupted with a not-so-very-nice comment concerning Sandro's parentage.

Angry or not, he listened and nodded several times. "Yes. We will cause a bigger show to happen, and soon. It is designed to test our, um, what was the word you used?" He slapped a hand against his forehead. "Ah. Readiness. Sí."

Sandro listened again and started to speak when the other party abruptly ended the call, leaving him holding a silent phone coupled with a growing grudge. When the phone chirped again, he was about to throw it against a wall. But he thought better of it and took the call.

.   .   .

Cleo told Kid upon returning to the table, "I spoke to the landlord's nephew. He's assured me that the flat remains available. He also provided directions." She fell silent while sounds of cutlery and chit-chat filled the void when all at once she got an amazed look. "Wait. I have a *scathingly* brilliant idea. Why not follow me there so we can see it together?"

"Sure." He stood and held her chair for her.

"Thank you, love. Now then. Let us see about your housing."

THE new digs were dismal—an illegally remodeled detached garage behind a retired couple's house in a last-chance neighborhood. The exterior brown paint hung in long curls and matters were worse inside, where rancid grease from a kitchenette hung in the air like a wet sheet.

The tiny living area doubled as a bedroom, the queen-sized bed had seen better days, and the sagging yellow fabric couch should have been tossed a decade ago. A micro-bathroom to one side filled in the blanks.

Kid cringed. Dirt, dust, and any number of vermin were a part of the place as evidenced by mouse droppings near the kitchen. In addition to the grease, it also smelled like a rugby locker room. Ancient pallid green paint was peeling from the walls, almost as if locked in a race with its exterior cousin to see which one shriveled away first, and noise from honking cars and backfiring trucks intruded. He also thought it was all too convenient—a possible set-up. It's why he said, "I like it."

Wrinkles creased her forehead. "Really? I should think this is rather a dump. You do have money for far better lodgings."

"I'm trying to start a new life," he began. Between the lines, he meant that this dump would have to do since she was probing to see if he had indeed renounced his wealth. He swept a hand at the room. "A new bed and sofa wouldn't hurt."

"Yes," she said. " I see it in my mind's eye, and I'm quite certain you can freshen it up. Might I venture to suggest that you begin by razing the entire building while yelling 'piss off' and starting anew?"

Her accent pleased Kid's ear, and for the sake of the mission he hugged her. "Thank you for all you're doing."

"It has been my pleasure. Also, love? I find your confidence to be quite charming." All at once she kissed his mouth and held it until his hands spanned her waist. "You are so lovely."

Kid in his Mata Hari role spoke from the heart. "Mmm. If only I were single." He offered an enchanting smile that said, *I'd love to be with a woman as fascinating as you. But—*

Her chest heaved but she spoke with a humorous glint in her eyes. "Wow, mate. Too bad you are spoken for."

"More or less." Then he pressed against her to make his needs known, and when she smiled he began grinding against her with sensual male appetite until quipping, "Yes. Quite."

She released a moan and tapped his zipper, and when he didn't protest she eased it down and exposed him and slowly sank to her knees until he gripped her arms and tugged her back up.

Cleo stood still and showed white teeth. "Well, as you said earlier, you're married. Too bad. Well, shall we meet at the café on the morrow? We'll talk then. Let us say, one hour before noon?"

"I'd love that," he whispered and winked at Cleo while she stowed his rapidly relaxing penis back where she found it, and zipped him up.

Easing away from him, she went to the door only to pause and glance over her shoulder. "What have you planned for the rest of the day?"

He shrugged. "Shopping. And I'll need to haul ass if I'm to fix this place up."

"Brilliant." She hesitated. "Shall I stop by tonight to tuck you in?"

A silence followed while he deliberated with his soul. He finally met her stare. "I love my wife. Yeah, I know... I got carried away just now. Hell, who wouldn't with such a wonderful woman? So if you come it'll be as a friend only. Which is what you've become."

After she nodded, he walked her outside and waved as she drove off. Then it was back inside where his eyes searched the room without seeming to. If there were hidden cameras or mics, he didn't spot them.

And yet he had to assume they existed. He even saw an advantage to being bugged: if everything he said or did was recorded, he could employ words and deeds that validated his reasons for leaving home.

But then a lightning bolt of heaviness descended upon him as he pictured his wife, children, and unborn son. If only for their benefit alone, he had to commit himself to the mission; he just had to.

Minutes later he was at a low-budget store where he purchased bedding, cookware, dishes, towels, and a broom. After returning, he spruced the place up and cooked a modest dinner. By ten he was exhausted, and Kid, who'd slept in the buff since childhood, stripped and fell naked upon the bed.

POUNDING. Followed by more pounding. Kid's eyes fluttered open. The door. Cleo. He shook away the sleep, then raised up on an elbow to flick the bedside lamp on. "Come in," he mumbled.

Cleo stepped inside wearing a pin-striped ivory blouse and black linen shorts. She made a point of looking around until her white teeth gleamed in the subdued light. "Love what you've done with the place." When her eyes settled on him, she showed a lovely sleepy-cat smile.

"I'm glad you came," he said drowsily. After working some moisture into his mouth he looked full-face at her. "I wanted you to come."

She offered a subdued glance. "Cheers, then. But are you not married?"

Kid hesitated for only a heartbeat before offering a most sophisticated reply: "Shut up." Then he touched the spot next to him and said as a hidden camera kicked on, "I'm inviting you to my bed. As a friend. Because I like you a lot. Only, there'll be no sex."

She frowned. "My. Aren't we big on ourselves?"

He looked directly at her and said in a way that didn't invite rebuttal, "Final offer." Then he shifted to make room for her, secure in the knowledge that she would join him.

SOMETIME later he jerked awake while wondering who was at his side. *Oh. Cleo.* He winced and then left the slumbering woman's side and went to the sole window. After crossing his bare ankles, he leaned against the window frame and peered through the darkness for quite some time before turning to study Cleo. Right now a wan beam of moonlight shouldered its way past the flimsy curtains and highlighted her most invitingly.

Kid released a sustained sigh and said a silent prayer for Jennifer and their daughters while reminding himself that Cleo and her cohorts were the enemy and that a clock was ticking away. It helps explain why he decided that if he had to be a Romeo to block these zealots bent on destroying the world — a world his children had every right to embrace — then he would be a ruthless one.

Vowing to make it happen, he returned to bed and draped an arm around the naked enemy. Following that act of marginalized intimacy, he fell into a deep and untroubled sleep.

CLEO touched Kid's arm as the new dawn's light filtered into the room. "Lad?"

He stirred and cleared his throat. "Yes?"

"Did you make love to them?"

Creases etched his forehead. "Huh? To *them,* who?"

"The models. From *Cosmo* and *Vogue.* Who else would I mean, you mad Yank."

"Oh." Kid studied her face while wondering, *Why do I always get asked* before providing his stock answer. "Don't ask, don't tell. That's my motto." He idly stroked her forearm while awaiting her reaction.

"Ah. Understood." She raised up on an elbow and traced a fingertip along his sternum. "I once aspired to become a model. It's why I have such a keen interest in knowing what takes place behind the scenes. That's all. No offense intended."

"None taken." Kid kissed her mouth and guided her cheek to his chest. In the silence that followed he felt so much older than even the day before. The rest-stop attack had certainly matured him; accepting Cleo into his bed even for a sleepover had further aged his soul. His only consolation was that he hadn't consummated a sexual relationship with the anarchist.

Anarchist or not, he could not deny her beauty—that power of her gaze, combined with her full sensual mouth, satiny skin, and clean hair. Pulling her close, he luxuriated in the feel of her body against his. Cleo meanwhile played her fingers up and down his flanks and atop his long legs before taking delicate hold of his penis and flopping it back and forth as if she did this to him every day.

"Kid? I respect the vow you made to your wife. Mind you," she began with a broad smile, "I should have preferred that you'd provided me with a good go betwixt the sheets. My gosh! I shan't say that I didn't feel gutted when you rejected me."

"Sorry to disappoint," he said with just the right shade of British slang. "I truly did wish to give you the proper shagging that you are so demonstrably entitled to."

She threw her head back and laughed with total release. "You are too much. Are you quite certain you were not raised in a Commonwealth Country?" She gave his penis a little tug. "Christ, you are so much a British bloke, down to your uncut willie." She let go of it and sighed. "Where was I? Ah, yes. I shall respect the vow you made forbidding you from cheating. Am I making sense?"

"Like a raving banshee," he said with enough goofiness to lend intimacy to their non-starter adventures.

"Ah. Well, love?" She wagged her eyebrows. "Now to make good on my wish to kiss your arse." In a teasing way that spoke of casual friendship, she urged him onto his belly and planted sensuous lips against his bottom. After making a juicy SMACK sound she looked up, and when she found him smiling at her in a most pleasantly inviting manner, she entered his open arms. They kissed, they touched, they talked. But nothing more.

"Well," he began with killing casualness sometime later. "Time to hit the shower."

He left her side and walked naked into the tiny bathroom, where he twisted the water knobs and got busy to give her time to plant a bugging device or two.

"Love?" she began when he stepped from the shower. "I trust you won't mind, but I came bearing gifts." She angled her head toward an air freshener that was now plugged into an outlet near the bed. "A plug-in, don't you know? To freshen this decidedly unseemly air."

His smile dazzled. "Aww, you're so sweet." He tossed the towel aside and kissed her while making a mental note to examine the gift later.

Moments later he pulled his pants on, and they talked while he fixed a breakfast which they ate with relish. Once she downed her third cup of coffee—not tea, he noted—he wrapped his arms around her neck and kissed her with a deep feeling.

"You're incorrigible," she said with a wink and a smile and went to the door.

Kid waited until she drove off before examining the air freshener. A tiny mic was indeed embedded within its white plastic housing. *Very slick, masking it this way. Constant source of power; no wiring required. So, yeah. I'll activate my phone speaker during calls and let them hear both ends of my conversations. Only, my end's gonna be edited for effect. Betcher ass.*

He did the dishes and broke out the textbooks while wondering, *the 4th of July's still seven weeks away, so where's the friggin' urgency? Why am I here?*

•   •   •

Alessandro "Sandro" Costa had edged closer to the screen earlier in anticipation of watching the very pretty boy have steamy intercourse with Cleopatra. But when the person of interest balked, Sandro shouted, "Bah!"

Angry or not, he decided that this boy—who in fact was only two or three years younger than he—had a degree of honor. And that meant everything to this self-styled Spanish nobleman who had fallen so far from his father's grace.

After Malee walked over as quietly as a ghost and regarded him with her blue eyes, he smiled. "Malee, do you know I have for you so much of the love?"

While the Siamese licked her paws in response, Sandro picked up a small hand mirror with its three lines of cocaine and snorted one of them. When the high-octane product slammed home, he vigorously rubbed the tip of his nose and blinked several times, "Whoa."

Following another *whoa*, he hit the video machine's PLAY button and smiled at the part where the boy undressed for bed. His smile grew as he invited Cleo into his bed, and his interest knew few bounds while he watched the images of her playing with his manhood.

All of this justified the monthly stipend he paid his uncle to only rent the converted garage to the clueless young men that Sandro sent to him. Although these rentals were short-lived, the occupants usually stayed long enough for the Spaniard to record their actions and words from a hidden mic and video lens.

But it was this new renter's global agenda as reported by Cleo that had piqued Sandro's interest. Was he legit? Or was this young man a special agent of the F. B. of I.? A surveillance could be crucial in discovering an answer.

This required two courses of action: one to reveal the truth; the other to lure the world-famous model into his own bed. But according to Cleo, this boy was devoted to family—which meant toppling his wife's faith in her husband before Sandro could lure him to his bed.

Luckily for Sandro, he began exploring deepfake technology over a year ago. He had already invested several thousand U.S. dollars for a Graphics Processing Unit. Then he acquired a Generative Adversarial Network, or GAN. It creates new images from latent source materials that mimic reality with remarkable precision. These images then evolve into a zero-sum event that makes deepfakes exceedingly difficult to protect against.

The Spaniard then devoted months of learning and practice to train a model program and fix imperfections. All this just to generate deepfake porn. Now he got to work.

Thanks to the GPU and GAN software, he replicated the models—in this case, the nude Kid and Cleo—until they generated a continual flow of motions that learned from each other due to the GAN's ability to mimic reality.

By twelve noon he said to the empty room, "All it requires is time. Sí."

The blue-eyed Malee meowed in affirmation.

Chapter Thirteen

. . . .

That afternoon • May 16

SANDRO TOOK ONE look at the caller ID and answered at once. "Sí?"

The detached female voice filling his ear was all business. "Pay attention. This assumes of course you can sustain that minimal level of cognitive thinking. I think not. However. The new one. He has proven his trustworthiness. I want him. Vet him thoroughly and report your findings."

A buzz filled the Spaniard's ear after she hung up on him.

• • •

Kid dressed in casual clothes and drove to the café, where he found Cleo drinking tea rather than her usual coffee. After getting some orange juice he joined her just as a scattering of customers began filling the air with the usual dull roar, their conversations light and trivial—like a thistle blossom falling without a sound and without any weight.

As steam rose from her cup of tea and circled her head like playful clouds, she narrowed her eyes at him. "Well?"

"Well, what?" Kid had his own steam going. Too much coffee; too much heat from a caffeine dump that had him tweaked like a twenty-dollar hooker after snorting her fifth line of the evening, then shoving cotton up her nose to stem the coke-induced bleeding.

A heavy silence filled the room. Not even those thistle blossoms invaded. Cleo waited it out before asking, "How far are you willing to go in your fight against those who offend nature?"

Kid replied with iron in his voice. "I didn't come this far not to go all the way."

"Suppose the only feasible solution should cause two million global deaths before our planet can reap any benefits?"

"You ask a revealing question. I've no idea what such an action entails. But I'll argue that the United States alone killed half a million civilians during World War II with fire-bomb raids on Dresden, Hamburg and Tokyo. Or must I add Hiroshima and Nagasaki to prove my case?"

"Which side of that argument do you advocate for."

He stared at her and bit the next words off. "We did what had to be done at the time."

Cleo nodded while a young couple engaged in animated conversation swept by, then said as if discussing the weather, "I might have a mate who knows this guy who has joined a cause. Perhaps he can use you." She caught Kid's eye. "He'll want to vet you."

"He would be crazy-foolish careless not to."

Cleo sipped her tea and looked past Kid. "Shall I ring this mate?"

Kid went in-role by pressing his lips tight and staring at some unseen thing before saying with a sudden excitement, "I didn't leave home to spin my wheels. My answer is, yes."

• • •

Sandro, garbed in black, stood behind Ag with imperial grace and watched the computer whiz move the mouse until the cursor brushed a message in bold red letters:

WARNING—AUTHORIZED PERSONNEL ONLY

The message marked a Maginot Line of sorts; a technician's feeble effort to steer hackers away from the Federal Reserve Bank's Eighth District Office in Little Rock.

Sandro suspected the basement air was infested with mold and other allergens. So after rubbing his nose, he reached without thinking into his trousers and pulled out a tiny bottle of fluticasone. He sprayed some into each nostril, and mumbled while pocketing it, "Do you not ever clean this place?"

Ag snapped at him. "This room's cleaner than Mission Control."

In fact, his high-end CPUs and huge screens did mimic Mission Control. "You're welcome to leave if you don't like it." He made a noise and left-clicked the mouse.

One of his three huge concave screens lit up with a glaring light before softening to a dull blue. All at once a menu appeared.

"We're in," Ag said, as much to himself as to Sandro.

The Spaniard reached for the fluticasone and sprayed it again while thinking he might call that bitch and say, *See? This was the readiness test that I made the mention of to you. Having entered this new phase, we can now proceed. Now please to show me some respect.*

. . .

Later that evening Sandro sat hunched over his desktop and reviewed the video of last night's aborted lovemaking.

The boy let Cleo into his bed, he reassured himself. *He did not make to her the love. Perhaps not in the fact. But possibly in the imagination? Sí. Bravo! Ah, but no imagination is required when Cleo fondles him, or kisses his bottom. The scenes are so choice. Also? His ass? Que bella!* He put his fingers to his mouth and pulled them away while making a kissing sound.

Then Sandro smiled and sent the video through a ghost server to Jennifer Bailey's email account.

A ding from Jen's smartphone yanked her from sleep. She felt weary — the pregnancy, the children; her absent husband — all combined in an alliance to defeat her. But when she saw a Pacific time zone stamp, she figured Kid had sent a text and danced feverish fingers across the password.

"Huh." Jen squinted at the sender's address and mumbled, "An email. But not from Kid." Furrows erupted across her lovely forehead until she whispered, "Maybe he's using another device?"

Ever wary of malware, she slipped out of bed and went down the hallway, sniffing the air while drawing closer to the nursery's open door, the scent of baby oil reassuring her in ways that lifted her heart. She lingered at the door briefly before going downstairs.

Jen had purged an old iPad of personal information long ago so the twins could use it to acquire basic computer skills. It was on the kitchen table right where she last saw it, and she clutched it to her breasts while letting a flood of memories inside her heart.

A minute later she had it booted and on the web. More curious than ever now, she opened the message: *You must watch the video of Kid.*

Her breath caught. She took a step back. Then she felt a flood of caution screaming, *Don't open the attachment.* Yet she was too intrigued not to. So she downloaded the attachment and after sending it to a media suite, her trembling index finger hovered over the keyboard. Then she clicked PLAY.

Thirty minutes later she placed a hand against her growing abdomen and tried not to cry. "Oh, Kid."

She knew of course that her husband might have to sleep with other women. But seeing him making love to this very beautiful black woman triggered a deep pain that sent tears streaking down her cheeks. She swiped at them though while thinking, *I'm tougher than this. I also know what had to be going through Kid's mind.* She hit STOP and sat in silence.

A moment later she got up and did something she never thought possible—especially while at seven months: she poured a shot of bourbon and tossed it back.

Then she nodded, and after saying a prayer for the man she loved more than life itself she returned to bed and slept the sleep of those who've been blessed with peace of mind.

·   ·   ·

Kid gasped and sat up in bed, his eyes wide from a nightmare that had him locked in mortal combat with Goliath. He took a few deep breaths while reassuring himself that the ex-con could never threaten him again. Then he went to the kitchen and poured a shot of bourbon.

He gulped it down and returned to bed, where he closed his eyes and pictured Jen and Lana and Lara. He was snoring seconds later.

Chapter Fourteen
· ·

May 17 · Olympia

KID CHECKED THE time again and scowled. Bill hadn't shown up at the café, and Kid was keen on picking his brain to see if he socialized with other morbidly obese poor souls—one of them might even be the elusive Agamemnon.

At least Marty hadn't failed him. Kid wasn't in the café five minutes before he spotted the business-casual operative in a dark corner, where for all the world he appeared to be engrossed in his laptop.

But Marty left a short time later, so Kid was studying an anatomy textbook when an attractive young couple sauntered in. He had on blue scrubs, and she was wearing her neon red hair over a revealing white halter top and ultra-skimpy blue shorts. They were Dr. Jake Berg and his wife Gillian Robertson.

Neither of them glanced his way as they went to the barista, and they ignored him again when they shuffled along with coffee and snacks in hand and plopped onto a faded blue couch against a far wall.

Kid thought, *Christ. This spy crap sure as shit takes a lot of energy.*

Later on when Bill still failed to appear, Kid stepped outside to call home. When Jen picked up he said, "Hey, babe"

"I, um... hello."

He frowned. "What's wrong?"

"Oh, you know. The usual. Fatigue."

Kid couldn't tell if she was playing the required role of the rebuffed wife, so he kept their talk neutral before asking her to put her cell on speaker and hold it close to the twins. He tried his best to electronically reach out and hold them by making cartoonish sounds and asking about their play. But when their girls' chatter died away, he signaled Jen that he needed to end the call.

Following a glance at the low, greasy Pacific Northwest skies, he went inside feeling deeply depressed and kept glancing at a wall clock over the service counter.

As its minute hand moved with the sureness of Earth's rotation to officially make it 1:00 PM, Kid gave up on Bill and got up to leave when the main door banged open. Then Bill barged inside, looking as if he were wearing a large sack.

"You're late," Kid announced.

"Late?" The huge man scowled. "What're you yakking about? I'm right on time."

"We agreed on noon sharp."

"No. We settled on one."

"I... shit!" Kid slapped a hand against his forehead. "Right. We did say one. I must still be locked into East Coast time. Or something."

"Or something," Bill said, but his face showed a deep interest in Kid. "You didn't abandon me, though. Christ, nobody's ever waited for me." He reached out a hand.

As Kid shook it amid a burst of laughter from a clutch of college students, he said, "My friends matter to me."

"Is—" Bill drew in a little breath. "Is that how you see me? As your friend?"

"Of course. I also see myself as hungry. How about you?"

An hour later the man Kid knew only as Bill dabbed a napkin at the corners of his mouth and folded it. Then he spoke without shame for perhaps the first time in his life. "I am grateful for your friendship. It means a lot—" His mouth opened and closed several times like a beached carp's before he mumbled, "It means almost as much as my wife and children mean to me."

"Yeah?" Kid edged forward with genuine interest. "You never did tell me her name."

"Huh?" Bill's face turned ashen. "Um, well you see, her name's Katarina. Yeah," he said with a new energy. "Katarina. From Italy, you know?"

"Ah! *Italia!*" Kid's enchanting smile brightened the room. *"Parli Italiano?"*

Bill's eyes darted back and forth. "Um, no. I don't. Wish I did speak it, but—" He swiped at some sweat on his forehead. "I take it you do?"

"Fluently." Kid's eyes lit up with real excitement. "Do you think Katarina would let me practice my skills with her? And hey… your children. Tell me about them. Also, photos. You must have photos." Kid was radiating nothing less than pure interest in another person's life.

Bill cheerfully said, "Do I have photos? Is that what you're asking? Well of course I do." But after making a show of searching his pockets he grimaced. "Damn. Must've left my primary phone at home. I'll be sure to bring it next time. If that's okay with you, I mean."

Something was not okay, but Kid kept a poker face while his gut spoke to him. "Of course, Bill. Anytime." A pause, then, "Who else do you hang out with around here?"

A sudden shadow crossed Bill's face. "Nobody. Just um, family. And you."

Sensing Bill's pain, Kid tried to put a positive spin on it. "Yeah, sometimes I also want some alone time. I'm guessing that's how you feel."

Bill looked at him gratefully, and Kid's heart went out to the big man. Yet he needed to stay on point with his instincts, which led him to ask Bill to meet again. Tomorrow. Same place and time. Finally, he offered to trade phone numbers. But when Bill shied away, Kid shifted gears and turned the conversation toward world events.

Later, after Bill left, Kid scribbled his evaluation of the big man onto a napkin, hid it in his palm, and walked toward the barista only to stumble against Jake Berg. "Sorry," he mumbled while offering his hand. "The name's Kid."

Jake took the proffered hand while cupping the note inside it. "Howdy, stranger."

•   •   •

That evening the Spaniard sat back and stroked his chin after concluding that the young Latino he had been seeing, this Cain, must be yet another undercover FBI agent. Why else did Cain avoid having sex with him? More importantly, why did Cain's Ohio driver's license feature his photo with a different name? *Julio Solla*, it read, although Cain told Sandro his name was Cain Perez.

These issues led Sandro to a conclusion, so he got up from the chair in search of Malee. After finding the Siamese atop his bed, he mock-scolded her. "You are always making with the hiding." Then he smiled and used Catalan Spanish to explain his problem with Julio, aka Cain. When Malee meowed what he saw as her affirmation, he armed himself with his .40 automatic.

Moments later he parked in front of Cain's rooming house and began banging on the door. When Cain opened it, Sandro snarled at him and spoke in English rather than in Spanish. "Let's go"

The frail young man blinked sleep from his eyes. "Go? Where? What's up?"

"We go for a ride. This instant." He put on a show of excitement. "Yes, there is something you will want to see."

Cain/Julio shrugged and peered at Sandro. "Mi amigo, are choo not going to tell me?"

"And spoil the surprise? No, my friend. Let us go now. I promise to have you back in one hour." Sandro showed an endearing smile. "Perhaps you will add a modicum of insight to the enigma that I shall reveal to you, yes?"

Five minutes later Julio plopped onto the passenger seat of Sandro's decrepit Nissan and fastened his seatbelt as required by law. Because Julio was an illegal alien with a fake ID and could not risk drawing a cop's attention.

Unfortunately for Julio, Sandro interpreted the action as something only cops do out of habit, even when under-cover. But he said nothing while he drove up one lane and down another under a canopy of dark clouds, finally stopping alongside a secluded river.

"We get out here."

Furrows covered the younger man's forehead. "Why? What's here?"

"You shall see. As I explain, it is the surprise."

A hesitation, then, "Sure. Who does not like surprises?" Cain/Julio opened the door, stepped out, and bolted toward the river.

Sandro grabbed his night vision goggles and tore off in pursuit while drawing his pistol and mockingly calling out, "Julio? Why do you run?"

When his prey didn't answer, Sandro muttered, "You run because you have the alias. This is because you are F.B. of I."

The Spaniard knew which trails weren't marred by under-growth and face-slapping ferns. He also knew which way Julio had gone, and what shortcut to use to trap the fleeing imposter.

"Ah," he said a moment later as he pulled off his night vision equipment and aimed the pistol at the trembling wide-eyed young man.

"So now you tell me," Sandro began. "Why did you lie about your name? Who are you really?"

Julio said in a voice fraught with fear, "I am illegal. Also, I left my lover. He's cruel and I don't want him to make the finding of me. So I..."

Julio was dead before he could finish his sentence.

Sandro laughed at the look of utter shock on this liar's face. He laughed at the entrance wound dead center between the liar's eyes. And he laughed while trumpeting, "Ha! Right between the running lights, just as the Norteamericanos say."

Chapter Fifteen

· ·

May 17 · Vanguard International · Washington, D.C.

LEVI HART GRIPPED the back of Hacksaw's Aeron chair and peered at the Ops Center's main screen. "Come on, Kid. Give us some feedback."

Hacksaw had been posting daily log entries from Marty, Jake, and Gillian on the screen. They detailed Kid's café visits along with his lack of progress. But Levi felt spurred with a new urgency in the wake of the Amtrak incident. "Come on."

Hacksaw swiped a broad hand across his coffee-colored cheek and spoke in the soft, well-modulated rhythms of the Virginia tidelands he hailed from. "Easy does it, Boss Man. You've worked enough deep covers. Sure as the hands on a clock go around, you know how long it takes to make headway."

"You're right, Hack. I do know. It's why I'm pissed at myself for acting like a mother hen."

"Better than acting like a motherfucker," Hacksaw chided, when all at once he sat upright. "*Un momento, jefe.*"

Hack squinted at an encrypted message before announcing in a rush of words, "All right. Here we go. Jake Berg's reporting in. Kid met a six hundred pound guy at the café, name of Bill. Claims to be married with children. Except the guy had no family photos on his smartphone. Kid adds that our person of interest also refused to exchange numbers.

"Let's see, what else… okay, to reiterate: he's at least six hundred pounds and he visits our targeted café. Coincidence? Kid doesn't think so."

After reading a few more lines, Hacksaw pushed forward in his chair with some sort of excitement. "Looky, looky. Kid asked the guy to meet him tomorrow, same time and place. He wants Marty to tail him when he leaves. Said to find out where he lives and see if he really is married."

Levi sniffed. "Could be nothing; could be everything."

"Ya think, Boss Man?" Hacksaw was all smiles.

"Hmm." Levi knuckled his long jaw. "Tell you what. Grab Michael and join me in my office."

The three men were seated in Levi's office ten minutes later with drinks in hand, the ice tinkling in two of their glasses when Levi pulled a high-end Arturo Fuente cigar from a humidor and held it up. When the others demurred, he clipped the end off and pulled out a thick kitchen match from the humidor which he scratched across his shoe's leather sole. When the match erupted into a sulfur-smelling blaze, he lit up and blew a smoke ring.

After settling deep into his chair he briefed Michael on Kid's message. Then he turned to Hack. "How about providing a rundown of the typical cyber threats."

Hacksaw Jones held his drink to his eyes and studied its golden contents while speaking. "There are Deep Webs and Dark Webs. There's D-DOS—aka, Distributed Denial-of-Service in the form of D-DOS attacks. We've also got these pesky things called *botnets*. Damn things generate floods of internet traffic with the singular goal of creating chaos."

He ticked off other threats on his short fingers. "There are your everyday Advanced Persistent Threats. These involve stealthy actors who gain unauthorized access to a network and remain undetected for years... tha's right folks, we're talkin' *years*. Then there's code injection, which is designed to exploit computer bugs." He raised a third finger. "Fork bombs, also known as 'rabbit virus,' or *wabbit*. It's another DOS attack that replicates itself to deplete available system resources until the system crashes. An' land's sake, did I mention the wipers that erase hard drives of their data and programs?" He grunted. "That 2012 attacks on Iranian oil companies? Wipers, baby. Wipers."

Michael said, "Meanwhile, the world's nation-states rely on Continuous Diagnostics and Mitigation programs, along with back-end databases. Not much help, are they Hack?"

Levi said, "I'll play the devil's advocate. We know that DHS uses the CDM program, which is *somewhat* effective. And DHS reached out to NCA to form a partner-sharing program."

Hacksaw showed a slight smile. "Ah, yes. The UK's much-vaunted National Crime Agency. Love 'em or leave 'em, right?"

"And lest we forget AI," Michael added. "Performing faster than humans can control it."

• • •

The Next Day • Olympia

Kid showered, fixed breakfast, and after cleaning up he settled in to study. At noon he drove to the café to meet Bill, stepping inside only to be greeted by the usual coffee smells, clattering dishes, and subdued talk.

Jake and Gillian were seated at a corner table, where they appeared immersed in the talk of lovers. He didn't see Marty or Bill.

When a plump neon-blue-haired fiftyish woman wearing a shapeless dress and Doc Martens brushed past Kid, he noted her tatted neck, earlobe spacers, and the stud in one side of her nose. She was also sporting a cheap perfume that had his nose crinkling in disgust.

He completed his scan before getting coffee and a vegetarian breakfast. Fortunately for him, he stumbled upon one of the few empty tables that were left. Minutes later he was sipping coffee and chewing a croissant when a pleasant-looking young man came to an abrupt stop in the middle of the floor.

Kid looked him over. Very friendly face. Late twenties. Tall and slender with riveting blue eyes and thick blond hair reaching halfway down his back. Kid decided that he could have been a model, had he chosen that path.

The guy's lazily unbuttoned green flannel shirt revealed a long lean torso, he wore three strings of multi-colored beads around his neck, and his faded blue jeans with *de facto* ripped knees—coupled with his bare feet—also spoke volumes, as did the marijuana odor clinging to his clothes like a well-worn mantle.

Kid called out, "You're welcome to sit here."

"Thanks." The guy put his tray down and sat across from him. "'Preciate it."

"I'm Kid," he said while sticking out his right hand.

The young man half-stood and clasped it. "Nice to meet you. I'm Huck."

"*Huck?* As in, Huckleberry?"

"My folks? They like, loved the book? Plus I never wear shoes? Well, almost never. And my last name's Quinn? So they named me Huckleberry." He flicked his eyes at Kid's wedding band, then glanced around the room. "Are you here with your husband?"

A miffed Kid's eyebrows knitted together. "I have a wife."

Huck said with good cheer, "Oh. 'Cause I like, made you for gay? For sure you're a twink. *Totally* fem. So what're you, like, transitioning?" He smiled with a total lack of malice.

For some reason, this didn't irritate Kid. "I get the girlish stuff a lot."

Huck's head bobbed in total acceptance. "You think? Me? I identify as straight. But straight lines aren't much fun if there aren't, like, a few bends in the river?" He flashed a smile. "So I'll like, get to the point? You're very pretty and I'm horny as hell? So I wanna do you." He smiled at Kid, then sipped his coffee and closed his eyes. "Mmm. Nice!"

Kid regarded Huck anew. He came across as a gentle soul, one he might let his sister marry—if he had one. It's why he felt comfortable enough to rest his elbows on the table and say, "You might not believe in serendipity, but my wife and I considered naming our unborn son Huckleberry."

"A son? Say, that's great." Huck smiled at first, only to look beyond Kid and turn quiet.

"What about you?" Kid asked. "Married? Single? Are you a local?"

"Single. Doing all the babes. Planning on nailing you before the day's over." His smile dazzled just before he leveled Kid with his eyes. "So like, seriously. Are you up for that? Gettin' butt-fucked? 'Cause you're fuckin' hot an' I need to like, fuck *some*body." His face turned serious. "Hey? Don't worry. 'Cause I'll like, be gentle?"

Kid said in a droll way, "If only I wasn't married."

"Hah. Good comeback. Yeah… I like you, Kid. You're a real smart-ass, just like me. It's why I've been messin' with ya; bustin' your balls an' all about doing ya."

Huck fell silent and got busy with his coffee before saying in the most off-handed way, "Last year? Me and this girl-friend, we like, had a baby? We named her Cher. Like the singer? Only, she died a week shy of turning one. Pancreatic cancer. Can you believe that? In an infant?" He pressed his lips tight and shook his head.

Kid reached out and gripped Huck's hand. "I'm so sorry. Jesus, I can't begin to imagine what you and your girlfriend suffered through. The pain; the *grief* at the end. Oh my god. Listen, I'll say a prayer for Cher tonight. I'll ask my wife to do the same, and we'll keep you and your girl in our daily thoughts."

Huck looked gratefully at him. "Anyway, after Cher died my girlfriend up and left. Said she couldn't handle being, you know, reminded of the baby? Whenever she saw my face? Sooo—" He seemed to run out of words.

A protracted silence followed while he pulled a purple fabric hair tie from a pocket and held it between his teeth while running his fingers through his long blond hair. Once he formed a ponytail he slid the scrunchie in place and sat quietly while sipping his coffee.

Kid said to break the spell, "Huck? Any time you need a friend to talk to? Man, don't hesitate."

"Sure. Like, thanks."

Seconds later they had their smartphones out. After Huck proudly showed off some photos of Cher, Kid pulled up images of the twins. Following the usual ooohs and ahhhs, Huck fiddled with his coffee cup while regarding Kid with an animal stare. "I like to get stoned? Maybe you do, too?"

Although Kid had experimented with recreational drugs, he didn't enjoy using them very often. However, he wanted to see where this would go, and said while stirring his coffee, "Of course I do."

Huck nodded rapidly. "Right on."

Kid stifled a smile. *Right on. Hmm, I guess it's true. Northwesterners really do cling to that old phrase. Probably no different than Bostonians saying 'wicked' all the time.*

The young man narrowed his eyes. "So like, I don't drop acid or do Molly or coke. No smack, nothing like that. Weed; hash. That's all. So like, let's hook up and do some puffs?"

Kid made himself perk up. "Sure, I'll do some with you."

"Really? Great." Huck beamed and bobbed his head repeatedly. "Right on, right on."

"Right on," Kid echoed, his gut telling him that Huck was good people. He also seemed the sort who might know people who might know Agamemnon. But there was one other thing: Kid needed to establish himself as a low-level doper to quell suspicions that he might be FBI, and this could be an opening.

It's why he felt relieved when Huck said, "So I'm gonna give you my phone number? For when you're ready to do some puffs? Or for me to do you? Or whatever?"

After exchanging numbers, Kid told Huck why he left his family to come here. Huck nodded often and readily agreed with Kid's take on intrusive governments, only to ask, "You're like, dedicated? Leaving your family and everything? Only, wouldn't you do more for 'em by being home?"

"Maybe. But I have to at least try, or I won't be able to look in a mirror."

Huck said, "Got it," and pantomimed smoking a joint. "Just remembered. I have some edibles? If you wanna get high? As in, right now?"

"Yeah?" Kid scooted forward in his chair. "What've you got?"

"These." He pulled a red and white Altoids container from a pocket and opened it to reveal several red gummies.

A single glance told Kid that they were almost certainly infused with the usual five or ten milligrams of THC, and probably much more. And since Bill hadn't appeared—although to be fair, it wasn't one o'clock yet—and because it would help Kid fit in, he plucked a gummie at random and put it beneath his tongue.

Huck's infectious smile said so much, and he popped one. A few minutes later he popped another gummy and signaled Kid to come closer. When he did, Huck abruptly put his lips to Kid's and deep-kissed him while transferring the gummy from his mouth to Kid's. "Mmm, maybe I'll fuck you up the ass after all." A pause, then, "You up for that?"

Several long seconds passed before Kid said, "I've... never been with a guy. But who knows?" Kid figured the non-answer would let him come across as a player. He even encouraged Huck to repeat the kissing transfer after the stoner popped another gummy.

Then they were laughing hilariously at anything and everything, and when Kid got up to buy some much-needed sweets, he learned the hard way that he'd lost his depth perception when each step he took sent him staggering and grabbing chairs and tables for support.

The time passed. Once they were sober, Huck got to his feet and pulled Kid up. Then while pressing close, Huck ran his fingers through Kid's heavy brown hair. "I'm like, jazzed that I met you? An' I can tell you want me? So like, let's go 'cause I'm taking you to my bed?" He showed a gleaming smile as he grabbed Kid's hand and dragged him toward the front door.

But Kid laughingly sidestepped the offer. "Um, not now. But how about a rain check?"

Huck's deep-throated chuckle spoke well of him, and he deep-kissed Kid and said, "Mmm. You're so pretty." A second later he padded off.

Kid followed him outside, and after watching him drive away he walked through the parking lot just in case Bill was here but unable to get out of his car. Kid saw nothing.

. . .

Another day passed with Kid agonizing over the assignment and its effect on his family. The dismal weather didn't help either, prompting him to take solace by immersing himself in his smartphone's family photos, and by plunging into his textbooks.

To his great relief the following day, Cleo told him over the usual café lunch, "I want you to meet a friend."

"I'm listening."

"Tomorrow. Noon. The shopping mall near Evergreen State." She sat back and sighed. "Fair warning? He's a git."

"I—" Kid jumped a bit when his phone chirped, and after checking the caller ID he excused himself and walked outside under a cloud layer to answer it.

It was Jen. "Some guy appeared on our doorstep asking about you. Wanted to know about your political beliefs and your cut-and-run to Olympia. Even asked about your sexual proclivities. As if I'd respond to such a question."

Kid reminded her in code that they had been told to expect the visit.

It proved fortuitous seconds later when Jen's voice turned harsh. "Some dude also dropped in on my folks. Jesus, Kid.

Don't you see what you're doing to us? In case you don't, you'd better believe that Mother ripped into him about what she thinks of you running out on us."

They spoke some more before ending the call mere seconds before Britney rang in.

"A suit in shades came by asking about you. Wanted to know if I'd heard anything about you knocking up some coeds."

He gripped the phone. "Jesus. What'd you tell him?"

"Only that I'd heard rumors to that effect. Next, he asked if it was true that you also put the proverbial bun in my oven."

Kid stiffened. "Christ."

"Anyway, I told him my pregnancy was none of his business. Oh, he wanted to know if you're a Greener. So I said yes and mentioned the library staff marking you as rebellious for wearing flip-flops." She laughed, only to quietly add, "Kid? I love you very much."

He thanked her for calling, and after pocketing the phone he rejoined Cleo, who regarded him with cool eyes before saying she had to leave. He saw her off but remained at the café on the off-chance that Bill might appear. But he didn't.

THE next day Kid dressed in a black cotton T and jeans, ate a quick breakfast, downed two javas, then drove to the mall beneath the usual layer of gray scud. After parking, he got out only to shudder from a late May chill. So he pulled a gray fleece-lined jacket from his trunk and shrugged it on before marching toward the mall's inviting warmth.

Kid found the food court easily enough. It was clean and precise yet as drab and ordinary as its patrons. He got a Diet Coke and was about to sit at a yellow Formica-topped table when Sandro came into view. The tall slender young man with dark features, black hair, and gray eyes sure did match his photo. He was wearing green army combat pants and a dark blue U.S. Navy pea coat, which made Kid scoff at the military motif clothes.

The Spaniard went directly to him without stopping at Go or collecting his two hundred. "You must be the one called Kid."

"That's me." Kid sat and watched him warily while sipping his soft drink.

"Ah, good. I am Alessandro Costa. Please to call me Sandro." The pleasant accent seemed to fit the handsome Spaniard.

Kid spotted a gold Hublot watch worth a cool twenty-six grand on Sandro's wrist, signifying that he came from money—as did Kid. It's why he knew the timepiece's value.

Sandro meanwhile looked Kid over with obvious appetite before extending his hand.

Kid's instant thought as they shook: Sandro reminded him of the rest-stop thug. His next appraisal came while they were still shaking hands when the Spaniard tickled Kid's palm with a crooked finger in a decades-old way of determining if the other man was gay. Kid nodded ever so slightly as a way of saying; *I might be available at some point.*

Sandro smiled at that, and when he took off his pea coat Kid spotted three faded track marks inside his left elbow. "After Cleo told me about you, I searched for and found the *Vogue* and *Cosmo* editions that featured your photo spread. Also the shots from Paris with the, how do you say, the burlap bag you were wearing?"

Kid grunted. "Not my usual style."

"Hmm. Perhaps." He gave Kid a direct look. "Your pa*pa*, the man who raised you. He was polic*í*a, s*í*?"

"Yes." Kid started to say more when a group of high schoolers with their noses buried in smartphones rudely pushed past them. He waited until they walked off. "He was *un capitán*."

"*Veo que hablas Español*. You have no accent, either. Bravo." Sandro clapped lightly before tilting his head and drilling Kid with his eyes. "Your p*a*pa. You think I perhaps do not like him for the reason that he is polic*í*a. Yes? No?"

Kid refused to rise to the bait. Instead, he sipped his soft drink while Muzak filled the silence. In time, he set the drink down and met the Spaniard's eyes. "Sandro? I don't give a flying fuck if you like him or hate him. Now are we done here?"

"No, Señor *Bailey*. We are not."

"Well, I see *this* is going to be a vibrant discussion." Kid arched an eyebrow. "It stands to reason that you also dislike my biological father."

"This is correct. He also has had the law enforcement career. Therefore I do not like him too." Sandro crossed his arms over his chest and raised his chin in a Mussolini-like pose, only to smile. "You I do like. Why? I refer once again to the countless *fotografías* of you."

Kid cocked an eye. "Jesus. You are *so* friggin' FOMO." When Sandro flung a questioning look at him, Kid said from the side of his mouth, "Fear Of Missing Out."

Sandro narrowed his eyes. "I have *no* fears! Do you hear me? You, you... *rich* boy."

Kid pointed amusedly at his chest and pantomimed, *moi?* and darted his eyes at Sandro's watch. When Sandro glared, Kid changed the topic to keep the options open. "I find you to be very interesting."

Sandro smirked. "Ah, sí. Why would you not? So. Let us discuss another topic. You have the reputation for cheating on your wife with women *and* with men. Also, it is widely known that you have sired children with other women. Is this not so?" He arched an eyebrow.

"All talk predicated on envy, fantasy, and supposition."

The Spaniard grunted. "I think perhaps you are telling the lie."

Kid leaned into Sandro. "Do you actually think I care about what you believe? Jesus."

"I tell you this, then. Once you are away from your wife for the long enough time? You will sleep with others. By that I mean, with me."

Kid stared at him as if bored. "Don't forget to take an Iberian breath now and then while waiting for that to happen."

"I am *Catalan*," Sandro growled. "Not the Iberian." Then as if someone had flipped a switch, he smiled. "Your friend. The Señorita Britney. She tells us that you have the love of all things natural, along with your hatred of the menace that industry poses to nature. It means you are true lover of Earth, and this makes you true friend of us."

Amid the background chatter and the sudden, shrill sound of a crying infant, Kid shrewdly asked, "Us? I don't understand. Do you mean you and Cleo?"

"Hah. Not so fast, *Señor Norteamericano*. I am part of larger group. I say this with the knowing that Cleo mentioned to you this possibility, *sí*?"

"*Sí*. So tell me about Cleo." He cocked an eyebrow. "*¿O es ella un escaparate?*"

"Window dressing? No, my friend. Cleo, she is, how do you say, a C.E.O." He leaned back in his chair. "Now we play the games no longer. First, I shall tell you that you are the shallow rich boy. You are also homosexual. Is this not so?"

Kid yawned while odors of chicken and soy sauce from a Chinese food vendor brushed past his food-sensitive nostrils. "Sandro? You really need more filler in your diet."

Sandro glared. "We shall see who receives the filler—and who gives the filler." Then he abruptly stood and said, "Come. Cleo awaits us at the café."

THEY drove separately and found Cleo at a corner table with a Gauguin-inspired silk scarf hanging from her divine neck.

The men pulled up chairs at once, and Sandro jerked a thumb at Kid. "This young man you sent to me. I like him a lot and I will have him as my lover. I wish also to discuss with you having him as our associate. Well?"

"That depends on him." Cleo faced Kid. "Your wife has filed for divorce."

Kid needed no role-play, for he felt a true stabbing pain as he enunciated each of his next words: "What... the... hell... are... you talking about?"

"I just this moment read it in the newspaper. An official notice from her solicitor, as required by law. She claims adultery and has sworn that you've impregnated two women."

"All lies," Kid whispered.

"Your fellow students named names: Britney Chadwick and Tisha Kimani, among others. It appears you've acquired quite the reputation for fecundity."

Kid made a show of slumping in his chair. "All right. Here it is. Britney and I are friends. Tisha? Well, we're running partners. Yeah, we shower at her place afterward. What's wrong with that?" He raised his hands. "Look, I run into girls on campus. They invite me to their place. You know, just to talk. Only, we end up doing some molly. Before you know it we end up in—"

Cleo looked sidelong at him. "So it's true. All of it. Not to mention another two that you stand accused of impregnating and six more whom you are rumored to be sleeping with. Well? Are these numbers accurate?"

He gripped her arm. "Listen to me. None of 'em can prove I fathered their babies." This non-answer had the benefit of providing a multitude of interpretations, any one of which he could later deny or deflect.

"Apparently your wife's able to prove it. Ergo, the divorce."

"Well, she's wrong." The news still hurt despite its role-play basis, and his face was twisting in genuine pain, when…

BLAM!

Kid whirled.

Three young Hispanics in thrift store clothing stood in the doorway. One held a .38 revolver.

"Nobody better move," Gun Guy shouted. "Or call no motherfawking cops!"

Sandro's eyes turned huge, and he bolted through the rear door. Other customers, so shocked by the sudden violence, got busy examining their shoes.

As the armed thug approached, Kid stepped in front of Cleo to shield her.

"We gonna fawk you people up," Gun Guy shouted. He had rugged good looks. But his tall, skinny frame came with heavily tattooed arms, strangely lit eyes, and decayed teeth.

"Tha's right," the second one growled. "An' don't look for no policía to help choo, 'cause we done swatted 'em. Jes! We call the nine-one-one. We say some white dude kidnapped his bitch. We tell 'em, 'this hombre, he is boarded up in a house. He is shootin' at everyone.' The policía? They are runnin' *there*, while we are here."

All at once Gun Guy swept the room with his revolver and yelled, "Toss your wallets on the floor. Cells, too. Also, jewelry! Why? Because *ime cago en todo lo que se menea!*"

"Oh my god," Cleo said from behind Kid. "They shall kill us."

"Don't worry," Kid whispered. "I'll protect you."

As if on cue, Gun Guy pointed the revolver at Kid's head and jutted his jaw at him. "Choo! You are very pretty. Choo also look like you got money. Maybe in some bank, no?"

Kid felt a cold shiver. These thugs had crazed eyes, and their decayed teeth all but shouted, *meth users*. Yet he felt a surge of confidence when a burst of espresso machine steam startled the trio of daring banditos.

The other customers were tossing wallets and cells to the floor when Kid looked out the window in time to spot Jake and Gillian in the parking lot. Jake held a Browning Hi-Power 9mm pistol in his right hand, and Gil had a phone to her ear.

All at once Gun Guy lurched toward Kid while holding the revolver sideways, gangsta-style. "Choo are pretty, like a gorl. We take you with us. We find ATM and you're gonna get money for us. Maybe then we take choo somewhere an' use you like a gorl."

Cleo trembled behind Kid and made a wounded animal sound when the doper jammed the .38's muzzle against Kid's forehead. "Hands up, hombre! Or I keel you now."

Kid slowly raised his hands—but only to shoulder height while he examined the revolver and saw that it wasn't cocked. This meant Gun Guy would have to exert three pounds of pressure to pull the trigger. Having been trained at length on how to disarm a gun-wielding menace, Kid gauged the distance between his hands and the revolver.

Then he went wildcat.

He jerked his head to the left and simultaneously slammed his left hand against the handgun. With the muzzle now facing away from him, he gripped the barrel and trapped the thug's finger inside the trigger guard. Then he viciously twisted the weapon up and to the left with a sudden force.

Snap!

As the trigger guard broke Gun Guy's finger, he howled and dropped to the floor where he flopped like a gut-shot redhead.

The second thug bolted for the door, but when Gillian slammed the side of his head with a round kick he went bug-eyed and dropped like a pole-axed ox.

Jake stopped the third bandito in his tracks by aiming his 9mm at the punk's nose while speaking in a low voice. "Reach for the sky, varmint."

Kid meanwhile turned and took Cleo into his arms. "Are you all right?"

"Am I all right? Oi! You are my knight in shining armor. You—" She shook her head in disbelief before flinging her arms around his neck and kissing his face all over.

"Hang on," Kid said, and quickly frisked Gun Guy to make sure he had no hideout weapons before stepping closer to the married couple.

Gillian stood watch over the thug she'd taken down while Jake looked at Kid and showed a shy smile. "I always wanted to say that. *Reach for the sky.* Yup." He remained aimed in on the punk.

Kid handed the revolver to Jake. "Here. I don't want it."

As police sirens filled the air, Sandro magically reappeared. "We must leave. It will not do for the policía to get the, how do you say, the tabs on us." In a lower voice, he told Cleo

and Kid, "The bandito leader? I know him. He hates me."
He shrugged helplessly.

Kid figured it to be a liaison gone bad, and after facing
Jake and Gillian he spoke in OPSEC terms: "I don't know
who you two are, but we owe you."

Jake shrugged. "Don't sweat it, stranger." He met Kid's
eye, and both men nodded.

"I hope we don't remain strangers."

Gillian said loudly enough for Cleo and Sandro to hear,
"My husband and I come here often. Maybe you'll buy us a
couple of double lattes the next time we meet."

While still keeping his pistol trained on the bandito, Jake
turned to Cleo and touched a finger to his eyebrow. "Afternoon ma'am. Hope these hombres didn't hurt you none,
ma'am."

"Don't call me ma'am. It's sexist."

Jake deadpanned with, "Can't help it, ma'am. I'm from
Wyomin'. It's how we talk to our women folk."

Cleo glared and opened her mouth until Sandro tugged
her arm. "We must go."

Kid said, "I agree. Let's clear out."

Sandro nudged Kid's ribs and pointed at a battered gray
Nissan in the lot. "Follow me."

Chapter Sixteen

• •

May 19 • Olympia

KID TAPPED THE Beamer's phone icon while hugging the Nissan's rear bumper and called Jennifer. Since he assumed his car was bugged, he went in-role the instant she answered by beseeching her to reconsider the divorce.

She replied with a hard-edged voice. "You have been legally notified of my intentions. There's nothing else to discuss."

"Jen, wait!" But the call had already gone dead.

"Jen," he whispered. "Jen—" The terrible suddenness gripped him with panic. Sure, Kid knew it was an act... still, just the thought...

THE phone in Sandro's Nissan chimed at almost the same instant. He thumbed his Bluetooth. "Sí?"

A woman's voice came across with great power. "Kid is a fighter. I've awaited someone of his caliber for quite some time. See to it that he's welcomed into the fold. You may also sleep with him if you wish." A pause, followed by a teasing, "See? Do I not give you toys to indulge yourself with when you are a good boy?" She abruptly ended the call with a *click*.

FOLLOWING a short drive, they arrived at a solitary cottage in a heavily wooded area. Kid shifted mental gears and shook off his Oscar-worthy pain and joined Sandro on a soapstone step just large enough for two people.

After going inside Kid surveyed the single-bedroom home. It was clean and tidy, despite a few too many microwave-able dinner trays with partially eaten contents. The place also reeked of marijuana, and he saw heroin paraphernalia spread across a small dining table.

Sandro glanced at Kid and narrowed his eyes. "You do not look good."

"My wife," he said from the side of his mouth.

"Ah. Yes. Forgive me. She has filed the papers, no?"

"Yes. Now she's told me—" He regarded his phony wedding band and choked back a phony sob before pulling it off and tossing it into a nearby trash can.

Sandro went to him at once. "Oh, my friend. Please. Let me give to you the comfort." He kissed Kid's forehead. "I hope this helps."

"She ditched me," Kid growled, and jutted his jaw at the trash can. "So I've ditched her."

The Spaniard pointed to the kitchen table and the plastic bags of fine white powder. "Let us soothe your anguish. You have a taste for the opium?"

Kid's emotional profile showed that he was resistant to habituation—a fortunate thing since he needed to be a player. Even so— "Um, I considered trying it a few times."

"Ah. This is wonderful. Then you will join me. Yes?"

"No. Not now, anyway. I'm not in the mood. You under-stand." While licking his lips he added, "But I need some-thing after what went down." Kid meant it. His unspent adrenaline had left his hands trembling. "I won't say no to some scotch. Or weed." All at once he got a semblance of a smile. "Who is *this* beautiful girl?"

Sandro's head jerked. "Huh? Oh. That is my darling Malee. Do you like the pussy cats?"

"Are you kidding? I love 'em. Also dogs, whales... *elephants*." He stooped down. The Siamese went to Kid at once, and after rubbing against him, the blue-eyed beauty deigned to let him pick her up. "Hi," he whispered. "I'm Kid. It's nice to meet you, Malee."

The Basque Separatist watched with approval when Malee rubbed her head against Kid's neck and began purring. But after Kid reluctantly put her down, Sandro pointed at a pantry door and said, "Scotch." Then he dimmed the lights, and when he pressed another switch rage music instantly blared from four speakers. When he hit another switch, strobes began bouncing chaotic flashes throughout the room, sending Malee scurrying away.

Kid opened the pantry and grabbed a bottle of low-end scotch.

Sandro meanwhile gathered some heroin and went to the gas stove, where he got busy cooking up a dose. While the drug began dissolving into a dirty brown liquid, the Spaniard said over his shoulder. "You were quite the hero. Sí. Your bravery, it is commendable."

"Luck," Kid shouted above the rage music. "Luck in learning how to fight."

Sandro grunted. "You learned your lessons with the great vigor."

"I guess." Kid poured a shot and tossed it back. "Fuck," he muttered as the cheap booze went down his gullet. He poured another shot, then a third while the burnt Band-Aid odor of heated heroin filled the room.

"Why do you know that robber?" Kid didn't expect an answer, but Sandro surprised him with a candid response.

"I know him from the bed. We… did not get along. So. That is all." His eyes glazed over as he watched the heroin cook.

A connection to an armed robber. Hmm. I'll pass this on to Uncle Marty.

Kid did one more shot before Sandro's heroin cooled enough, when he drew a dose into a syringe and plucked a yellow medicinal-smelling rubber tourniquet from the table. Working quickly, he wrapped it around his bicep and raised a vein while the rage music and hectic strobes blasted in the background.

"Ah, this one is ready," he announced and swabbed a swollen vein with an alcohol prep pad. Next, he put the needle against the vein and pushed until it went in with a soft *plop*. After pulling back slightly to get a blood return, he smiled at Kid and eased down on the plunger. "Mmmmm," he began a second later. "Yeahhh. Mmm—"

Kid killed the rage music and strobes, and he was pouring a fifth shot when a roach skittered across the floor just as Sandro began walking unsteadily toward Kid.

"You are pretty," he said with a voice from the dead. "Sí, I like you very much."

Damn, Kid thought. *Here we go. They said I might have to be a Romeo. But nobody said anything about being a gay one. Now what? Do I yield for God, King, and Country?* He drew a deep breath and thought, *Fuck it. I wanna go home, I wanna do whatever it takes to finish this crap, and I wanna get the fuck out of here… because at the end of the day, I'm either all in, or I walk away.* Even so, he felt like reaching into Army Field Manual 2733 for a solution.

The Spaniard said while something worked behind his eyes, "Now that your marriage is no longer? Now I can be like the wife to you. Hmm, perhaps for you I shall change my name to Katarina. Sí, I like that name. *Katarina.*"

Kid's antennae went up at once. Bill claimed his wife was named Katarina. Coincidence?

Sandro kept talking. "This State of Washington? It will let me get the marriage license with that name. *Katarina*. We will get married, and I shall become Katarina Bailey, your legal wife. Yes?"

Kid had yet to reply when Sandro clamped a hand around his arm and pulled him into the bedroom, where he shuddered without seeming to. *Dad and Papa were right; this guy's psycho. Do I play along? Will he even accept me for what I'm coming across as? I… Jesus.* His decision made, he gripped Sandro's shoulders and roughly forced him to his knees, then peered down at him while wrapping his words in steel. "Now that I have no wife to be faithful to? I'm gonna make you my bitch-boy. Know what I'm sayin'?"

When Sandro nodded six times in rapid succession, Kid unzipped and taunted Sandro by tapping his penis against the Spaniard's lips. "Well? What're you waiting for? Gobble the goo. After you do that? I'm gonna bend you over and do you like a dog."

IT was midnight when Kid got up from the Spaniard's bed and went to the bathroom to relieve himself. After finishing, he framed himself in the doorway and stared at Sandro while he grasped the determination of the Israeli agent his dad mentioned.

Seeing that Sandro was awake, he said, "I'm gonna grab a shower."

Sandro nodded and watched Kid until he stepped inside the stall. Once he heard the water taps twisting and the shower running, he dashed somewhat unsteadily into the kitchen and pulled Kid's wedding band out of the trash can.

After a thorough examination, he put it back and composed a smartphone text: *He is not the federal agent we expected. He threw away his wedding band. I checked; it has their wedding date inscribed. Also, it is well-worn and matches the one in the wedding photo our man found on his hometown society page. He is not so squeaky clean, either. Not like the F.B. of I. agents. It is why I trust him. Also, we are now lovers.* Sandro smiled and sent the message that would reach two recipients within a minute.

He got a reply within thirty seconds. *We fully accept him now.*

THE shower's hot water combined with a liberal use of soap helped Kid physically cleanse himself of Sandro, the person. The gay sex itself hadn't troubled him in the least. It was simply something he'd never engaged in until this very day. Kid even quipped to himself, *Guess I'm gay-for-pay now.*

Likewise, he accepted the risk of STDs in his efforts to prevent Armageddon. No, Kid only wanted to purge himself of Sandro the person. The biting irony was that the very attractive Spaniard lacked any sense of technique or soulfulness in bed.

Now that steam clouds were embracing him, Kid planted his forehead against the wall and closed his eyes. But depression still engulfed him half an hour later, so he eased away and returned to bed.

LATER that day, Kid pulled shorts on and padded into the kitchen while Sandro followed in his birthday suit. Kid reached for the scotch. Sandro cooked a dose of heroin and shot up. Minutes later a languid Sandro slid into bed and patted the spot next to him.

"Hold on, big guy." Kid gulped a shot of liquor before stretching out next to him and asking, "How come you don't have a boyfriend?" He was hoping Sandro would mention Special Agent Dustin Smythe. To his great amazement, Sandro did just that.

"I make the friendship with a young man. Very pretty. Like you. Only, he will not have the sex with me. So I tell this pretty boy, this… Dustin… to leave and make the visit again when he decides to no longer be in the denial."

Kid screwed his eyes tight for effect and said, "Dust-pan? What a weird-ass name."

Sandro hesitated. But after licking his lips several times, he looked at Kid. "This Dustin, he did not have for me the respect. So I killed him."

"Yeah? Humph. Probably deserved it." Kid narrowed his eyes and said in a bored way, "Sandro? I think this is the beginning of a beautiful friendship." And just like that he jabbed a cruel elbow into Sandro's ribs. "Give me some head, bitch."

•   •   •

Gun Guy, who turned out to be a Honduran named Jorge, maintained his tough-guy routine for all of three minutes before he caved and asked, "What is it choo need to know?"

The bull-like detective inside the dim interrogation room stared at the large cast on the tattooed punk's arm that was needed to immobilize the thug's broken finger. "Talk to me," the bull bellowed.

Jorge's orange prisoner scrubs were the only color in the desolate room. After repeatedly licking his lips, he began talking. "So maybe I see this hombre at the café, choo know? He is Español. Young. A faggot. I think he is up to something bad. I can find out for choo."

The detective snorted. "Really? That's all you've got? That he's up to something and you'll do me the honor of checking?"

Jorge opened his mouth to say more when the detective stood and pointed at the door.

"Get out. You're wasting my time."

•   •   •

At that same moment, Kid was asking Sandro, "Am I wasting my time with you guys? Or is there something worthwhile in the works?"

A heartbeat passed. And when Sandro began spilling it all, Kid listened with an intensity he'd never known — especially after the Basque Separatist mentioned the Holy Grail of names: Agamemnon.

Chapter Seventeen

. . . .

Two days later · May 21

KID CRACKED OPEN an eye when late morning light filled Sandro's bedroom. They had been holed up for two days, Kid now had a slight scruff, he was exhausted and now he stared at the empty Jameson's bottle atop the nightstand—the third he'd emptied in as many days in his quest to dull the searing pain of this mission's requirements.

And yet the varsity sportsman was keeping to game strategy. July 4th would soon be here, so he kept Sandro high and kept having sex with him to get his tongue wagging. Luckily for Kid, the Spaniard spoke recklessly each time, prompting Kid to think Sandro no longer suspected him of being an agent. It helped that law enforcement operatives are restrained by regs coupled with internal prejudices from resorting to gay sex to further their goals, or from indulging in other behaviors.

Kid meanwhile had snooped around as any good investigator would, and discovered a .40 Glock pistol inside the nightstand drawer. *Did this motherfucker kill the agent with this?* He needed to get word to his handlers.

The next morning, Kid prepared a breakfast of Canadian bacon and potatoes. While they dug into the meal, he asked, "How many global deaths will our action trigger?"

"How many?" Sandro regarded him with jaded eyes. "Do you get off on knowing that many, many people will die?"

"Get real. Innocents die even when the cause is just."

"*Mierda*. You are the son of *federales*. How can you take the detour from the noble causes they profess to stand for?"

Kid put down his fork and studied Sandro's face. "What's your father's occupation?"

The Spaniard lifted his head high. "I told you this already. He is *el abogado*."

"An attorney. And yet you didn't follow his path?" Kid picked up his fork and held it aloft.

"No. I do not care for such things."

"Ah. I see. *You're* permitted to make a radical departure from a normal life, yet I cannot shun the road my parents traveled?" Melee rubbed against Kid's leg while he peered at Sandro. "Because I've gotta tell you, I began veering away from their life years ago."

Sandro bobbed his head up and down. "Yes. You have made your argument well. Bravo."

From that point on the back and forth flowed like river rapids, emboldening Kid to ask, "If we shut down all the grids, won't they be back up and running within weeks?"

Sandro dabbed a napkin to his mouth before speaking—the elegant Euro-trash terrorist about to dispense wisdom. "This is a prudent question. You see, once we launch our cyberattack we will follow up with AI. It will replicate and infect the million or so invasive programs that foolish employees everywhere download to their office computers. It will go global."

Kid arched an eyebrow. "Riiight. Wipers and wabbits."

Sandro said while forking potatoes into his mouth. "Precisely. Also? The world's stock markets will have crashed.

The global economy? Wiped out. Okay. Even if they repair the grids? Big deal. There will be no money to buy the means to run them; no customers with funds to purchase the electricity. Also? I want you to make the love to me."

Kid looked at him as he would a young child. "Hold that thought on the sex, because I'm impressed by the level of thought you've put into this. Well? When do we do it?"

"I, um… am not certain. Perhaps on Christmas Day. Our gift to the world."

"A brave new world," Kid offered before asking, "Hey, will I ever get to meet this Ag guy?"

Sandro turned sullen at first, only to smile. "I think a meeting might come soon. Why? It is because we see now that you are one of us. Particularly because you do not ask too many questions, only the ones that show your interest in our idea but not our methods."

Kid said, "Right on," and offered a silent prayer of thanks for having yielded to Sandro's demand for sex. *If I hadn't given in I'd have remained suspect. By not asking questions afterward, I didn't come across as too anxious. Yay, team!*

But to lend greater credibility to why he'd come here, he grabbed Sandro's arm. "Hey? I want my children at my side when it all goes down."

"Not your wife?" Sandro peered at him and waited.

"My wife? Why the fuck would I want her? She and I are history." He paused before carefully adding, "Besides, you'll be my wife by then." When Sandro's jaw dropped, Kid rushed to say, "My children, though. I'll need time to grab 'em. Will you tell me when we're a week away from pulling the plug?"

Sandro smiled at once. "Anything for you."

"Good." Kid abruptly began clearing the dishes. After dumping them in the sink, he turned to Sandro. "I'm going to my place and hang for a couple of days. Maybe I'll get my things and move in with you. While I'm gone I want you to shave your legs and your pits." Kid also wanted this bastard to pay for killing the agent, and what better way than through chemical castration. "Start taking estrogen, too. And don't say you won't. Because you will."

"To grow the tits," Sandro said with a sudden excitement, his eyes now following Kid's progress as the young man combed fingers through his unkempt hair while grabbing his car key.

AFTER driving along a sparsely traveled road, Kid stopped and opened his trunk to retrieve one of several burner phones he'd purchased. Verbal phone calls were out of the question due to eavesdropping. Even text messages can be retrieved from the Cloud. So he used burners.

Following a text to Levi about a possible connection between Sandro and Gun Guy, he relayed Sandro's boast that he killed the FBI agent. Kid added that he found a pistol inside Sandro's nightstand and typed its serial number from memory. Finally, he mentioned Bill's absence at the café.

•   •   •

Cleo remained hidden near the entrance to Evergreen State while she fumed and ground her molars while waiting for Ag. Faint puffs of vapor hanging over the sodden trees were making her shiver as she checked the time yet again.

When he drove up in his mother's SUV a moment later, she sprang from her concealed place and stormed his car like the troops on Omaha Beach. She yanked the passenger door open and shouted, "Where have you been? I've been waiting."

Ag tilted his head like a dog listening to its owner. But what he did next surprised even him. "Cleo? I am on time. You are early. Do not ever again accuse me of tardiness or direct your micro-aggression at me. Not... *ever*." He held up a hand at once. "You are the second person who has committed a scheduling error."

Her anger vanished at once. "Cheers. I deserve that. No worries." She sat in the passenger seat and rested a hand on his thigh. "Pet? Who is this other person?"

"A friend. His name is—" He started to say Kid's name. What came out instead was, "You needed to see me?"

"Yes, love. I do." She patted his thigh while reminding him of their ultimate goal, that of living together. "The time has arrived for the next dreadful event. A minor one as we agreed upon, yes?"

"Affirmative. Tonight. Twenty-four hundred Zulu."

"Brilliant, that." She stroked his thigh. "When this is all over, you and I will have our special place to live."

He flushed red and looked puppy-eyed at her. "Sorry for being rude toward you."

"Not to worry." Cleo gave his thigh a very sexy squeeze. Then she got out and vanished.

·   ·   ·

At precisely midnight Greenwich Time, some 20,000 drawbridges throughout the United States began opening on their own. Whether awash with traffic, sunshine, or rainwater depending upon the time zone, the synchronicity of the bridges' actions eluded human intervention.

Enraged motorists leaned on horns while bridge tenders scratched their heads. Only a handful of them knew how to operate the hydraulic valves that can manually lower a bridge, but those few were retirees and they moved with the speed of a sloth on Librium.

Exactly three hours later to the very *second*, every drawbridge in the nation resumed its normal functioning.

. . .

The next day Jen told Nadia, "That's something about the drawbridges."

"It is."

"I um, haven't heard from Kid lately. Have you?"

Nadia scoffed—all in-role since they assumed their conversations were monitored. "Jen, what did you expect? Come on, you filed against him. I mean, couldn't you have waited to confront him to his face?"

"No, Mom. He cheated on me. He's knocked up other women. He…" She sobbed aloud. "I'm so angry!"

They talked a bit more until Nadia cleared her throat. "I'll pass along what you said. And Jen? Michael and I love you very much."

"I know you do, Mom. I um, thanks." The call went dead.

Nadia held her phone for a moment while admiring the way Jen ended the call. To the empty room, she said, "Good move, girl." Then she called her son to implement the next stage of this three-act play.

"MOM, I've done nothing wrong." Kid was standing inside his dismal rental while pulling on a worn-out pair of BDUs—Battle Dress Utility pants. "Jen's bent on this wild notion that I've turned my back on her. I haven't."

"Jesus, *Kid*. What don't you understand? You go off on this positively lunatic jaunt of yours? And you expect Jen to just accept it?"

He said more quietly, "She's also on about me knocking up some girls at school. Only, there's no way she can prove I did."

"Are you overlooking DNA testing for some even mildly plausible reason?" She sighed and quietly asked, "How many?"

A subdued Kid mumbled, "Campus talk has me knocking up anywhere from three to six girls."

"Give me a damn number."

He released a long breath. "Four that I'm certain of. *Okay*? The word is also out that I'd been sleeping with five other babes—and one of them might also be… you know. Then there's these two guys that I was seeing."

"For god's sake, Kid. *Four* girls."

"Mom, I can't help it if my swimmers are always doing their thing."

"Jesus—"

At this point they steered the conversation in another direction while assuming Cleo was listening in to the carefully worded back-and-forth. He ended the call a minute later, and when he felt a headache coming on he got in bed and clamped his eyes shut.

CLEO closed her eyes tight and shook her head after listening in on Kid's conversation, courtesy of the air freshener's concealed mic. *He did sleep with other girls Not to mention some lads. So why not me?*

Chapter Eighteen

·······························

May 23 • The Café

"THERE'S OUR HERO," a chorus of regulars shouted when a bare-chested Kid entered the café.

He mumbled, "Thanks," and gave his head a toss that sent his unkempt hair flying with untamed abandon.

"Ooooh," a Gen Z girl in mismatched clothes began. "You look so... *savage.*" She jumped up and hurried to him. Then she wrapped her arms around his neck kissed his mouth before breathing, "Call me," all while thrusting a slip of paper into his hand.

He thanked her with his eyes and looked around hoping to spot Marty. No luck. But he saw Cleo sitting at a table, so after getting coffee and a tofu burger he sat across from her.

She looked sidelong at him. "Oh, my. I hadn't realized how utterly gaunt you've become. Now without your shirt, I—" She regarded him kindly. "I daresay you've lost nearly a stone. Have you not?"

Stress had indeed caused weight loss. "Yes, a bit over."

"Righto, lad. Now tell Auntie Cleo what's wrong."

"It's Jen. She—" His face dissolved in anguish. "She accused me of adultery." He winced and said to the floor, "So maybe I did fool around. I mean, it's those damn photos. All these girls asking me to do 'em." He held up the slip of paper and met Cleo's eyes. "I'm not perfect, *okay?* I—" His shoulders slumped, and he spoke quietly. "I guess you and Sandro won't want me in the group now. Well, don't worry. I'll go quietly. But um, thanks for being so kind to me." Ignoring his food, he stood and began walking away.

Cleo said, "Sit down and listen." She waited until he sat again. "Only someone genuine would bow out as you just did. It's one more reason why we want you." She looked into his eyes. "Bollocks that things have gone so awry with your wife. I mean it, Kid. I feel for you."

He stifled his relief at the positive outcome of this portion of his three-act play and said, "Thanks." Now he narrowed his eyes. "I wish now that I had made love to you that night. Hell, I don't know what I'm thinking anymore…"

"It's fine, love."

"You're just being gracious." But he regarded her with bedroom eyes before abruptly saying, "That's something about the drawbridges." When she offered a shrug but nothing more, he leaned forward in a conspiratorial manner. "It's okay. Sandro gave me the scoop."

She looked up as if beseeching the heavens. "Kid, you are such an innocent. As I live and breathe, just who do you think brokers his conversations with you?"

"I ah, just assumed he mentioned it because we're lovers—" He was showing a shy smile when Sandro suddenly appeared and sat next to him. Hard on his heels was a mousey girl in dusty western wear who ambled up to them.

She nodded at Sandro and Cleo in turn, then glanced at Kid. "Howdy do?"

He thought her mid-western twang was a refreshing slice through the café's perpetual mellow speak. But his nose crinkled while he rose to greet her. *What is she,* he wondered. *A wrangler?*

"I'm Roo," she said while pumping his outstretched hand.

"Kid Bailey."

She withdrew her hand and looked him over. "Say, you're durn purty. I like the thin look, too. Kinda wild-like." In a response as age-old as the sea, her pupils dilated and she took a step toward him, only to stop and face Cleo. "Dang! I ain't seen you in I don't know how long."

"About twelve days," Cleo said without a hint of emotion.

"Well strike me twice on a Sunday if you ain't right. Yup, you durn sure are." Roo pulled up a chair and sat. "Well, Sandro? I reckon this purty fellow here must be a homma-sexal like you. An' I'm a guessin' he's your new boyfriend."

The Spaniard gestured at Kid, "Yes, he is. Also, he is the reason why Cleo and I asked that you join us today."

She whomped the tabletop with her palm and trumpeted, "Yup, you got yerself a good catch, Sandro. Girlish as all get out, only I don't doubt that he's toppin' the fuck outta you. Hell, I'll wager a dollar to a doughnut that he's doin' you ever single night."

Kid broke in and said, "You're a long way from west of the Brazos."

Roo regarded him with interest. "Very good. Don't too many Easterners know that part of West Texas."

"I traveled there back in the day." He noted the brown patches beneath the eyes along with her ruddy complexion. "Have you been here long?"

"'Bout two years," she said, and swiveled her head back and forth like a radar dish before saying, "Well fuck me! Ain't nobody gonna come an' take my order?"

Kid swept a hand at the counter. "What would you like?"

"Why, that's right decent of you to ask. Yessir. It shore is. But I kin git my own stuff. So if all y'all will excuse me? Or even if ya don't? Either way, I'll be right back."

He watched the direct manner in which she walked to the counter. Small and slight as she was, Kid knew she could hold her own in a confrontation. He thought, *Too bad she wasn't here during the robbery.*

Roo returned a minute later carrying a coffee and a biscuit slathered with gravy. "Durn good thing this here café ain't no veggie-tear-on place."

Kid asked as she sat next to him, "Do you live nearby?"

"Yup." She tore off a piece of biscuit with clean white teeth and talked with her mouth open. "I got me this here job on a horse farm."

"A horse farm? In this area?" Kid was honestly amazed.

She popped more food in her mouth and pointed in a northerly direction. "Yup. T'ain't far from here either. Place called Boston Harbor. 'Longside the Nisqually Reach."

"Sorry? The Nis— what?" He was playing dumb. In nautical terms, a reach is a straight portion of a stream or river.

"Nisqually *Reach*. It's a sorta small river what runs offa South Bay, what comes offa Puget Sound. You know, from up 'round Seattle?"

She bit into her biscuit again and said while chewing, "I don't drive much. Mostly I git 'round in a skiff. It's got a sixty-horse Merc an' hellfire, that's all I need. If I do make landfall, why I jist call me one a them there Ubers to take me inland."

Roo grunted. "Too bad you're a faggot. Or what's that new-fangled term? Not, gay. Um—" She snapped her fingers. "Got it! Non-binary, right? Shee-it. Gimme jist a little break."

Kid raised an eyebrow. "Blow me."

"Blow—" She cackled and slapped a knee. "Tell you what, Kid. Girlish or not, I'd mount you in a heartbeat—an' that ain't me talkin' shit." She scratched a rib and continued eating.

Kid liked her. Direct. Honest. Authentic. Not someone he would sleep with, although he might've sought her friendship if she wasn't the enemy. "What do you do on the horse farm?"

"Do? Why, I work the horses. Feed 'em, groom 'em; keep 'em outta trouble an' suchlike. Oh, an' I also hang with Cleo an' Sandro. Why, you might ask? 'Cause they're my kinda folks." She turned quiet all at once and stole a glance at Sandro, who then elbowed Kid.

"Others of our acquaintance are to join us in a moment. I—" A black guy abruptly appeared at the table as if he'd been waiting in the wings.

Cleo said as the man sat with them, "Kid? Meet, Jamal."

The tall, slender Jamal had ebony skin and all-black clothing. A narrow shock of bleached-blond hair was done up in small dreads that sprouted from the top of his otherwise black hair. Other than that he appeared average.

Kid figured him for early thirties and was about to greet him, when Huck showed up in his trademark undone shirt, faded jeans and unshod feet. Kid cried out, "Huck! What're the chances?"

Sandro looked from one to the other. "You hombres know each other?"

Huck settled lazily into a chair and regarded Sandro through half-closed eyes. "That would be a yes… Alessandro."

Kid felt an instant drop in barometric pressure. *Whaddya know; Sandro defers to Huck. Might even fear him. Does this mean Huck's the one calling the shots?*

Huck told everyone, "Kid an' me? We was like, here? A while back? An' we like, got to talkin'. So like, we hit it off. Plus, I wanted to do him. Now here we are again."

Kid noted Huck's take-charge manner. *I'll bet Cleo called him the day she and I met, meaning he and I didn't meet by accident. Probably been vetting me ever since. Now he's telling the others what an okay hombre I am.*

Huck smiled almost on cue. "We know you're not like, perfect? I mean, knocking up those other babes? An' like, who knows how many others you musta been nailing? Maybe it's also why you cut and ran from home? Anyway, we want you to join our family."

When Roo and Jamal nodded their acceptance Kid tried not to show his relief at being in. But now that he had the E-Ticket, it meant climbing aboard for the ride. Only, he had no road maps or nautical charts to reveal what lurked around the next bend. So he caught Huck's eye and pantomimed smoking a joint as a signal that he wanted to get high. *Maybe I can prompt him to cut loose with some details.*

Chapter Nineteen

· ·

May 23 • Evening • Olympia

HUCK APPEARED AT Kid's door that evening and immediately swept Kid into his arms to hug him. "So like, what's going on with your wife?"

Kid let loose with a theatrical sigh. "She's done with me. I—" He swiped at an eye.

"Damn." Huck held him again. "I'm glad to see you're dealing with it. 'Cause I like, care about you? And I know you feel the same about me. Right?"

"I do."

The slacker's smile dazzled. "Right on. So like, let's party?"

He brought some quality marijuana and a bong, and soon they were sitting cross-legged atop Kid's bed. Half an hour later they were stoned and talkative.

At one point Kid asked, "What's with Jamal?"

"Jamal? Naval Academy grad. I hear he made like, lieutenant commander? Then this one day he saw a destroyer dumping fuel at sea…"

"Why would they do that?" Kid knew why but wanted to play innocent. That way he could come across as justly outraged at the very idea of dumping oil.

"There's like, some rule? About not having too much fuel when they enter port. In case of fire? So Jamal, he like, calls 'em on it. Only, they call *him* on it for running his yap.

And zip, before ya know it they kick him out." Huck took a hit from the bong and exhaled. "Jamal's been like, bitter ever since."

Kid peered at him through fluttering eyelids. "This is why I hate governments. They do shit like that—discarding oil in the ocean."

Now that he'd expressed his outrage and filed away the info on Jamal, he changed the subject and they chatted on. A bit later when a sudden urge for sugar hit the pair, they raided the pantry and gorged on Kid's dried-fruit snacks.

They smoked some more, and both were quite high by the time the sun went down, leading Kid to invite Huck to stay the night. "Take my bed. I'll crash on the couch."

"That works," the ever-agreeable Huck replied, only to strip off his pants to reveal nothing on underneath. "I've always gone commando," he explained.

"Me too," Kid said, and undressed while feeling Huck's eyes on him. After stretching out on the couch he pulled a sheet up to his chest and killed the light.

But in the darkened room Huck cleared his throat. "Word on the proverbial street is like, you and Sandro are lovers now?"

"Friends with bennies. Nothing more."

"Hey, I'm cool with it. I'm—" A brief silence ensued until he got up from the bed and sat naked on the sofa's outermost edge. "Hey? The day we met? I didn't know Cleo had already run into you. I saw only some friendly dude who offered me a place to sit. Then you said you'd pray for my daughter? And like, I felt a spiritual connection with you." Huck got busy combing his long fingers through Kid's mop of thick hair before saying, "Maybe we can deepen our bond?"

"Friends with bennies?" Kid figured as much but wanted to hear Huck say it.

Huck smiled as he pulled the sheet down and caressed Kid's skinny flanks. "I told you earlier about how I care about you. Then like, tonight? The more we shot the breeze? The more I admired you. I also like, find you fascinating? Now I'm starting to fall... well, you know." He patted Kid's cheek.

"I'm glad you clarified how we met." He drew a breath and edged over to make room for Huck. "Join me?"

Huck gazed into his eyes until without fanfare he bent forward and kissed Kid's mouth; he kissed with feeling, and after drawing away he grazed his fingertips along Kid's naked thigh before padding off and returning to the bed.

AT dawn, Huck yawned and made other noises meant to rouse Kid from his slumber, and on finding his host awake, he said, "Gotta run. It's my day to open the store."

Kid nodded and pulled on his distressed BDUs to walk Huck to the door.

Once there, Huck paused. "I liked hanging with you. Let's like, do it again? Also, I work at a state-licensed store. We sell gummies an' ganja and... whatever. So here's a gift." He handed over a small paper bag.

His host peered inside and found a new bong, an ounce of weed that Huck assured him was within Washington's legal limit, and a Zippo lighter. Kid winked at him. "You're the best, brother." He meant it. Huck's companionship had certainly buoyed his spirit.

Seconds later he saw Huck out to a ratty Volvo, where Huck kissed his mouth with a balance of passion and non-sexual fun, only to grip Kid's head between his hands with a sudden, fierce passion and look into Kid's eyes while saying, "I think I love you."

Kid's breath caught because a part of his soul was also building deep feelings for the ever-amiable Huckleberry. But he kept quiet and watched him drive off.

· · ·

Marty Fischbach entered the Olympia Police Department's Headquarters through the rear door and produced his law enforcement credentials. Then he asked to see Gun Guy, aka Jorge.

The young Latina staffer scrunched her face and delivered the bad news: the prisoner had bonded out just minutes earlier. "A white girl picked him up. I have his address? If it helps?"

"I'll get that motherfucker," Jorge snarled. His American girlfriend cringed and focused on driving the rust-bucket light blue Chevy through heavy traffic. A torrential downpour wasn't helping, and she had to brake hard to avoid a pickup while Jorge asked, "Choo know where he lives, no?"

"Of course. I saw him at Sandro's. Then I followed him to where he's been staying."

He scoffed. "Sandro thinks I did not see him? Did he think he could run out the back without me knowing? Also, that *hijo de puta* he sleeps with—that bastard thinks he can break my finger?" Jorge held his cast up. "I show him. I break his skull." Turning to his girl, he pinned her with a stare. "Choo got the gun?"

She jutted her jaw at the glove compartment. "In there."

He opened it and seized the cheap Saturday Night Special with relish. "Sí. Maybe I put a bullet in that bastard's head."

KID was drinking coffee when his phone began a persistent chiming. He was reaching for it just as someone pounded on his door. Expecting to find Huck on the other side, he ignored the phone and opened the door.

The first thing he saw was the pistol pointed at his heart. Next, he caught a flash of the cast on the right arm. Then he was looking into Goliath's hate-filled eyes.

The ex-con boomed, "Motherfucker!" and bulled his way through the door.

No you don't, Kid's brain shouted as he took it all in: *Pistol's in his left hand. Goliath's right-handed. He's stepping forward on his right leg. So... .*

Kid instantly stepped into Goliath's left side, drove his hip against the ex-con's, wrapped an arm around Goliath's waist, and executed a hip throw.

The ex-con roared with anger as he flew upward. He roared even more as he reached apogee, when Kid flexed his hip and drove the thug into the floor.

Goliath gasped, the wind driven from his lungs.

Kid hammered a fist squarely between the ex-con's eyes.

But the big man was insane with rage, he still had the pistol, he was swinging it toward Kid, and he had his finger on the trigger.

But Kid gripped the barrel and savagely twisted it until the muzzle was pointed at Goliath's head, and then... *BANG!*

The .32 bullet crashed into Goliath's temple.

Blue smoke trailed from the muzzle as Kid stood in stunned silence but while keeping the pistol trained on Goliath—the ex-con might be dead; then again he might not be. From that point on, time stood still for Kid. He fell into tunnel vision. Sounds were distorted.

But when he sensed someone coming through the door, his heart made like a trip hammer as he whirled and prepared to shoot.

"Whoa," a white-haired senior citizen said while reaching for the sky.

Kid recognized his landlord at once. "Sorry. You came rushing up on me, and…"

"Is okay. I see this hombre coming through your door with the pistola. So I arm myself to come to your aid." He held up his right hand to reveal a 9mm pistol. "I see it all. You defend yourself. You had not the choice. So, perhaps it is a bad drug deal. I not know. But I must call the 911." He pointed at Goliath's lifeless body, his sightless eyes now frozen in time. "Keep watch on him. Just in case, sí?"

"Thank you, sir."

Even as the landlord pulled his phone out, Kid grabbed his own and made a different call. It was answered after one ring. "Dad," Kid began. "We have a situation—"

THE instant Levi Hart finished talking to his bio-son, he entered a phone number in his cell and held it to his ear. A female voice answered almost instantly. "White House."

"Levi Hart for the President. Code name, Stranger."

"Putting you through at once, sir."

JORGE gripped his girlfriend's arm. "What is with the policía? Chit! Slow down!" She let off the gas, and they drifted past the yellow DO NOT CROSS tape at the bottom of Kid's driveway. A uniformed officer standing in front of the tape was using a nail file on her left fingers, and she idly watched the looky-loo drive by in a ragged light blue Chevy sedan.

Jorge craned his neck and announced, "An ambulancia is also there. Hmm. Ho-kay. We go now."

The girlfriend nodded. Cops made her nervous. She sped off.

THIRTY minutes later a platoon of crime scene techs and officers were trailing in and out of Kid's place like so many soldier ants. They were also swarming his BMW.

A tech held up an AirTag she'd discovered taped inside the car's rear fender. An on-spot analysis revealed Goliath's fingerprint on it.

When the homicide investigator mentioned this, Kid surmised that Goliath arrived at the Wyoming rest stop without knowing how many people were in the men's room, or if anyone was armed—a real possibility in that region. So he attached the AirTag thinking he could find the car later and steal it. It explained how he found Kid's residence.

Chapter Twenty

May 24 • Olympia

LONG BEFORE THE crime scene techs began their thorough search, three federal government officials of the highest ranks held a series of telecons in the following order: the Governor of Washington; the local district attorney, and finally Olympia's police chief.

These calls prompted a mammoth effort by on-scene investigators, crime lab personnel, and forensic pathologists who asked no questions when the police chief appeared at the scene and instructed them to carefully perform their duties.

Once the chief made his wishes known, he took Kid aside and he was about to speak when Kid held up a palm. In the ensuing silence, he pulled up Notes on his smartphone and wrote that he couldn't speak due to potential eavesdropping devices.

The chief motioned for the phone and wrote, *Not sure who you are or who you're with, but you've got juice. Yep, you definitely have juice.*

Kid thanked him with his eyes while he used the back cursor to erase the notes. That seemed to be all until everything hit Kid at once, and he turned his head in time to avoid spewing all over the chief.

The chief planted two strong hands on Kid's shoulders afterward and looked him in the eye. "Did the same thing the first time I killed in the line of duty. You're strong, son. But for whatever my opinion's worth? Call a crisis helpline." He opened his mouth to say more when he appeared to remember the covert situation. So he patted Kid's back instead and walked off.

LEVI texted Kid on a burner phone later that day to inform him that a speed-of-light effort had cleared him of any wrongdoing. Goliath's thirty-nine-page rap sheet helped Kid's case since it included rapes, aggravated assaults, and homicides. His fingerprints on the AirTag also made it clear that he'd gone after Kid with a vengeance, and the landlord's eyewitness account sealed it.

Kid read Levi's follow-up text: *The crime techs found a plug-in room deodorizer with a mic, along with a very well-hidden video camera and another mic. The landlord claims to have no idea how they got there. He suggests a previous tenant with a reputation for making videos with girlfriends might've left them behind.*

But Kid quickly wrote, *They're Sandro's. I already knew about the plug-in but not the other devices. It's what we expected. Hence the role-play.*

Levi replied: *A forensic computer tech gleaned portions of some videos from Cloud. He found one of you defending yourself from the man you killed. How're you doing with it, Son? Do you need someone to talk to?*

Kid felt his heart go out to Levi. *Thanks for asking. You always know the right thing to say. Yeah, it's all surreal. I tossed my cookies earlier. The police chief was there and did his best to comfort me. I'm sure I'll be jerking awake in a cold sweat for a few days. I'll deal with it. I'll even see a psychologist if necessary.*

Levi responded at once. *Good. Anything else I can do for you?*

No, sir. Kid felt more was needed, so he worked his fingers rapidly. *Thank you so much. And? I love you.*

· · ·

"So that's it," Marty told Kid. "I wanted to interview the guy from the café about his relationship to Sandro. Only, he'd just made bail. So I was calling to warn you about him when Goliath showed up."

They were at an obscure location far from their respective cars—although Kid still had to wait until Marty swept him with an electronic detector before either of them could speak.

"Got it." Kid paused. "I know my father gave you the word on Bill, and on Sandro's connection to the dead agent. Also, um—" Kid grunted and said without shame, "Uncle Marty? I'm sleeping with a dude, I'm doing potent pot with another gang-banger, and what else? Oh! There's a sale at Macy's. Whaddya say we haul ass there before all the good stuff's gone?"

Marty said at once, "It's a lot of pressure on top of what just happened." Marty put a hand on Kid's arm. "Hey? You're not alone in any of this. I'm right here, and I won't leave you. Let me know if you need a shoulder. Okay?"

Kid's eyes misted. "Thanks, Uncle Marty."

· · ·

What Kid could not realize despite being pre-med was that the rest-stop attack, coupled with Goliath barging into his home and the ensuing violence had taken a great toll on him. On top of that, he now had to be on the lookout for the guy whose finger he broke.

The medical process that eluded Kid is a fundamental one: The body releases cortisol to help those in immediate peril. But with stressors always present now, his body's natural fight-or-flight reaction could not shut down. Too much cortisol along with other stress hormones were flooding him. The divorce play-acting added to this. These chemicals were now disrupting his body's processes, which leads to anxiety, depression, and disruption of reasoning and focus.

It's why Kid couldn't bear to step foot inside his rental, which led him to ask Huck, "Can I stay with you? And would you retrieve my belongings for me?"

Huck of course picked up Kid's things and brought them to his micro-mobile home. Because it had a queen-size bed but not even a couch for Kid to stretch out on—they slept together. In the nude. Neither one complained.

• • •

Jennifer glanced at the time. It was eight in the morning, five on the west coast. Too early to call. Besides, she had to bathe and feed the twins. So she responded to maternal instinct by taking care of her children while her mother watched with raised eyebrows.

Precisely at noon, she picked up her phone.

KID groaned when his cell chirped. He'd been dead to the world and would rather remain in that state. He even considered ignoring the call before remembering Marty's desperate attempt to reach him moments before Goliath appeared. So he grabbed the cell and felt his spirits lift when he saw Jen's number. He went into role-play. "What do you want?"

"I haven't heard from you in so long."

"What'd you expect. You filed against me."

"Since you're going to be that way, tell me this: Did you have fun fucking all those Harvard girls? How many were you doing, by the way? And how many are you doing now?"

He leaped to his feet and began talking with wide sweeps of his arm. "Jen, I don't know where this is coming from."

"Yes, you do… and fuck you."

The call went dead.

JEN turned to Cati. "Did I do okay?"

"Sad as it sounds, you were wonderful." The older woman ran her fingers through Jen's black hair. "I can't imagine how difficult this must be for you, especially with what happened to him the other day."

She touched Cati's forearm. "I'm made of tough stuff. Listen, Marty said the bad guys bugged Kid's place. So I get it. It's why Papa Bailey gave me a special cell phone if I needed to call him. Or you. Or…"

DESPITE knowing full well that Jen had put on an act, Kid still felt an ache deep in his heart. To make it all worthwhile he made another vow. *I'll get these people. Even Huck. Even though I'm beginning to love him.*

CATI gently said, "Jen? Darling? It's time we take the next step in our little theater play."

·   ·   ·

Kid was in bed with Cleo the next morning, having finally made love to her in order to solidify his role, when Jen's attorney called.

"This is Gary Ronalds, of Beck, Jensen, and Ronalds. I am informing you that your wife has affirmed her decision to pursue a divorce. She cited irreconcilable differences in addition to adultery..."

"Wait! This is crazy. What're you talking about?"

The attorney was unfazed. "You cannot contest this under the laws of the Commonwealth of Massachusetts. Accordingly, in nine months a judge will sign a divorce decree with or without your consent. Now please be so kind as to provide your address. A process server will visit you shortly."

Feeling that he'd been punched in the head despite expecting this next higher level of acting, Kid sank back against the pillow in shock and disbelief. A full minute passed before he could tell Cleo what happened without his voice breaking.

She did her best to console him, while unknown to her the camera Sandro had hidden in her bedroom long ago was catching everything.

THAT night when images of Goliath bursting into his home jerked him awake, he touched Huck's bare hip and asked in a low voice, "Hey? Talk to me?"

"Of course," Huck said, and pulled Kid into his arms and absently stroked Kid's bare back while they talked. In time, he put his mouth close to Kid's ear and whispered without shame, "I love you. Do you hear me? I have fallen in love with you." He shifted a bit and watched Kid's face.

Kid searched Huck's eyes before he kissed Huck's chest. "I wish I were in love with you. I'm not, at least not yet. But I want to be. Okay?"

Huck's grin knew no boundary. They talked on, and in time they fell asleep.

Chapter Twenty-One

· ·

That Same Day • May 27 • Washington, D.C.

LEVI HART STOOD looking out his office window while telling Michael Bailey, "Christ! If only he'd check in more often."

"Knock it off," Michael snapped. "We do have eyes on him. Or have you forgotten?"

Levi turned and bit off the next four words. "No. I have not."

"Kid had a tough enough sell to make. Now he's killed a man. Don't you think he's feeling tremendous pressure?" He gave Levi a look that said, *We've been through so much together. Now let's keep faith in others to do their job.*

"I suppose," Levi mumbled, only to stare at a blank spot on his office wall and rub his chin. "Logic tells me you're on target. My heart doesn't agree. I doubt yours does, either."

"You're beginning to sound like my grandma," Michael scolded good-naturedly.

"You never had a grandma," Levi fired back, only to cringe. "Sorry. You know I didn't mean it."

Michael offered a smile. "Of course, brother. Listen. They've accepted him. Sandro's promised to make the intro with Ag." He mimicked an old Jewish man's voice. "Vhat! That's not progress?"

Levi cut him off with a sharp look and even sharper words. "I'm not stupid."

Michael grunted and went to the mini bar where he grabbed a bottle of Chivas Regal. After pouring two fingers each into a pair of Salviati crystal tumblers, he handed one to his best friend and took the other for himself.

Levi said as they clinked glasses, "To Kid."

"To Kid," Michael echoed. "And to that other brave soul in this mission; Jen."

After they tossed one back, Levi said, "Let's take a ride."

They arrived at the J. Edgar Hoover Building minutes later and were brought to a SCIF. Once the door was closed, Levi turned to Michael. "The Bureau's latest intel suggests a growing likelihood of a global shutdown."

Michael's breath caught. "Mother of God. It would mean a return to medieval times; an entire planet without fuel, electricity, or running water. Without water to cool reactors, even nuclear power will be wiped out."

He stared at some distant thing. "No motor vehicles or aircraft to rush people to E.R.s in hospitals that no longer function. There'll be no medicines to offer. No grocery stores. Absolute chaos. A complete breakdown of civilized behavior."

"Lest we forget the goddamn Gang of Eight," Levi said from the side of his mouth. "Talk about a breakdown."

The *Gang of Eight* are the eight Congressional leaders who get briefed on ultra-classified matters. The Gang includes both parties from the Senate and from the House, along with the intelligence committee chairs. Under an ironclad mandate, the executive branch must consult with the Gang on major concerns. By design, the Gang of Eight can be an asset. Or they can be a royal pain.

"Jesus, Michael. Two of the ranking minority members want to dodge a full-court press so they won't offend Pacific

Northwest voters. One of them—and I'm not mentioning any names—but she said, and I quote, 'I don't want my constituents to feel they've been *othered* by being lumped together as 'requiring government intervention.''"

Michael grimaced. "Damn."

Levi sighed and said in a low voice, "The President's begun briefing the G-7 leaders on the worst possible scenario."

"It's why we must keep Kid going strong."

· · ·

At that very moment three time zones away

Another day. Another cup of joe at the café while Kid, Sandro, and Cleo made small talk about myriad subjects that included the environment, the war in Ukraine, and the best way to make a soufflé without it falling in on itself. Sandro opened his mouth to say something when a female voice called out, "There you are!"

Kid's breath caught at the sight of the blonde woman in a white blouse, gray skirt, and black pumps. He peered at her and said, *"Britney?"*

She hurried over and showered him with kisses. "I hadn't heard from you in such a while. So I decided to fly out and soothe your weary brow." Her eyes showed her concern. "Oh, baby. You look terrible." She sprinkled the air with laughter. "You haven't killed anyone, have you?"

Feeling as if in a dream, he stood and wrapped an arm around her shoulder. When she lay her head against his shoulder, he kept it all upfront by introducing her to Cleo and Sandro as an unexpected visit from a friend at an unexpected time—but a friend whom Cleo and Sandro believed was carrying Kid's child.

Cleo was polite and remained seated. Sandro offered a deep scowl and muttered, "Excuse me. I must use the toilet," and stormed off.

Although Cleo was only feet away, Kid asked the obvious question. "Brit, how did you know where to find me?"

"Does it matter?" She gave him a fresh appraisal. "I like your new look. Nothing on but these old pants. Of course, you look so much more delicious au naturel. Mmm," she began dreamily. "Remember our last day in bed?"

Kid could only say, "Of course."

She paused. "I suspect you've forgotten our conversation? When I offered to come to your side if you got lonely? You gave the name of this café, and what luck! I had three days before I start prepping for the summer session. So, darling? I flew into SeaTac and here I am!"

He smiled. "Well, I'm glad you are."

As if oblivious to Cleo's presence, Britney said, "Kid? Can you ever forgive me? I was so intent on surprising you. But after flying in last night I was so thoroughly jet-lagged, that I only now woke up."

She tried to smile. "Now I have to fly home in a few short hours. My carry-on's already in my rental."

The polite response would have been for Kid to suggest she remain another day. He could not, of course. Instead, he took her hand and asked, "Where are you parked?"

Sandro, who had been recording them on video from behind a pillar, quickly jockeyed for a new position when they walked outside in time to watch the shirtless and shoeless Kid and the girl crossing the parking lot to a forest green rental in a secluded corner. After zooming in from afar he hit a jackpot of sorts when they got in the back seat and closed the door. Unable to risk getting closer, Sandro was forced to wait and see.

When Kid finally emerged, his pants were hanging open and he was zipping up and fastening them when Britney appeared with her blouse undone. They laughed and exchanged foolish grins while she buttoned up, and after running her palms across the skirt to smooth its wrinkles she clung to him and pressed her face against his chest.

In time they kissed, holding it until he stepped back to watch her speed off.

Sandro immediately ducked inside the café and found a quiet corner, where he hit PLAYBACK and smirked at the images of Kid and Britney stepping inside the car and getting out later with their clothes in disarray. This was all he needed for a deepfake.

．　　．　　．

That night Kid went to Cleo's apartment and they got in bed at once, and now he was holding her firmly in place as she arched and bucked beneath him; Kid whispering to her; spurring her on by prompting her to let go of everything that had been before and was yet to come; urging her to be in the moment rather than the past, the time sweeping by as he skillfully touched her everywhere, all the while suggesting in her mind's eye a union of milk and honey; of rough textures and ancient harmonies; of lovers moving as one, their energies subdued, their hushed sounds paired with the murmur of pulsing waves kissing the shorelines of their imaginations; of fingertips dancing like butterflies along each other's backs and buttocks while they edged closer and closer, until the lovers finally cried out and shuddered against each other before collapsing in a sweaty, gasping heap.

They slept and woke and loved again.

· · ·

Sandro watched the video of Britney and Kid talking inside the café until it segued to the parking lot and showed them getting in the back seat. Then the camera seemed to be looking through the car's window as Kid's bottom bobbed up and down between Britney's open naked thighs.

From the parking lot scene, the video shifted and portrayed Kid and Britney engaged in lavish intercourse atop a bed. Never mind that after filming Kid having real intercourse with Cleo the other night, and again last night, he'd substituted Britney's face and hair for Cleo's, and colorized Cleo's body to match Britney's skin tones.

He reviewed the tape once more while thinking, *You are my lover. Yet you go with this woman to her car? You sleep with Cleo? Bah! No wonder you do not commit to marrying me. Therefore I must ensure that your wife sends your marriage into the darkest reaches.*

A moment later he sent the video to Kid's wife, along with a caption: *Britney Comes to Play With the Man Whose Baby She Carries.*

· · ·

"Oh, Kid. What are you doing?" Jen had watched the parking lot portion of the video, from when they entered the backseat and had intercourse, to when they got out with their clothes in disarray. But while watching the next video of them atop the bed, she recognized Kid's rhythm; heard his whispers, his love talk—the very words he so often spoke to her.

All at once tears were streaming down her cheeks, and she instinctively placed a hand on her very round belly to shield the fetus from its father's betrayal.

In time she turned angry, and that anger evolved into fury.

• • •

Kid's phone chimed and Jen's number appeared. "Jen," he said.

"Tell me one thing, Kid. It better be the truth. Did Britney come to see you?"

He frowned. "Yes, she did. Jesus, how did you know?"

"Did you have fun fucking her? You bastard, you've been having an affair with her all along. Haven't you?"

"Jen, let me explain. She invited herself. She... she literally appeared from nowhere. So okay, we ended up in the back of her car. And yeah, I was no saint. We fooled around. But..."

But he was now talking to a call that had gone dead.

• • •

Marty met with Kid on a rural side road later that day and gave him the terrible news. "Jen's divorcing you for real."

The young operative nodded and said in a small boy's voice, "A girl I know from Harvard dropped in uninvited. Now someone's filling Jen's head with lies about us."

Marty held up a hand. "Did you have intercourse?"

"Of course not! I mean, sure. We messed around a bit, the same as when we study. Christ, I tell Jen everything we do. But having sex with Brit? Or getting a blowjob? For god's sake, I would never do that. Never. It's a set-up, I tell you. A set-up." He stepped closer and quietly said, "Will you help me? Maybe you can call and explain it to her?"

"Yes. Right now, in fact. But if we're going to discuss the set-up, then we'll have to be on secure phones."

Kid could barely stand still as he replied. "She has one,"

"Got it." Marty stepped away and made the call. He spoke, listened briefly, and abruptly held the phone at arm's length.

Marty pocketed the phone and returned to Kid. "Jen said she has proof that you screwed Britney and ended the call." He rested a fatherly hand on Kid's shirtless shoulder. "I'll call Levi and Michael. It's better that they reach out to her."

He made the calls and they waited quietly until Marty's phone chirped. He answered and spoke in low tones. Afterward, he looked at Kid. "She hung up on both of 'em." He worried the end of his nose. "I don't know what to say, Kid."

AFTER thanking Marty, Kid went to Huck's. But he wasn't there so he fell onto the bed and sobbed as never before, the tears coursing down his cheeks in torrents while his nose ran nonstop. In time, he crawled into a fetal position and was still sobbing two hours later.

"Why?" he kept asking. "Why, God? *Why?*" He clung to this one hope—that she was hormonal and acting irrationally. Yet he knew this to be a worn-out excuse that far too many men use—one that women find so offensive. Besides, he reasoned. Jen hadn't been hormonal with the twins and shouldn't be now. So he cried on.

A while later he stepped inside the bathroom, where a glance in the mirror revealed red-rimmed eyes and snot-covered lips and chin. So he cleaned himself up, and then he got in the car and drove to the café—but not until he deleted every photo he had of Jen from his smartphone.

SINCE that day he began dealing with his heart-wrenching misery in the same toxic manner that countless others have done before him—through sex. In his case, it was with Sandro and Cleo.

But the sex did no good because Kid felt so lost; so utterly alone and in a black despair from losing Jen, his daughters, and his unborn son.

Even so, he didn't back down, steeling himself instead with a renewed vow to get the job done. Or as he bitterly reminded himself, *Hell, aren't I supposed to be a Romeo? Well goddamn it then.*

He slept with Cleo that night—Cleo, who at dawn looked into his eyes and whispered, "There, you handsome devil. You've gone and done it. I've fallen helplessly in love with you."

                    •   •   •

Ag said to himself at almost the same instant, "Cleo has fallen along some wayside. Why else hasn't she called?" He banged a fist on the computer table and shouted, "Goddamn it! I will not be the one to call first."

Cleo's lack of communication had riled him, so to clear his mind he adjusted his blue bathrobe and shifted a bit, making his chair squeak. It creaked again when he leaned forward to check the monitor for the social media poker-playing tells he needed before he could penetrate the next three firewalls. When he wasn't seeing them, he scowled and whispered to the empty room, "I'll get in, damn it All of 'em, and show the world who I am. And *fuck* her for not calling!"

His cell sounded at that very instant, and after grabbing it with shaking hands and seeing the caller's name, he reared back, his heart hammering against his chest as he pushed the green icon. "Hello?"

Cleo's energized voice burst forth. "I'm sorry for not calling these past few days. I have no excuse to offer. So please bear with me when I say that I've been chock-full of duties."

"I um, was wondering why you hadn't. Not that I, ah, noticed now that I think about it."

"Sorry, pet. My life's been falling apart. But everything's back on track now."

"Oh." Ag felt a selfish relief that she hadn't rejected him. "Please tell me what's going on."

She gave him a rundown about a friend who had almost been murdered. Ag went limp. "Gosh, I don't know what to say. I'm ah, glad you called." He swiped at his eyes, and once he could trust his voice he said with forced cheer, "I hope to see you again. Hey, come over now if you'd like. You're welcome to stay the night. Well?"

"Thank you so much for the invite. And you can wager without risk that I shall be there ASAP. Can't stay the night, though. A girl's got to sleep in her own bed." She added, "At least until we've done our thing, after which we shall move in together. I'm sure you understand."

"Of course." Ag felt his pulse race. "Hey? Stop by? Even for just a few minutes. Please?"

"Of course, my pet. Not to worry; I shan't dilly-dally. Quite the opposite… I shall be there straight away."

. . .

Two days passed before Kid saw Cleo at the café again. Goliath's attack, combined with Jen's continued refusal to believe him, had taken its toll on him. He barely ate now, leaving him so gaunt that his ribs were clearly etched into his shirtless flanks. Dark rings encircled his hollow eyes. He felt listless. And he hadn't even been here a month yet.

He watched her eat a spare lunch, then asked, "Will I ever get to see Agamemnon?"

"The bloke remains unavailable," she said at once. "He answers when we ring him. Yet he has refused to grant any audiences. Ag assures me however that he's nearing comple-tion of his goals. Not to worry, love. It shan't be much longer before you and he meet up."

Kid sniffed and said, "Know what? The hell with it. It's not as if I *need* to meet him. You guys think he'll deliver? Great. Introduce us after we've done our thing." When he saw a new light of trust growing in her eyes, he excused himself and got some cream for his coffee.

• • •

Cleo's *It shan't be much longer* evolved into a week and Kid groused inwardly about this. But he had Huck in his life now, and he looked forward to their time together.

In the meantime, Cleo moaned about his ill-fitting cloth-ing and his habit of going barefoot 24/7.

Then there was Sandro, who was locked in battle with a growing anger. In his world, Kid should be with him and nobody else—not with Cleo, and he most assuredly must not sleep with Huck. What galled him even more was that he'd done as Kid had commanded: he'd shaved his legs and other body hair. He was also taking daily estrogen shots, despite knowing the estrogen would literally burn up his balls.

Unknown to Sandro however, Kid had been visiting a downtown walk-in clinic to get checked for STDs following every sexual encounter.

• • •

A day later Cleo touched Kid's forearm at a café table. "I think we might be ready to see our man Ag. I'll know more in a fortnight."

Kid made a show of slumped shoulders. "Jesus, make up your minds, will ya? No, forget I said that. I mean, it's going to happen. Right? Our goal, I mean. A complete…"

"… and total shutdown of this planet that we all love so much."

He smiled a North Star smile, and his eyes shone like those of the mystics. "Think about it. No more pollution. People running naked if they wish; me for certain. Children able to—" He clammed up when he saw Cleo's amused look. "Okay, I deserved that." He smiled as a way of saying, no harm, no foul.

. . .

"Slow down," Jorge screamed into his girlfriend's ear, only to sit back against the car's seat and try once again to scratch an unreachable itch inside the cast. "Chit! It is not there." He pounded the dash as she drifted past the address. "This is how many days now that we do not see his car?"

"Several." The meek girl instinctively shrugged her shoulders to protect her neck and head in case he lashed out at her. Others certainly had, and she felt he would eventually get around to doing it too.

"Ho-kay. We keep looking until we find him. When we do? I will make the bastard pay."

. . .

"What else do you have for me?" Marty asked.

Kid sighed amid traces of pine scent. "They promised to introduce me to Ag."

"Good." The retired pilot rested a hand on Kid's shoulder. "How're you doing?"

"Dead inside," the unofficial nephew said to the ground.

Marty ended it there, and an instant later he walked away from the obscure side street they'd found for their meeting. Kid waited until he was out of sight before barefootin' it in the opposite direction.

·   ·   ·

"Bill!" Kid shouted later that very day when the big man entered the café. Kid hadn't seen him in three weeks. Under normal circumstances, he might have wondered whether Bill had taken his wife and children on vacation. But his instincts kept him wary enough not to believe it.

Once Bill plopped into a chair at Kid's table like an aircraft carrier's anchor hitting the sea bed, they chatted it up. Nothing heavy. Family, friends; current events. After an hour of this, Bill said goodbye.

"Gotta get home to the missus. Wouldn't you know it? She's pissed at me for something. Don't ask me what." He looked at Kid in that conspiratorial way husbands do.

Kid guffawed. "I know what you mean. By the way, when do I get to meet her?"

The blood drained from Bill's face. "Katarina? Um, why?"

"I dunno." Kid offered a good-natured shrug coupled with a laser focused interest. "Guess I just wanna meet the woman who takes such good care of my buddy." A pause. "Katarina's such a beautiful name. Not that common. No sir, not common at all. Actually, I don't know anyone else by that name. Do you?" He watched Bill's face for tells but got a quick shake of the head for his effort.

At least he got Bill to exchange phone numbers. Then while Kid waved goodbye he glanced at Marty at the far end of the café, who got up a heartbeat later to follow Bill.

• • •

"Pay attention," Levi told Hacksaw and Michael moments after Marty phoned to say he'd tracked Bill to his home. "Hack? I want 24/7 surveillance. Draw teams from other assignments if necessary."

Hack nodded. "Got it, Boss Man."

"Michael? I told Marty to check with local zoning and planning for diagrams, building permits and you name it on this guy's residence. He'll also conduct a search of any architectural drawings. We must know Bill's house to the tiniest detail if we conduct a raid. You'll coordinate between Marty and Hack."

"I'm on it," Michael said.

• • •

The next day Marty slipped inside the café, and when Kid looked his way he tugged an earlobe to signal him that they must talk. They met on a rural side street an hour later.

"I've discovered Bill's residence: 1023 Montrose Avenue. We have it under surveillance and so far there's no sign of a wife or children. I even sent someone to pose as a florist delivery girl. When she knocked on the front door an elderly woman answered, but our agent saw no signs of a family life. One other thing. There's a rear entrance to a basement that's been modified as a living area. Hell, our anarchist even got the required building permits."

Kid blew air from his cheeks. "I was almost hoping Bill did have a family." His shoulders slumped. "At least now I can focus on any failsafe systems."

"Good plan," Marty said. "By the way, your friend Huck's comments about Jamal were spot-on. Annapolis grad.

Meteoric rise to the rank of lieutenant commander and XO on a frigate when the Navy canned him for not being a team player."

· · ·

"We're going to pull an action," the Naval Academy grad told Kid the next night as they stood in the café's parking lot. "It's a political action to raise enough cash to fund some food co-ops. We could rob a bank or even take down an armored car. But the risks outweigh the rewards. So we'll do a midnight burglary of Saunders & Son Fine Jewelers. Do you know it?"

Kid nodded at Jamal, whom he could only see as an outline against the overcast sky's blackness. "Half a block southwest of Kernan Mall."

"That's the one. I chose them specifically because they exploit the workers of the African diamond mines run by white-skinned Europeans..."

Kid thought, *Sure, and the miners are friggin' grateful to have a paying job in a destitute land. But maybe that's just my take on it...*

"... I have the necessary tools and I'm told you know how to handle yourself with a pistol." He grinned, "I heard about you and that ex-con."

Kid bridled at once. "Yeah, that's right. I fuckin' killed him. What of it? Because I don't see the humor in it."

Jamal sniffed and said, "Understood, and I apologize. Hell, I know men who've killed in combat who felt the same way. It's why your soulfulness speaks well of you." He patted Kid's shoulder. "We good?"

"Sure," Kid said. Only, he wasn't. The nightmares continued, along with his weight loss and hollow-eyed look.

"Very well. We'll meet for a planning session four days from now. Questions?"

"No, sir."

Jamal smiled. "We're going to get along fine. Very well. You're dismissed."

Kid was about to turn away when his phone chimed. When a glance at the caller ID shot his eyebrows into upside-down V's, he jammed the phone to his ear. "Mom. What's wrong?"

"Hi, Kiddo. Congratulations. You're the father of a baby boy."

"I—" He clenched the phone until his knuckles blanched. "Mom, what do you mean?"

"He was born just hours ago, earlier than expected. Jennifer's fine. She'll stay a night in the hospital."

"*Mom*. I…" He swiped at his eyes while Jamal studied his face. "How, um, so how's little Michael? He has all his fingers and toes?"

"He's a healthy boy. A miniature *you*."

Kid brightened. "How are the girls? They must be jazzed at having a brother."

"You can't imagine how much so."

They spoke a bit more before Kid put away his phone and regarded Jamal with a set jaw. "My son. I'm flying to Boston and I'm doing it tonight. I should be back in a couple of days." His emotions were running the gamut: he wanted to see his newborn son. Yet he risked losing headway with these terrorists who had torn his family apart.

And, he would have to fly.

. . .

June 6 • The next day • Boston

Kid walked down one bleach-smelling maternity corridor after another before finding the nursery's eight-foot-wide observation window. There were no other visitors to be seen, so he slouched against the glass and stared lovingly at his son before asking to hold him.

A nurse seated at a desk among the talcum powder-smelling newborns regarded the malnourished, pretty boy slacker with unkempt hair in rumpled black clothes with concern, only to offer a half-smile.

He smiled back while a beautiful self-assured woman marched through the hallway. As she drew closer her eyebrows knitted together. Now frowning at him, she pointedly stopped at the far end of the window to peer through the glass.

Kid watched her with interest before saying, "He's gorgeous, isn't he?"

The woman turned and faced him, only to rear back and jam knuckles to her mouth, her eyes bulging in horror as she gave him a new once-over. "Kid," she croaked. "Oh my god, *Kid*."

The young father pulled his mother into his embrace and hung on fiercely. "Mom, what're you doing here? I never told anyone I was coming."

She dabbed at her eyes and said with wonder, "Son, I didn't even recognize you. You're positively *scrawny*. How much weight have you lost?" Without waiting for an answer, she touched a cool palm to his face. "These rings around your eyes, they…"

Because the gang might be monitoring him even here, he reverted to role-play. "Speaking of rings? I tossed my wedding band."

Her eyes turned down. "No. Tell me you didn't."

"Jen wouldn't even hear me out. As far as I'm concerned, she flat-out betrayed me."

"Give her time, Kid." She met his eye before brushing past him to gaze at the newborn. "He is so you, isn't he?"

Kid grinned. "Right? I can't wait to hold him." He shifted gears. "Mom? Please don't tell Papa I'm in town. I'd rather remain under the radar."

Nadia stiffened. "It wouldn't be a good idea anyway. Monica's taken a turn for the worse. The doctors doubt she'll make it through the day."

"Oh, no!" Kid jammed a hand to his eyes. "Mom. Please tell Papa how sorry I am." He looked at her in anguish. "The mother of Papa's daughter is about to leave us, and I just don't know what to say or think anymore."

"I'll pass along your thoughts." Nadia turned quiet for a moment. "So, Kiddo. Shall we visit Jennifer next?"

His mouth formed a straight line. "No. We're through." He looked at her with an intensity that signified that he wasn't acting. "Let's drop it, or I'll begin to hate her." He exhaled in a rush. "I want to hold little Michael."

Nadia winced and traced a long tapering finger along his cheek. "Kid? Jen named him Huckleberry."

"She... damn it. I—" He glared and said through clenched teeth, "Huckleberry's fine."

Minutes later they were in an anteroom where a nurse brought the newborn to its father.

Kid said while holding his son, "He's beautiful, Mom. He's—" He swiped at a joyful tear, and after kissing his son's forehead he handed the boy to its paternal grandmother.

An hour later Kid was ready to leave. "Tell Papa I'm keeping him and Monica in my thoughts. And Mom? Don't worry about me. I'll be fine. Now that's it. I've a flight to catch."

He did have a flight. He also wanted to see Britney, who lived fewer than two miles from the hospital. But despite feeling free to make love to her now, deep down he knew he shouldn't. So he continued on his way.

Chapter Twenty-Two

· ·

June 8 • Olympia

KID'S STOMACH FLIP-FLOPPED the instant he turned onto the street and spotted two sheriff's patrol units blocking the hospital driveway. They were there in the wake of Jamal's false active shooter call which was meant to draw deputies away from the jewelry store. So he took a fresh grip on the stolen tow truck's steering wheel and drove on. Roo sat quietly at his side while Jamal and Sandro followed in a sedan rented with phony ID and stolen plastic.

The plan was straightforward. Occam's razor. Keep it simple. Now that they'd eyeballed the chaos at the hospital, Jamal would monitor police frequencies on a hand-held scanner to guard against an outlier.

They drove another two miles along deserted streets before the red brick, single-story building housing Saunders & Son Fine Jewelers materialized straight ahead of them, prompting Kid and Roo to tighten their seat belts and pray that the truck's airbags would cushion the blow. Then he sped up to twenty and drove the truck through the store's large glass window.

An audible alarm instantly pierced the air, its tone rising and falling sharply while they unbuckled amid a cabin fogged by airbag chemical residue, and they were already hopping out when Jamal parked behind them. He and Sandro emerged seconds later with hoods over their heads and masks covering their faces.

While Jamal positioned himself next to the shattered window, the others climbed through the raw opening and went for the display cases. Smash and grab. That was the plan. Get all you could carry within thirty seconds, and haul ass.

Kid's heart pounded against his chest and Sandro's eyes were huge, but Roo remained cool and collected as they hammered the glass display cases. After sweeping up what they could, all four of them sped off in the sedan.

"IS that all?" Kid cried out as they examined the loot. They had gone to Sandro's where they spread the take across the kitchen table. "Fuck, man. That's not much."

Their grab in fact did not amount to much—twenty grand at the outside, since the really valuable stuff was in a vault for the night.

"Pocket money," Jamal replied. "Just for drill to let me see how everyone works as a unit."

Yeah, right, Kid told himself. *You people have tons of money. How else do you afford high-end investigators? So why the big grab? Was it because creating havoc is in your guys' DNA? Or was it all about seeing if I'm all in?*

Minutes later after they burned their hoods, masks, and clothes in the fifty-five-gallon drum placed out back for that purpose, Jamal collected the goods. "Don't worry," he told Kid and Sandro. "I've got a fence lined up and he's champing at the bit."

ONCE Jamal and Roo were gone, Kid shut the door and started for the bathroom. He smelled from too much sweat, his neglected hair looked creepy, and the rumpled, ill-fitting street clothes he'd changed into while Jamal drove the getaway car itched in places he'd rather not think about.

Minutes later he was standing under a steaming shower when Sandro, who had been miffed at Kid for days now, joined him uninvited. "I am your lover. Why do you sleep with Huck? With Cleo? Huh?"

"Get over it," Kid snapped.

"No! Look at me. I have shaved my body for you. I have begun to grow the titties. I feel my manhood burning up. All for you. No, I will not, as you say, get over it."

While the shower's water cascaded upon them, Kid realized he needed to change tactics if only to remain on Sandro's good side—at least until they introduced him to Agamemnon. And so he said, "Sorry, Sandro. I just haven't been myself since I killed that guy. You understand, don't you?" To show his contrition, he put on a charming smile and spun Sandro around until he faced the wall. Then he pressed Sandro against it and growled, "Oh, and thanks for going the estrogen route for me. Now? Shut the fuck up while I use your ass."

They went to bed afterward, and Kid went hunting once Sandro was snoring. Although he'd spotted the hidden camera lenses and mics in the bedroom, the main room and the kitchen long ago, he felt restless. Doing something—anything—might help him calm down.

It took less than a minute to see that the cameras and mics were still in place. But he frowned as it hit him that Sandro must have taken videos of him during his intimate encounters with Cleo—and was almost certainly behind Jen's total rejection of him. But because he'd been a varsity sports player, he winged it by fighting past the pain as he developed a game strategy that would involve using the surveillance devices to his advantage.

Afterward, he shook Sandro awake. "Baby? Listen, I need a couple of weeks to myself. You have my number."

A clearly disappointed Spaniard frowned. "Okay. Well, you will return soon?"

"Of course. In fact, before I leave? Hands and knees, punk. Ass high, back arched. That's if you still wanna be my wife."

A smiling Sandro complied at once, with Kid telling himself while taking the Spaniard, *this one's for you, Dustin.*

.   .   .

The next day Sandro, clad in white and walking with stiff jerking movements stepped closer to Ag until he loomed over him. When the big man edged forward in his chair, Sandro sliced a hand through the dense air. "Well?"

"Don't rush me." Ag focused on his screens and left-clicked his mouse. "There," he triumphed.

Sandro pumped an arm like an NFL referee announcing a penalty. "Ah. Very well, my friend. So, you have also the first-responder frequencies?"

Ag looked over his shoulder and made a face. "Whaddya think I run here? A Chinese fire drill? Anyway, it's all deep web stuff. Easy access." He pointed to a wall-mounted speaker and said under his breath, "Wait for it."

Four minutes later every police and fire department radio downstream from a Minnesota earthen-works dam came alive, their chatter disoriented and distressed as the dam opened.

With another left click, Ag sent a time release code to scramble the entire Florida Keys' power supply—although by design it wouldn't happen until midnight.

Sandro patted Ag's shoulder. "You did the very good job. I also have the confidence that you will reverse these actions once the point has been made."

"Count on it," Ag muttered. Yet as he stared at the multiple screens, he began wondering about those who would lose what they'd accumulated over a lifetime of effort and sacrifice. Or, those who might lose something worse. After all, he didn't want to hurt anyone. Then again, he wanted people to pay for the years they spent ostracizing him and so many others.

Sandro left a short time later, unaware that two Vanguard operators were watching him from inside a plumber's windowless van parked half a block away.

"I make it eleven-zero-niner hours," one operator said. Her partner nodded and logged Sandro's time of departure.

• • •

"Bill," Kid began in a pleasant voice while pressing the phone against his ear. "I'm at the café and I haven't seen you for so long. Have you stopped coming?"

"I've been busy."

Kid said as a clatter of café dishware filled the air, "It's just that I miss your company."

The sound that escaped Bill's lips carried even over the phone. "Really?"

"Sure," Kid said, his eyes narrowing. "Why wouldn't I?"

"I, um, it's just that nobody ever gave a damn for me."

"That's strange. Not even your wife and children?"

"My what? Oh. Them. Well, they're family."

Kid digested this for the lie that it was and pressed on. "When're you coming to the café again? I miss you and, heck… why not bring your family for dinner? My treat. Well?"

"That... would be nice. I'll ask my um, wife. Only, she's not been feeling well. Hey, maybe I could drop in by myself. When's a good time?"

"Why, anytime." His smile glittered as he set the hook. "You're the busy one, not me. Not to mention that you're my buddy. Hey? I always make time for friends."

"Wow. Thank you for that. I'll ah, get back to you."

The call went dead. Kid thought he heard Bill sob just before it did.

LATER that day Kid moved into a shabby waterfront hotel with a red neon sign above its lobby that flashed, *The Apollo* — although a broken lowercase L had rendered it, *The Apol o.*

Although Kid would rather remain with Huck, he needed distance for operational purposes. Huck took it well enough, and even tagged along to help Kid move his things.

Kid stowed everything within two minutes, after which they kicked back and talked about fast cars and even faster women. They also got stoned, and as daylight capitulated to dusk, Huck crawled into bed with Kid.

They spent a moment adjusting their arms and legs until Huck rested a palm on Kid's hairy thigh and whispered, "Kid? I love you."

"I—" The cortisol-challenged Kid searched Huck's eyes before edging closer. Neither of them said anything. Not at first. But soon they spoke quietly, their whispers transitioning to kissing and touching, until Kid looked up and found the power of Huck's gaze focused on his eyes.

And so when Huck gently positioned him on his stomach, Kid craned his neck to meet Huck's eyes and nodded. He then willed his muscles to relax while Huck patiently claimed his naked body, slowly and gently, until the earth fell away when Huck took Kid to various levels of rapture with his tender, spiritual lovemaking, the two of them letting go completely until they were both utterly consumed.

HUCK caressed Kid's cheek afterward and whispered, "Are you okay?"

After Kid replied with a smile, Huck took him into his arms, and they lay in silence while trembling from wondrous sensations. Following their pillow talk they loved again, and then once more.

In time they drifted off with their arms and legs entwined, and with Huck's palm resting possessively on Kid's bottom. And in that final instant before Kid surrendered to sleep, he realized that he was falling in love with Huck.

But he promised himself that he would kill Huck if that's what it took to save the planet.

· · ·

Despite his deepening feelings for Huck, Kid knew he still had to all but shout to the gang, *Look at the clean break I've made from my old life. Sex. Drugs. Getting it on with guys...*

It's why he still slept with Cleo while also enjoying assignations with women he met at the mall—elegant ladies who were drawn to this savagely beautiful boy.

Then there was Enzo—the very attractive Italian wannabe rock star who washed dishes to pay for gas and grass. The pre-med student thought the black-haired, olive-skinned slacker's numerous faults were completely mitigated by his adventurous, amorous, and mischievous behavior—a true Italian stud who made it a fun thing for Kid to be in the lad's bed.

And of course he had Huck, to whom Kid always gave himself completely during Huck's frequent overnight stays.

•   •   •

When Kid's cell jerked him from a deep sleep, he groped for his phone. Then while Enzo stirred at his side, he peered through sleepy eyes at the time. Just after midnight.

"Hello?" he mumbled.

"It's me. Jamal. Sorry to call so late. I only just now got the word. Kid? Be at the café by twelve hundred hours tomorrow so can I introduce you to someone."

Chapter Twenty-Three

. . . .

June 9 • The Café

THE NEXT DAY Jamal led Kid across the barren café parking lot to a dilapidated grey Ford van sitting off to one side. Huck was already in the front passenger spot with Cleo seated behind him. Sandro had taken a third-row seat, and Kid settled in next to him while Jamal got behind the wheel.

Ten minutes later the tires were crunching against an indifferently graveled driveway that led to a weather-beaten house with a fading white exterior. Jamal stopped and said, "Let's go, people."

Kid got out and peered at the clear sky. It was warm and clear for once, and conflicting flora odors were saturating the air like a streetwalker's perfume.

Once everyone fell in behind Jamal, he started across the front yard toward the west side of the house, where a gradual incline ended at an exterior basement door. Jamal knocked and pushed it open while the hinges squeaked in protest.

The Annapolis grad went first. Kid followed, and once he stepped into a darkened room he smelled electronic ozone and heard the soft humming of CPU cooling fans. Someone coughed from within a shadowy corner.

Jamal closed the door and waved a hand at the shadow. "I am pleased to introduce you to Agamemnon, whom we call Ag for short."

The instant Ag appeared from the shadow, Kid blinked and feigned shock by crying out, "Bill! Christ, what're you doing here?"

The large man's jaw dropped. *"Kid?"*

Yet no one was more astonished than Jamal, whose eyes narrowed while his hands formed knife edges. Yet he said as if at a dinner party, "Ordinarily introductions would be in order. But it seems you two have apparently already made each other's acquaintance."

"THAT'S it," Ag summarized. He shifted in his chair, which stretched his tent-size T-shirt to its max. "I ran into Kid at the coffee shop about six weeks ago. We got to talking. Next thing you know, we're friends."

Kid frowned. "How come you told me your name's Bill?"

"Because 'William' is the name on my birth certificate. My grandma always called me Bill. Agamemnon's a boyhood nickname." He appeared sheepish. "I thought it'd be cool to use that name now and then. Nothing more."

"I see."

Ag's voice caught. "Kid, I never meant to deceive you. I freakin' sure never knew you'd joined our cause."

"I'm guessing you're the real brains. No surprise there, huh? Hell, I've always been in awe of you."

Sandro guffawed, only to be cut short when Ag shouted, "Shut up! Kid's my friend and I'm in awe of his humanity. He's why I'm in this fight—to teach a lesson to bullies who poke fun at people like me. Bullies like you. I..." His voice trailed away. He'd said enough.

As Kid's instincts told him that Ag was ashamed to be seen in this new light, he thought, *Maybe I can use that shame against him. But I'll need to start with positive reinforcements.* And so he swept an arm at the computers and the large concave monitors that lined the walls and theatrically intoned, "Ladies and gentlemen, I am standing inside Mission Control."

Ag's chest swelled. "Wow. Thank you for that."

Kid then pointed at a processor case near Ag's chair. "What's that?"

"A CPU. I built it myself and you can bet that it's far superior to the most expensive ones on the market. Those store-bought buggers run from nine to twenty grand." He patted the CPU. "I could sell this for fifty. Only, I won't. Also? Wanna see something?"

"Sure." He thought Ag was walking on air, he sounded that buoyant.

When Ag slid his computer chair to one side, its wheels rolled soundlessly across a faux hardwood floor. "See those four CPUs against the wall? They're identical to this one and I networked 'em. That boosted my ability to search the 'net by several thousand exponentials."

"Damn, Bill. I mean, Ag. I am very impressed." Kid jutted his jaw at the monitors. "What about those?"

"Forty-five-inch curved ultra-wide QHD free sync monitors, with HDR. I'd rather have 4Ks, but I'd have to be flush with cash to afford just one."

Kid nodded, but then he squinted at the equipment and cried out, "Wait. Where are your surge protectors? Your standby battery backups?"

"Bah! They're the devil's devices. Built-in spyware, all of 'em. No way I'm poisoning my network with such crap."

"Well," Kid began in an agreeable voice, "There certainly are perils out there." Now that he knew about Ag's fear of surge and backup devices, Kid began formulating contingency plans that would involve their absence.

And then it was time to leave—but not before Ag stared at the floor and spoke in the manner of a child asking if Santa would be coming for Christmas. "Kid, I'm sorry for lying about having a family." He looked at Kid with puppy dog eyes. "Will you ever forgive me?"

"What's there to forgive?" Kid rested a hand on the big man's shoulder. "Don't ever think I'd feel less about you."

But to himself, he was shouting, *I finally fucking found you. Only, you had to turn out to be a nice guy, didn't you? Fuck… that's gonna make it harder when I take you down. But I will. Bet your ass I will. Because there's no way I'm letting you take civilization back to the stone age. No way, Ag… no* fucking *way.*

During the return trip Kid began taking stock. Less than a month remained before the Fourth of July, but at least he'd verified Ag's identity and location. Now he could focus on tackling the other prime directive: find their failsafe plan.

·   ·   ·

After they arrived at the café Kid had to wait for everyone else to disembark before he could get out. It's why he didn't see the beat-up Chevy that slowed on the main road while the passenger shouted to the girl behind the wheel, "Look! There's that Beamer."

·   ·   ·

Kid typed a text one hour later, finishing with, *However do NOT move against Ag until I've given the signal. This is non-negotiable. I've made a major hit on some related details but need time to develop them.*

After pressing SEND, he stared at the placid lake until the reply came in the form of a single word, CONFIRMED.

"Damn," he said aloud. "Now I really do wish I smoked."

Next, he opened the burner phone's back, and after ripping out its innards he walked along the shoreline while tossing a chip here, a circuit board there and other parts at random, the water's calm surface offering a *plunk* each time.

Tedious as this method might be, he had no choice. It's why he also came up with a credible explanation for why he had several burners stashed in his trunk in case Cleo or Jamal discovered them: he would say that he gave them to his lovers so they could shield his calls from their significant others.

He also assumed that a tracking device was attached to his car at all times, as happened with Goliath. So he could justify stopping at the lake by saying he took a whiz en route to the Apollo. And despite the exhausting nature of this spy biz that was now weighing more heavily upon him, Kid could not deny the thrilling life that attaches.

LATER that evening while preparing for bed, Kid conceded that sleeping with women and men outside of the tribe appeared to have tempered any doubts that he had been having sex with Cleo and Sandro just so he could worm his way into the tribe.

For in the final analysis, day by day Kid had been transitioning away from the spurned husband to the male prostitute—a ravisher of women's bodies along with their hearts—but also the twink who posed little threat to total-top guys like Huck and Enzo. He only hoped that these tactics would help him prevail against his clever adversaries.

Or as he recalled reading, *Prostitution is a calling with many hazards, sadness, and tragedy. But it accepts human nature.* He added a coda: *It sure as fuck does. Now I see why governments find ways to accommodate it for their clandestine needs.*

In a prayer to his very soul, he justified his lifestyle as the means to getting him home. *But home to what? Holy mother of god, do I even have a family to return to? Or has this mission fucked me up too much? I've killed a man. I've lied and burgled some poor slob's jewelry store. On top of it all, I have to save the world within three weeks. Jesus, I need to bring things to an end before it kills the rest of my soul.*

THAT night Kid stared up at his crummy, mold-smelling hotel room ceiling for hours, the enormity of the mission's massive violation of his soul and his heart now awakening a sleeping giant within. But when a moonbeam fought its way past the usual cloud cover to shine down on him with the speed of a hypersonic missile, Kid reached into a dark corner of his soul, and while the fury within him became a living thing, he made a vow. *I will get these people no matter what it takes. Starting with Sandro. So help me God.*

PART III

. . .

Chapter Twenty-Four

· ·

June 10 • Olympia

THE NEXT MORNING Kid donned his predictable militaristic garb and sped off to the café hoping to arrive before the lunch crowd descended. He lucked out, only to appreciate how nice the place smelled of coffee beans, breads, and sweets. There were also soothing sounds of clattering mugs and cutlery scraping across plates.

When he spotted Cleo, Roo, and Jamal at a table near a murky corner, he nodded at them on his way to the barista for a cup of wake-up juice.

Minutes later and with coffee in hand, he started toward the others only to stumble against a business casual-attired Marty. Kid turned on him in an instant. "Why don't you watch what you're doing?"

"Hey, pal. I'm sorry. Listen, let me help…"

"How 'bout you just shut the fuck up?" Kid turned on his bare heel and joined the others.

Marty closed his laptop a few moments later and left, leaving Kid to endure an hour of tedious prattling before mumbling something about wanting to wander around. "I need to get my mind off the divorce. Maybe I'll hang around the mall."

H E drove a good two miles before Marty's car popped up in his rearview in response to Kid's signal that they meet. After turning down three streets at random, he found a suitable site flanked by concealing trees where he parked and got out. Seeing nobody around, he folded his arms across his bare chest and waited.

Marty appeared on foot within minutes and discreetly scanned Kid for listening devices.

"Here's the scoop," Kid began as he revealed additional details about Agamemnon's computers, even telling Marty what the place smelled like. "But I still don't know if they have a Plan B." He fidgeted and bit down on his lower lip. "At least I've established a partial case for the dead agent."

Marty grunted. "Anything else?"

"Not much." After describing the jewelry store heist he pressed his lips tight. "I'm getting mixed signals from Jamal. I don't think the tribe completely trusts me yet."

Marty tapped Kid's forearm. "Don't forget about our bandito friend. I think he's hunting you." He paused and worried the end of his nose, then said, "Why don't you take my pistol?"

"Nah, I'm fine."

"You sure?" He sighed when Kid gave a thumbs-up, and said, "All right. Now get out of here."

·   ·   ·

Nadia entered her restaurant's kitchen amid the usual clatter of pots, pans, and the chef's shouted orders. When a whiff of poached salmon teased her refined nostrils, she lifted her nose and was inhaling deeply when her personal iPhone chimed.

One look at the caller ID had her taking the call. "Yes, Jennifer?"

"Mom? I've not heard from Kid in quite some time."

"Jen, do you really expect him to call?"

Jen stifled a sob. "I don't know *what* to think anymore."

"I'm sure you don't, darling." Nadia chose her words with care in case the call was being monitored. "Jen? I didn't even recognize Kid at the hospital. My own son! He's lost weight. His eyes are sunken and dark."

Jen gasped. "If only he'd stopped by my room after seeing our son."

Nadia felt everything inside go still as she realized how distraught Jen was.

"Mom, I want very much to speak to him. Only, he won't answer my calls." A pause, and then she cried out like a wounded animal, "Oh, no! I've lost *everything*."

Nadia did her best to soothe her. Yet there was little more to say, so they ended the call with a promise to speak again.

Chapter Twenty-Five

. . . .

June 13 • Olympia

AS DAWN SIGNALED a new day, Kid kissed Cleo's mouth. Following some small talk and caressing, he got up from the bed and pulled on the usual olive-drab BDU pants. After saying farewell, he walked outside under scattered clouds and got behind the wheel of his beloved BMW. But he had neglected it to the point of shame. It was filthy, two tires needed air, and an amber CHECK ENGINE icon lit up every time he turned the ignition.

He ignored the warning as always and drove without a destination, hoping to open his mind to the sort of epiphany that could come by doing this. When nothing lit his neurons he sighed and drove to the shabby Apollo.

He could not have selected a more secluded place. The derelict, musty-smelling hotel overlooked one of Olympia's myriad waterways, the Eld Inlet. Staying here left him off-grid while letting him ease his tortured mind by watching the inlet's currents and tides. As a bonus, nobody in this hotel of mold and destitute wallpaper cared about his grimy hair and unshod status.

He was parking just as a light blue Chevy slowly cruised past the hotel. Kid eyed it and mumbled, "Another poor traveler wondering whether to check in. I would tell 'em to run while they stiff have a chance. But that's just me—"

He spent the morning studying until just before noon, when he got up to take a piss. But he postponed that when someone knocked on the door. Then, forgetting to the point of recklessness the lesson he should have learned from Goliath, he opened it.

The always-mellow Huck flashed an endearing smile. Like Kid, he was shoeless and shirtless. Unlike Kid, he held a gym bag containing drug paraphernalia. A moment later they were sitting cross-legged on the bed, and once Huck prepped the bong Kid used his new lighter to get it going. After taking a hit he passed the bong to Huck, who drew from it and exhaled khaki-colored smoke.

Huck's eyes followed the rising smoke while he said to the ceiling, "One day at the café? About a year ago? I kinda stumbled onto Cleo. We like, hit it off?"

Kid understood at once. "And you and she are still lovers."

The young man answered without fanfare. "Of course."

"It's how you ended up in the group."

"Yep. Also, she's big-time into white guys. Especially us blue-eyed devils."

"You think? Christ, she tried recruiting me through the bed. Only, I was still married." He looked away, "Well, at the time anyway."

"Yeah, I heard. Also heard you're poking her on a regular basis. But you're a gentleman who keeps things private." He took a hit. "So. You an' this Enzo guy. What's going on there?"

"What's to say? I've got the friggin' hots for him." He laughed. "Other than sex, we actually do have some things in common. Travel, for example. That sort of thing. Now that I think about it, traveling's what connects me to Sandro."

He didn't disclose that he wouldn't be sleeping with Sandro much longer now that he knew Ag's identity.

Huck gave his head a toss which sent his long blond hair flying. As the strands cleared from his face, this superb young man's blue eyes turned dark in a way Kid never thought possible. "I've heard how psycho Sandro is? So if he like, ever threatens you? Let me know? 'Cause I guarantee he'll never threaten you again."

Kid's pride kicked in. "I know how to fight."

"Yeah, maybe." All at once Huck gripped Kid's shoulders with strong hands, and his eyes blazed with a fierce light. "Listen to me! Sandro's poison. So if he gets like, too toxic? Tell me." Huck's face hardened. "He knows there's a line he'd better not cross with me."

Kid's hunch that Huck might be the group's power broker now seemed more likely. But there was more to Huck—a gentle soul who adored the daughter who'd been ripped from his heart. On impulse, Kid said, "Just so you know? I make sure my lovers are STD-free, like me."

"I trust you to do the right thing," a clearly relieved Huck said and fell silent. After a moment he shifted his long legs and looked sidelong at Kid. Then in a reverent tone, he said, "Come live with me, okay? We can build a life together. It'll be like, a good thing."

The emotionally battered yet mission-oriented Kid hadn't nurtured this bond with Huck for mission purposes only. He'd also done it for his soul. But he still had to perform Romeo duties, so to buy time he touched Huck's knee. "I'd like that. Can you give me a few days to get my shit together?"

"Of course," Huck whispered.

Their eyes met, they kissed, and in time Kid gently urged Huck onto his back and unzipped him. When the slacker released a pent-up moan several minutes later, they undressed completely and whispered and touched for almost an hour, until Huck joined his body to Kid's.

HUCK arched his far leg afterward and planted his foot flat atop the mattress, and once Kid entered his open arms, he smiled and planted a palm on Kid's bottom. Then an extraordinary thing occurred during their pillow talk: they began asking those questions people ask when they are truly in love: *Where were you born? How many siblings?* And most importantly: *Who was your favorite character in the original 'Star Wars'?*

But when a silence eventually hung in the air like smoke that wouldn't rise through a chimney, Huck cleared his throat. "Be careful when you leave Sandro. 'Cause once he's tired of his boyfriends? Or feels betrayed? He kills them."

Kid raised his head and narrowed his eyes. "You know this for a fact?"

"Abso-fucking-lutely. He strangles 'em while they're asleep."

All at once Huck got up and walked naked to the gym bag to reach inside and pull out a pistol.

Kid took it in at once. "Beretta. 92F. Nine mil."

This caught Huck's interest. "You know firearms?"

"My Papa. Remember?"

"Ah, that's right." Huck rejoined Kid and offered the pistol. "Anyway, it's for you."

He took the pistol and hefted it. The weight told him it was loaded, so he exercised great care while putting it on the nightstand.

They talked for a few more minutes until Huck said, "Gotta go to work." So he swung his feet to the floor and showered and said while pulling his jeans on, "Hey, Kid? Thank you for being in my life."

A very quiet Kid nodded while also pulling pants on, and after seeing Huck to the door he abruptly clung to him and blurted, "I love you very much."

The forever chill young man smiled a North Star smile. But then it dimmed, and he pointed at the pistol atop the nightstand. "For Sandro. For that day."

AFTER locking the door behind Huck, Kid put on some coffee. To kill time while it brewed he got the Beretta and released its magazine. Next, he pulled back the slide to empty the chamber of any ammunition. A 9mm hollow point popped out.

He caught it in his free hand and rapidly field-stripped the pistol, his hands obeying the muscle memory that builds upon enormous levels of practice with handguns, long guns, machine guns, and shotguns that he'd acquired under his father's expert guidance.

Kid examined the barrel's interior. Clean. Bright. Free of residue. He held it to his nose and inhaled. It smelled faintly of solvent, while the barrel's exterior glistened from a fine coating of lubricant. He checked the other components and found no flaws, which meant that Huck had lavished great care on its maintenance.

That, or Huck the mellow stoner swiped it from a conscientious owner. Because Kid understood a singular fact: Huck was the enemy, and Kid would not let their relationship cloud his judgment. "Even though I love him," he said to the empty room.

Then he sighed and tested himself by reassembling the weapon with his eyes closed. And now that he knew who he must use it against and why, he loaded it.

Once the coffee maker stopped gurgling he poured a cup and stepped onto the balcony. After a pleasant first sip of coffee, he stared at boughs of sun-shot green leaves from trees lining the sluggish waterway. Next, he peered into the shaggy corridors of light streaming through the green canopies and said, "Damn."

Six months ago he had an adoring wife, twin daughters whom he revered, and a son on the way. Now he felt a dull ache from not seeing them, and now Jen was gone.

He swallowed the last of the java and scratched his exposed ribs while wondering what to do next. On impulse, he climbed inside his filthy Beamer and fired it up. Ignoring the engine warning lights, he burned rubber while speeding off—a man without a destination.

WHEN he spotted Marty's car in his rearview ten minutes later, they met on a side street where Marty first checked Kid for electronic bugs. Once Marty gave the nod, he peered at Kid. "I love you like I do my sons. That's why it hurts like hell to see you like this." He ran some fingers through Kid's filthy long hair, then pointed at the young man's bare feet. "Part of the new look?"

Kid scoffed and squinted against the sun. "It's not a look. It's me. Now are we done?"

"No. Listen up. There's a new urgency in the wake of that latest hit." When Kid replied with a blank stare, Marty said, "The dam? The other day?"

"Dam?"

"Jesus. It released millions of gallons of water. Aren't you even watching the news?"

A fury in Kid came alive, his face turning beet red and his hands becoming fists. "Shut up! Right now! Just shut the fuck up and don't you dare start in on me, *Uncle* Marty."

He must have surprised even himself because he stepped back until he got his breathing under control. When he spoke again it was with a respectful tone. "I was about to say I might be onto a new connection with one of the gang's leaders. Now what's this about a dam?"

"Identical scenario to the Beaver incident. Loads of water. Zero deaths or injuries. There's more. Last night the Florida Keys went dark for five hours to the millisecond. We must find out if Agamemnon has established a failsafe system; we *must*."

Kid scuffed a foot against the sidewalk, only to curse when he lost a bit of skin to the concrete. "No shit. It's why I've become a male whore." He looked sidelong at Marty. "Well? Aren't you gonna say how disgusted you are with me?"

Marty rubbed his chin, deep in thought. "You were briefed on this contingency."

"Briefings don't smooth out the rough edges."

"Even so, you knew this going in."

"Wait one goddamned minute." Kid narrowed his eyes. "Are you trying to read policy exemptions to me? Are we going down *that* road?"

"No." Marty draped an arm around Kid's bare shoulder and said to a distant hill, "It's tough, isn't it? Springing and spinning between two worlds? That of the fledgling physician, and a world inhabited by pseudo-intellectuals; self-anointed saviors who would thrust Earth into a state of barbarism while chanting, 'Happy, happy, joy, joy'."

"I get it," Kid said to his feet.

Marty showed soft eyes. "I believe we were discussing your conversion into a male whore."

"Yeah, we were." Unable to help himself, he flashed a smile at Marty. "Here it is. I'm sleeping with women, but more and more with guys. It seems that sucking dicks and taking it up the ass helps intellectual snobs feel good about themselves. Jesus, I'm being buggered senseless."

Marty said, "On the plus side? It seems you're crazy good at being used."

Kid surprised even himself when his chest swelled with pride. "Isn't that what I hired on for? To be the Romeo everyone thinks I am?"

"No. Not really." The older man studied the younger one before saying, "I'm here if you want to talk."

Kid grimaced. "Have you the slightest idea how much I wanna kill Sandro while I'm screwing him? So, yeah. You're spot on. Talking and compartmentalizing helps." He looked at Marty and offered a heartfelt, "Thanks for listening to me."

"Anytime, Kid. Anytime. Just know that we have complete trust in your ability to finish this assignment. Turning to other news, your papa's doing fine. There'll be a memorial service for Monica two days from now. He knows you want to come. Don't. He said to tell you, and I quote, 'the mission is priority one.'"

"Thanks for the word on Papa." He looked Marty in the eye. "Hey? I'll get these bastards even if it kills me."

Marty whispered, "I know."

"Wait. Losing Jen? When I needed her the most? I... oh, Jesus." All at once he buried his face against the taller man's shoulder and wept while Marty made soothing noises and gently massaged Kid's neck. Then the unofficial uncle began the chant Kid recited while putting down his beloved dog: "It's okay, it's all right. I'm right here…"

"THANKS," Kid said afterward. After swiping at his tears he said to the ground, "You must think I'm a pussy."

Marty touched Kid's chin and tugged until their eyes met and said with a heartfelt voice, "Totally." He offered an engaging smile and added, "Levi once said that it takes a strong man to be a *gentle* man. You're strong. Although, well, you're still a pussy. Just thought you should know." He playfully cuffed the side of Kid's head.

"In your dreams." Kid flipped him off but failed to stop the smile tugging at his lips. Once it faded he provided the details on Huck, adding, "I need you to run a check on him."

"Got it." Marty looked at Kid. "Any reason?"

"My gut's speaking to me." He opened and closed his mouth several times before saying, "He's one of their leaders. A short time ago he fingered Sandro as a possible threat and gave me a pistol."

He frowned. "Uncle Marty? Every fiber of my body… everything I know about reading people is telling me they want Sandro out of the way. They also want it done soon, because the Fourth is around the corner and they're ready to act. All that's left is the question of how to deal with Sandro… because they want me to do it. Probably another loyalty test."

He took a step toward Marty and rested a hand on the older man's forearm. "Uncle Marty? The thing is? I've fallen in love with Huck and, well, I need to know more about him in case—" He tightened his grip on Marty's arm. "In case I have to kill him, too."

The man Kid knew as Uncle Marty looked him over. "You possess great integrity, Kid. Draw from that." He added in a very kind voice, "You've grown up, son. Before my eyes. Yep. You sure have. Also? I love you. We all do."

Kid watched a flock of birds flying past before saying, "Thank you for always being here for me."

"Anytime. Now let's clear out before the violins begin playing." All at once he grinned at Kid. "In case I don't tell you often enough? You are one hot hunk of man flesh!" He winked while Kid flashed a broad smile and flipped him off again.

· · ·

Kid waited a few minutes after Marty walked off before returning to his car. "Where to now?" All at once he knew, and following a short drive, his tires were crunching the gravel on Bill's driveway.

He began the visit by discussing politics amid the electrical odors and humming HEPA filtering machines—although at one point Ag sniffed pointedly and asked, "Don't you ever bathe?"

"Sorry," Kid said, and said as if wondering about the weather, "The day Jamal introduced us, I got to wondering. What happens if you get sick and can't do your thing on the 4th?"

Ag looked away. "Um, we've been working on a stand-in. Someone I can teach. You know, just in case." But after disclosing this he clammed up.

To counter any suspicion, Kid turned the conversation to other topics until he play-punched Bill's shoulder and said, "Gotta go. Thanks for letting me stop by."

MINUTES later he was en route to the Apollo. But while entering the parking lot he looked up in time to see that same blue Chevy coasting by. He waited until it was out of sight before shutting off the Beamer's motor. As its heated pistons and cylinders made their cooling sounds, Kid saw the wisdom in Marty's advice to arm himself and decided to carry the Beretta at all times.

· · ·

It was almost five by the time he turned on the TV and found a news station still reporting on the latest dam event. Following this, he grabbed the bottle of Glenlivet he'd developed a personal relationship with lately and stepped out onto the river-view balcony. Three fingers of the good stuff helped him unwind enough to think.

As he grew mellow he reached two conclusions: he no longer had anything to go home to—no wife, and perhaps no Harvard Med. In the plus column, he had Huck and Britney—one to love and be loved in return, the other to make babies with.

Another finger of booze went down his gullet while he wondered, *What if I follow Marty's path as a full-time operative? I'd pack heat while traveling the world and loving the adventures, along with lots of ladies.*

There could be no answer. Not yet anyway. His current role remained the only certainty. So he gamed some scenarios involving Sandro and took a final slug of the Glenlivet. Seconds later he stood to go inside when he heard the whine of an outboard engine. A skiff appeared a moment later as it turned into the Eld. As it drew closer he spotted Roo in a patchwork flannel shirt at the tiller.

She killed the engine while still thirty feet from the hotel dock and coasted to a perfect stop, then secured the skiff and climbed a shallow bank leading from the dock. She knocked at his door a minute later.

"Howdy do?" she said by way of greeting.

He invited her inside with a sweep of an arm. "Howdy do, yourself."

"Doin' okay." She looked at him with an animal stare. "I hear you been banging the hell outta Sandro… along with every woman you look at. Yes, sir. From the sound of it, I'm danged if you ain't randier than a three-balled tomcat."

"Oh? You've known a few three-balled toms?"

Roo burst into laughter. "Well if'n I ever did, I'll bet a ticket to a rodeo they never got as much tail as you been gettin'. 'Course, I hear talk about a few guys who're havin' at it with *your* tail." She looked pointedly at the bed, then at him.

THEY rested afterward, and once they were dressed Kid led her to the balcony. As dusk began a slow fade-in, they watched the inlet's changing colors in silence—at least until Roo hawked up a lunger and spat a huge gob onto the grass below, and said without looking at him, "Be careful with that there Cleo. She's manipulative."

"I can handle her." Turning to her, he asked, "How did you and she meet, anyway?"

Roo sighed and said as if bored, "At university."

Kid picked up on the British expression. "Oxford? Or Cambridge?"

She glanced at him as if dealing with a dullard. "Sure as shit you don't know much, do ya boy?" Roo rolled her eyes and broke into perfect grammar, minus the Texan twang. "I had the good fortune to be offered a Rhodes Scholarship. So, Oxford. Cleo and I shared a room."

"What did you read?"

"Ah, I see you know the colloquialism. Excellent. In answer to your inquiry, I read Economic and Social History."

"PhD?"

"Naturally." She showed a tiny smile. "Although the Brits call it a DPhil."

"Admirable. Your variable speech patterns?"

While looking out over the water she asked, *"Eres fluido en Portugués, ¿verdad?"*

"Yes, I'm fluent in Portuguese. Also Italian, French, and Spanish. You know this."

"Ja osaa saksaa ja suomea."

Kid nodded. "Yes, and conversant in German and Finnish. By the by, you speak the latter without an accent. What's your point?"

"I should think that you switch between languages without effort. Ja? Oui?"

"Good analogy. Your Texan speech patterns are…"

"Native to me. T'ain't nothin' to it, neither. Switching to upper-class English, that is."

He was about to say something when a bird cried out from the dense green trees. So he took her hand in his instead and held it. When she squeezed his in return they sat until Kid broke the hush. "Is Roo your real name?"

"Hells bells, no. It's Katarina."

Kid thought his heart would seize up as new tumblers fell into place. "Has a nice flow."

Roo added, "Katarina Ruth Jones; Roo's short for Ruth." She drew a deep breath. "Anyway, you also need to be careful 'round Sandro. He's cruel. That no-good sumbitch just don't know how to treat people right. Nossir, he sure don't. 'Course, I reckon you already done found that out fer yourself. 'Specially in bed."

"He submits to *my* will, not the other way around. He…" Kid stifled a gasp as it hit home. Then following a brief pause—a rest between the notes on a piece of sheet music—he said, "You've slept with him."

She said to the darkening trees, "Reckon I have."

"Huh. I didn't know he slept with women."

"He don't."

"Then why…"

"He needed his Green Card. So him an' me done got married."

Kid said a silent Ah. "Guess you're not the first couple to go that route and then divorce."

"Oh, we ain't divorced. Balls walls, Kid. Him an' me? We got us a passel of children."

"*Whaaat?*"

"Sure. Come on, son. Sandro *is* handsome. An' smart." She showed a little smile. "Okay, so maybe the sumbitch is *bain dramaged.*"

Kid laughed at the little joke out of politeness.

"So, yeah. What the hell. I decided to breed with him. Yessir, we got three young'uns. Cody? Just turned six. As fer Sarah Jean? The little princess is gonna be four next month. Zane? Danged if he ain't already pushin' three." A breeze ruffled her hair. "Guess it's how it is with you faggots. You sleep with women an' give 'em babies jist fer show. Except deep down all yer thinkin' about is gettin' that next dick."

He nodded as the scent of fir hit his nose with a sublime quality. "So no divorce."

Roo said in a slow deliberate way, "Nope. 'Cause there ain't no way I'm lettin' him off no hook. I jerk that rein, an' he goes the direction I want."

"But you don't live together."

She smiled, the teacher regarding the slow student. "Well hell, boy! He is a gol-durned *faggot* ain't he? No offense meant. Anyway, now that I ain't got nothin' that varmint wants? Now that he's got his Card? Nossir. He lives his life, I live mine. Ain't that a hoot?"

She cackled on while Kid nodded. *It's a hoot, all right. Because it means Roo's the driving source. Not Cleo, not Huck; surely not Sandro.* The logic seemed spot-on. Except for one wrinkle: logic doesn't exist among off-grid terrorists.

Then for a reason he would never be able to explain, a switch tripped his brain's synapses. *Wait! The name Katarina could mean Roo's simply a connecting force. Because she just doesn't quite seem to be their leader. No. It's Jamal. He's their top dog; the real key. An' danged if that don't fit the lock to their sanctum sanctorum. Yee haw.*

Roo glanced at him as if she were telepathic. "We done got a new job lined up for you."

His eyebrows formed arches. "I'm listening."

"Boat crew. Ya see, we done earmarked an island fer us to use. Patos Island, in Upper Puget Sound? It's uninhabited but it's got an old lighthouse, 'long with the lighthouse keeper's cottage. We can live in the cottage, an' won't nobody else will wanna come there fer survival 'cause there ain't no food or stuff. Right about now Jamal's seein' a man 'bout buyin' a large sailboat fer us to git back an' forth on. He heard you crewed on some racing yachts."

Leaping at the opening, Kid asked, "So what's in it for you? Pulling the power?"

Roo reverted to her learned speech patterns. "You shouldn't be at all surprised to learn that global collapse shall inevitably visit our planet. Every key indicator is in place—the social and economic tumblers; the *pain*." She shook her head. "Earth's inhabitants have become an animal in a cage that doesn't dare leave it—not even if the door's opened. It paces instead."

Kid grimaced. "Rilke. *The Panther*."

She spat another lunger onto the grass below. "Give the man a see-gar."

"Sooo, our task is to prod people with a stick and get them moving."

She spoke to the river as it passively flowed past. "Yes. The pressing question then becomes, why wait? Have we not already polluted our planet enough? Have not a sufficient number of the world's scientists declared that climate change may doom our planet by this century's end? Do you not see that we're already bordering on collapse?"

"Put a stop to it all while we're ahead."

Her face shone with a sudden radiance even as the sky turned darker, and she began speaking with the passion so often born of a pathological disorder. "Kid? I've awaited your arrival for months. In fact, I've *yearned* for someone of your depth; a man who sees what I see." Her eyes began to glow. "You're the one I've sought for so long."

"Why?"

"Dunno. T'ain't somethin' I can 'zactly git a handle on. So I jist try an' trust my guts an' my liver." She squeezed his hand and began speaking to the planet again—to the river, to the trees and to the sky. "Your task in our new order is clear. With your brains? Your looks and charm? An' bein' pre-med? We'll press you into rebuilding a new generation.

Yessir, we're going to pass that torch to those who shall continue fighting for our grand cause."

"Kennedy's inaugural address," he whispered.

"Oh, Kid. I could kiss you for that. Yes, an' we want your torch."

Kid's gut clenched when he understood. "You mean my penis. Don't you?"

"Hell, darling. Of course… along with yer sperm-makin' balls. Yep, we're gonna put you out to stud. You're gonna breed babies, boy. Fact is, you're gonna give *me* some babies. Hell, fer all I know, you mighta put one in me just now."

She stared at the darkening sky. "Huck's also gonna breed. An' Christ if he ain't already got himself a harem." She smiled. "That leaves Jamal. He'll mate with Cleo."

"Cleo's in love with me." He said this while a breeze ruffled his hair.

"Yeah. I already done seen that fer myself." Roo looked at him with something that bordered on respect. "Danged if you don't know women."

Kid said in a low tone, "I know pain."

She gripped his hand. "Reckon you do. Else you wouldn't be here." She hesitated. "Sandro's gonna have to go his own way soon enough—an' you're the one who's gonna make sure he does."

"Anything for the cause," Kid told the river, and with his cautionary conversation with Marty so fresh in his mind, Kid's instincts went on full alert—instincts that were validated after Roo invited herself to stay the night and avail herself of Kid's other instinctual qualities.

Chapter Twenty-Six

. . . .

June 14 • Flag Day • Olympia

SANDRO'S UPPER LIP curled into a snarl. "Because I said so."

But Agamemnon was also stoking his boiler, and his deep scowl revealed itself even in the darkened room. He felt like kicking Sandro up one side, and down the other. Following a micro-sec of contemplation, he swiveled his head away from his monitor screens and looked Sandro in the eye. "Not good enough. Tell me the reason why, you bloodless bastard."

It was just after eight in the morning, he hadn't slept well, his coffee had yet to kick in and he didn't like Sandro even on the best of days.

"Very well. I shall humor you. It is to send a message. One that informs them that we are not to be dismissed." Sandro's shapeless black shirt rustled as he jabbed a finger at the mouse. "Now do it!"

Ag's face flushed purple against his blue bathrobe and he said between clenched teeth, "People will die."

"They will. Sí. Also, even more will meet their demise when we implement our plan's final phase."

Cleo rested a bejeweled hand on Ag's shoulder. "It's for the greater good, love."

Ag grumbled. "Same excuse the Nazis gave for the Holocaust." But Cleo still had her hand on his shoulder, and since he wanted her to keep it there he sighed and left-clicked the mouse. "There."

She bussed his ear. "Lovely that, pet."

In the meantime, Sandro grinned as he visualized what was unfolding seven thousand and five hundred miles to the west.

Bangkok's Siriraj Hospital sits on the west bank of the Chao Phraya River. It was late evening in the Thai city, yet the hospital remained locked in its myriad daily activities of surgical procedures, MRI sessions, and the constant mayhem of its walk-in clinic.

Mere seconds before Ag clicked the mouse a thoracic surgeon made an incision that exposed the heart of a child who'd been rushed to the O.R. for emergency surgery. The surgeon repositioned the scalpel and was about to incise next to an aorta when the room went pitch dark.

Generators failed to kick in. Machines that pumped blood and oxygen seized up. There were no emergency lights beyond a dozen flashlights.

No power, no way to keep the child alive, and no hope. The child died minutes later, just before the power mysteriously returned.

"Now do that hospital in Madrid," Sandro said.

Ag positioned the cursor and was about to click it when the exterior basement door banged open and a voice boomed, "Halt!"

Huck's command still hung in the air even as he dashed in and gripped Ag's hand. "No," he said and brushed the mouse aside. He glared at Cleo and Sandro and chopped a hand through the air. "Ag's like, proven his ability? So we don't need to take out any more people? Or God forbid, any kids? We like, know we're ready now? To proceed?"

Sandro grumbled while managing to avoid Huck's eyes. Cleo winced but said nothing. Ag's shoulders slumped from relief.

· · ·

Kid's shoulders slumped from weariness; a weariness that came from the roles he felt forced to play. There were the lies required of him, and of course he had his Romeo assignments. Then for some reason he would never understand, he recalled Mr. Miyagi's line from *The Karate Kid*: "You karate do *guess so*, get squish, just like grape."

These anarchists were a threat to the entire world. Kid had to go all out or get squished. With that soul-rattling issue settled, he spent the day studying.

· · ·

"Papa?"

Michael Bailey flinched at the sound of her voice. He had lost ten pounds following his wife's death and didn't feel like talking. Not to Jen, not to anyone. Still, he felt a higher duty, so after verifying that she was using the secure phone he'd given her, he stared outside his Vanguard office window at the passersby navigating the noon time streets. "Hello, Jen."

"I heard about Monica. I called to offer my condolences."

"Thank you. Now I hate to cut you short, but I have some urgent business…"

"Papa! Please hear me out. I'm so sorry for this big mess with Kid. The thing is, I'd have given him a pass for sleeping around. That is until he invited his Harvard hottie to Olympia.

"Papa, he did her in bed. He did her in a damn parking lot. He did her who knows where else. Now it's clear that he's been carrying on an affair with her for months. But what's worse is that he lied to me. I... I could've worked things out with him if he would've admitted to it all. He didn't, and I find that intolerable."

"Why don't you believe him?"

"Because I saw videos of him screwing that bimbo till she couldn't walk!"

Michael narrowed his eyes at a Diamond Taxicab swerving to avoid a motorcyclist on a dark green Harley with black leather saddlebags. "Videos?"

"Yes. I... well, someone sent them to me."

He frowned and dropped his voice an octave. "Who?"

"I don't know." She sniffled. "But I saw them going at it like rabbits until... until—" Her voice faded away. "I'm now given to understand that he got her pregnant."

"Jesus." Michael went to the mini-bar and reached for a bottle. He didn't care which one, so long as it dulled the pain. But with his hand halfway around a Woodford Reserve, he stepped away to gather his thoughts.

When he felt ready, he asked, "Jen. Sweetheart. Why didn't you come to me? Or to Levi? We'd have reviewed the videos. *Jen.* Don't you see? They could be deepfakes."

"... Deep—? Oh my God! Of course. I... that never occurred to me."

Michael switched off his grief long enough to use the kindly voice of the father-in-law who had loved this girl since she was five. "Think about it. What reason would someone have to send videos to you, or to say he fathered a child?"

"I don't know. The sender's anonymous."

"Of course." Michael drew a deep breath. "Let's review. Kid told me and Levi that Britney showed up uninvited. He admits to fooling around, but that they did not have sex. It's why we called you." He paused. "What did Kid tell you?"

"The same. Claimed she showed up unannounced. I—" All at once she broke down, and Michael's heart went out to her while she blubbered like a child.

In time he said, "Jen? Kid's gone deep-role. Now for the love of God, if you care about the father of your children, do not call him. I repeat, *do not call* or otherwise attempt to reach out to Kid, or you'll place him in grave jeopardy." He paused and said with nothing but kindness in his voice, "Hey? Email the videos to me. We'll examine them. Also, Jen? I'd like to stop by and see you. I can leave D.C. in ten minutes and reach your home in two hours. Would that be okay?"

NADIA'S secure phone vibrated. A glance at the caller ID sent her walking out of her daily staff meeting to a more private space. "Jen?"

"Mom, I... oh god—" Jen erupted into a keening wail.

"*Jen.* Tell me what's going on."

Jen described her conversation with Michael, ending with, "... Anyway, that's what Papa told me. Mom? Did Kid sleep with his college friend, or not?"

Nadia's charcoal gray linen skirt wrinkled as she sat on a folding metal chair in a hallway of industrial tile walls and a popcorn ceiling. After crossing her ankles, she said, "Kid insists that he did not. He's never lied to me and I've no reason not to believe him now."

"Then it's..." Her voice caught. "Then it's true? He didn't?"

"Yes." After a prolonged silence, Nadia asked, "Jen, darling. Why don't I stop by?"

HACKSAW Jones put aside his coffee mug, and while its steam swirled around his head and laced his nostrils with a double-jolt aroma, the small man of Congolese descent looked up from his Vanguard Ops monitor and glanced from Levi to Michael. "They're deepfakes."

Michael edged closer. "How can you be sure?"

"Through DVD… Deepfake Video-Detection system. Its programs are ninety-nine percent accurate and constantly honed. Feds have been using it for years. These videos are fake."

Levi rubbed his chin, deep in thought. "So that's not really Kid in the videos?"

"Oh, it's him all right. At least in one of them." Hack swept a hand at his monitor. "Our strapping young prince is in bed with Cleo, and they are engaged in intercourse. Only, he didn't deny doin' it with her to Jen. The video showing him and the Harvard gal standing in the parking lot is also real. However, the ones purporting to show Kid and Britney having intercourse in the car and in bed were faked."

Levi peered sidelong at Michael. "Well?"

"We say nothing to Kid. It'll only upset him further. I'll have a face-to-face with Jen and explain why she must not mention knowing they're fake until the mission's completed."

"Concur," Levi said. Then while pointing at Hack's cup of steaming coffee, he asked, "Any more where that came from?"

Hack grunted. "Why? You feel the need to doctor some java with a bit of Jameson's?"

"You read my mind. Hack? Michael? Join me?"

Chapter Twenty-Seven

· ·

June 15 • Olympia

"BASTARDO! YOU ARE late, you... you bastard!"

Kid looked over his shoulder in time to see flecks of saliva flying from an enraged Sandro's lips.

The Spaniard jabbed a finger at him. "You are my lover. This means you must check with me when you do not come home in time."

Despite the evening's warm temperature, Kid was wearing an unbuttoned brown shirt for the sole purpose of concealing the 9mm Beretta in the small of his back.

"Well?" Sandro demanded.

"Hey. Deep cleansing breath. I stopped at the mall for something to eat." He held up an index finger. "Now here's the thing. I don't answer to you. It's the other way around." Without seeming to, he got ready to go to Duke City if Sandro went psycho on him.

Sandro did in fact appear headed in that direction when he tapped an index finger against his temple and shouted, "If you only knew what I want to do to you, up here!" He jabbed his temple a final time and leveled dark eyes at Kid just as someone knocked at the door.

"I'll get it," Kid said at once—if only to leave Sandro fuming. Throwing caution aside, he opened the door.

He saw the silver pistol first… then the cast and the hate-filled eyes. "Shit!"

Too late. Gun Guy barged inside and leveled the pistol at Kid's chest. "Hands up, you *pendejo bastardo*." Then he pointed the muzzle at Sandro, who screamed like a eunuch and ran into the bedroom.

Gun Guy charged after him.

Malee meowed in anger.

Kid drew his pistol.

Seconds later the sounds of glass shattering were followed by an eerie silence.

Malee ran beneath the sofa.

Kid slipped out the front door, and let the India-ink night cloak him while he padded away and took cover behind Sandro's Nissan.

Gun Guy appeared in the doorway seconds later, his eyes burning with fury. He was tall and wiry, his black hair was cut short, and two thin strips were shaved to the skin on both sides. There were small black spacers in each earlobe, he wore dirty leather pants and black engineer boots, and his shirtless torso revealed about fifteen gang tattoos.

Nearly all of the tatts were in black ink, save for about four red ones. A few depicted guns and knives; others, eyeballs of various designs, several girls' names, along with a star tattooed around his navel. A silver chain dangling from his neck featured a miniature gold-framed painting of the Virgin Mary.

After peering through the dark night he pointed a finger at Kid. "There choo are. So. That bastard Alessandro, he has crashed through the window." He stepped forward while waving his pistol around. "That *fawker* is making the running through the woods. Me? I not chase him. Why? Because he will be gone all night. Making the hiding, jes? So I will catch him later." He edged closer. "And choo are the ass-a-hole who break my finger, no?"

They were close enough for Kid to smell tobacco, earth, and sweat—a masculine odor that was neither pleasing nor off-putting—and the thug's leather pants creaked whenever he moved. But even though Kid had his Beretta pointed at his chest, Gun Guy didn't appear to see it in the consuming darkness.

As Gun Guy's black eyes drilled holes through Kid, his breathing grew heavier in a sign of pending violence. Sure enough, he held up his cast and growled, "Choo mother-fawker. Look what you do to me. I should keel you. Also that cocksucker Allesandro. But first choo are going to get on chore knees and lick my *huevos*. Then choo will suck my cock." He was stepping closer with murder in his eyes and pistol aloft when to Kid's utter surprise he pocketed it and studied Kid's face.

"So ho-kay. Still you no show the fear. But choo remember me, jes?"

Kid bit the next words off. "I remember breaking your finger."

The darkly handsome thug threw his head back and laughed. "Sí. You did. Well ho-kay, I am Jorge. And you?"

"Me? I'm the guy aiming a Beretta at your heart." He held it aloft for Jorge to see.

"Hmm. So maybe you choote me now, no?"

"Or maybe not. And kudos for not showing fear." Kid slid the pistol into the small of his back.

The thug grunted. "So. Choo got me again, just like you got me the last time. Hey, I respect you for that, even though choo are a pussy boy. A very pretty one. Mmmmm, jes."

Kid snorted. "Pussy boy? So you're telling me that pussy boys routinely disarm you, break your finger, and leave you on the floor crying like a schoolgirl? Is that it?"

"Fawk you." Then as if they were high school buddies greeting each other behind the gym during lunch, the thug pulled a pack of Marlboros from his pants pocket and stuck one between his lips. After digging an anodized metal Zippo lighter from another pocket, he lit up, closed the lighter's cap with a careless flick of the wrist, dragged deep at the cancer stick, held the smoke, and finally exhaled while sending twin jets of gray-blue smoke from his nostrils.

As the smoke climbed in the heat of the night's air, he took another drag and squinted at Kid. "That day? At the café? So... I never would have shot you. So ho-kay. Choo did not know this at the time. Is why I have for you the respect. But? It does not mean I will not pay you back for what choo do to me, my friend. I must. It is for the honor."

"I understand," Kid replied.

"Hmm, choo must be Allesandro's bitch-boy. Therefore I *must* fawk you. For the honor."

"As if," Kid muttered. He gave his head a toss which sent his long hair flying. Then he studied his adversary. Jorge's syntax and subject-verb agreements differed from Sandro's equally laborious sentence structures, which Kid attributed to Sandro's Catalan dialect versus Jorge's provincial Spanish.

Jorge's teeth were another puzzle. Although the thug enjoyed deadly attractive looks to go with his taut rawboned body, his meth-decayed teeth at the café had ruined the effect. Only, the teeth were no longer decayed.

Kid narrowed his eyes. "That day at the coffee shop. You had bad teeth. Meth mouth."

The bandito grunted. "*Mi amigos* and me? We put on them the black stuff. To make the disguise, no? People see rotten teeth, they no look up to see the handsome face I have."

"Good idea," Kid admitted before adding, "Now listen up. I broke your finger righteously and you speak of respect. Yet you're coming after me. Why?"

Jorge reared back in surprise. "Huh? Choo? Sheet, man. I not here for you. I not even know choo would be here. I came after that cocksucker Sandro."

Kid frowned before nodding. "Ahh, that's right. He said you were his lover."

"He say *whaaat?*" A sudden fury began working behind his dark eyes. "He was never my lover. And I am no faggot!" He spat on the floor. "That *pendejo*... that ass-a-hole... that—that *Español* bastard. No... *Julio* was his lover."

Creases erupted across Kid's forehead. "Who's Julio?"

"Julio is my leetle brother. And that fawking Sandro, he keel him."

"Hold on." Kid stood still beneath gloomy skies that were mercifully laced by evergreen scents and nightbird songs. Then while stroking his chin he asked, "If you're out for Sandro, why the hell are you following me around? And don't deny it. I've seen your car driving by."

"You? Why would I follow you? Choo I respect, even though you are not a man, but only a gorl." The thug showed a very male smile. "Hmm. I think choo would like to be *my* gorl. Jes?"

"Doubtful." Kid drew himself up to his full height and narrowed his eyes into slits.

"Hah. You make with the joke. But choo have no choice. Because now I take you inside and fawk you on that *pendejo* Sandro's bed. He will hear that I did this, and be too mad to see the straight lines." Jorge edged closer, his eyes glinting with pure masculine interest as he gripped Kid's arm.

When Kid resisted, the thug snarled. "I am not making the kidding around. Let's go, bitch. Or I will fawking hurt choo."

Kid shook free and rolled his eyes. "Get serious for a moment. Tell me why you've been driving past wherever I go?"

Jorge regarded Kid with intense curiosity. "If you see me drive by, is because I have been searching for Julio's car. My girlfriend, she last saw it here, at this place. She thinks Julio and Sandro have the sex, so she follows Julio to a new place he was staying. I search for him. Here. There. All over. Many times. Then I am told today Julio is been keeled. Shot in the head."

"I see." Kid tuned into the warm inviting soil against his soles, smelled the forest's fertile mosses, and listened to the night sounds while running the numbers. Finally he asked, "How well do you know Sandro?"

A flash of anger darkened Jorge's face. "Why do you want to know this?"

"Shut up and listen. Do you know if he had a Caucasian lover? A good looking young guy?"

"Dustin," the thug said at once.

Kid's heart raced. "That's the one."

"Sí. Julio, he tell me that Sandro made the brag about killing Dustin. Sandro say to Julio, 'This Norteamericano, he no sleep with me. Also, he knows too much. Then Sandro brags about knowing another hombre. His name is Agamemnon. Sandro says this hombre visits your café."

A bolt of electricity shot through Kid. *Christ! There's so much more to this. I need to get this punk aboard.* "What do you know about Agamemnon?"

"Only what Sandro say to my brother: *Este hombre es muy grande.*"

"This man is very big," Kid translated, and figured Jorge wasn't giving him a snow job.

But this presented a problem. What Jorge told him about Sandro and Dustin is hearsay evidence, and therefore inadmissible in court. However, the raw info could lead investigators to tangible evidence. Feeling his way with great care, Kid focused on Julio and Sandro. "Did Julio say *where* Sandro killed Dustin?"

The thug drew from his cigarette and exhaled. He took another drag while regarding Kid with half-lidded eyes, almost as if trying to make up his mind. All at once he dropped the cigarette, his leather pants squeaking as he ground it under the heel of his boot, his eyes turning cold and cruel. "Choo are a twink; a fawking pussy. It is not your place to ask questions of a man. Chore job is to cook for chore man, and to take care of his needs."

Kid put on his street fighter look. "Shut the fuck up and answer me before I break the rest of your fingers."

Jorge's hands turned to fists. But he hesitated and finally said, "Julio, he say to me that Allesandro kill Dustin near this cottage."

"All right. Next question. When do you come to trial for that café job?"

"Not until October." He looked daggers at Kid and lifted his chin in anger. "Why do you want to know this, you fawking faggot?"

"Because you might swing a deal with the prosecutor to avoid prison by testifying against Sandro for killing Julio. But you'll also disclose everything you know about Dustin."

"Fawk that. I will hunt Allesandro down and cut off his huevos. After I feed them to him? And I will… I will put the bullet through his brain. Then I come back here and bend you over and fawk you for what choo do to my finger." He raised his cast high.

"Sure. Take revenge. End up in prison. Be the forgotten nobody." Kid paused for effect. "Or, be *el familia* hero. The respected son who put Julio's killer away for life; the son who put him in a prison with vicious inmates who will knock his teeth out on day one so that he'll give better blowjobs."

The thug regarded him with deep suspicion. "What do choo got against him?"

Kid knew he was walking a tightrope between passivity and a guy ready to fight, and that he must provide a motive to explain his anger. "He's been stealing from me." He raised an eyebrow. "Well? Do you want to cut a deal?"

"Hmm. This would be good for the vengeance for Julio. But this would be all I would make the contract over—for Julio."

"No good."

"What else, then? Huh?"

"I already explained. You'll help link Sandro to Dustin's murder."

Jorge fell silent and looked away, eventually scuffing his boot against the dirt and asking, "What else is in it for me?"

Kid peered at him in the blackness and asked the question he already knew the answer to. "What else do you want?"

The thug lit a fresh cigarette and stared at Kid. "Choo. That's what else."

"Forget it. I'm not gonna be your lover."

The thug got an amused look. "Hey, I tell you before. I am not the *maricón*."

Kid mentally translated: faggot.

"I only want to make choo my bitch for breaking my finger. I also want that cock-sucking Allesandro to know I fawked his husband. Which I will do. An' then I will sell choo to my friends, and they will turn choo into a bored-out whore."

"Not gonna happen."

"Then we do not have the deal."

"I—" Kid thought fast. *Fuck it.* '*You karate do guess so, get squish, just like grape.*' "All right. I'll go to your bed—and only yours—but only after you talk to the authorities."

A smile tugged at the corners of Jorge's lips and curled itself into a snake. "Sí, I think we make the deal."

Kid's brain reeled. *If this thug knows Ag's name, he could open who knows how many other doors.*

"Wait. You'll have to give up something else." Kid was thinking of Sandro's pistol since forensics could show if it had been used to kill Sandro's victims. But despite having lawful access to the cottage, he couldn't let the Spaniard's surveillance cameras see him taking it. They must show Jorge stealing the pistol as part of a theft, instead of a search for evidence.

So he said, "Sandro has a pistol inside his nightstand drawer. There's also a ton of heroin on the kitchen table." He pinned Jorge with a stare and jutted his jaw at the cottage. "Bring the pistol to me, keep the smack for yourself."

The thug looked sidelong at Kid. "I have never used drugs. Not ever." He chuckled. "Choo are surprised to hear this, no?"

"I'll admit that I am. I'm also happy to know you don't."

"Ah, good. So you see? I am not that bad. No drugs. So ho-kay, maybe the marijuana. Also, Tequila. Mostly the *cerveza*. The robbery? So jes, I did the wrong thing. We

266 • RICHARD CRAIG ANDERSON

wanted money to send to our homes. *Para enviar a nuestras familias.*"

Kid nodded. *To our families.*

"Also, I say again—I would not have used the *pistola* on you that day." He made the sign of the cross and looked intently at Kid.

"Ya know what? I believe you."

"Hmm. Good." Jorge turned quiet before saying, "I think choo are right. That ass-a-hole Sandro, he will suffer much more in the prison. They will make him die each day."

"Go get the pistol. Once you've done that we'll exchange phone numbers. It could take days before someone's ready to discuss a deal. But they will, and I'll call you with instructions."

Jorge nodded and said in a no-nonsense voice, "If these others say there is no deal? You will come to my bed anyway. For the payback. Jes?"

Kid had to concede, if only to bait Jorge into doing his bidding. "All right. Now get going. We don't have much time left." Kid flicked his eyes at the cottage.

The instant Jorge began walking toward it, Kid called Sandro to make sure he wasn't somewhere nearby and watching everything unfold.

Sandro's phone rang four times before he answered with a loud, "Is he gone?"

Because he didn't hear the Spaniard's phone chiming, or hear his loud voice except through his earpiece, he concluded that Sandro was a fair distance away. "The guy's still inside. Me? I'm hiding out front. Where the fuck are you?"

"I am near the small river."

Kid knew the one he meant. It was at least half a mile away, and he heard the tinny whine of an outboard motor coming through the phone. Then Sandro cried out. "Malee. Is my precious Malee safe?"

"I saw her run under the sofa. Listen, I can't even get to my car. It's why I'm hiding. This guy? I think he's waiting for you to return, so you'd better stay far away. I'll call when he leaves. Could be a couple of hours, though."

"Yes, I will go now to Cleo's. I will sleep there."

"Good idea." A breeze graced Kid's cheek as he whispered, "Gotta go."

The thug returned a minute later with Sandro's pistol and a plastic bag. When he offered the pistol, Kid took it gingerly to avoid leaving fingerprints. After making sure it wouldn't fire by accident, he slid it into a pocket.

Jorge upended the bag next and dumped Sandro's heroin into the dirt. "Allesandro, you *pendejo*. Now you have no motherfawking junk." He spit on the dull white powder and ground it under the heel of his black engineer boot.

"You have honor," Kid said, impressed.

A brief silence followed until the thug narrowed his dark eyes. "Julio, he tell me Dustin mention to him a word. Encryption." Jorge worried his good hand against his forehead. "He add a word to this. Only I cannot remember. I don't know why this is. Perhaps choo suck my cock right now, to help me remember."

He abruptly unzipped and waved his penis at Kid. "Choo like what you see, no? It is *muy grande*, jes? Choo also see that I am not a fawking Jew. So, you drop to chore knees and lick my huevos. Then the blowjob. After? Maybe I remember what is that word. Or not." His eyes turned dark, and he said in a low, threatening voice, "Suck my cock, bitch. *Now*."

A stone-faced Kid said, "Love to. First, hold your breath and count to a thousand."

Jorge actually smiled while zipping up. *"Tu madre,* she mated with a fox."

Kid replied with a set face, "Wait for my call."

He meant of course to wait until Marty called an Assistant United States Attorney with enough authority to strike a deal.

Jorge looked at Kid. "What if maybe after I talk, you have the sudden headache and don't honor your part of the deal?"

"You've been around. You've seen things; done things. It's why you know I'm a man of my word."

The thug grunted as he lit up and blew a smoke ring that somehow managed to hold its shape in the breeze-swept night sky. After blowing another ring, Jorge squinted and spoke to the night sky as the ring rose higher and higher. "Is funny, but I now remember Sandro's other word that my brother Julio mentioned. *Keys. Sí.* Encryption keys."

Kid's shoulders slumped. "Thank you."

"Thank choo? No. Fawk you, bitch." The thug skewered Kid with his eyes. "I want something in return. Right now. Jes?" While still staring at Kid, he reached his good hand inside Kid's unbuttoned shirt and caressed his smooth torso. "Mmmmm," he began with pure male appetite. "Choo have a gorl's body. *Muy* feminine; *muy cimbreño.*"

Kid translated to himself: Cimbreño; willowy.

The thug then traced a nicotine-stained finger around Kid's lips, only to shove the finger completely in and work it back and forth, in and out. "Chore lips will look good wrapped around my cock. Also? Choo are berry pretty." Pulling his finger free, he dragged at his Marlboro and exhaled in Kid's face. "Now, bitch. Do it. Lick my balls and suck my cock."

The young operative knew what he must do if only for the sake of his children. *You karate do 'guess so,' get squish...* So he resigned himself to it by pointedly glancing at Jorge's midsection. "I couldn't help but notice how horse-hung you are earlier. Guess I missed what you were telling me about not being Jewish. Maybe if I take a closer look?"

"Chore," the hood replied with an air of conquest and unzipped, making his leather pants creak from excitement. "Jes. Take a look. Only, *tú chupar? Tú* swallow the *leche. Sí?*"

"Shut up," Kid muttered as he knelt and dug his toes into the loamy soil before humbling himself with this thug.

JORGE chain-smoked for the next fifteen minutes, often tapping ashes into Kid's hair until finally he gripped Kid's head in his hands and cried out while driving his hips forward.

The somber-faced operative stood afterward and swiped the back of a hand across his mouth, his sweat-streaked body shimmering despite the cooling breeze.

The smug Honduran's leather pants now hung limply from his hips, and he regarded Kid with utter contempt while zipping up. After dragging at his cigarette and carelessly tossing it aside, he sniffed and said, "Ho-kay. I will talk to these people choo want to send me to."

"Good. Wait for my call."

"I will. But choo better still come to my bed after... you fawking *bitch.*" With that, he spat at the dirt next to Kid's foot. Then he walked off and blended with the darkness.

Kid waited until he heard a car door open and close. Seconds later he saw tail lights and heard tires crunch the dirt road. The sound grew distant, and when he could see the lights no longer he stood still for a moment with just the stars overhead for companionship, along with a cooling breeze that was whisking his body with its breath to provide emotional comfort. He might have been thoroughly humiliated, but he was able to shove it into a compartment within his mind so he could move on with his mission.

A moment later he padded back to the cottage. Once he spotted Malee under the sofa, he cradled her in his arms while closing the bedroom door to keep her from cutting herself on the broken glass. Then he put her down in the kitchen while he cleaned her litter box and put out fresh water and food. Once he'd taken care of Malee, he called the Spaniard. "Malee's safe and that guy's gone."

Following a final look around, he got in his car and drove off. Eventually he stopped in a shadowy place to text Marty with the details concerning Jorge and encryption keys. After adding the young thug's phone number, he arranged a time and place to meet so he could transfer the pistol to Marty.

Then he destroyed the burner, and after tossing its innards in various directions he used his smartphone and called Jamal to describe what happened at Sandro's, adding that the Spaniard was nowhere to be seen.

"I'll handle him," Jamal said while trying to conceal a growing fury in his voice. "If he remains AWOL for more than half a day I'll hunt him down and *end* him." He paused, and said, "Meet me at the marina tomorrow morning." Jamal told him when and where and ended the call.

Kid put away his phone and nodded at the dark night, one that was now growing darker still with the arrival of high cumulus clouds. So he drove into town and stopped at the walk-in health clinic.

Chapter Twenty-Eight

. . . .

June 16 • The Marina • Olympia

JAMAL, CLAD IN khaki shirt and trousers, stood waiting on the dock as Kid walked toward him. After shaking hands, Jamal waved a majestic hand at the yawl. "Here she is. $297,000, cash money. Not bad for a fifty-foot '76 Hinckley Sou'wester."

"I love it," Kid said with great vigor.

The former naval officer with his thatch of bleached dreadlocks met Kid's eyes. "Thanks for coming on short notice. Now then." He cleared his throat and spoke with the deep rumbling voice of a military officer accustomed to addressing subordinates. "Our Sandro popped up on the radar not one hour ago. However, I'm having difficulty believing his version of events. It's why I've restricted him to his assigned quarters."

Kid took this to mean the cottage. He also interpreted Jamal's tone to mean Sandro had become a liability and might not be around much longer.

"Very well," the vessel's new captain said. "Shall we do a walk-through?"

"Absolutely," Kid said at once, and fell into step behind Jamal for a tour of the ultra-sleek blue-hulled, teak-decked sailing vessel.

Jamal paused while still topside. "It sleeps eight in relative comfort. More if needed."

Even eight aboard a fifty-footer's a lot, Kid thought as he spread and braced his bare feet on the wooden deck boards, while also lifting his nose to the fresh air coming off the water.

They went below, where Kid was pleased to find the topside breeze was also freshening the below-deck spaces. A wave of nostalgia coursed through him as he listened to the reassuring rhythm of tiny waves lapping against the hull.

Jamal stopped at the galley. "Well? What do you think of her?"

"Lovely lines. Centerboard design. Easily handled with the right crew."

"Spot-on assessment." Jamal regarded him with a new respect. "You must have crewed several sailing vessels."

Kid shrugged in that helpless way which only the truly modest people are capable of. "I grew up on Chesapeake Bay."

"So I heard." Jamal blew air from his cheeks. "Very well. Let's get moving. I'll show you the rest and then we'll get down to specific duties."

Fifteen minutes later found them back on the main deck, where Jamal pointed to some boxes near the yawl's cockpit. "I'm adding a solar device for electricity and a passive nav system with the most current charts. I also purchased sounding lines, real charts, two compasses, and a pair of sextants." A gull flew overhead while Jamal narrowed his eyes at Kid. "Will you help me install the systems?"

"Of course."

"Outstanding. With your assistance we'll complete the tasks in only a day or two."

"What about a name?" Kid asked.

Jamal's sudden smile revealed Ivory Soap teeth. "I am so pleased you asked. Yes, sir. Proves you're a true mariner. Tell me what you think of christening her, the *Arcturus*."

Kid nodded. "Arcturus. Third brightest star of the night sky and the brightest in the northern hemisphere. Arcturus has been a reference point for celestial navigation ever since mariners pushed beyond landfall."

"Very good. For make no mistake; celestial navigation will be a must after all GPS and radio nav systems cease functioning. It's why we plan on establishing Patos Island as our shore-based home."

"Upper Puget Sound," Kid said. "Roo mentioned it."

"I know she did. Now here's the Patos plan in broad strokes: after dropping anchor we'll send the park rangers packing. Then we'll rotate our squadron, with half of us living in the lighthouse digs while the other half remains aboard Arcturus. Patos is small and easily defended. The lighthouse will serve as a handy lookout post. I'll also ring the island with solar-powered surveillance and motion detectors. Arcturus will be our redoubt."

"Good plan," Kid admitted.

"Glad you approve."

Following this they spent the next few hours installing mounts for the new array until Jamal called it a day by saying, "Gotta run an errand." All at once he pointed a finger like a pistol at Kid's chest and cocked it. "Have your sweet ass back here tomorrow morning. Zero seven hundred sharp. We'll finish the array and tackle another chore."

Kid all but saluted. "Aye, aye, Captain."

·   ·   ·

Early the next morning Kid left the slumbering Huck's side and met Jamal on the rain-drenched dock, where the captain silently pointed at the boat's stern. Kid looked and smiled at what he saw painted across it: *Arcturus*. Jamal beckoned with a finger. "Follow me."

The rain had left Kid feeling cold and miserable—not to mention that trying to determine the existence of a failsafe system had his anxiety level growing with each passing day. Yet he felt hogtied since making out-of-hand inquiries would raise too many eyebrows. Of course, ignoring this challenging task could result in millions of deaths.

At least he felt warmer once he descended the yawl's polished teak steps to the main salon. The large space smelled of varnish, Murphy soap and brass polish, leaving Kid wondering at the incongruity of an anarchist running such a taut ship.

Jamal looked over his shoulder at him. "You performed well at the jewelry store. Even so, I won't deny being shocked by the fact that you'd met Agamemnon long ago."

"Why can't you trust me? I mean, come on. I've given up everything for my beliefs. *Everything.*"

"Do you blame us? Christ! You appear out of nowhere, the son of government operatives. I mean—" Jamal faced Kid and pressed his lips tight.

"People defect all the time, Captain. But yeah, I get it. Guess I'd feel the same way."

Jamal put a hand on Kid's shoulder. "What strikes me is that you do feel. So okay, maybe I don't get the entire homosexual scene... although I must concede that an undercover operative would never indulge in *that*. Our investigator also spoke to some students who heard you were sleeping with some guys, so you're clearly not out to deceive us."

A strange shudder so out of place in Jamal coursed through his body. "But I see your soul. It's why I've come to admire you. That, and I think you're so very casually amazing."

"Thank you, Captain. I'm honored."

Jamal winked. "The honor's mine. It's why you're my first mate, effective immediately."

"Thanks! Hey, I won't let you down." But then Kid looked him in the eye. "I want my children with me... with *us*."

Jamal cocked an eyebrow. "Know what? I'd think less of you if you didn't. Yeah, don't worry. We'll make it happen. Now come along. We've lots to do."

The rain had stopped by the time they reappeared on deck, and they spent the next few hours working on the solar array and other add-ons. Once they put everything aside for the day, Jamal checked his Rolex Submariner and said, "This way."

They went below to the aft bulkhead, where Jamal slid a finger into a chrome ring recessed in the deck. When he pulled up, he revealed a vast storage space. "Let's go outside."

Kid followed him to the parking lot, where Jamal looked around and mumbled, "Should be arriving any moment."

Seconds later a small yellow rental van emerged from a patch of the breeze-fanned firs that lined the main road. Huck was at the wheel, and he smiled at Kid and led the way to the rear, where he opened the loading door to reveal four long wooden crates.

They smelled of pine and creosote, and when Jamal gripped the end of the nearest one and pulled, Kid hopped to it and grabbed the other end. Once they had the weight balanced between them, they carried it aboard the yawl and set it next to the open storage space.

It took the three men forty minutes to unload the crates and position them throughout the passageways. Following a brief rest that incorporated the consumption of two cold beers per man, Jamal produced a crowbar and popped the first crate's lid. Inside were a dozen heavy machine guns.

Jamal cleared his throat. "These are SAWs…"

"Squad Automatic Weapons," Kid said.

"Right. So here's the deal. We swiped everything from an armory a long time ago in a galaxy… well, you get my drift." Jamal pried open another crate and pointed at its contents. "M-16s…"

"The M-4 versions," Kid said in a matter-of-fact voice.

"Hmm." Jamal grabbed an M-4 and thrust it to Kid, then watched his first mate smartly draw the receiver's charging handle back and lock it in place.

After exposing the breech, Kid did a visual inspection before sliding his little finger inside to check for live ammo. Next, he turned the weapon around and peered into the muzzle. With a curt nod, he brought the weapon to a position of *present arms* and offered it to Jamal.

"So. A pussy boy who knows weapons. Very good." He looked at Huck.

Taking his cue, the stoner grabbed the next M-4 and performed an identical inspection.

Kid raised an eyebrow and chided himself for not considering this possible side of Huck. "Which branch were you?"

"Marines," Huck said while returning the weapon to the crate. "Two combat tours. Afghanistan."

Jamal pointed a long finger at the other crates. "We have 40mm grenade launchers. We've got Stingers in case someone with an aircraft gets too nosy. U.S. Navy twelve-gauge shotguns to repel boarders with. Also? A .50 caliber

machine gun with four thousand rounds, plenty of handguns, and a ton of ammo —"

He gave Kid a hard look. "Once things go tits up people will
want to take from others." He swept a hand at the crates. "We
will defend Patos and Arcturus. *Nobody* will take from us."

Kid said, "We're sure as hell not going down without a
fight."

"Certainly not you," Jamal said while staring at him.
"Cleo told me you're a fighter. It's among the reasons you're
here." He paused, and said, "We have fishing tackle. We
have MREs; seeds to raise crops, and we'll acquire chickens,
pigs and goats. I've also hidden extra sails, lines, and other
gear at strategic shoreline locations. All right. Let's stow
everything."

Rivers of perspiration were streaming down their faces
and soaking their clothes by the time they finished. Following a break, Huck wiped his face and said, "I'd better get
going. I gotta have the truck back by six before some *barney*
reports it stolen."

As soon as the amiable slacker departed, Jamal jabbed
Kid's shoulder. "This is your new home effective immediately. Gather your belongings and bring them here." He
pulled a spare key from a pocket and offered it.

Kid took the key and was about to leave when Jamal
gripped his arm and gazed into his eyes. "We planned on
making our move Christmas Day. But with the weapons
aboard I see no need to wait. It's October. Already cold in
parts of the country. Let's do it tonight. Stroke of twelve."

Creases etched Kid's forehead. "I won't have time to fetch
my children."

"I—" Jamal locked eyes with him. "We have a higher priority. If we had time then I'd say, get 'em. We don't. Besides,

call me old-fashioned, but children are better off with their mamas. I'm also betting on their grandfathers ensuring their survival."

Kid rubbed his chin, deep in thought. "I do want my children. Then again, I left 'em behind. Didn't I? Guess I can't complain now." A pause. "One thing, though. We're preparing as if the world will go dark forever. But how is shutting down the grid not temporary?"

Jamal looked over his shoulder before speaking in a conspiratorial voice. "Ag's installed a failsafe code designed to scramble every global grid within a micro-sec of coming back online. From that point on the AI programs he launched will take over." He glowed. "Yes, my friend. It's gonna be dark for decades at the very least."

Kid put on an 'I'm impressed look' and said, "Speaking of failsafe codes, what happens if Ag drops dead in the next hour? I like the guy all right. But damn… he's a heart attack waiting to happen."

"You asked a good question. Here's a good answer: it's why we're doing it tonight *before* he croaks."

"I see." Kid appeared thoughtful before shrugging and saying with a happy-go-lucky voice. "Well, I guess that's why you're the skipper… because you're on top of things."

"Pretty much, yeah." He caught Kid's eye. "All right. Be at Ag's by twenty-two hundred hours."

Although this fresh imperative troubled Kid, he all but barked, "Aye, aye, skipper."

PART IV

. . .

Chapter Twenty-Nine

· ·

June 16 · Later That Day

THE TWO MEN secured the yacht and Kid drove off, traveling a mile before stopping along a river shoreline to text Levi.

The message included a strong reminder that there were no surge protectors or battery backups at Ag's. He finished with: *They're pushing up the schedule. No info on a failsafe system. But Jamal mentioned using surveillance and motion detectors at their island redoubt. He might have installed some around Ag's house.*

These are the facts as I know them. Except something's not right. You cannot close in. Not yet. You must trust me on this. I have a pistol. If I'm wrong and Ag's about to pull the plug, I'll put a round through the base of his skull. I'll also kill the others if needed. He pressed his lips tight at how quickly the moral lines he'd grown up with had blurred. Now he asked this question of his soul: what else am I willing to do in this all-or-nothing mission? When the answer came, he added this to the text: *What's happening with Jorge? Is there a deal yet?*

Levi's replied, *Got your message. We're giving you your reins but will have backup nearby. We have ECM gear to detect surveillance hardware. The AUSA made a deal with Jorge. He gave a depo and mentioned Ag. No connection yet to any encryption keys. Could it be a component of Ag's password? Finally, forensics matched Sandro's pistol with the homicides. Good work!*

Kid texted, *Thanks for showing the faith. Also, I love you.*

He finished just as his real phone chirped. The caller ID read, *Papa.*

"What's up?"

"Son? Jen stopped the divorce proceedings. She said to say she's sorry and desperately wants to talk to you."

"Papa? Jen turned her back on me at the darkest moment in my life. Please tell her that if she won't follow through with the divorce, I'll file my own. That's it, gotta go." He pressed END and shoved his cell into a pocket, then stared at the water as he ripped the burner phone apart with a violence he'd never known and flung its components into the water.

•   •   •

WHACK!

Kid whirled, his eyes huge and shoulders instinctively hunched against attack. "Wha—?"

Sandro stood at the front door after slamming it shut, his eyes bright with an unnatural light. "That Jorge!" he roared. "He stole from me. My *pistola*, my… my heroin! Why did you not stop him?"

"Why? Hey, fuck off. You ran and left me to deal with your mess."

Sandro stepped closer. "I see. In that case—" All at once he charged with crazed eyes and flailing arms.

But Kid crashed a fist against Sandro's jaw and dropped him in his tracks. After frisking him for weapons and finding none—and with the reassuring weight of the Beretta in the small of his back—he slapped Sandro's cheeks until he stirred. Once his eyelids fluttered open, Kid shoved his nose to within an inch of the Spaniard's and fixed him with a street fighter's glazed eyes.

"Do not take me on. I will hurt you. Also, punk? In case you've forgotten, your sad ass is due at Agamemnon's in thirty minutes. Now get moving."

He added a P.S. by growling, "By the way, you can thank me later for saving Malee during the home invasion."

．　　．　　．

Jamal glared at Kid. "Where've you been? It's almost time."

Other than Ag, everyone in the ozone-smelling basement wore black military clothes and were watching Kid with the shimmering eyes of zealots.

Kid lifted a defiant chin. "Get over yourself, Jamal. Now listen up. I had a run-in with Sandro. He attacked me. I settled his hash. End of message." To himself, he said, *Christ, you anarchist types are shameless. You rail against authority, but only so long as others obey you.* After a brief stare-down Kid said with a modicum of contrition, "Okay. I should've called to say I was running late. I'm sorry."

Jamal stepped closer. "Good display of decision-making skills." He started to add to this when the basement door opened, and Sandro stepped inside. A large bruise on his jaw testified to Kid's well-planted fist.

Jamal got in his face at once. "What are you thinking these days? Huh? Tell me, because at this point I…"

"Knock it off," Huck shouted. After shooting a pained glance at Kid, he growled, "We're here to like, do it! What're we waiting for?"

"Nothing," Jamal fired back as he smacked his palms together and let them fly apart. "You heard the man. Let's move."

Ag had been watching in silence. But when Cleo touched his shoulder, a fresh energy gripped him, and he straightened his back and settled a finger on the mouse. "Two clicks and I'm in. One shift of the cursor puts us seconds away from lights out. After that, it's 'Good night Mr. and Mrs. America and all the ships at sea.'"

Kid studied Huck's face. His eyes appeared so animated that Kid decided he was stoned. Next, he studied the flop sweat on Cleo's Ghanaian forehead. Then there was Jamal: cool and calm. No surprise there.

No surprise, and yet Kid frowned. *Wait. Who's missing?*

Jamal's voice blasted his concentration apart. "Ag! Anytime you're ready."

"Roger that." Ag stole a glance at Kid as if asking, *is this what we really, really wanna do,* before turning to watch a countdown clock. "Two minutes."

The room's palpable tension was approaching a flash point when Kid's gut shouted that an element of some kind was out of kilter; that none of this was authentic. Still, he slid his hand under his shirt, ready to draw his pistol and shoot Ag in the head.

In the meantime his belly flip-flopped from fear—fear of what would happen if he were wrong; fear for his children most of all, and for his parents and his brother and the rest of Earth's eight billion-plus inhabitants; fear for Jen.

"One minute and counting," Ag announced, and after dabbing a handkerchief against his brow he stared at the countdown clock.

Kid also watched it. Forty-five seconds. Thirty. Twenty. All eyes were on Ag's finger when Kid gripped his pistol. He eased it out and got ready. *I've gotta shoot him… now!*

WHAM!

The basement door burst open.

Men rushed inside.

"FBI," they shouted. "Freeze!"

Jamal raised his arms. So did everyone else. All but Kid.

He whirled. Caught the four-man FBI SWAT team in the corner of his eye; caught sight of their MP-5 submachine guns.

"Down!" The SWAT leader shouted.

Kid squinted; did a micro-eval; said to himself, *Something's not right.* He didn't know what. And yet he did.

All at once he fired three rounds into the closest agent's chest. He crumpled to the floor while wisps of blue smoke rose from the Beretta. As cordite stench filled the room the other agents screamed like pre-pubescent girls—then they were shoving each other aside in their panic to escape the danger.

Kid stood over the downed agent and aimed at his nose, his finger on the trigger. "Say bye-bye."

Jamal shouted, "Kid, *halt!*"

"He's here to kill us," Kid barked. "It's him or me."

"Jesus," Huck said from behind him.

"Mother of God," Cleo whispered.

"I think I crapped myself," Ag advised.

CLEO did her best to soothe Kid after the last of the phony agents drove off in a rickety car. "We're so sorry to have doubted you, Pet."

"Tell it to the motherfucker I shot," he said with rage-filled eyes.

The agent in question had remained motionless for thirty seconds after Kid shot him multiple times. "You shot me," he kept screaming. "You fucking shot me!"

Kid had indeed shot him. A blink of an eye. It's all he needed for his gut to shout; *These aren't real agents!*

And what did he see in that blink? Agents with submachine guns but no side arms; agents who failed to shout "Clear!" upon making entry. There were also no noises from other SWAT members who should be just outside the door. And there'd been no back-and-forth chatter; no SITREPs given over mics at their mouths.

Kid's micro-sec eval had all but screamed that this was a set-up; that Jamal and the others were testing his loyalty. Had Kid shouted, "Thank god! You guys made it just in time," he would have blown his cover. But when Kid saw the fake agent's very genuine ballistic vest, he plugged him three times knowing that while it would hurt like hell, it wouldn't kill him.

It's also why he remained in-role by angrily turning on the others. "Fuck you! Fuck all of you. Especially you, Huck."

Huck hung his head — and yet Kid had the strangest sensation that Huck felt disappointed in him as well. But Kid squared off and growled, "You set this up. Didn't you, Mister Marine?"

Huck appeared both stunned and hurt. "Kid, I swear. I had nothing to do with this."

"It's all on me," Jamal said while stepping between them. "I got spooked when it turned out you'd already met Ag. I had to make certain of you. Sure, you're sleeping with dudes. It still proved nothing. But then you friggin' shoot a SWAT guy? You... you put your life on the line to defend us? Jesus, Kid. You're my hero."

But the husband/father/Harvard pre-med student wouldn't hear him out. "Fuck the hero bullshit and fuck all of you! I'm outta here."

Cleo grabbed his arm. "Please see it from our perspective, pet."

"I've got your perspective. The only one you care about. Right here." He grabbed his crotch and thrust his pelvis at her before storming out.

KID gripped the steering wheel to keep his hands from shaking more than they already were. *Fucking close; too close. What if I'd been wrong? Those punks would've shot me dead. Yeah, Jamal claimed their MP-5s weren't loaded. But something else was out of kink. What, though? What else was wrong with that setup?*

Ten minutes later he was still trembling from unspent adrenaline when he called Jamal. "Listen up, *Commander*. I'm pissed. *Okay?* But I'm still in." He said in a quieter voice, "Just give me a day to get over this... this betrayal. I'll be fine after that. I promise."

"Good to know, Kid. Listen, will you forgive me? Are you still with us?"

"Of course. Our cause is just... but um, just give me some space. That's all I ask. I'll call later and tell you where I end up."

"Got it," Jamal said, adding, "Kid? I think you are among the most remarkable people I've ever known. It's a pleasure to be serving with you. Listen, go do... whatever you've gotta do. Is a day long enough? Do you need more time?"

"Just tonight. I'll be aboard Arcturus by noon tomorrow. And, thanks."

Kid ended the call. Then with a pledge he felt honor-bound to keep coupled with a duty to his country, he made another call. When a dubious voice answered, Kid said, "Jorge? Where do you live?"

Chapter Thirty

. . . .

June 17 • Olympia

KID PULLED UP to a tiny, dilapidated trailer minutes later. It seemed to be held together by rust, and was surrounded by a forest of ferns and weeds. He parked and got out just as the heavily tattooed thug appeared buck-assed in the doorway with a delicious half-naked brunette in tow, whom he shoved out the door while shouting, "Do not come back until I call you. Maybe tomorrow night. Maybe not. Now get out!"

Jorge raised his right arm to show that the cast had been removed, and once Kid drew closer, the thug stepped aside to let him enter.

Kid walked inside only to find empty pizza boxes, unwashed dishes, and piles of dirty clothes strewn all over. The place reeked of stale tobacco, the sickly-sweet odors of mildew and rotting food, and recently spent energy. A filthy bare mattress with a blanket and two soiled pillows took up the middle of the crummy floor, and a dozen cockroaches were skittering across both the floor and the mattress.

Kid wordlessly stripped and faced the nude and well-hung thug, who simply jutted his jaw at the soiled mattress.

Chapter Thirty-One

· ·

June 18 • Olympia

THE RISING SUN stabbed Kid's eyes with great malice, and he blinked several times while wondering what was tickling his lips—only to bolt upright and shout, "Fuck!" when he realized it was a huge, bloated cockroach. He swept it away and shuddered, only to spot another crawling across his scrotum. "Bastard," he shouted and flung it aside before settling back against the stained mattress.

He didn't feel good, having had less than an hour of sleep after slavishly servicing the Honduran hoodlum throughout the night—for Jorge proved to be both virile and voracious in sexual appetite. And yet he'd been quite skilled, surprisingly gentle, and even attentive to Kid.

Jorge watched him with amused eyes while absently brushing at a brown cockroach atop his own hairy thigh. Then he smiled and said, "Choo got a hot little ass. You know that?"

An exhausted Kid mumbled, "So I've been told."

"Hmm. I bet choo have. Also? I own it now." He turned jaded eyes toward Kid and said in a menacing tone, "Don't I?"

When Kid clamped his eyes tight and nodded, the thug smiled in victory. "Good. Because I liked using it an' I will make the use of it again." The hood released a sated moan and stretched his long legs while saying, "Choo also liked it, didn't you? Each time I fawked you."

Kid looked away as his role required, and replied with a guttural, "Yes."

Jorge grunted. "Sí, I knew you did. Also, choo enjoyed it every time you gave to me the blowjobs. Jes?"

"I… yeah."

The thug smiled in victory and lit a Marlboro. After dragging deeply at it he exhaled and said as blue smoke jetted from his nostrils, "Choo proved your honor by coming here last night, instead of making the excuses. For that, and because I have now paid you back for what choo did to my finger? I will say to you another thing that Allesandro told my brother."

He took another drag and contentedly exhaled. "That *pendejo* bastard, he tell Julio that he has been taught how to use a computer to bring an end to the world."

Kid's pulse stormed out of the starting gate and began charging down the track. Yet he felt like a hapless jockey struggling to stay in the saddle while the payoff for trading in his manhood loomed just ahead. Would it be a photo finish? He might never know. But he believed he'd hit a trifecta and that it might provide a handle on the failsafe method.

And so they talked awhile longer, with Kid at one point idly plucking a roach from within his abundant hair and tossing it against the wall with such force that it went *blat* and oozed a reddish-black juice down the wall.

All at once Kid faced Jorge. "You're very bright. With a little help, you can get into college and can make a good life for *tú madre*."

When the Honduran hoodlum gave him a dismissive look, Kid shrugged and walked stiffly to where he'd dropped his clothes. He was so inured to the obscene trailer by now that he didn't even flinch when a black mouse shot across his toes while he got dressed.

He'd just reached the door when Jorge said, "Wait." After lighting yet another Marlboro, he said, "I have chore number. If I hear anything else I will call you."

A sudden panic gripped Kid's soul; there were his children and other children across the globe to consider — so on the off-chance that Jorge was withholding additional information in exchange for sex, Kid tossed his pride and said, "Jorge? Can I come back tonight?"

"Why?"

"Because I want to be your girlfriend. Okay? Yes? *Please?*"

Jorge looked at him with interest before saying, "I meant it. I have not any other words to give to you. Also? I am not the homosexual. I only fawked choo for breaking my motherfawking finger. But I no want you again. So get out."

"Got it." Kid went to the door, but there he paused and craned his neck. "Jorge? You don't have to live like this. Education can take you to a new level."

Jorge sniffed as if bored by the conversation. "What the fawk do you talk about?" But when the thug broke eye contact rather than admit to a weakness, Kid figured the Latino code of machismo was at play.

Perhaps it's why Jorge studied the ash of his burning cigarette while mumbling, "Maybe I call, and we talk about it. Not for me... for one of my amigos." Then he looked at Kid with unwavering eyes.

"I look forward to that call," Kid said, and paused before adding, "Jorge? Swear to God, I will kick your ass all over this fucking dump you live in if you don't accept the opportunity I'm offering. Then I'll butt-fuck you till you beg me to stop. Are we clear... bitch?"

Jorge nodded, and surprised Kid by saying, "I am glad choo came here last night. Also, I like it that you want to be my gorl. Choo *are* berry pretty, and I —" He looked away and got busy with his cigarette for a few seconds before facing Kid. "Hey? No hard feelings for the other night? And last night?"

"Never in a million years, man."

Jorge pressed his lips tight and nodded, only to look full into Kid's face. "Maybe we can be the amigos, choo and me. Jes?"

"That'd be good," a mildly surprised Kid replied, only to be amazed when Jorge locked eyes with him and patted the mattress. After the briefest pause, Kid undressed and joined him.

After leaving Jorge's bed some two hours later, Kid stopped along a deserted roadside to text Levi about the probable connection between Sandro and the failsafe issue.

From there he drove to the 24/7 walk-in clinic and got new instant tests for STDs.

.   .   .

Jamal smiled when Kid boarded Arcturus a bit later. "Listen, I owe you a huge debt of gratitude for defending us from that ill-conceived raid. I also wish to thank you for returning." The skipper suddenly pulled Kid into his arms, and after hugging him he led Kid to the yawl's main salon and pointed at a cushioned chair.

"Sit," he commanded. Kid plopped down and smiled when Jamal offered him a very nice cigar. Soon they were both smoking and sipping some great Kentucky bourbon.

As clouds of cigar smoke spread across the overhead and streamed out through an open hatch, Jamal edged forward in his seat and locked eyes with Kid. "We've ramped things up."

"I'm listening."

"We go on Tuesday. Twenty-four hundred hours local time."

"Got it," Kid said, and made his eyes shine with the fanatical brightness he'd seen in Cleo's. After a nod and a smile, he gulped a slug of bourbon and monkey-grinned Jamal.

Awhile later Kid mumbled something about gassing his car, adding, "In case we need it once there's no more gas." The instant he found a quiet place, he sent a text to Levi with this new imperative. Once Levi confirmed receipt of the message, Kid tore the phone to shreds and tossed the pieces into the forest.

Having not heard from Jorge, he drove to Enzo's for the night because he still felt on the outs with Huck—and because he didn't want to feel lonely.

THE next morning Kid slid out from under Enzo's arm and stepped inside the shower, only to be joined by the Italian stud whose needs were obvious. When Kid finally emerged and dried off, he pulled on faded olive drab army pants and drove shirtless and shoeless to the café.

He found Cleo and Huck quietly sitting at a table, and he went to them at once. Huck swore again that he'd had nothing to do with the fake raid, and mouthed, *I love you.*

Kid felt a flood of relief, and he tapped his bare foot against Huck's as a signal that he wanted to make love. The young stoner's chest swelled in response.

•   •   •

Levi Hart gripped the Civil War-era chair's arms with such force that his knuckles blanched. "Mr. President, we cannot send the Bureau."

President Mark Cohen's West Wing leather chair creaked when he leaned back and made a teepee of his fingers, and then tapped them against his chin. "I'm listening."

Not caring that the Bureau's Director sat four feet away, Levi argued his case. "The stakes are too high. We need Delta Force."

The President frowned. "Yet here you are—a former Bureau alumnus. A rather high-level one at that. Nevertheless, you lack confidence in their Hostage Rescue Team. Why is that?"

Levi glanced first at the Director and then at Cohen's National Security Advisor. "Today's agents are immature. Few have served in the military and fewer still have worked as street-savvy cops.

"Sir? Last month I witnessed a training exercise involving the Bureau's premier HRT. Their ineptitude was outmatched only by their arrogance. The team leader even told a Delta Force bull colonel who'd been invited to observe them to shut up when the colonel offered a spot-on critique. Whatever the teams might have been, they are no more. Sir? We need Delta."

The President spoke from deep inside his chest. "Both the Constitution and federal law prohibit their use for domestic purposes."

"I'm aware of the legal proscriptions. But these are terrorists. Two of them are foreign nationals. It's why the Gang of Eight authorized intervention." Levi squinted at Cohen. "Sir? You gave me the mission. It's my party, my call."

Cohen frowned and replied in a frosty tone. "I know this, Levi."

The Director cleared his throat. "Under my personal guidance, our HRTs are greatly improved. Don't concern yourselves with them. They're up to the task." He made a grumbling sound and pointed a finger at Cohen. "This debate is pointless. I'm sending in my HRT, and *that* is how it shall be. Discussion over."

Cohen glared at him. "Just who do you think you are addressing? I am the President of the United States of America, and you shall not presume to lecture me or to override my authority."

The Director regarded him with contempt. "You're nothing but an elected official who has been in office far too long. I'm sending my boys in." He stood and started for the door.

"Sit down," Cohen barked. "I have not dismissed you."

The Director said while walking, "I don't need your permission."

"We'll see about that," Cohen said, and called out, "Secret Service!" When the agent just outside the door glanced inside, Cohen stabbed a finger at the Director. "Seize that man and place him under arrest for sedition."

The agent didn't even blink. "Very well, Mister President."

The Director drew himself up to his full height of six feet and said in a baritone, "You're not arresting anyone, sonny boy. Now go home to your mommy." Turning away, he signaled to his aide to follow and began walking.

Levi watched with detached interest as the agent grabbed the Director's elbow, quickly spun him around, and cuffed the Director's hands behind his back. "Sir, you are under arrest. And you," he told the aide, "are next if you interfere."

The President called out to the Director. "You are fired, effectively immediately." He waited until the agent hustled him out of sight, then picked up his phone and told the operator, "Get me the Attorney General."

A moment of silence followed before the President spoke into the handset. "Roger? I just had my protective detail arrest the Director." He explained why, listened, and said, "Yes. That's right. Draw up the charges. List me as the complainant. Mr. Levi Hart and the national security advisor are witnesses." He listened and nodded. "Don't worry. I've already fired him."

Cohen ended the call and returned the handset to its cradle. After a moment he regarded Levi with a set face. "I must send in the HRT."

"My people are better, Mr. President."

"I'm quite certain. However, the Gang of Eight lacks the authority it presumes to hold. Me? I'm as much a slave to the law as our good Director was supposed to be. They're going in."

A blood vessel jumped in Levi's temple. "Then I demand the right to use my recon people."

Cohen flared in anger. "Don't you *ever* presume to make demands. I don't care what our relationship is. Are we clear?"

Levi drew a deep cleansing breath. "Yes, sir. I'm sorry to have offended you, sir. It won't happen again."

Now mollified, Cohen regarded Levi with soft eyes. "Go on. Use your recon people." He added with a slight smile, "But for God's sake, do not also inform me that you'll have a backup team in place should the HRT drop the ball. Otherwise, I'll be obligated to stop you."

A stone-faced Levi answered with a crisp, "Understood."

"Good. Now why don't you tell me about your recon people?"

"Sir, I have an on-call contract pilot with the appropriate security clearances. He'll fly a single-engine aircraft five thousand feet up, and five miles west of the target. The aircraft has a high-resolution camera with high-def and infra-red capabilities. The camera can read a magazine page from twice that distance, and I can slave it to my laptop."

Cohen glanced at his security advisor. When he didn't object, Cohen said, "Very well, Levi. Make it so."

"Thank you, Mr. President." He rose to leave.

The President held up a hand. "Wait. I need Delta and our other elite military units close at hand. Should the anarchists prevail, I'll need all available assets to restore order. It's why I have little choice but to send the HRT."

"Understood, sir." Levi knew Cohen would not have both-ered to explain his decision to anyone else other than him. So he added a heartfelt, "Thank you, Mr. President."

· · ·

When Kid got up to leave the café a short time later, Cleo said she would walk him to his car. They crossed the parking lot in silence until they reached the Beamer, where she wound her long tapering fingers within Kid's.

After moving closer to him, she looked into his eyes. "I've fallen even deeper in love with you, as if that were possible." She sighed, and her shoulders slumped. "Also? Some test results came back yesterday. I'm pregnant."

Chapter Thirty-Two

· ·

June 21 • Olympia

KID DREW UPON every ounce of emotional strength to push back from Cleo's stunning news. Besides, it could very well be Huck's child—although he didn't mention this to Huck that night, not even during their pillow talk.

But it still troubled him the next day while he sent an update to Levi. It also remained on his mind later that evening, when he donned black clothing and slid the 9mm Beretta into the small of his back as he prepared for the big event. And following all of this he said a silent prayer for his three children... and one for Jen.

Thirty-three minutes later he walked inside Ag's basement only to find everyone else already there. Even Sandro, who'd been keeping a low profile ever since Jamal looked him in the eye and said, "I will ice you if you create so much as one more problem."

With only minutes left before midnight, the fear was palpable not only on their faces but in the sudden stench of uncontainable perspiration.

At a nod from Jamal, Ag adjusted the cursor on his program to end the civilized world. Perhaps in a nod toward dark humor, the primary screen displayed a red field with this simple blue label: START HERE.

Ag craned his neck at Kid. "Won't say I'll miss things now that I've got at least one friend in the world."

Despite himself, Kid's heart went out to this lonely man who had engineered the trial disasters that resulted in deaths. But he brushed that aside, and after glancing at the custom-built CPUs with the planet's destiny in their hard drives, he checked to make sure Ag hadn't installed battery back-ups or surge protectors at the last minute. Finally, he checked the clock and intoned, "One minute."

"One minute," Ag echoed—the co-pilot running through a pre-flight checklist. When he settled a meaty hand on the mouse, everyone edged closer while he chanted the count-down. "Nineteen, eighteen, seventeen..."

At *fifteen*, Kid clamped a hand on Ag's shoulder and shouted, "Wait!"

Everyone went bug-eyed but he didn't care. "Maybe we should re-think this."

Ag looked at him. "What are you saying?"

"I'm saying that if you're my friend you'll call it off long enough for me to bring my children here."

"Kid? You're the only person to ever call me his friend." He moved the cursor to another part of the screen and left-clicked the mouse. "There. We're done for tonight. We..."

"No," Jamal boomed with a bullhorn voice. "Do it *now*. Or swear to god I'll kill you!"

Ag reared back and stammered, "If... if you do that, then... then." He swallowed hard, about to say more when thunder-ous explosions and lightning bolts erupted outside.

Every computer monitor went blank.

The room turned India-ink dark.

While a door at the top of the stairs opened and closed.

And then a six-man HRT team was storming the basement.

They wore night-vision gear and were shouting, "FBI! Down, down, down!"

An agent moved his submachine gun left and right. A light attached to its muzzle probed the dark room's spaces.

Another agent shouted, "Clear!" and spoke into a mic attached to his ballistic helmet.

A third team member brought in a battery-operated floodlight. Its dazzling LED light caught Sandro, Cleo, Huck, and Ag staring open-mouthed at the team.

When Levi and Michael in SWAT uniforms and hefting M-4s brushed past the agents, Kid shouted, "Wait! We're missing Jamal." It wasn't until Marty and Hacksaw entered in SWAT gear that it hit him. "Holy shit! Jamal went out through the upstairs door!"

Michael meanwhile went to Kid. "Son! My son my son. Are you all right?"

"I'm fine," he replied in a rush, only to grip Michael's arms. "Papa, listen up. We have Sandro and he's right there." He tilted his head at the Spaniard. "He's their failsafe asset. But we're missing Jamal. He must've escaped through a door at the top of the stairs."

Then it all made sense. "Son of a *bitch*! Roo's also missing. Why didn't I see it before?" He gripped Michael's arms anew. "*She's* their Plan fucking B! Probably their backup to Sandro. We find her? We find Jamal and we stop both of them." He nodded and said as if to himself, "The good news? I know where she is."

Levi swore under his breath and turned on the lead agent. "I told you to surround the entire house."

The lead glared back. "I don't answer to you. I..."

"Shut it," Levi said in a voice so edged with steel that it commanded instant attention. "You might have tactical command, but I've got strategic command and yes, you do answer to me. By god, you sure do." He looked at Michael and barked, "Outside. *Now*."

THE pair were clustered around Levi's laptop sixteen seconds later. Kid joined them and said in a voice meant to be obeyed, "Pull up a map of South Bay."

Levi typed the commands. Once the graphic appeared, Kid ordered, "Zero in on Boston Harbor. Then go to Sat Photo and look for a horse farm."

Seconds later he pointed at the screen. "There. That small river. See it? The Nisqually Reach. Search for a dock. It might even show an outboard-equipped skiff."

Levi's fingers flew across the keyboard. Once the location sprang up he said in the calm manner of a NASA mission controller, "Got it," and pulled up another app. His fingers danced again. "Recon's got the coordinates. Let's give him time to zero his camera."

"I should have known," Cleo said from a few feet away. Kid turned to see the face of a woman scorned, her wrists held tight by handcuffs. "I fell in love with you," she said in a voice laced with bitter acid. "Yet this is how you repay us? *Me?*"

Kid pinned her with a flinty stare and bit the next words off. "Are you *that* nuts? You were ready to kill my children; my *children!*"

An agent urged her along just as two others came by with a handcuffed Sandro. Kid was giving him a withering look, when to his total shock an agent brought Huck to Kid's side. Only, the stoner wasn't cuffed.

Huck revealed a slight smile. "Kid, you had me worried there. Hey, like, who do you think tipped the Bureau off? To these guys? And their plans?"

Kid's mouth opened, closed, and opened again. "You?"

"The one and only. Ya see…"

"Kid!"

He spun and saw Michael staring at him. "Is this the skiff?"

"Let's see." Kid needed only a glance at the recon plane's image. "Yep. And that's the horse farm. Now pay attention. Roo's the leader and Jamal's either going to her, or to this marina." He pointed to its real-time image. "Look for a yawl. The *Arcturus*."

Meanwhile, four HRT members appeared out of the gloom with Ag in their clutches. He cried out, "Kid! You must believe me. I wasn't gonna do it. Not after you asked me not to." He stammered a bit. "Only, Jamal devised a failsafe plan."

Kid gripped Ag's elbow. "Holy cow! Finally! Tell me what it is."

"Sandro made me teach him everything. The codes. The commands. He said they might use me as a decoy while *he* pulls the plug." Ag paused. "It wasn't until yesterday that I realized he taught someone else. You know, just in case. But they won't be able to…"

His next words were lost to Kid as he stared at the aerial image of Roo's skiff and cried out, "Holy mother of…" He looked into his papa's eyes. "I was right. Roo's the fall-back—and now *she's* about to pull the plug!"

Michael jabbed an index finger at him and growled, "Go."

Kid nodded, leaped into his Beamer, burned rubber, hit fifty in a posted thirty, and turned onto a dark road. As he sped down it with the engine roaring, he thumbed the car's automated assistant and spoke to the concealed mic. "Take me to Nisqually Reach." The location and directions instantly appeared on the nav screen. Next, he had the robot call Levi.

Kid said when Levi answered, "Dad! I'm heading for Nisqually. My car has a compass." He glanced at the GPS. "ETA is six-point-seven minutes. But I can shave some time. Listen. There's a side road leading to the river's opposite shore. Give me compass headings from that far shore to the dock with the skiff. Copy?"

"I do. Listen, we're watching you in real time from above and the cavalry's right behind you." A pause, then, "Okay. I see the road you're heading toward. Now stand by—"

Levi's voice echoed through the car seconds later. "From the opposite shore, determine a heading of two-niner-four degrees."

"Got it." Kid ended the call, force-shifted down to third, smoked the tires while rounding a curve, stomped on the accelerator, and jetted out of a blue cloud of tire smoke just as a call came through. He thumbed the ANSWER button. "Yes?"

"I treated choo like the dog. But you have been a good gorl to me... *for* me. Also, you stayed and pleased me when you did not have to. Plus I have the caring for you after choo talk to me about school. So now I tell you what I forget until this minute. You know those words I give to you? Encryption keys? I must be *estúpido*. For I remember something."

Kid gasped and thought *Holy fuck* and swerved to avoid a raccoon sauntering across the road. Then he said as if discussing the weather, "You have my total interest."

"That *hijo de puta* Allesandro, he tell Julio something else. He say that one other person can do the computer thing—whatever this means. This person is named *Roo*. Does this have for you the meaning?"

Kid sped up to seventy on a narrow road while saying, "It does. *¿Qué dijo tu hermano?*"

"Ah, *lengua Española*! My brother, Julio say only that Allesandro brag that he give to Roo these keys. What does this mean?"

"No time to explain. Maybe later. I…" Kid braked hard to avoid a slow-moving Camry. Then he bided his time until he saw a place to pass, and stomped on the gas. He was still trying to put the pedal through the floorboard even as he shot past. "Anything else?"

"No…"

But by now the Honduran thug was talking to air because Kid had ended the call. He must focus on the immediate task: stopping Roo no matter what it might take.

HALFWAY to his target Kid screeched to a halt at a fork in the road. He checked the nav screen and turned right. After a short drive, he screeched to a stop beneath a canopy of sheltering trees.

Seeing the river just ten yards away, he turned the wheel and moved the car in a slow circle while watching his compass. When it nudged the heading of two-nine-five, he glanced up and found a landmark on the far shore.

"Got it," he whispered and killed the engine. Next, he ran to the water's edge and studied the landmark. Sure enough, the dock was just below it. He calculated the distance involved and mumbled, "It'll work."

Rushing back to the Beamer, he jerked the rear door open, gripped the bottom edge of the back seat, yanked up smartly, and nodded with satisfaction when the seat came out.

"Car seats will float," his papa taught him years ago.

But while the seat might float, the drugs and booze he'd been using had taken their toll and he found himself laboring for breath while carrying the seat to the water's edge. But he got there, and after easing it into the water he said, "Damn. It does float. Thanks, Papa."

With no time to waste, he stripped completely and put his clothes and the Beretta on the seat. Then while an owl hooted from nearby, he slid the seat deeper into the water. The owl hooted once again, and then Kid was up to his chest and shuddering. *Holy fuck this water's fucking cold! As in holy fuck cold! And it's almost July!*

Ignoring the cold, he eyeballed the landmark and swam toward the far shore. It was two hundred feet away, but the shortcut sliced his travel time by road in half. As a bonus, this let him avoid any headlights or car sounds that might alert Roo.

"There's the dock," he whispered if only to keep his teeth from chattering more than they already were. "And the skiff."

He glided the seat to the dock and emerged from the river. Rivulets of water streamed down his torso as he dressed, his shivering so bad that he had trouble tying his shoes. After sliding the pistol into his waistband, he stepped into the skiff and removed the outboard motor's gas can. After emptying its contents on the shore, he flung the can into a distant clump of shrubs.

Where to now? he wondered. Fortune favored him by placing him downwind, so he let his nose guide him toward the horse and manure odors. The smells grew stronger as he stole his way along the unfamiliar ground until a barn materialized. But when he stopped to devise a plan, a breeze hit his wet skin and chilled him to the core.

Luck graced him again when he spotted a shaft of light peeking past some window curtains in the upper part of the barn. *Could be her apartment*, he thought. *Or an office. No wonder she always smells of horses.*

Now that he knew where to find her, he knew what to do—and due to another of life's quirks, he gave thanks to all the doping he'd done with Huck. Otherwise, he might not have the Beretta. Or the lighter in his pocket. And he would need both.

By planting one foot in front of the other, he reached the barn's huge sliding door and slipped inside, then paused until his eyes adjusted to the darkness. After spotting some stairs, he looked up and saw a weak light peeping from under a closed door.

He surveyed the barn next and counted twelve stalls occupied by horses. When they turned to examine him with idle curiosity, he whispered, "Sorry to have to do this, guys."

Working fast, he gathered enough straw to form a pile on the dirt floor. Then he held the Zippo close and flicked its wheel.

Nothing.

He tried again and again, and he was cursing himself for failing to keep it filled when for some unfathomable reason, he recalled watching a homeless man shake a reluctant lighter to life. So he shook his with vengeance and brought it close to the straw. Then he held his breath and flicked.

A flame leaped out. It lapped at the straw. A small fire burst into life. The straw began giving off white smoke. Then billowing clouds that anyone could smell from a country mile away were filling the barn.

The horses were stamping their hooves and snorting as he'd expected. When the smoke spread even more, they began squealing and kicking against the stalls.

Kid drew his pistol and crouched behind an upright support beam. The upstairs door whomped open seconds later and Roo appeared, her eyes narrowed as she stared at the fire.

"Dang! What the hell?" She clomped down the steps, and Kid waited until she reached the bottom before stepping from the shadow.

"Don't sweat the fire, Roo. It won't spread."

She peered at him through a haze of smoke. "I mighta knowed it was you. Sumbitch! An' here I am, carrying your baby." She grunted at Kid's shocked look. "I tested today. Yeah, it's the one you done put in me the other day. Well? Ain't ya gonna say, reach fer the sky, pardner?"

"Reach for the sky, pardner."

If he expected a feminine voice in response, the masculine one he got instead startled him into V-Tac.

"Drop the weapon," Jamal said. "Drop it right now or swear to god, I'll blow your fucking head right off."

"I'll drop it, Jamal. But you're smart enough to realize it's over with. There's no escape and the SWAT team's en route." Kid wanted to say more but good sense prevailed, so he let go of the pistol and let it fall to the dirt with a muted thud.

"Might be that Roo and I have an escape. Might be we don't. Either way, we're still gonna pull the plug. Now take three steps away from that puny Beretta."

Kid complied and turned to face Jamal, who trained a .45 automatic on Kid while asking Roo, "How much time do you need?"

"I reckon eight minutes. See, one of the codes Ag done give Sandro ain't workin' quite right. Wouldn't surprise me none if that fucker Sandro wrote it down wrong. But I think I done got it figgered out."

Jamal nodded and waved the .45 at Kid. "What about him?"

"Kill him," she said without emotion, and after turning away she took the stairs two at a time.

Kid told himself, *Whaddya know? Roo's been in command all along. Christ, lot of good it does me now.*

Jamal leveled the pistol at Kid's chest. "You put on a good goddamn act. When you shot our fake SWAT guy? Yessir, that did it for me." He waved the barrel up and down. "How'd you know he was one of ours?"

"Trade secret."

"Hmm. All Right. I can respect that. Just as you'll have to appreciate our multi-layered plans. You know the ones I'm talking about, you little faggot. For fuck's sake, I never could stand having to be around faggots."

Kid remained poker-faced. "In denial of our own sexuality, are we?"

Jamal spit on the dirt. "Imagine, a man sucking another man's cock. For crying out loud."

"There's still time for you to go down on mine," Kid said, only to narrow his eyes. "Give it up. You don't need a murder charge on top of everything else. Besides, you can't escape."

"Wrong. We have Roo's skiff."

"Not anymore. I put it out of commission."

The sudden rage on Jamal's face grew into a living thing. "That's it!" he roared. "Die, motherfucker! *Die!*"

POW!

Kid cried out in pain when the heavy slug pierced his sternum. He clutched at his chest, but blood still streamed through his fingers. Then a blackness began to descend, and his final thought as he fell to the dirt was *Fuck. Jamal shot me; he fucking shot me. But I'm gonna go down fighting. Fuckin' right I am. Now where's my pistol?*

For reasons he could not understand, he felt a new life force. He scrambled for his Beretta, and damned if he didn't find it. Though still in deep shock he looked for Jamal. But the terrorist was nowhere to be seen.

It took Kid a few microsecs to realize that it was part of Jamal's skull and not a bullet that struck his chest—a conclusion he reached upon spotting Jamal face down in the dirt with the top of his head missing.

Kid ripped his shirt open anyway and didn't relax until he found a dime-sized bone fragment embedded in the skin over his sternum. And although it hadn't penetrated, it sure as hell knocked him on his ass. It also cut the skin, which explained the blood.

So who in hell shot Jamal?

The answer arrived when Jake's voice filled the stable. "Sorry about that, Kid. Didn't think you'd end up taking shrapnel. Had to take the shot, though. Hey, I'm from Wyomin'. It's what we do."

Kid spoke with a reverent voice. "Jake. You saved my friggin'…"

Gillian suddenly materialized at Jake's side, jolting Kid back into the moment enough to point at the upstairs door and shout, "Roo's up there. She has the codes, and we only have a few seconds!" Leaping to his feet, he bellowed, "Follow me!"

Kid pounded up the steps three at a time and kicked the door open. Roo was sitting fewer than eight feet away with her hand on her desktop's mouse.

She looked over her shoulder at him.

Kid raised his pistol.

Roo gave him a look of utter contempt.

He fired.

Her head whipped forward while at the same instant a gunshot erupted near Kid's ear. Then Roo's right elbow exploded, and her arm jerked backward.

A wide-eyed Kid examined his pistol in disbelief until Levi stepped next to him with his SIG Sauer in hand.

"Good job, Kid. Your round found its mark. Base of the skull. Killed all motor functions. But I had to ensure against a cadaveric spasm."

Levi explained while keeping his .357 trained on Roo's lifeless body. "She had her hand on the mouse. She could've clicked it spasmodically. But I was at a thirty-degree angle to her. Taking out the elbow caused a reflex that forced her hand from the mouse. It's why I took the shot. Too much at risk."

"Dad, I..."

"You stopped 'em, Kid. Stopped 'em cold."

Jake reached their side and let loose with a low whistle. "Danged if she ain't deader than graveyard dead. An' if any varmint needed killing then that one shore did."

Kid struggled with a flood of emotions before saying, "She had children, Dad. I took her from them. She was also carrying *my* child. I—" He turned his head to one side and vomited.

Levi put a hand on Kid's shoulder while he retched a second time. Then he looked into his son's eyes and said, "She would have caused the deaths of your children and a billion others worldwide. You did the only thing possible. Okay?"

Chapter Thirty-Three

· ·

Olympia · Wait, there's more.

"WAIT, THERE'S MORE," the special agent said as she turned to another item on her list. It was the next day and Kid, Levi, Michael, and Huck were enduring a grueling debrief. The topics included Ag's revelations that he'd given corrupted encryption keys to Sandro as a bargaining chip to guard against being murdered. Ag added with total certainty, "They were powerless without my codes."

As for Jorge's good-faith late-breaking details concerning Roo, they had only solidified Kid's belief that she posed a mega-threat to the world, and it ranked high in the criteria he used to justify using deadly force against her.

The debrief finally ended when Michael's phone chirped. After a short discussion, he smiled at Kid and pulled him aside. "You're to report to the White House in five weeks for a private ceremony. Cohen will award you the Presidential Medal of Freedom, with dinner to follow with The Man and the First Lady."

"I'm honored." But Kid grew quiet from the enormity of it all.

In a case of bad timing, Michael's face darkened. "Kid? There's something else."

"Wait. I want to say something about Cleo. I'll adopt the baby and…"

"Son?" Michael said this in such a quiet voice that a new fear tore through Kid. "I was about to tell you. We just got word. The stress and pending criminal charges got to her. She miscarried."

"Oh my god." Kid closed his eyes and said a prayer for the child's soul—whoever its father might be. Then he said one for the baby that Roo would never give birth to.

Now Michael wrapped an arm around Kid's shoulders. "I think now's the time to tell you that your mother and I remarried a few days ago. I've already moved back in, and we painted one of the guest rooms pink for my daughter."

Kid beamed. "Papa, that's great!"

"Listen, there's something else." Michael urged Kid to the end of a hallway, where he pushed through a door marked STAIRS. As they stood on the landing he wrapped his hands around Kid's upper arms. "Son? You've been through hell. So has Jen. We told you about the videos she saw. On top of that, she had the children to look after." He lifted a hand to the ceiling. "The pressure affected her judgment."

"Forget it, Papa. Her brain's one thing, her heart's another. She couldn't hold onto it, so she broke mine out of spite."

Michael sighed audibly. "Kid? I understand what you're going through. You've suffered, and I think it's clouding your thinking. But hasn't she also suffered? At least consider sitting down with her to discuss it."

"No."

When there seemed to be nothing else to say, Kid said goodbye and drove to the community health clinic for a follow-up exam. That night he stayed with Huck.

On the third day following the event, Levi informed Kid that some upper-level decisions had been made: DOJ had all but cleared Levi and Kid for their roles in Roo's death. Cleo faced life in Supermax, locked away in perpetual solitary confinement where her brains and beauty would wither. Sandro? The psycho punk had been charged with killing Dustin. Unfortunately there wasn't enough evidence to charge him with Julio's death, although that could change.

As for Ag? He would be permitted to plead guilty and avoid prison, but only if he worked to the end of his days to help the FBI deter, detect, and demolish cyber warfare sites.

LATER that day Kid stepped inside the field office's secure conference room for a session with a Bureau psychiatrist. The doc even held a security clearance, which would let Kid speak openly.

As they sat in a stark impersonal room, Kid told the octogenarian PhD that he felt numb. "I took a life when I didn't need to. If only Ag had told me earlier about those damn encryption keys. So you see? I didn't have to kill her after all. I... Doc, she had children. Christ, she was carrying my baby!"

"Son? Look at me." The good doctor waited until Kid complied. "You didn't have this information at the time. You only knew that she posed a threat of such enormity that I'm not permitted to know the details. But I've been assured that it was beyond substantial." He paused and looked at Kid with accepting eyes. "You see where I'm going with this, right?"

"No." In fact, Kid's ravaged brain really could not see it. Not yet, anyway.

KID called Jorge following the session. When the Honduran hoodlum answered, Kid said, "I need to see you. I'll be at your place in thirty minutes."

The thug met him at the door, naked but for white boxers that were stark against his olive skin and his even darker tatts as he regarded Kid with heavy-lidded eyes. "I knew choo would want me again."

"I do," Kid ad-libbed. "Good god, man! Don't you know I fantasize about you every waking moment?" He rolled his eyes and started to enter.

But Jorge planted a palm against his chest while he looked at Kid with concern. "Choo look like chit. Tell me what I can do to be of the help to you."

Despite being taken aback at how awful he apparently looked, Kid regarded Jorge in a new way, one that flirted along the borders of fondness. "Thanks," he mumbled and stepped inside only to be shocked to find everything spotless and tidy.

Although the place still smelled of tobacco, the odor had been tempered by Pine-Sol, which in turn had been underscored by an air freshener. The seedy mattress was gone, and a futon had taken its place. It wasn't a bed, but it was certainly an improvement. There were even fresh sheets and new pillows atop it. Kid also noted a complete absence of cockroaches.

Jorge swept a hand at everything and spoke humbly. "I did this for you, so choo would like me. I also stopped the cigarettes." He met Kid's eyes. "I am sorry for how I treated choo. Also, for how I made choo get on chore knees at Allesandro's. I cannot make the change of what happened. I also called you the names. Only, I did not mean it. My brother, he is also the homosexual, and I have for him the love. But..."

"But you live by a code." Kid tapped a finger against Jorge's tattooed sternum. "Don't sweat it, mi amigo. I didn't take it personally."

Jorge smiled and said with a typical gang-banger mentality, "That's because you like me. Hey, maybe choo stay and be my girlfriend. Is that not what you said you want?"

Kid was ready with a wise-ass reply until he saw a sadness in Jorge's eyes, and Kid's recent experiences of deprivation and uncertainty served to create a soulful connection with this thug who'd come up from hard times.

Sure enough, Jorge gripped Kid's arm and said in a husky voice, "I mean it. I want choo to be my woman."

"I—" Kid had always been honest with himself. It's why he could not deny Jorge's animal magnetism. But there was more to this thug, and Kid saw it now. Finally, he said, "The thing is, I already have a boyfriend." Then he touched Jorge's cheek and said, "Anyway, we need to move on. Listen, I came here to tell you a few things."

He described working deep cover to nab Sandro for the two murders without disclosing the mission's real purpose, since it remained classified. Next, he planted a hand on Jorge's naked shoulder. "You did the right thing by calling me about Roo. For that, you're being rewarded with a college education, all expenses paid."

"College?" Jorge canted his head to one side and stared unbelievingly at Kid.

"A good one. You're already enrolled, and a tutor's been hired to get you up to speed. Here's her number." Kid handed him a slip of paper. "Everything's arranged. Tuition, living expenses; monthly allowance."

The thug shifted from one bare foot to the other. "How did this thing come about?"

"Don't question the gift, okay?" It was actually Levi's doing, which led to Kid adding, "When you graduate there'll be a job waiting for you."

"I… chit, man." The Honduran took Kid into his arms and kissed his mouth with great tenderness, and on drawing away he spoke slowly while feeling his way.

"Thank choo for all of this. Also, give to my—how do you say—ah, my benefactor. Please give to this person my most gracious thanks. Now make me feel the more happier by saying choo will live with me."

"Jorge—" Kid sighed. "I can't…"

"Wait. Listen. I promise to be a good man to you. I will treat choo well and give to you the pretty things to wear. And you? Choo are going to be the good gorl who shaves her legs and takes care of her man's needs. Only, we will tell others that we are only roommates."

Kid offered a non-answer. "I mean, anything's possible." Then he narrowed his eyes. "But why do you want me? You don't even know who I am. Or is it just sexual?"

A stillness took hold of Jorge until he said with great nobility, "Choo have the courage. The honor. The dignity. And I want to learn to be just like you."

He stepped closer and planted a hand on Kid's waist. "Choo have also given to me the kindness. Something I never know before. So—" He seemed to peer into Kid's soul while he undid the non-resisting Kid's shirt and slid it from his shoulders. As it fell to the floor with a muted rustle, he deftly undid Kid's trousers and let them drop while whispering, "Now I make the love to you, jes?"

"I have a boyfriend."

"I know. I heard choo the first time." He lowered his eyes and spoke with a subdued voice. "I do not wish to come between choo and your man. So I am sad. Why? Because I wanted choo for my friend; for us to live our lives together. The sex? It is how do you say, the icing only. Not the real cake of having the caring for each other. But it is with the regrets that I must say goodbye. Only, I will make the prayers that we can still be good amigos." Jorge put on a brave smile and took a step back.

The repentant thug's response touched the emotionally and physically exhausted Kid deeply, prompting him to quietly say, "If only you knew how right your words were; what they mean to me. Jorge? If I should become single again I would very much like to live with you."

The joy in the Honduran's face was such a palpable thing that Kid put a palm against Jorge's naked back and glanced at the futon. "Let's relax a bit and talk."

So they stretched out to talk. Before long they were laughing. Soon enough they crossed an unseen line, one that signified sincere friendship. When their talk turned into whispers, the Honduran took Kid into his arms and began kissing him with mounting passion, his tongue thrusting deeply until Kid let go and looked into Jorge's eyes. After that, he accepted all that the bareback Latino offered. Later—afterward—they shared a rare and intimate smile.

And then it was time to leave, the host walking his guest to the door where Kid embraced the tearful Jorge and looked into his face while telling him, "I'm proud to call you my friend, and I promise to keep in touch."

HE told Huck everything, and at six they dressed in their best and joined Levi and Michael at an elegant restaurant. They ate well, and following dessert Michael placed a hand over one of Huck's. "Thank you for being in my son's life. I can't imagine him finding anyone better than you."

Levi touched Huck's other hand. "Welcome to our family."

Later that night, Kid and Huck settled into bed to hold their own debrief. It began when the ever-amiable Huck rested a palm on Kid's thigh. "You still have a lot of crap on your mind. Don't you?"

"I killed two people. I've lost my wife."

"Hey? It's time to love yourself enough to let go of those you can't have. Love Jen so you can understand her side of things. Then forgive her. Once you've done that? Forgive yourself for what you were forced to do in two life-threatening situations."

Kid peered at Huck as if a pot plant had sprouted from his forehead. "When the hell did you begin speaking in declarative, active voice sentences?"

Huck elbowed Kid's ribs. "Come on. I only speak slacker to fit in." He paused and cleared his throat. "So like, after I tipped off the FBI? And you showed up? I figured they'd sent you. Only, you started getting it on with guys. And getting stoned?"

"All role-play. I got high. Robbed stores. Became gay for pay. Whatever it took."

Huck spoke quietly. "The day my baby died? I'd have gone down on a hundred dudes if it would've brought her back to life." Now he regarded Kid with haunted eyes. "But you *did* do it. For your children. You..." His voice caught. "Fuck, dude! You're my idol."

Kid's chest heaved. "Wow. I, um... thank you for that. I—" He got quiet until a moment or so later, when he said, "I hope others will grasp that having sex with guys didn't bother me. As in, not at all. Sure, it's *different*. Just wasn't my game. But wouldn't you know it? Now I see its virtues."

"Hmm. That's like, interesting? So do you consider yourself gay now? Or bi-? Or..."

"I consider myself 'Kid.'" He gripped Huck's hand. "And Kid's sexuality has become semi-permeable; new horizons, and all that."

Huck grinned. "We'll settle for Metro. How's that?"

"Sure, that works."

"Good." Huck stretched his long legs. "It's no state secret that I've come to feel the same way... well, at least where you're concerned. But um, listen. The day we met? I came on to you just to see if you were a special agent. But then? Later? I fell in love with you, and... and it's the best thing that's happened to me."

Kid smiled for perhaps the first time in days. "Back to the gay stuff. Enzo? Damn, Huck. He was sooo fucking great in the sack. Then there's Jorge. Wow, what a pleasant surprise. I assumed he would be brutal. He turned out to be quite nice. Now he..."

"Now he wants you to live with him." Huck's smile dazzled. "I'm glad you found each other, and that you guys like, shared some intimacy today. Hey... I'm good with it, 'cause you needed some good loving."

"Can we not talk about what we did?"

"Of course." He patted Kid's thigh. "Man, until we met? I never thought I'd even sleep nude with a dude. Only, I found it to be different with you." His eyes narrowed. "I guess it's because we're natural about it, and 'cause we act from the heart. Which is all that really matters. I mean, if I'm gonna be philosophical."

Kid was regarding Huck anew when all at once he saw in Huck's eyes the river that Herman Hesse's *Siddhartha* loved so much: '... *the water continually flowed and flowed and yet it was always there; it was always the same and yet every moment it was new...*'

Following a quiet moment, the stoner nudged Kid. "When you shot Jamal's pretend SWAT guy? I figured you were beyond doubt a for-real terrorist. Which killed me, 'cause I'd already grown to love you."

Kid's face revealed his gratitude. "Thank you for caring so much about me."

"Wait. I need to say this. I had my own nine mil that night, an' I was ready to blow Ag's brains all over his fuckin' computer. Then the other night? I was seconds away from killing him when you asked him to stop. If you hadn't? Or if you'd tried to fight me? I'd have shot *you*."

"I'd have shot me too," Kid murmured. Then he shifted against Huck and squinted at him. "I have to know. Your daughter."

Huck wiped away a sudden tear. "All true. It's why I couldn't sit by and let 'em carry out their agenda. Death. Destruction. A total takedown of the world? No way. So maybe karma put me inside the café? Like, the day after Cher's funeral? 'Cause it's when Cleo came onto me."

The young slacker winced. "I was sad and like, lonely. She brought me into her circle of friends. It only took me a month before I saw what they were all about. So I was think-ing of Cher and the rest of the world's kids when I called the Feds. Only, there's another reason I called? Because first and foremost I was a Marine. And I love my country. So I dimed in on 'em."

"Got it," Kid said, only to hesitate before looking at Huck. "I hope you won't mind if I dump on you again." His mouth worked soundlessly until he said, "It's just that I still feel dead inside. I mean, Jesus. I've felt that way since Jen dumped me. Then the killings…"

"Aww, shut the fuck up," Huck snapped. "Just fucking shut up and stop feeling sorry for yourself." But then he looked at Kid with soft eyes and spoke with a reverent voice. "You had all that stuff going on in your head. Yet you moved forward. You like, advanced as if in battle. You were even wounded. I don't just mean that bone hitting your chest. Emotionally, too. But you never stopped; you carried out your orders."

Kid grew quiet and settled a hand on Huck's thing before asking, "You've seen combat. Tell me. Did I do what's expected of a man?"

Huck gazed unwaveringly into Kid's eyes and said in a hushed voice, "Kid? Whenever I see you now? I see a hero."

"I—" Kid could say no more at first. Finally, he said, "Ask me if I'd risk losing my wife and children by doing it all over again, knowing just how bad the threat turned out to be."

"Would you?"

"In a heartbeat. Otherwise? I never would've met you."

Huck stared open-mouthed at Kid until he whispered, "Fuuuck. Have I been that good a friend?"

"Your love sustained me even when I considered you an enemy. Sure, I stayed on top of the Stockholm Syndrome. But I needed to feel loved. And it's why I've grown to love you so completely in return."

•   •   •

Two days later Kid got the Beamer cleaned, detailed, and serviced for the drive back east. Next, he drove the gleaming car to the nearest salon where he got a facial, a mani-pedi, and had his hair cut short. Yet despite this sense of renewal he was still feeling numb inside when he called his mother.

She picked up and asked, "How are you doing Kiddo?"

"I'm um, okay. Lots of stuff going on. Listen. The car's gassed and ready to go. And, Mom? I know Papa told you about Huckleberry. Do you mind if I bring him home? Don't worry about a guest room. We'll bunk together in my old room."

"Your papa told me all about your boyfriend and what you two mean to one another. Listen, Kiddo. Huckleberry's welcome to stay for as long as he wants."

THEY made the trip in four days and arrived on Saturday, July 3rd. Before checking out of their last motel, Huck arranged his long blond hair into a ponytail and fixed it in place with a scrunchie. Then he dressed in the dark suit he'd bought for his daughter's funeral.

For Kid's part, he put on a white long-sleeved Isaia shirt, coal-black trousers and gleaming black Dolce & Gabbana lace-ups.

The air was sparkling when they arrived at his childhood home, and Kid used his key to open the door. He led Huck inside, and while turning a corner they nearly collided with Nadia, who gasped and said, "Ohhh, Kid. You look even worse than at the hospital."

Huck, who had been too close to Kid these past weeks to notice, hadn't grasped until this moment how emotionally scarred Kid had become—or that he hovered just above being in a state of shock.

Nadia recovered and approached her son's lover with understated grace. "My, aren't you quite the beautiful man?" She kissed Huck's cheek. "You're family now, so please call me Mom." Then she told Kid, "I put extra towels in your bathroom."

Now Michael in a navy blue blazer, light blue shirt, and chinos approached and embraced Huck. "Thank you again for loving my son. Now why don't you two get settled in. Huck? When you're ready? Please join me for drinks while I discuss a position I'm holding open for you."

But even as Huck thanked him, Nadia's face turned somber. "Bad news, Kid. The twins have come down with something. The physician fears a possible exposure to that newest COVID strain. Sorry, but you won't be able to see your children for several days."

"Thanks, Mom." Kid did his best to hide his disappointment before he and Huck went upstairs to unpack.

Michael had a sweaty martini shaker in hand by the time they returned, and he was pouring for them when Nadia clutched Huck's hand and led him to their elegant library.

The bright room featured a slate fireplace, Brazilian Jatoba wood shelves, and a bay window overlooking a wide river. After guiding him to a beige sofa of Italian fabric, she sat at his side. "Kid told me what you've done for him."

"Mrs. Bailey? I love him. He's…"

She put her fingers to his lips. "Please call me Mom."

"Thanks, um… Mom." He tilted his head toward the main room. "Kid's my whole life. But I guess he like, mentioned my daughter?"

"He did. And rest assured that my husband and I shall keep her in our nightly prayers."

Huck took her hand. "God bless you for that, and for accepting me into your family." He pushed some stray hair from his eyes and wet his lips. "Um, Mom? Just so you're aware? Kid and I are discussing marriage. But all during the trip I've been like, trying to talk him into getting back together with Jen." He worried his thumb against the martini glass and looked away while saying, "I'll be okay with it if, you know, you wanna invite her over so they can like, talk?"

"Oh, Huck." She wrapped her arms around him and whispered into his ear, "No wonder my son worships you."

THE others arrived the next day, the 4th of July—the day that might have ended all days. Since it fell on a Sunday, family tradition meant that everyone dressed in evening wear. Kid had on Versace, while Huck glowed in his host's Ralph Lauren tux and Bally lace-ups. Cati was elegant in Adrianna Papeli and Levi looked dashing in a tuxedo. Marty, Hacksaw, and their wives were also radiant in exquisitely tailored clothing.

But when Kid's brother Nick appeared with his girlfriend, he looked at Kid and said as only a brother could, "Whoa, you look like shit."

Kid said poker-faced, "You like it? I did this look just for you."

Nick started to flip him the bird, only to reel it in and trace a finger around his brother's hollow, dark-rimmed eyes. "Hey. Anytime you wanna talk. Okay?" Then he hugged Kid with a fierceness that comes from seeing a loved one survive the unimaginable, and when he drew back the brothers kissed each other's cheeks.

Nick turned to Huck next. "I always wanted another brother. Now here you are." He embraced Huck and said into his ear, "I'm so grateful to you for looking after Kid. Also? I hope you and nut-job get married." He kissed Huck's cheek, then stepped back and smiled.

At five o'clock everyone took their seats at the dining room table to enjoy Kid's Boeuf Bourguignon. He'd spent the day preparing it to keep his mind occupied, yet he didn't speak more than three words during the meal.

Following dessert, Michael put his daughter to bed while the others adjourned to the living room. The conversation began to sparkle. Kid laid his head on Huck's shoulder and sighed when the mellow ex-Marine began running long fingers through Kid's short hair. But Nadia appeared nervous in a way so out of character for her, and she kept glancing at a wall clock.

Michael returned just as the doorbell chimed.

Nadia leaped up. "I'll get it."

She reappeared a moment later and said, "Son? Someone wishes to say hello."

"Huh? Who?" Kid stood and looked around, only to stiffen and glare when Jen appeared. "Who the hell invited *you*?"

The room turned quiet. Nobody said a word or made a sound as she took a tentative step toward him. But when she got close enough to see beyond his gaunt appearance to the haunted, hunted look in his eyes, she gasped and ran to him.

"No," he said with an upraised palm. "Go away. I want nothing to do with you."

"Oh, Kid. Please talk to me. *Please.*"

Kid said to his mother, "Get her out of here." It was a command, not a request.

"Son?" Michael tilted his head at the library while Jen buried her face against Nadia's shoulder and shook from heart-wrenching sobs.

Levi entered the library just as Michael said, "Kid? Knock it off. Go talk to your wife."

"No!" Kid chopped a hand through the air, his eyes fierce; his facial muscles standing out like a relief map. "She turned her back on me when I needed her at the lowest point in my life."

Michael's face was unreadable. "Do you hate her that much?"

The son said through hooded eyes, "Jen killed something in me. Then she tossed me aside like garbage."

"Damn it," Levi began. "Can't you see she's devastated? She wants to explain herself."

Kid replied in the quiet voice reserved for funeral homes, "No."

"Bullshit," Levi said in a sudden, sharp voice. "Your papa and I discussed the videos with you. Listen, I'd have *sworn* you were having full-blown intercourse with Britney. Imagine how Jen must have felt."

"Nobody held a gun to her head and made her watch."

"Jen thought you lied. Sure, from your perspective you were telling the truth. But from a mother-to-be's viewpoint? Don't you see? She felt betrayed. Right or wrong, there it is."

Michael added, "Son? You're a wreck and I'm afraid it's affecting your judgment."

"Papa? Dad? Thank you for your concern. Now I'll only say this once. She wouldn't hear me out. She rejected me, she broke me, now she can live without me."

Michael edged closer and wrapped an arm around his son's shoulders. "Your newborn son needs his father. So do the twins. At least be civil to her for their sake."

Kid was mumbling a reply when Nadia and a tear-streaked Jennifer entered the room.

"We're not doing this," Kid said at once.

He stood to leave until Jen made a sound like a wounded animal. "*Please.* I'm begging you. Please talk to me, Kid." She gasped for air and said, "I made a mistake. And I'm so, so sorry for what I've done. Kid! I love you. I always have." Her voice hitched. "Can't we sit and talk? Please?" Her lip quivered as she looked at him in desperation.

But he pinned her with a flinty stare. "Don't ever ask me to sit and talk again. Is that clear?" He marched away and didn't see Levi catch her just before she fell to the floor.

The party ended. Nobody wanted to go into town to watch the fireworks, Kid most of all.

LATER that night as he and Huck settled into bed, Kid asked, "Go on. Let's hear it."

Huck's reply was sharp. "Betcher ass you're gonna hear it." But he relaxed his shoulders and idly stroked Kid's inner thigh. "I'd give anything to have my daughter back. *Anything.*"

"I know," Kid whispered. But he swept a hand at the window and the darkness that lay beyond. "What's here for me anymore?"

Huck said in his gentle way, "Your children. They're here for you." He grazed the backs of his knuckles along Kid's cheek. "Jen made a mistake. You're being a prick by not accepting this. Besides, hasn't she suffered? I'm like, saying she suffered as much as you. Maybe more. So cut the shit and get your friggin' act together." He gripped Kid's chin and turned his head until they could see each other's eyes. "And that's all I'm going to say."

Kid nodded and thanked him for caring enough to speak his mind. But as Huck shifted his slender frame and began turning onto his side, Kid touched his arm. "Tell me more about Cher."

"Cher?" Huck looked at him in gratitude as he lay on his back and opened his arms. Once Kid entered them and put his cheek on Huck's chest, the amiable slacker rested a palm on Kid's bare bottom and spoke with a new-found joy. "Well, my daughter *Cher*. She had this funny face she'd like, make? It always gave me a belly laugh. What she'd do is…"

HUCK stayed two weeks, during which Kid mulled over what he had said. And with each passing day Kid was shedding more and more of the mission's cortisol-induced stress. The hollowness in his eyes also began to fade; he no longer jumped at sudden noises. He smiled more often.

Then the morning arrived when Huck put on business casual and grabbed a carry-on. After saying his farewells to Nadia and Michael, Kid drove him under a blast of hyperthermic heat to a regional airport so Huck could visit his parents before reporting to Vanguard.

Before going through security though, Huck pulled Kid aside and wrapped his arms around him. Then while sounds of luggage scraping floors and impatient passengers threatened to smother their words, he said, "We all make mistakes. We all need to forgive. Also? I'm so in love with you, and *that's* no mistake."

But then he peered into Kid's eyes. "Do you remember what we discussed our first night here? When I pointed out that you have your children, along with a wife you once adored? And that she worships you?" Huck paused and pressed his lips tight. "You have all of that, and it's *here*. And—and now it's time for me to get going."

Kid felt a rock in his chest, and he hugged Huck tighter while smelling on him the scent of clean water and fresh soap. "Okay, okay. I get it."

Still, he held on a moment longer before easing away with an aching slowness, yet while putting on a brave face. He even managed a smile that mirrored a sense of a new dawn. "You're right. About having to go. Yeah, clearing the way and all that. And I love you so very much."

"Ohhh, Kid." Huck blinked rapidly and brushed non-existent lint from Kid's shirt. "You're gonna be a great surgeon one day."

"Forget about me. You're gonna be a great daddy once more. I just know it."

"Yeah, well… get your ass back to your wife and children. As for me? I—" All at once the combat veteran had no more words. So he embraced Kid and kissed his mouth and held it for a long moment before walking off.

Kid ignored the few nasty glares he got, and once Huck's flight was airborne he ventured out onto the parking lot beneath gathering cumulonimbus clouds. With no destination in mind, he drove to Assateague Island—that frozen-in-time barrier island with its roving herds of wild ponies. He knew of a difficult-to-reach beach at the north end where few ever ventured to. It's where he had to be right now.

He was parking behind a dune under leaden clouds just as harsh summer winds began buffeting the beach. After gauging the clouds and their potential to evolve into a storm, he doffed his flip-flops and grabbed a rain jacket.

Minutes later he was trudging along a deserted beach when the clouds released their heavy burdens, the rain coming down in torrents. But he donned the jacket and pressed on until in time he stopped to watch the storm-tossed waves howl and roar and heave, all while carrying on their crests reminders of the past.

As the waves crashed ashore with stuttered sounds, others marched forward. They too sought the future, and their growls, though furious, were underscored by a sublime murmur. Kid felt it was a great noise, as haunting as it was reassuring; as tragic as it was beautiful.

"Oh my god," he whispered, because all at once he understood Huck's wisdom and the lesson of Siddhartha's timeless river—a new insight that reminded him of Huck's tremendous loss and great pain. Yet Huck still managed to smile; he still loved. It was the same with Kid's papa, who had moved forward despite an unspeakably cruel childhood.

As Huck's message about mistakes began to penetrate the bitterness he still wore like a garment, Kid walked on even when the rain turned violent. He kept going until he felt a great upheaval in his soul—a precursor to change—and though it wasn't a complete change, it signaled a turning point.

"What've I done to myself?" he asked aloud, surprised at how grateful he felt to be alive. Now he looked beyond his own needs to give thanks to Huck. *If he hadn't ratted the others out, the world might've folded beneath my children; if not for him I might have lost all touch with love. And whaddya know? My son's name is Huck. Talk about karma. Yes, sir! And if I'm ever blessed with another daughter? I'll name her Cher. Yeah, betcher ass I will.*

And Jorge. He nurtured my soul the other day. Yep, he sure did, and I hope our paths cross.

When a new line of rain gusts knifing through Kid's jacket convinced him to seek his car's respite, he turned to go only to spot a distant herd of brown and white ponies. They were free and unbridled, and his breath caught. *Now I'm free, too. Free to let go of having killed two people; free to understand and appreciate the life raft Huck pulled me into.*

Yeah, he offered me refuge when I needed it the most. Then he coaxed me from it; he told me to sort out my unfinished business with Jen. It's why I love Huck; he sees that she's the only one, the genuine one, for me—and that my happiness means more to him than his own.

He whispered, "Yeah. She made a mistake. That's all. A damn mistake. Sure, I watched those goddamn deepfakes. Damn, they must've really hit her hard. But not as hard as I did by rejecting her."

Now he faced the ocean and quietly spoke to it. "So. It's here at last. It's time. Time to say goodbye; goodbye to the mission. Goodbye to pain and killing and sleeping with others. But I'll always love Huck; that'll never change. Only, I love Jen so much and it's time we start healing." He clutched his chest. "God, I only hope I can win her back now."

Minutes later Kid roared off in the Beamer, and following a short drive, he parked in front of the single-story stucco home he knew so well. He knocked on the door. It opened. And when he saw the look of complete shock mixed with unutterable joy on her face, he took her hand in his.

"Hey... Jen? Wanna sit and talk? Because I love you so much and I need you in my life and I was so, so wrong to storm off the way I did. Jen? I'll do anything to get you back."

"Kid," she whispered. "Oh Kid, Kid, Kid." As a new light entered her eyes, she undid a small gold chain from around her neck. On it was Kid's real wedding band, and after removing it from the chain, she slipped it onto his ring finger. Then she flung her arms around his neck and kissed his face again and again. And when the twins began running down the hall toward them, he closed his eyes on all that was—and held on dearly for all that could be.

. . .

ACKNOWLEDGMENTS

To Joe Coleman, Joyce Emge, Mike Furnari, Dave Hobson, Janice Hobson and Jane O'Brien for your beta readings: thank you for your heartfelt beta readings. You helped me keep the story true to itself, and I could not have done it without your guidance.

And of course I must extend my gratitude to Levi, Michael, Quenton, Marty, Jake, and Gillian for giving parts of themselves to the story.

Finally, here's a shout-out to my friends at the dog park for your encouragement and support. Everyone helped me in so many ways. Thank you.

ABOUT THE AUTHOR

RICHARD CRAIG ANDERSON started out as a fire fighter in 1971, became a highly decorated Maryland State Police trooper, and went on to accept a position as a counter-terrorist operative. An accomplished aviator, world-class scuba diver and global traveler, Rick has enjoyed a life well lived thanks to the relationships and friendships he's forged along the way.